The River of Dancing Gods

Jack L. Chalker

A Del Rey Book

BALLANTINE BOOKS • NEW YORK

For David Whitley Chalker,
who, being born 12/19/81,
did his crying best to prevent
the completion of this novel.

A Del Rey Book
Published by Ballantine Books

Copyright © 1984 by Jack L. Chalker

Library of Congress Catalog Card Number: 83-91125

ISBN 0-345-30892-1

Manufactured in the United States of America

First Edition: February 1984

Cover art by Darrell K. Sweet

Map by Shelly Shapiro

TABLE OF CONTENTS

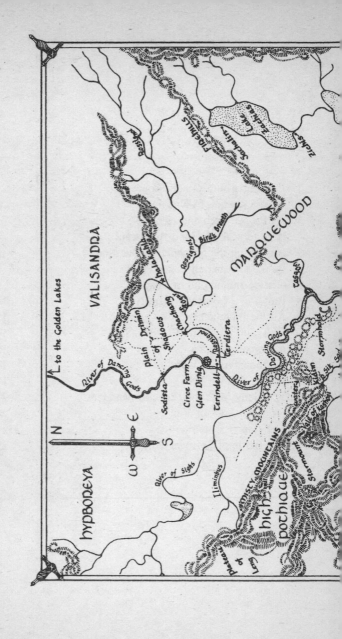

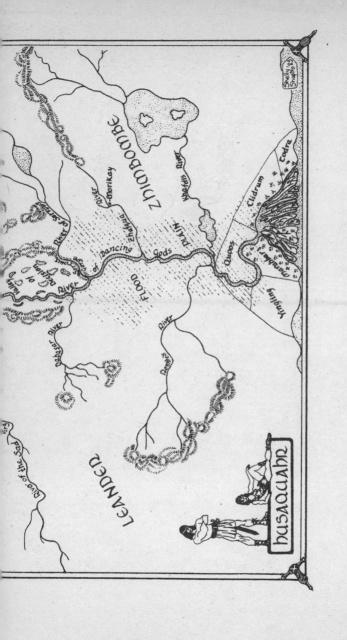

CHAPTER I

ENCOUNTER ON A LONELY ROAD

People taken from other universes should always be near death.
—The Books of Rules, XX, 109, 234(a)

JUST BECAUSE YOUR WHOLE LIFE IS GOING TO HELL DOESN'T mean you have to walk there.

She was walking down a lonely stretch of west Texas freeway in the still dark of the early morning, an area where nobody walked and where there was no place to walk to, anyway. She might have been hitching, or not, but a total lack of traffic gave her very little choice there. So she was just walking, clutching a small overnight bag and a purse that was almost the same size, holding on to them as if they were the only two real things in her life, they and the dark and that endless stretch of west Texas freeway.

Whatever traffic there was seemed to be heading the other way—an occasional car, or pickup, or eighteen-wheeler with someplace to go and some reason to go there, all heading in the direction she was walking from, and where, she knew too well, there was nothing much at all for anybody. But if their destinations were wrong, their sense of purpose separated the night travelers from the woman on the road; people who had someplace to go and something to do belonged to a different world than she did.

She had started out hitching, all right. She'd made it to the truck stop at Ozona, that huge, garish, ultramodern, and plastic heaven in the middle of nowhere that served up anything and everything twenty-four hours a day for those stuck out here, going between here and there. After a time, she'd gotten another ride, this one only twenty miles west and at a cost she was not willing to pay. And so here she was, stuck out in the middle of nowhere, going nowhere fast. Walk, walk, walk to nowhere, from nowhere in particular, because nowhere was all the where she had to go.

Headlights approached from far off; but even if they had

1

held any interest for her, they were still too far away to be more than abstract, jerky round dots in the distance, a distance that the west Texas desert made even more deceptive. How far off was the oncoming driver? Ten miles? More? Did it matter?

It was at least ten, maybe fifteen minutes before the vehicle grew close enough for the woman to hear the roar of the big diesel and realize that this was, in fact, one of those haunters of the desert dark, a monster tractor-trailer truck with a load of furniture for Houston or beef for New Orleans or, perhaps, California oranges for the Nashville markets. Although it had been approaching her from the west for some time, its sudden close-up reality was startling against the total stillness of the night, a looming monster that quickly illuminated the night and its empty, vacant walker, then was just as suddenly gone, a mass of diminishing red lights in the distance behind her. But in the few seconds that those gaping headlights had shone on the scene, they had illuminated her form against that desperate dark, illuminated her and, in the cab behind those lights, gave her notice and recognition.

She paid this truck no more attention than any of the others and just kept walking onward into the unseen distance.

The driver had been going much too fast for a practical stop, a pace that would have upset the highway patrol but was required to make his employer's deadline. Besides, he was on the wrong side of the median to be of any practical help himself—but there were other ways, ways that didn't even involve slowing down.

"Break one-nine, break, break. How 'bout a westbound? Anybody in this here Lone Star truckin' west on this one dark night?" His accent was Texarkana, but he could have been from Maine or Miami or San Francisco or Minneapolis just as well. Something in the CB radio seemed automatically to add the standard accent, even in Brooklyn.

"You got a westbound. Go," came a reply, only very slightly different in sound or tone from the caller's.

"What's your twenty?" Eastbound asked.

"Three-thirty was the last I saw," Westbound responded. "Clean and green back to the truck-'em-up. Even the bears go to sleep this time o' night in these parts."

Eastbound chuckled. "Yeah, you got that right. I got to keep pushin' it, though. They want me in Shreveport by tonight."

"Shreveport! You got some haul yet!"

"Yeah, but that's home sweet home, baby. Get in, get it off, stick this thing in the junkyard, and I'm in bed with the old lady. I'll make it."

"All I got is El Paso by ten."

"Aw, shit, you'll make that easy. Say—caught something your side in my lights about three-two-seven or so you might check out. Looked like a beaver just walkin' by the side of the road. Maybe a breakdown, though I ain't seen no cars on your side and I'm just on you now. Probably nothin', but you might want to check her out just in case. Ain't nobody lives within miles o' here, I don't think."

"I'll back off a little and see if I can eyeball her," Westbound assured him. "Won't hurt much. That your Kenworth just passed me?"

"Yeah. Who else? All best to ya, and check on that little gal. Don't wanna hear she got found dead by the side of the road or something. Spoil my whole day."

"That's a four," Westbound came back with a slight chuckle. "Keep safe, keep well, that's the Red Rooster sayin' that, eastbound and down."

"Y'all have a safe one. This is the Nighthawk, westbound and backin' down."

Nighthawk put his mike into its little holder and backed down to fifty. He wasn't in any hurry, and he wouldn't lose much, even if this was nothing at all, not on this flat stretch.

The woman was beginning to falter, occasionally stumbling in the scrub brush by the side of the road. She was starting to think again, and that wasn't what she wanted at all. Finally she stopped, knowing it was beyond her to take too many more steps, and looked around. It was incredible how dark the desert could be at night, even with more stars than city folk had ever seen beaming down from overhead. No matter what, she knew she had to get some rest. Maybe just lie down over there in the scrub—get stung by a tarantula or a scorpion or whatever else lived around here. Snake, maybe. She considered the idea and was somewhat surprised that she cared about that. Nice and quick, maybe—but painfully bitten or poisoned to death by inches? That seemed particularly ugly. With everything else so messed up, at least her exit ought to be clean, neat, and as comfortable as these things could be. *One* thing in her life should go right, damn it. And for the first time since she'd jumped out of the car, she began to consider living again—at least a little bit longer, at least until the sunrise. She stopped and looked up and down the highway for any sign of lights, wondering what she'd do if she saw any. It would just as likely be another Cal Hurder as anybody useful, particularly at this ungodly hour in a place like this.

Lights approaching from the east told her a decision was near, and soon. But she made no decision until the lights were actually on her, and when she did, it was on impulse, without any thought applied to it. She turned, put down her bags, and stuck out her thumb.

Even with that and on the lookout for her, he almost missed her. Spotting her, he hit the brakes and started gearing to a stop by the side of the road, getting things stopped fully a hundred yards west of her. Knowing this, he put the truck in reverse and slowly backed up, eyeing the shoulder carefully with his right mirror. After all this, he didn't want to be the one to run her down.

Finally he saw her, or thought he did, just standing there, looking at the huge monster approaching, doing nothing else at all. For her part, she was unsure of just what to do next. That huge rig was really intimidating, and so she just stood there, trembling slightly.

Nighthawk frowned, realized she wasn't coming up to the door, and decided to put on his flashers and go to her. He was not without his own suspicions; hijackers would use such bait and such a setting—although he could hardly imagine somebody hijacking forty thousand pounds of soap flakes. Still, you never knew—and there was always his own money and cards and the truck itself to steal. He took out his small pistol and slipped it into his pocket, then slid over, opened the passenger door, and got out warily.

He was a big man, somewhat intimidating-looking himself, perhaps six-three, two hundred and twenty-five pounds of mostly muscle, wearing faded jeans, boots, and a checkered flannel shirt. His age was hard to measure, but he was at least in his forties with a face maybe ten years older and with very long, graying hair. He was dark, too—she took him at first for a black man—but there was something not quite of any race and yet of all of them in his face and features. He was used to the look she was giving him and past minding.

"M'am?" he called to her in a calm yet wary baritone. "Don't worry—I don't bite. A trucker going the other way spotted you and asked me to see if you was all right."

Oh, what the hell, she decided, resigning herself. *I can always jump out again.* "I need a ride," she said simply. "I'm kind of stuck here."

He walked over to her, seeing her tenseness and pretty much ignoring it. He picked up her bag, letting her get her purse, and went back to the truck. "Come on. I'll take you for a while if you're going west."

She hesitated a moment more, then followed him and permitted him to assist her up into the cab. He slammed her door, walked around the truck, got in on the driver's side, released the brakes, and put the truck in gear. "How far you going?" he asked her.

She sat almost pressed against the passenger door, trying to look as if she weren't doing it. For all he knew, she *didn't* realize she was doing it.

She sighed. "Any place, I guess. How far you going?"

"El Paso. But I can get you to a phone in Fort Stockton if that's what you need."

She shook her head slowly. "No, nobody to call. El Paso's fine, if it's okay with you. I don't have enough money for a motel or anything."

Up to speed and cruising now, he glanced sideways over at her. At one time she'd been a pretty attractive woman, he decided. It was all still there, but something had happened to it, put a dull, dirty coating over it. Medium height—five-four or -five, maybe—with short, greasy-looking brown hair with traces of gray. Thirties, probably. Thin and slightly built, she had that hollow, empty look, like somebody who'd been on the booze pretty long and pretty hard.

"None of my business, but how'd you get stuck out here in the middle of nowhere at three in the morning?" he asked casually.

She gave a little sigh and looked out the window for a moment at the black nothingness. Finally she said, "If you really want to know, I jumped out of a car."

"Huh?"

"I got a ride with a salesman—at least he said he was a salesman—back at Ozona. We got fifteen, twenty miles down the road and he pulled over. You can guess the rest."

He nodded.

"I grabbed the bags and ran. He turned out to be a little scared of the dark, I guess. Just stood there yelling for me, then threatened to drive off if I didn't come back. I didn't—and he did."

He lighted a cigarette, inhaled deeply, and expelled the smoke with an accompanying sigh. "Yeah, I guess I get the picture."

"You—you're an Indian, aren't you?"

He laughed. "Good change of subject. Well, sort of. My mom was a full-blooded Seminole, my dad was Puerto Rican, which is a little bit of everything."

"You're from Florida? You don't sound like a southerner."

Again he chuckled. "Oh, I'm from the south, all right. South of Philadelphia, anyway. Long story. Right now what home I have is in a trailer park in a little town south of Baltimore. No Indians or Puerto Ricans around, so they just think of me as something a little bit exotic, I guess."

"You're a long way from home," she noted.

He nodded. "More or less. Don't matter much, though. I'm on the road so much the only place I really feel at home is in this truck. I own it and I run it, and it's mine as long as I keep up the payments. They had to let me keep the truck, otherwise they couldn't get no alimony. What about you? That pretty voice sounds pure Texas to me."

She nodded idly, still staring distantly into the nothingness. "Yeah. San Antone, that's me."

"Air Force brat?" He was nervous at pushing her too much, maybe upsetting or alienating her—she was on a thin edge, that was for sure—but he just had the feeling she wanted to talk to somebody.

She did, a little surprised at that herself. "Sort of. Daddy was a flier. Jet pilot."

"What happened to him?" He guessed by her tone that something had happened.

"Killed in his plane, in the finest traditions of the Air Force. Sucked a bird into his jets while coming in for a landing and that was it, or so I'm told. I was much too young, really, to remember him any more than as a vague presence. And the pictures, of course. Momma kept all the pictures. The benefits, though, they weren't all that much. He was only a captain, after all, and a new one at that. So Momma worked like hell at all sorts of jobs to bring me up right. She was solid Oklahoma—high school, no marketable skills, that sort of thing. Supermarket checker was about the highest she got—pretty good, really, when you see the benefits they get at the union stores. She did really well, when you think about it—except it was all for me. She didn't have much else to live for. Wanted me to go to college—she'd wanted to go, but never did. Well, she and the VA and a bunch of college loans got me there, all right, and got me through, for all the good it did. Ten days after I graduated with a useless degree in English Lit, she dropped dead from a heart attack. I had to sell the trailer we lived in all those years just to make sure she was buried right. After paying out all the stuff she owed, I had eight hundred dollars, eight pairs of well-worn jeans, a massive collection of T-shirts, and little else."

He sighed. "Yeah, that's rough. I always wanted to go to college, you know, but I never had the money until I didn't have the time. I read a lot, though. It don't pay to get hooked on TV when you're on the road so much."

She chuckled dryly. "College is all well and good and some of it's interesting, but if your degree's not in business, law, medicine, or engineering, the paper's only good for about thirty-eight hundred—that's what I still owe on those loans, and it'll be a cold day in hell before they see a penny. They track you down all over, too—use collection agents. So you can't get credit, can't get a loan, none of that. I got one job teaching junior high English for a year—but they cut back and laid me off. Only time I ever really enjoyed life."

"So you been goin' around from job to job ever since?"

"For a while. But a couple years of working hamburger joints and all those other minimum-wage, minimum-life jobs gets to you. I finally sat down one day and decided it was fate, or destiny, or something. I was getting older, and all I could see was myself years later, sitting in a rented slum shared with a couple of other folks just like me, getting quickies from the night manager. So I figured I would find a man, marry him, and let *him* pay my bills while I got into the cooking and baby business."

"Well, it's a job like any other and has a pretty long history," he noted. "Somebody's got to do it—otherwise the government will do *that*, too."

She managed a wan smile at the remark. "Yeah, well, that's what I told myself, but there are many ways to go about it. You can meet a guy, date, fall in love, really commit yourself— both of you. That might work. But just to go out in desperation and marry the first guy who comes along who'll have you— that's disaster."

"Works the other way, too, honey," he responded. "That's why I'm paying five hundred a month in rehabilitation money— that's what they call alimony these days in liberal states that abolished alimony—and child support. And she's living with another guy who owns an auto-repair shop and is doing pretty well; she has a kid by him, too. But so long as she don't marry him, I'm stuck."

"You have a kid?"

He nodded. "A son. Irving. Lousy name, but it was the one uncle he had on her side who had money. Not that it got us or him anything. I love him, but I almost never see him."

"Because you're on the road?"

"Naw. You'd be surprised what you can work. I'm supposed to have visitation rights, but somehow he's always away when I come visiting. She don't want him to see me, get to know me instead of her current as his daddy. Uh-uh."

"Couldn't you go to court on that?"

He laughed. "Honey, them courts will slap me in jail so fast if I miss a payment to her it isn't funny—but tell *her* to live up to *her* end of the bargain? Yeah, they'll tell her, and that's that. Tell her and tell her and tell her. Until, one day, you realize that the old joke's true—she got the gold mine in the settlement and I got the shaft. Oh, I suppose I could make an unholy mess trying to get custody, but I'd never win. I'd have to give up truckin', and truckin's all I know how to do. And I'd probably lose, anyway—nine out of ten men do. Even if I won—hell, it's been near five years." He sighed. "I guess at this stage he's better off. I hope so."

"I hope so, too," she responded, sounding genuinely touched, with the oddly pleasing guilt felt when, sunk deep in self-pity, you find a fellow sufferer.

They rode in near silence for the next few minutes, a silence broken only by the occasional crackle from the CB and a report of this or that or two jerks talking away at each other when they could just as easily have used a telephone and kept the world out.

Finally he said, "I guess from what you say that your marriage didn't work out either."

"Yeah, you could say that. He was an Air Force sergeant at Lackland. A drill instructor in basic. We met in a bar and got drunk on the town. He was older and a very lonely man, and, well, you know what I was going through. We just kinda fell into it. He was a pretty rough character, and after all the early fun had worn off and we'd settled down, he'd come home at night and take all his frustrations out on me. It really got to him, after a while, that I was smarter and better educated than he was. He had some inferiority complex. He was hell on his recruits, too—but they got away from him after eight weeks or so. I had him for years. After a while he got transferred up to Reese in Lubbock, but he hated that job and he hated the cold weather and the dust and wind, and that just made it all the worse. Me, I had it really bad there, too, since what few friends I had were all in San Antonio."

"I'd have taken a hike long before," he commented. "Divorce ain't all that bad. Ask my ex."

"Well, it's easy to see that—now. But I had some money for the first time, and a house, and a real sense of something permanent, even if it was lousy. I know it's kind of hard to understand—it's hard to explain. I guess you just had to be me. I figured maybe kids would mellow him out and give me a new direction—but after two miscarriages, the second one damn near killing me, the doctors told me I should never have kids. Probably couldn't, but definitely shouldn't. That just made him meaner and sent me down the tubes. Booze, pot, pills— you name it, I swallowed it or smoked it or sniffed it. And one day—it was my thirtieth birthday—I looked at myself in the mirror, saw somebody a shot-to-hell forty-five looking back at me, picked up what I could use most and carry easy, cashed a check for half our joint account, and took a bus south to think things out. I've been walking ever since—and I still haven't been out of the goddamned state of Texas. I waited tables, swept floors, never stayed long in one spot. Hell, I've sold my body for a plate of eggs. Done everything possible to keep from thinking, looking ahead, worrying. I burned out. I've had it."

He thought about it for a moment, and then it came to him. "But you jumped out of that fella's car."

She nodded wearily. "Yeah, I did. I don't even know why, exactly. Or maybe, yes, I do, too. It was an all-of-a-sudden kind of thing, sort of like when I turned thirty and looked in the mirror. There wasn't any mirror, really, but back there in that car I still kind of looked at myself and was, well, scared, frightened, maybe even revolted at what I saw staring back. Something just sorta said to me, 'If this is the rest of your life, then why bother to be alive at all?'"

He thought, but could find little else to say right then. What *was* the right thing to say to somebody like this, anyway?

Flecks of rain struck his windshield, and he flipped on the wipers, the sound adding an eerie, hypnotic background to the sudden roar of a midsummer thunderstorm on a truck cab. Peering out, he thought for a moment he saw two Interstate 10 roadways—an impossible sort of fork he knew just couldn't be there. He kicked on the brights and the fog lights, and the image seemed to resolve itself a bit, the right-hand one looking more solid. He decided that keeping to the white stripe down the side of the road separating road and shoulder was the safest course.

At the illusory intersection, there seemed for a moment to be two trucks, one coming out of the other, going right, while the other, its ghostly twin, went left. The image of the second truck, apparently passing his and vanishing quickly in the distance to his left, startled him for a moment. He could have sworn there wasn't anything behind him for a couple of miles, and the CB was totally silent.

The rain stopped as suddenly as it had begun, and things took on a more normal appearance in minutes. He glanced over at the woman and saw that she was asleep—best thing for her, he decided. Ahead loomed a green exit sign, and, still a little unnerved, he badly wanted to get his bearings.

The sign said, "Ruddygore, 5 miles."

That didn't help him much. Ruddygore? Where in hell was

that? The next exit should be Sheffield. A mile marker approached, and he decided to check things out.

The little green number said, "4."

He frowned again, beginning to become a little unglued. Four? That couldn't be right. Not if he was still on I–10. Uneasily, he began to think of that split back there. Maybe it *was* a split—that other truck had seemed to curve off to the left when he went right. If so, he was on some cockeyed interstate spur to God knew where.

God knew, indeed. As far as *he* knew or could remember, there were no exits, let alone splits, between Ozona and Sheffield.

He flicked on his interior light and looked down at his road atlas, held open by clips to the west Texas map. According to it, he was right—and no sign of any Ruddygore. He sighed and snapped off the light. Well, the thing was wrong in a hundred places, anyway. Luckily he was still ahead of schedule, so a five-mile detour shouldn't be much of a problem. He glanced over to his left again for no particular reason. Funny. The landscaping made it look as if there weren't any lane going back.

A small interstate highway marker, the usual red, white, and blue was between mile markers 3 and 2, but it told him nothing. It didn't even make sense. He was probably just a little crazy tonight, or his eyes were going, but it looked for all the world as if it said:

∞? What the hell was *that?* Somebody in the highway department must have goofed good there, stenciling an 8 on its side.

At the 2, another green sign announced Ruddygore, and there was also a brown sign, like the kind used for parks and monuments. It said, "Ferry—Turn Left at Stop Sign."

Now he knew he had gone suddenly mad. Not just that he knew that I–8 went from Tucson to San Diego and nowhere near Texas, but—a ferry? In the middle of the west Texas desert?

He backed down to slow—very slow—and turned to his passenger. "Hey, little lady. Wake up!"

She didn't stir, and finally he reached over and shook her, repeating his words.

She moved and squirmed and managed to open her eyes. "Um. Sorry. So *tired* . . . What's the matter? We in El Paso?"

He shook his head. "No. I think I've gone absolutely nuts. Somehow in the storm we took an exit that wasn't supposed to be there and we're headed for a town called Ruddygore. Ever heard of it?"

She shook her head sleepily from side to side. "Nope. But that doesn't mean anything. Why? We lost?"

"Lost ain't the word," he mumbled. "Look, I don't want to scare you or anything, but I think I'm going nuts. You ever hear of a ferryboat around here?"

She looked at him as if he had suddenly sprouted feathers. "A what? Over *what*?"

He nodded nervously and gestured toward the windshield. "Well, then, you read me that big sign."

She rubbed the sleep from her eyes and looked. "Ruddygore—exit one mile," she mumbled.

"And the little brown sign?"

"Ferry," she read, suddenly awake and looking very confused. "And an arrow." She turned and faced him. "How long was I asleep?"

"Five, maybe ten minutes," he answered truthfully. "You can still see the rain on the windshield where the wipers don't reach."

She shook her head in wonder. "It must be across the Pecos. But the Pecos isn't much around here."

"Yeah," he replied and felt for his revolver.

The interstate road went right into the exit, allowing no choice. There was a slight downgrade to a standard stop sign and a set of small signs. To the left, they said, were Ruddygore and the impossible ferry. To the right was—Oblivion.

"I never heard of any town named Oblivion, either," he muttered, "but it sounds right for these parts. Still, all the signs said only Ruddygore, so that's got to be the bigger and closer place. Any place they build an interstate spur to at a few million bucks a mile *has* to have something open even this time of night. Besides," he added, "I'm damned curious to see that ferry in the middle of the desert."

He put on his signals, then made the turn onto a modest two-lane road. He passed under the highway and noted glumly that there wasn't any apparent way of getting back on. Well, he told himself, he'd find it later.

Up ahead in the distance he saw, not the town lights he'd expected, but an odd, circular, lighted area. It was particularly unusual in that it looked something like the kind of throw a huge spotlight, pointed straight down, might give—but there were no signs of lights anywhere. Fingering the pistol, he proceeded on, knowing that the road was leading him to that lighted area.

And it *was* bright when he reached it, although no source was apparent. The road, too, seemed to vanish into it, and the entire surface appeared as smooth as glass. Damnedest thing he'd ever seen, maybe a thousand yards across. He stopped at the edge of it, and both he and the woman strained to see where the light was coming from, but the sky remained black—blacker than usual, since the reflected glow blotted out all but the brightest stars.

"Now, what the hell . . . ?" he mused aloud.

"Hey! Look! Up ahead there, almost in the middle. Isn't that a man?" She pointed through the windshield.

He squinted and nodded. "Yeah. Sure looks like somebody. I don't like this, though. Not at all. There's some very funny game being played here." Again he reached in and felt the comfort of the .38 in his pocket. He put the truck back in gear and moved slowly forward, one eye on the strange figure ahead and the other warily on the woman, whom he no longer trusted. It was a great sob story, but this craziness had started only after she came aboard.

He drove straight for the lone figure standing there in the center of the lighted area at about five miles per hour, applying the hissing air brakes when he was almost on top of the stranger and could see him clearly.

The woman gasped. "He looks like a vampire Santa Claus!"

Her nervous surprise seemed genuine. Certainly her description of the man who stood looking back at them fitted him perfectly. Very tall—six-five or better, he guessed—and very large. "Portly" would be too kind a word. The man had a reddish face, twinkling eyes with laugh lines etched around them, and a huge, full white beard—the very image of Santa Claus on all those Christmas cards. But he was not dressed in any furry red suit, but rather in formal wear—striped pants, morning coat, red velvet vest and cummerbund, even a top hat, and he was also wearing a red-velvet-lined opera cape.

The strange man made no gestures or moves, and finally the driver said, "Look, you wait in the truck. I'm going to find out what the hell this is about."

"I'm coming with you."

"*No!*" He hesitated a moment, then nervously cleared his throat. "Look, first of all, if there's any danger I don't want you between me and who I might have to shoot—understand? And second, forgive me, but I can't one hundred percent trust that you're not in on whatever this is."

That last seemed to shock her, but she nodded and sighed and said no more.

He opened the door, got down, and put one hand in his pocket, right on the trigger. Only then did he walk forward toward the odd figure who stood there, to stop a few feet from the man. The stranger said nothing, but the driver could feel those eyes following his every move and gesture.

"Good morning," he opened. What else was there to say to start things off?

The man in the top hat didn't reply immediately, but seemed to examine him from head to toe as an appraiser might look at a diamond ring. "Oh, yes, you'll do nicely, I think," he said in a pleasant, mellow voice with a hint of a British accent. He looked up at the woman, still in the cab, seemingly oblivious to the glare of the truck lights. "She, too, I suspect, although I really wasn't expecting her. A pleasant bonus."

"Hey, look, you!" the driver called angrily, losing patience. "What the hell *is* all this?"

"Oh, dear me, forgive my manners!" the stranger responded. "But, you see, *you* came *here*, I didn't come to you. Where do you *think* you are—and where do you want to be?"

Because the man was right, it put the driver on the defensive. "Uh, um, well, I seem to have taken a bum turn back on Interstate 10. I'm just trying to get back to it."

The big man smiled gently. "But you never *left* that road.

You're still on it. You'll be on it for another nineteen minutes and eighteen seconds."

The driver just shook his head disgustedly. He must be as nutty as he looked, that was for sure. "Look, friend. I got stuck over here by accident in a thunderstorm and followed the road back there to—what was the town? Oh, yeah, Ruddygore. I figure I'll turn around there. Can you just tell me how far it is?"

"Oh, Ruddygore isn't an 'it,' sir," the strange man replied. "You see, *I'm* Ruddygore. Throckmorton P. Ruddygore, at your service." He doffed his top hat and made a small bow. "At least, that's who I am when I'm here."

The driver gave an exasperated sigh. "Okay, that's it. Forget it, buddy. I'll find my own way back."

"The way back is easy, Joe," Ruddygore said casually. "Just follow the road back. But you'll die, Joe—nineteen minutes eighteen seconds after you rejoin your highway. A second storm with hail and a small twister is up there, and it's going to cause you to skid, jackknife, then fall over into a gully. The overturning will break your neck."

He froze, an icy chill going through him. "How did you know my name was Joe?" His hand went back to the .38.

"Oh, it's my business to know these things," the strange man told him. "Recruiting is such a problem with many people, and I must be very limited and very selective for complicated reasons."

Suddenly all of his mother's old legends about conjure men and the demons of death came back from his childhood, where they'd been buried for perhaps forty years—and the childhood fears that went with them returned as well, although he hated himself for it. "Just who—or what—*are* you?"

"Ruddygore. Or a thousand other names, none of which you'd recognize, Joe. I'm no superstition and I'm no angel of death, any more than that truck radio of yours is a human mouth. I'm not causing your death. It is preordained. It can not be changed. I only know about it—found out about it, you might say—and am taking advantage of that knowledge. That's the hard part, Joe. Finding out. It costs me greatly every time I try and might just kill *me* someday. Compared with that, diverting you here to me was child's play." He looked up at the woman, who was still in the cab, straining to hear. "Shall we let the lady join us?"

"Even if I buy what you're saying—which I don't," Joe responded, "how does she fit in? Is she going to die, too?"

The big man shrugged. "I haven't the slightest idea. Certainly she'll be in the accident, unless you throw her out ahead of time. I expected you to be alone, frankly."

Joe pulled the pistol out and pointed it at Ruddygore. "All right. Enough of this. I think maybe you'll tell me what this all is, really, or I'll put a hole in you. You're pretty hard to miss, you know."

Ruddygore looked pained. "I'll thank you to keep my weight out of this. As for what's going on—I've just told you."

"You've told me nothing! Let's say what you say is for real, just for the sake of argument. You say I'm not dead yet, and you're no conjure spirit, so you pulled me off the main line of my death for something. What?"

"Oh, I didn't say I wasn't involved in magic. Sorcery, actually. That's what I do for a living. I'm a necromancer. A sorcerer." He shrugged. "It's a living—and it pays better than truck driving."

The pistol didn't waver. "All right. You say I'm gonna die in—I guess fifteen minutes or less now, huh?"

"No. Time has stopped for you. It did the moment you diverted to my road. It will not resume until you return to the Interstate, I think you called it."

"So we just stand here and I live forever, huh?"

"Oh, my, no! I have important things to do. I must be on the ferry when it comes. When I leave, you'll be back on that road instantly, deciding you just had a nutty dream—for nineteen minutes eighteen seconds, that is."

Joe thought about it. "And suppose I do a flip, don't keep going west? Or suppose I exit at Fort Stockton? Or pull over to the side for a half hour?"

Ruddygore shrugged. "What difference? You wouldn't know if that storm was going to hit you hard because you were sitting by the side of the road or because you turned back—you can never be sure. I am. You can't avoid it. Whatever you do will take you to your destiny."

Joe didn't like that. He also didn't like the fact that he was taking this all so seriously. It was just a funny man in a circle of— "Where does the light come from?"

"I create it. For stuff like this, I like to work in a spotlight. I'll turn it off if you like." He snapped his fingers, and suddenly the only lights were the truck headlights and running lights, which still illuminated Ruddygore pretty well.

Suddenly the vast sea of stars that was the west Texas sky on a clear night faded in, brilliant and impressive and, somehow, reassuring.

Joe heard the door open and close on the passenger side and knew that the woman was coming despite his cautions. He couldn't really blame her—hell, this was crazy.

"What's going on?" she wanted to know.

Ruddygore turned, bowed low, and said, "Madam, it is a pleasure to meet you, even if you are an unexpected complication. I am Throckmorton P. Ruddygore."

She stared at him, then over at Joe, half in shadow, and caught sight of the pistol in his hand. "Hey—what's this all about?" she called to him, disturbed.

"The man says I'm dead, honey," Joe told her. "He says I'm about to have a fatal accident. He says he's a conjure man. Other than that, he's said nothing at all."

Her mouth opened, then closed and she looked confusedly from one man to the other. She was not a small woman, but she felt dwarfed by the two giants. Finally she said to Ruddygore, "Is he right?"

Ruddygore nodded. "I'm afraid so. Unless, of course, he takes me up on my proposition."

"I figured we'd get to the point of all this sooner or later," Joe muttered.

"Exactly so," Ruddygore agreed. "I'm a recruiter, you see. I come from a place that's not all *that* unfamiliar to people of your world, but which is, in effect, a world of its own. It is a world of men—and others—both very much like and very different from what you know. It is a world both more peaceful and more violent than your Earth. That is, there are no guns, no nuclear missiles, no threats of world holocaust. The violence is more direct, more basic—say medieval. Right now that world is under attack and it needs help. After examining all the factors, I find that help from outside my world might— *might*—have a slight edge, for various reasons too long to go into here. And so I look for recruits, but not just *any* recruits. People with special qualities that will go well over there. People who fit special requirements to do the job. And, of course, people who are about to die and who meet those other requirements are the best recruits. You see?"

"Let me get this straight," the woman put in. "You're from another planet?" She looked up at the stars. "Out there? And you're whisking away people to help you fight a war? And we've got the chance to join up and go—or die?"

"That's about the size of it," Ruddygore admitted. "Although you are not quite right. First of all, I have no idea if *you* will die. I had no idea you would be in the truck. And, as an honorable man, I must admit that he might be able to save you if, after returning to the road, he lets you off. Might. He, however, *is* in the situation you describe. Secondly, I'm no little green man from Mars. The world I speak of is not up *there*, it's—well, somewhere else." He looked thoughtful for a moment.

"Think of it this way," he continued. "Think of opposites. Nature usually contains opposites. There is even, I hear, a different kind of matter, anti-matter, that's as real as we are yet works so opposite to us that, if it came into contact with us, it would cancel itself and us out. When the Earth was created, my world was also created—a by-product, you might say, of the creation. It's very much like Earth, but it is in many ways an opposite. It runs by different rules. But it's as real a place as any you've been to, and, I think, a better, nicer place than Earth in a number of ways."

Far off in the distance there seemed to come a deep sound, like a boat's whistle, or a steam train blowing off. Ruddygore heard it and turned back to Joe.

"You have to decide soon, you know," he told the driver. "The ferry's coming in, and it won't wait long. Although few ride it, because only a very few can find it or even know of it, it keeps a rigid schedule, for the path it travels is impossible unless you're greatly skilled *and* well timed. You can die and pass beyond my ken to the unknown beyond, or you can come with me. Face it, Joe. What have you got to lose? Even if you somehow could beat your destiny, you're only going through the motions, anyway. There's nothing for you in *this* world any more. I offer a whole new life."

"And maybe just as short," the driver replied. "I did my bit of soldiering."

"Oh, it's not like that. We have many for armies. I need you for special tasks, not military ones. Adventure, Joe. A new life. A new world. I will make you young again. Better than you ever were."

Something snapped inside the driver. "No! You're Satan come to steal me at the last minute! I know you now!" And, with that, he fired three shots point-blank at Ruddygore.

The huge man didn't even flinch, but simply smiled, pursed his lips, and spat out the three spent bullets. "Lousy aim," he commented. "I really didn't catch any of them. I had to use magic." He sighed sadly. The whistle sounded again, closer now. "But I'm not the devil, Joe. I'm flesh and blood and I live. I am not a man, but I was once a man, and still am more than not. There are far worse things than your silly, primitive devil, Joe—that's part of what I'm fighting. Come with me—now. Down to the dock."

Joe looked disgusted, both with Ruddygore and with the pistol. "All right, Ruddygore, or whoever or whatever you are. It don't make any difference, anyway. I can't go. Not if I can save her. You understand the duty."

Ruddygore nodded sadly. "I feared as much when I saw her in the cab. And for such a motive I can't stop you or blame you. Damn! You wouldn't believe how much trouble all this was, too. What a waste."

"Hey! Wait a minute!" the woman put in. "Don't *I* get to say anything about this?"

They both looked at her expectantly.

"Look, if I had a million bucks, I'd bet that I'm still sound asleep in that truck up there, speeding down a highway toward El Paso, and that this is all a crazy dream. But it's a great dream. The best I ever had. I'm on my way to kill myself. I've had it—up to here. I gave up on this stupid, crazy world. So I'm dreaming—or I'm psycho, in some funny world of my own. Okay. I'll take it. It's better than real life. There's no way I'm going back to that life. No way I'm getting back in that truck, period. I've finally done it! Gone completely off my rocker into a fantasy world that sounds pretty good to me."

Ruddygore's face broke into a broad, beaming smile. He looked over at the driver. "Joe? What do you say now?"

"Well, I heard her story and I can't say I blame her. But I'm the one who's gone bananas, not her."

"Dreams," Ruddygore mused. "No, this is no dream, but think of it that way if you like. For, in a sense, we're all just dreams. The Creator's dreams. And where we travel to is out there." He gestured with a cane, gold-tipped and with a dragon's head for a handle. "Out across the Sea of Dreams and beyond to the far shore. So take it as a dream, the both of you, if you wish. As a dream, you have even less to lose."

The pistol finally went down and was replaced in Joe's pocket. He looked back at the truck. "Maybe we should get our things."

"You won't need them," Ruddygore told him. "All will be provided to you as you need it. That's part of the bargain." The whistle sounded a third time, very close now, and Ruddygore turned to face the dark direction of its cry. "Come. Just follow me."

Joe looked back at his truck again. "I should at least kill the motor and the lights," he said wistfully. "That truck's the only thing I got, the only thing I ever had in my whole life that was real. This ferry—I don't suppose . . . ?"

Ruddygore shook his head sadly. "No, I'm afraid not. Your truck wouldn't work over there. The captain would never allow it, anyway, because we couldn't get it off the boat and it would take up too much room. But don't worry about it, Joe. It's not really here, you see. It's somewhere back there, on your Interstate 10."

With that the truck faded and was gone, lights, engine noise, and all, and they were in total darkness.

The whistle sounded once more, and it seemed almost on top of them.

CHAPTER 2

ACROSS THE SEA OF DREAMS

Travel between universes shall be difficult and highly restricted.
—XXI, 55, 44(b)

THE FERRY CAME OUT OF THE DARKNESS, FLOATING ON A SEA of black. It surprised them that it looked very much like the old ferryboats—an oval-shaped, double-ended affair with a lower platform for cars, and stairways up both sides to the upper deck, where the twin pilothouses, one at each end of the boat, flanked a passenger lounge of some sort with a large single stack rising right up the middle. The sides of the car deck weren't solid, but were punctuated by five large openings on each side, openings without windows or other obstructions, yet the car deck could not be seen through them.

Each one of the huge, round holes had a gigantic oar sticking out of it. The oars were in a raised position, seemingly locked in place. It was clear from the engine sounds and the wisps of white from the stack that the captain was using his engine.

"I never saw a ferry except in pictures," the woman remarked, "but I bet nobody ever saw one with oars before."

Ruddygore nodded. "The engine's in good shape for settling in on this side, but, once out on the sea and to the other shore, that kind of mechanical power just isn't possible to use." He paused a moment. "Ah! It's docked! Shall we go aboard?"

Joe stood there and stared for a minute. "Funny," he muttered, mostly to himself. "I swear I've seen this thing before someplace. Way, way back and long ago. When I was a kid." He scratched his head a moment, then snapped his fingers. "Yeah! Sure! The old Chester ferry. Long, long ago." He peered into the gloom, but the illumination from the passenger deck allowed him to see what he was looking for. "Yeah. There on the side. Kinda faded and peeling, but you can still make out the words 'Chester—Bridgeport.' I'll be damned!"

Ruddygore nodded. "It takes many shapes and many forms, for it's shaped from history and from memories, the backwash

21

of the world flowing backward into the sea whence it came. It is as it is because of your memories, Joe. But—come! I don't want to keep it waiting; as I said, it has a schedule to keep." He paused briefly. "You're not having second thoughts now, are you? Either of you?"

Joe looked at the woman, and she shrugged and gestured ahead with her hand. "Guess not," Joe replied dubiously. As Ruddygore led the way, first she and then the trucker followed, still more than a little uncertain of it all.

Even stepping onto the ribbed metal of the car deck, they both felt an air of dreamy unreality about the whole thing, as if they were in the midst of some wondrous dreaming drug or, perhaps, comatose and in some fantasy world of the mind. Still, both looked in at the cavernous car deck—and saw nothing. Nothing at all. It was totally and completely dark in there, with not even the other end of the boat showing.

Ruddygore led them to the right stairway and saw them peering into the dark. "I wouldn't be too anxious to see in there," he cautioned them. "The ones who row this ship are best not seen by mortal human beings, I assure you. Come. Climb up to the lounge with me and relax, and I will try to answer your questions as best I can."

Hesitantly, they both followed him, still glancing occasionally at the total dark that masked whoever or whatever could manage oars that had to weigh a ton or more each.

It was quickly obvious that they were the only passengers, and the lounge, as Ruddygore had called it, was deserted— but they had obviously been expected. A number of wooden chairs and benches were around, looking a bit shopworn but not too bad; in the rear, around the stack and its housing, was a large buffet table filled with cold platters and pitchers of something or other.

"Just take what you want whenever you feel hungry," the sorcerer told them. "The red jugs are a fair rose, the yellow a decent if slightly warm ale. Use any of the flagons you see— they're public."

The engines suddenly speeded up, and there was the faint but definite sensation of moving, moving back out into the dark. But moving where? And on what sea?

"What are we floating on—desert?" the woman asked.

Ruddygore cut himself a hunk of cheese, poured some wine,

tore off a large chunk of bread, then sat down in a chair that creaked under his great weight and settled back.

"We are heading across the Sea of Dreams," he told them between large bites and swallowed.

Joe decided he might as well eat, too, and followed Ruddygore's lead, except for taking some sliced meat as well and the ale rather than wine. "I never heard of a Sea of Dreams," he noted. "And it sure ain't in Texas."

Ruddygore chuckled, "No, Joe, it sure ain't. And yet, in a way, it is very close to Texas—and everyplace else, for that matter. It is the element that connects the universes. It isn't anywhere, really, except—well, *between*."

The woman wandered out onto the deck for a moment and stared down at the inky blackness. There was the strong feeling of movement; wind blew her hair, wind with an unaccustomed chill in it, but there was no sound of water, no smell of sea or brine.

She shivered in the cold and came back in to join the others. "That sea—is that water?"

Ruddygore reloaded with meat and half a loaf of bread and settled back. "Oh, no. But it has the consistency of water and the surface properties of water, so you treat it that way. In truth, I couldn't begin to explain to you what it actually is." He thought a moment. "The best way to give you at least a sense of it is to provide you with a little background."

Both passengers settled down. "Shoot," Joe invited him.

"Go back to the beginning. I mean the *real* beginning. The explosion that created your universe and mine. Where was the Creator before He created the universes?"

Joe shrugged. "Heaven?"

"But he created the heavens and the earth, also," Ruddygore reminded them. "Well, I'll tell you where He was. Here. And when He created your universe, He also created all the natural laws, the rules by which it all operates, and He generally has played by those rules, particularly in the past couple thousand years or so. But when He created your Earth, there was a backwash from all that released energy. As it surged from here toward your universe, an equal suction of sorts was created that resulted in the creation of another world—indeed, another whole universe on the other side of here. The force of it was such that it was totally complete—but it wasn't the universe

He was interested in. Realizing, though, that it was there, He turned it over to associates who were around. Angels, you might call 'em, although that's far too simple a term."

Ruddygore paused to stuff his face with gobs of meat and cheese, washed everything down with most of a pitcher of wine, then continued.

"The other universe was, of course, a mess, since it was more or less a backwash of yours. Much natural law held, but not enough to make any real sense out of it. It was chaos. How it was in reality is totally beyond imagination, I assure you, but it was an environment more alien than any other planet in your universe. It was madness beyond imagining, and it was obvious to those—angels—in charge that it must be stabilized, must have *rules* like those in the universe you know. But these were, after all, angels, not the Creator, and they could only shape what the Creator had wrought, not really change it. The result was a set of Laws, absolute Laws, governing how my universe and my world would operate. These Laws incorporate the basic physical laws needed for such a place to exist at all, but only the Creator can think of *everything*. Thus, the Laws of my world are, shall we say, soft. The simple ones, particularly on the local level, are subject to change."

"Huh?" the woman responded. "You mean, nine out of ten times that you drop a rock it goes down the way it should— but one in ten times it might go up? Or just stay there, suspended in midair?"

"Ah, something like that," the sorcerer replied. "Basically, that rock will drop every single time—unless someone with the knowledge and the will applies them to that specific rock. It won't do otherwise on its own, I assure you."

"This—place we're goin'," Joe put in. "It's got people and stuff?"

Ruddygore chuckled. "Yes, Joe, it's got 'people and stuff.' It didn't at the start, but the angels implored the Creator, once they'd gotten it set up, and He shifted a small group from your world over to mine. From that first tribe come the populations of today. And in the millennia that have passed since then, they've developed into different races, different cultures, just as on your Earth. Not quite as diverse, but diverse enough, and this despite the fact that there are far fewer languages there than on your Earth. It's not as important as you might think, that different language business. In your world almost all those peoples to the south of your own country, and many in your country, speak Spanish, I believe—yet there are many cultural differences among those peoples, and many countries that are quite different from one another. Geography and isolation do as much to make people diverse as language."

"You know a lot about our world," the woman noted. "Do your people visit us?"

"Oh, my, no!" Ruddygore laughed. "If they did, they'd soon be corrupted beyond belief. In fact, very few can cross the Sea of Dreams, and none as of now can do it until and unless *I* will it. You see, this is *my* ferry, and it's the only one. Oh, others can see the Sea and others can try the crossing, but it is tricky and dangerous. Impossible to cross, in fact, unless you know *exactly* how to do it. Fail and you will merge with the Sea, returning to the mind of the Creator—and you, yourself, will cease to exist. This is more than death. Your very soul is swallowed and merged back into the primal energies below us. You are gone in true death."

"You're telling us that there is a soul—an afterlife?" the woman pressed eagerly. "That's what it sounds like."

"Well, there is a soul, yes, Miss—just what *is* your name, anyway? We can't keep calling you 'that woman' all the time."

"Marjorie's my real name," she told them, "but mostly I just go by the nickname of Marge."

"All right—Marge," the sorcerer said, nodding. "At any rate, yes, you have a soul. All the humans have souls, and a few of the others. But as to the fate of those souls—there are a lot of things that can happen. Evil can destroy a soul—outside as well as internal evil—and leave the body empty. The soul can wander, or it can be trapped, or a million other things can happen. Otherwise it definitely goes *somewhere*, a *somewhere* from which it occasionally, but very rarely, returns. And there are, it seems, a *lot* of somewheres for that soul to go. Let's not get into that now."

"Okay," Joe agreed. "But I noticed you said all the humans have souls, and a few of the others. What kind of others do you mean?"

Ruddygore sighed. "An infinite variety, really. Those without souls are, of course, the creations of the original angels. To compensate, most are immortal or nearly so, meaning they don't age. They can still, of course, be killed—although, even there, they have a lot of charms and protections. They are not killed in the same way people are, usually. To that original band have been added, over the millennia, ones from your own world who were involved in the original creation but who have, through the dominance of man, been displaced and, by luck, or charm, or the help of me and my predecessors, or the mercy of the Creator, have made their way to my side of the Sea. A one-way trip, though. Some of these have souls, as the Creator Himself willed."

"What sort of—others?" Joe pressed nervously.

"Elves, gnomes, leprechauns—those sorts. The stuff of your legends the world over. The other folk who once shared your world, but for whom man had less and less need and far less room and tolerance. The stuff of your fantasies and legends. Their ties to their native Earth, in fact, are bridges between the worlds across the Sea of Dreams, in a way, for even today those artists and writers of fantasy and the fantastic in your world see them, experience them, if only in dreams, and write of their exploits. The fantasies, the myths, the dreams of your world, are the reality of mine."

Ruddygore sighed. "Look. We cross the Sea of Dreams, and the Creator is even now all around us. He sleeps, and as He sleeps He dreams. Some of the dreams are pleasant ones. Some are nightmares. But *His* dreams take root and flow to one side of the Sea or the other, entering the dreams of one and the reality of the other. This war we now face may be but one of His nightmares. Even now, some dreamer on your world may perceive it in his own mind and write it as a fantasy. You ought to think about that, anyway. You might well be the stuff of an epic fantasy novel in your own world, the dreamer there unknowing that he writes of your reality."

"I'd rather not think about that one," Marge said sourly.

"At any rate," the sorcerer continued, "you're going to a world that will be at once totally different and very familiar to you both. Like this boat. It is a familiar thing to Joe, yet it has not existed since he was a child. It is familiar—yet it is something else. Listen! Have you sensed that the engines have shut down?"

They were all suddenly quiet, attentive to the noises—and found that he was right. The thrumming of the engine had ceased, and along with it, the vibration against the glass windows of the lounge.

After a few moments of silence, they could hear the groanings of grommets larger than they as the massive oars were seized, freed, and dipped in unison down into the Sea of Dreams.

Below them, on that dark and mysterious car deck now began a deep, hollow sound, rhythmic and somewhat intrusive. It sounded like some giant drummer beating a slow tempo on some great kettledrum. It was all around them, yet not quite pervasive enough to drown out conversation.

"I know what that is," Joe said. "I saw *Ben Hur* nine times. They're rowing to the beat."

Ruddygore nodded. "That's exactly what they're doing. And they'll speed up when they can and maintain it for a long while."

"Just who are—they?" Marge asked apprehensively, thinking of the size of the boat and those oars.

"Monsters," Ruddygore replied casually, getting more cheese. "Real ones. Lost balls, you might say. One-of-a-kinds that didn't make it in either your universe or mine. Once evil and all defeated, they had no real choice. They row the boat, or they are cast adrift in the Sea of Dreams, unable to swim to any shore, even in dock. Oh, don't look so shocked. All of them deserve what they got, and all are volunteers, in a sense. I offered them a chance to row or sink, and they all chose to row. They are comfortable and reasonably kept and they are all now doing something constructive rather than the terrible things they did to destroy, way back in the past."

Marge shivered a little, suddenly even more aware of the beat of the great drum, and tried not to think of what might be beating it. She got up and went back over to the doorway, looking out at the darkness once more.

"Hey! There's something out there!" she called to them. Joe and Ruddygore walked over and joined her. The sorcerer slid back the door and walked out onto the deck. The other two followed.

The creak and groan of the great oars below was noticeable, but with their present better speed and rhythm, they and the drumming could be more or less tuned out. The breeze was still cool. Ruddygore stood at the rail a moment, staring off into the gloom and listening above the sound of the rowing and creak of the ship. "Just what did you see?" he asked her.

She shook her head in puzzlement. "I—I'm not really sure. Some large shapes and odd lights."

"You're liable to see just about anything out there if you stare long enough," the sorcerer told them. "All that was is drawn back to the Sea, and all that will be is formed and dispatched from it. Only what *is* is elsewhere."

In the night, after a while, they all could see what Marge had seen and more. Shapes, some familiar, some unfamiliar. Skylines and odd buildings, then at another time what looked like the fully deployed three masts of some great sailing ship, although the ship itself could not be seen. There were sounds, too—vague, low, yet omnipresent. The sounds of millions of voices talking together far off in some void; the sounds of great machines, of explosions, of building and destroying, all merged into a vague whole. For a while they were caught in its eerie spell, but finally Joe asked, "How long until we get to— wherever it is we're going?"

"A few hours," Ruddygore told him. "You might want to stretch out on one of the benches and catch some sleep—both of you. You've had quite a time so far this night."

"Maybe I will," Joe responded, scratching and yawning a bit.

Marge just shook her head. "No way for me. I'm afraid if I go to sleep I'm going to wake up on the outskirts of El Paso."

Ruddygore chuckled. "I understand your worry, but it won't happen, I assure you. Once we cast off from your world, you were committed irrevocably and forever. Only a few from my side may travel back and forth at will. For those like you, it is a one-way trip."

Joe did stretch out and after a while was snoring softly, but Marge was as good as her word, both anxious and too keyed up to sleep now. She sat down near Ruddygore, who was eating again, and tried to find out more.

"This place we're going to—does it have a name?" she asked him.

He nodded. "Oh, yes. It hasn't just one name, but many. Of course, the planet itself is simply called the world, or earth, just as you call yours. Why not? It's logical. But the nations and principalities are quite differently named and very distinct.

We are bound for Valisandra, my chosen land, to my castle there."

"You're the ruler of a country?"

"Oh, my, no!" He laughed. "Valisandra is a kingdom and quite well and fairly governed. The day-to-day administration of a nation is far too complex and boring for me, I'm afraid, and I'd probably do a very poor job if I ever got the chance. I'm more a—sorcerer in residence, you might say. Long ago I did a trifling service for the current king's grandfather and was given my castle and some land around it as a gift of thanks. With so much magic loose in the world, it gives comfort to the king and his people to have a powerful sorcerer living among them. I have great affection for the land and its people. I have been one among them for a very long time, and I have the same stake in its well-being and preservation as they do. They know this—and they also know that I have no political ambition whatsoever, and thus am no threat to them. There are few ranking sorcerers in the world today—thirteen, all told, including myself—although there are hundreds of slightly lesser lights that may one day replace us."

"This—Vali—"

"Valisandra."

"Valisandra, then. What's it like?"

He sat back, took another long swig of wine, and smiled. "It's a pretty country. The climate is mostly temperate, except in the far north, and the land is rich in good, black earth made for growing things. The people—about three million, all told— are pretty well divided between free farmers and townspeople and those on feudal holdings. The central government's fairly strong, with its own army, so the feudal hold is weak—more like sharecropping than the semi-slavery state some places have. There are still wild areas, too, where the unicorn and deer play free and the fairies come out to dance. Yes, it's a very pleasant place indeed."

She smiled. "It sounds nice. But you said something about a war. That doesn't sound so pleasant."

"It's a different world from yours," he reminded her. "In some ways more peaceful by far. There are no laser-guided battle stations in orbit, no ICBMs and strategic bombers ready to destroy the world at the slip of a politician's nerve. But there is war, and jealousy, and greed, and, yes, death there as well, as they are in every place that mankind exists. Think of a world where magic, not science, is supreme. There are no hospitals, no miracle cures or shock trauma units; and that means a higher mortality rate. There is, of course, medicine—folk and herbal, which can be surprisingly effective sometimes—and magical healers as well. No electricity or great engines for good *or* evil. Power is the wind and water and muscle, as it was in the old days on your world, although there is a cleverness in civil engineering that builds dikes and aqueducts and the like. On the surface, a more primitive, simpler world—but only on the surface. It would be a mistake to think of it as a medieval Earth, for the world is very complex and far more diverse than yours, and the magic is as complex in its own way as nuclear physics is in your world."

She nodded. "It sounds like a fairy story."

"It *is* a fairy story. It is the origin of all such tales. But it is very real—and right now, my part of it is in trouble."

"The war."

"Yes—the war," he responded. "The overall district is called Husaquahr. It's almost fifteen hundred miles from north to south, and more than half that from east to west. There are six countries, as well as five City-States around the mouth of the river which dominates the land. The River of Dancing Gods."

"The River of Dancing Gods," she repeated. "It's a charming name."

"It's more than charming. The river itself winds its way from the Golden Lakes in the north to the Kudra Delta far to the south. It is the blood of Husaquahr—its arteries are its many tributaries, and the system is life itself to the millions of humans and fairy folk who make up its population."

"Why is it named Dancing Gods?"

"There are all sorts of legends and stories about that, but I suspect its divinity derives from its importance to its people. The dancing part may have a thousand reasons in legend, but it is perhaps because it is a very old river that meanders greatly, so much so that to travel on the river the fifteen hundred straight-line miles to the delta from the lakes, you would actually travel over twenty-four hundred miles. It is a primary water source for irrigation, and it is navigable from the point where the Rossignol joins it to form the southwestern border of Valisandra. It is the Nile, the Mississippi, the Ganges, the Yellow, the Volga—and more, all rolled up into one. And, in a sense, it's what the war is about."

"Yes, we're back to the war."

He nodded. "The enemy force includes every destructive element in Husaquahr and from elsewhere besides. Evil, greedy, petty—you name it. It is a frightening force, commanded by a charismatic general known only as the Dark Baron. Who or what he actually is, is unknown, but he is, for certain, a great sorcerer who takes some pains to escape being identified. That makes me believe that he is the worst of all enemies, a fellow sorcerer on the Council that oversees the magic of the entire world. One of my brothers. Or, perhaps, sisters. The Dark Baron is so totally cloaked that it might be either."

"But if the sorcerer is one of your own—doesn't that narrow the field?" she asked. "I mean, it should be simple to discover which of only twelve others he or she might be."

"You'd think so," Ruddygore agreed, "but it's not that simple. Our skills may differ, but our powers are equal—and we are bound by our own rules and laws. No sorcerer may enter the lands or castle of another without the permission of the owner. Distances are great. Magical power being equal, there is no way to tell who is doing what. I assure you that it is quite possible to appear to be in two or even a dozen places at once. Spies within a fellow sorcerer's lairs are impossible—we smell each other too easily. And, of course, even if we knew, it would require incontrovertible proof before any action could be taken. Most of my brothers and sisters on the Council refuse to believe that one of their own could turn this way, and the Council would have to act in concert to defeat and destroy this enemy once and for all. So they sit idly by while the Dark Baron's armies march on Husaquahr, and unless those are defeated in battle, there's nothing that can be done. The Council will not stop something as petty as a war. They are almost traditional."

"But you're meddling," she pointed out.

He nodded. "Someone has to, I fear, and since I suspect that I am at least one primary object of the war, it is in my own self-interest to do so."

"You? They want to kill you?"

"No. I believe that the Dark Baron, with some of his great and powerful allies, could kill me if he wished. Kill me—but not capture me. You see, he has most certainly allied himself with the forces of Beyond—you might call it Hell itself—and that tips the scale in his favor. Oh, he's very clever about it— if I could prove that alliance, it would be the evidence needed to force the Council into action—but *I* know."

"This is starting to get complicated," she noted. "Who or what are these forces of Beyond?"

"Well, you know the story basically, I'm sure. Some of the angels of the Creator rebelled against Him and were cast out. Since that time those forces have been trying to get back, working through the actions of evil ones in your world and mine. Well, now they have their most powerful ally, and the assault's on my world, not yours, and thus more likely not to worry the Creator. They've been terribly frustrated that your own world hasn't yet blown itself into atoms despite their agents' best efforts. But now they have a chance—by getting back into Husaquahr and then, they hope, by forcing an accommodation with me—literally to invade your world, using my powers as a bridge."

She looked shocked. "You mean you'd *do* it?"

He shrugged. "They're not terribly interested in my world, because it's not a primary creation of the Creator. It's yours they want. But it's *my* world, after all. If they can seize and dominate it, they might force a swap, a trade. If they can gain control of the River of Dancing Gods, they will have Husaquahr by the throat, and that's exactly what they're trying to do. It's a slow, brutal conquest—but they are winning."

She sat back, a little dazed, and considered what he had said. The forces of Hell were after Earth—her native Earth— and were willing to conquer and destroy a whole different world to do this. She could appreciate Ruddygore's position, too. He alone knew the way across the Sea of Dreams. He alone could ferry them safely through the very mind of the Creator Himself. And since he controlled the pathway, he could be rid of them— by sending them one-way into Earth.

"Why don't you just send them all over and be done with it, then?" she asked him. "Wouldn't that solve your problem?"

He looked at her strangely and was silent a moment. Finally he muttered, "Yes, your world *has* treated you most unkindly, I see." He cleared his throat, and his voice grew loud and firm once more. "You seem to forget that your world is the *primary* object of creation. What you suggest is that I precipitate Armageddon. Disregarding the billions of souls I would have on my conscience for a moment, let me remind you that Armageddon would engulf everything, involve the Creator directly. My world would no more survive it than yours, and with less promise of rebuilding thereafter. There will be no Armageddon laid against my soul's account! I do not intend that—even if it means the total destruction of Husaquahr. But they will never believe that. Or they may believe, but not believe that they can not somehow get the secret, anyway. But I have a different plot in mind.

"I intend to beat them at their own game. Send them back into the abyss from which they crawled, they and all their ilk."

CHAPTER 3

"A PROPER HERO AND HEROINE"

Barbarians must be tall, dark, and handsome, exotic in race but of no known nationality.

—XL, 227, 301(a)

SHE SLEPT THEN, THE DEEPEST, SOUNDEST, MOST PEACEFUL sleep she'd had in recent memory, and so hard was it that she barely stirred when shaken the first time. Finally she became aware that somebody was trying to wake her, but she resisted. It was so very peaceful and felt so very good, and it had been such a long time . . .

At last she muttered, "All right, all right," to the mysterious shaker and, in a moment more, managed to open her eyes. She gave a little gasp and rubbed her eyes, a slow smile creeping over her lips. What she saw was the impossibly named and improbably dressed Throckmorton P. Ruddygore. "So it *was* real," she breathed.

He grinned. "Oh, yes. Come. Time to get up, get something into you, and get ready to begin. We're almost there now."

She yawned, stretched, got up, and looked casually out the

windows of the lounge. It was still dark right around them, but off in the distance day seemed to be slowly breaking.

Joe was already up and he nodded to her as she went back to the food table. It had changed somehow during the night and was now filled with pastries, cheese, crackers, brown bread, and condiments that made up a solid European-style breakfast. The pitchers and flagons, she found, were filled with various kinds of fruit juices—and there was a large pot of coffee.

Suddenly conscious of her hunger, she started in.

"No eggs or sausage or nothin'," Joe grumped. "A man's got to have something solid in him to start a day."

Ruddygore laughed. "I'm afraid you'll have to get used to this sort of thing, both of you. Everything's a bit more primitive in Husaquahr, and without refrigeration your American-style breakfasts just aren't practical. I wouldn't complain too much, though. There are times when you'll wish you *had* a breakfast like this."

"I don't mind at all," Marge assured him. "I never was much for the breakfast stuff, anyway."

Ruddygore looked at her with a satisfied expression. "You seem a lot more chipper today," he noted.

She nodded and sipped at the coffee, which was strong and bitter, but still what she needed to complete the waking-up process. "I woke up and you're both still here. That's enough."

Joe wandered over to the windows and looked forward. "Funny, I can see the dawn over there, but it's still dark as pitch right overhead."

"That's because it's never dawn on the Sea," the sorcerer told him. "What you're seeing is not dawn but the edge of the Sea of Dreams. You'll know we're out of it when we come into full light, although I've arranged for a bit of a fog. It wouldn't do to be seen putting in, you know."

Marge went over and looked out at the approaching sky. "How long?"

"An hour, maybe less," the sorcerer replied. "It's actually quite close, but particularly in this area we're going against the current."

Joe scratched and stretched. "I could use a shower."

"Me, too," Marge seconded, feeling just how grubby she'd let herself become. It was the first time in a long time that she cared about it one way or the other.

"Sorry. No facilities on the boat," Ruddygore told them. "You've seen the pitiful little johns—and they're more modern than you'll likely see again. There's little for showering at the castle, either, I fear, but I'm sure I could arrange for a bath. Just hold on until we get there."

Marge looked back out at the approaching division in the sky, then turned toward the sorcerer. "How long from when we land until we get to this castle of yours?" she asked him. "I seem to remember last night you said it was way up near the source of this big river."

"Indeed it is," Ruddygore told her, "but that won't bother us. The Sea of Dreams contacts all points in all universes. We will land within walking distance of the castle, I assure you. I could arrange even now for us to be met, but I think the walk will do us all good—and you'll get a look at the land." He turned and gestured toward the food table. "In the meantime, let us eat, drink, and be merry."

"Yeah, 'cause tomorrow we die," Joe responded grumpily. Clearly he was very much out of his element and most uncomfortable about it.

"We've broken through!" Marge called to them, and both men came to join her at the window. The darkness was gone— totally gone, with no sign fore or aft that it had ever been. They were now in a dense, white fog that obscured everything. Somewhere up there, though, was a bright point of light that had to be a sun, and that cheered both of the newcomers.

They heard the beat slow, heard oars being shipped, and realized now that they were drifting with a far different kind of current from that of the Sea of Dreams. There was no mistaking the feeling that the boat was coming in to dock.

They went outside on deck, and Marge in particular was cheered to find it comfortably warm, although the dense fog threatened to soak them through. She walked forward, around the pilothouse, and the two men followed. Neither Joe nor Marge could resist looking in the pilothouse, but there was nothing to be seen. Whoever or whatever the captain of this ghostly ferry was, he, she, or it was definitely not visible in the daylight, although the large wooden wheel moved with a deliberateness that said that something, someone, was there.

"The captain and deck crew are nice folks," Ruddygore told

them, "but rather sensitive about being seen. Among other things, unlike the rowing crew, *they* can and occasionally do go ashore, and what the passengers don't know about them can't someday be betrayed to an enemy."

Marge took a last look back at the apparently empty wheelhouse and shivered slightly despite the damp warmth. She wondered idly if Ruddygore was being completely honest and straightforward with them. Not that it made any difference right now. They were totally in his hands and at his mercy.

Somewhere aft, a loud bell clanged four times, and again some of the oars came down as the boat performed a steering maneuver. There was a sudden lurch, then a great bump that went the length of the boat, and abruptly the oars shipped again and the boat came to a complete stop.

"Well, we're home!" Ruddygore announced cheerfully. "Follow me." With that he made his way down one of the side stairways.

Joe looked out at the all-encompassing fog and shook his head. "Some home," he muttered to himself, but followed the other two.

They walked across the ribbed metal car deck and saw that there was a smooth area beyond the boat. Ruddygore stepped off onto it unhesitatingly, and after a moment, Marge and Joe did likewise.

The fog began to fade only a few paces from the boat, and before they'd gone fifty yards it had completely vanished, revealing an unexpectedly beautiful scene.

They were in a small wooded area beside a large river, the woods following and hugging the river itself, which seemed to be a thousand yards or more wide and whose other shore was apparently dense forest.

But ahead was cleared land, gently rolling and lushly green with tall, unmowed grasses. Everywhere, too, were wildflowers by the thousands, of countless colors and shapes and varieties, sticking up through the deep green grass. Insects, many very familiar-looking, buzzed and twitted to and fro; here and there small birds circled, dipped, or landed and hopped around in the grass.

Beyond was a hill, not very high, really. Beyond it was a bluff dominating the scene, and on top of the bluff was a castle of the kind both newcomers had seen only in picture books.

"Just like Disneyland," Joe muttered.

"Colder, draftier, but a lot bigger and more useful," Ruddygore responded. "That is Terindell. My home."

"It's beautiful," Marge told him. "Even more beautiful than you described last night."

Ruddygore led the way along a path that seemed well-worn, leading through the lush fields to the castle in an indirect, meandering fashion. It was not paved, but was dry and solid black earth and rock and proved no problem.

"The path is circuitous mostly because of erosion," the sorcerer explained. "As you might guess from the richness of the vegetation, this region gets a lot of rain, and a straight path would have worn its way into a crevass by now."

"I don't mind," Marge assured him. "It's so beautiful here, and I never felt better in my life."

Joe looked back dubiously. "Where's the boat?"

"Oh, it's not here," Ruddygore replied. "It never quite makes the whole trip either way. You might as well forget that boat, Joe. You'll never see it again."

The walk up to the castle took the better part of an hour, but it was time well spent in just enjoying life and feeling good. Marge was like a kid again, laughing and smelling flowers and chasing butterflies; even Joe seemed to be affected with a sense of well-being after a while. He didn't join in, but at least he laughed along with her.

Shortly before reaching the castle itself, the path intersected the main road leading up to it. It was a dirt and gravel road and not used very much, judging by the lack of real impressions in it, but it was well maintained.

As their elevation increased, they could look down and see the panorama that was Ruddygore's normal view.

"The river we just came from, back there, is the Rossignol," the sorcerer told them. "A gentle river that sings sweet, sad songs, but is a grand old lady in her own right. Over there, now, you can see her child, and the child of many other rivers great and small. The River of Dancing Gods."

Even this far north, there was no comparing the great river with its tributary. It flowed, shimmering golden in the sunlight, a broad, wide, powerful river. Although here it was not much wider than the Rossignol, they could see where the two rivers joined, and where they seemingly flowed along together in the same bed off into the distance, the dark of the Rossignol seemingly resisting the mix with its golden master. But when they joined, the River of Dancing Gods grew enormously, already a mile or more from bank to bank, a great river indeed, with more than a thousand miles left to grow in power and strength even more.

"The other side of the Dancing Gods is Hypboreya, a very different sort of country," Ruddygore told them. "Across the Rossignol is Marquewood, a republic that is even now threatened on its southern border by the forces of the Dark Baron. This little spot of Terindell is but a small finger of Valisandra pointing southwest."

After a last, long look at the stunningly beautiful scene, they regretfully continued around the castle and up to its great outer gate with its massive wooden doors.

Somewhere inside, a trumpet blared briefly, echoing through the inner courtyard, and a great gong sounded three times. At the third gong stroke, the huge doors opened inward, revealing, to the newcomers' surprise, a moat. The inner castle was still a good forty feet beyond. Now from the inner castle, the drawbridge lowered slowly on rusting hinges with a clatter of chains and a moaning of protesting timbers.

"Wow. Just like Robin Hood," Joe muttered, a bit awestruck in spite of himself.

The drawbridge hit with a clang, and, allowing Ruddygore to lead the way, they entered the inner castle.

The entire castle was more a complex than a single building—and complex was the word. The outer wall, including small guard towers and turrets, was thick enough to have almost an avenue along its protected top; inside, it presented a complex of ledges connected by elaborate stairways, all made out of granite. Beyond this was the moat—an ugly affair, oily on the surface and smelling as stagnant as it must be.

The inner castle was a second, thicker shell that definitely had rooms throughout. How many it was impossible to tell, but from the positioning of the windows they could see that there were at least four floors. It was perhaps a hundred feet thick.

Inside this structure was a broad, green courtyard, well kept and maintained, with decorative shrubbery and flower beds; it was broken by a series of blocky stone buildings of various sizes.

They stopped at the edge of the courtyard, and Ruddygore beamed with pride. "Terindell was built more than six centuries ago," he told them. "It has a grand and glorious history, since its position here commanded the heights overlooking the two great rivers and their junction—and, therefore, what commerce and use the rivers made possible. It is quite a fortress, and its location is still vital; but so long as it is mine and I am here, it is safe from the kind of violence it was built to withstand."

"They'd have a tough time getting anybody out of here who didn't want to go," Joe agreed. "They'd have to surround you and starve you out, most likely, and that would put *their* backs to the river in case you wanted out."

Ruddygore looked surprised at his new recruit. "You seem to understand the military factors of my world very well for someone from such a technological culture as your own. Do you have any experience in this sort of thing?"

"Naw. It just seemed logical, is all," the former trucker replied.

"Hmmm..." Ruddygore muttered to himself. "Remind me never to confuse ignorance and stupidity again." He cleared his throat and regained command of the conversation. "Staff quarters are in the inner ring, as we call it. I also do a bit of teaching here, and those students also stay there. Inside here we have the central kitchen, then the adjoining banquet hall. The two-storey, blocky L-shaped building over there contains my library, laboratories, and quarters. Come—we'll go there first."

He led the way across the courtyard. For the first time the two newcomers noticed others in the vast castle complex. Smoke was coming from the great chimney that abutted the kitchen, and from inside could be heard talking and the sounds of hard work. Around the courtyard, a few small boys were caring for flower groupings or trimming bushes. No, Marge saw, not small boys. About the size of nine- or ten-year-olds and dressed in green leotards and jerkins, but definitely not boys. One, at least, had a graying beard, and there was something odd, almost inhuman, about their wiry bowleggedness, oversized hands and feet, and disproportionately enormous and slightly pointed ears. Ruddygore caught her thoughts.

"Elves," he told her. "Nice, pleasant folk. Nobody better for landscaping and grounds maintenance work."

Even as they followed the sorcerer, both Joe and Marge could hardly keep from staring at the little men busily at work.

They reached Ruddygore's building and headquarters and were met at the door by a tall, exotic, and, again, not quite human creature. He was close to six feet and stood ramrod-straight, but he was oddly elongated. Joe thought of him as a four-foot-six man stretched somehow to that height. His face, too, was incredibly lean and thin, his ears large, thin, and sharply pointed. His skin was yellowish, and his eyes, black orbs set in deep red where white should be, darted this way and that like those of some beast of prey sizing up its victims. He was dressed in the same sort of jerkin and leotards as the elves, but his were a muddy brown. He wore no shoes; both hands and feet were long and had lengthy, eaglelike talons instead of nails. His jet-black hair was cropped very short, but a shock of it rose up and drooped slightly over his forehead. He was a formidable and fearsome sight, that was for sure.

"Welcome back, sir," the creature said in the stiff, emotionless tones of a butler or other professional servant. He neither looked nor sounded as if he were genuinely glad to see Ruddygore or anybody else. "Did you have a pleasant and successful trip?"

"Yes, yes, indeed," Ruddygore replied and started to go in. He was suddenly aware of his two guests' hesitancy, stopped, turned, and beckoned them in. "Please come in. Poquah— well, I won't say he doesn't bite, but he certainly doesn't bite friends."

Poquah gave what was probably meant as a disarming grin, but he showed an awful lot of sharp, pointy teeth and what looked like a black, forked tongue. The effect was more intimidating than it was hopefully meant to be.

Giving the creature something of a wide berth, they entered and found themselves in a large, two-storey open room completely lined by bookshelves going from floor to ceiling. The floor was covered with thick carpeting with elaborate designs in gold and silver against a burnt orange background. Around a central fireplace were four large, overstuffed chairs. The fireplace itself was reinforced with brick and stone and had a funnellike cap a few feet from the top that sucked up smoke and took it out the roof.

"My quick-reference library," the sorcerer told them with pride. "The bulk of the books are in storage rooms below the castle itself. The whole hill is really a man-made honeycomb of chambers."

They looked around the great library, and one thing immediately struck Marge, at least. "Very impressive," she told him. "I see all sorts of sizes and bindings on books on three of the walls—but all the books on that far wall look the same, with that red binding."

Ruddygore looked over at the wall and nodded. "Indeed, you're right in that they are related. You'll find a set of those in every town center, in every main city, and in the home of everyone wealthy enough to buy them or with any interest in the magical arts. Those, my dear, are the Books of Rules. Five hundred and thirty-seven leather-bound volumes with every little Rule that makes this place tick."

Poquah cleared his throat behind them. Marge jumped, not having heard him move at all. "Pardon, sir," the creature said, "but it is now five hundred and thirty-eight. A new one came in while you were away."

Ruddygore threw up his hands and looked to heaven. "By all the gods and demons and the Creator! This Council is the worst batch we *ever* had! No wonder the world is going to hell!" He let out a big sigh, then motioned to Joe and Marge. "Have a seat, you two, and I will try to explain this idiocy to you. Poquah, can you see about some cold ale for us and then rejoin us here? You're going to be involved in this, too, you know."

The creature bowed. "At once." He was gone so quickly they could hardly realize he had left.

Taking comfortable seats in the padded chairs, the two recruits waited for Ruddygore to begin.

"First of all," he said, "you have to remember what I told each of you in our different conversations last night. How this world was pure chaos, and how the angels in charge created order out of it."

They both nodded, each realizing now that the other had been given the same information.

"All right," the sorcerer went on, "What they did, they did

just to stabilize the place. They delivered the Laws. Needless to say, those Laws are complex and involved, and you could no more make sense of them than you could make sense of esoteric particle physics. But they're the operating Rules for the place. You follow me so far?"

They both nodded, and he continued.

"All right, then. Those Laws should be sufficient for everybody. They're very general and very universal, but they're all we really need. Unfortunately, several centuries ago, when this castle was an outpost in a major war, a new bunch of sorcerers came to the Council who were, let me say, rather pedestrian. All the really powerful magicians of the time had either perished in the wars or gone on to higher planes. This new Council was made up of pretty petty men—it was all male then, although that's changed—who decided that the Laws contained a large number of loopholes. They weren't specific enough. They didn't address modern problems. With that, the Council ceased being the guardian of the Laws and the integrity of magic and our way of life and became, alas, a bureaucracy. Oh, it was a creeping little thing—you never really noticed it, it was so agonizingly creeping—but, after a while, what we had were the Books of Rules to cover everybody's pet idea, theory, moral code—you name it. Anything they could get a majority of the Council to consider and pass on. Every generation of sorcerers brings some new stuff, and that's what you see behind me here. As long as none of the Rules break any of the Laws—nobody can do that—they are as binding and restrictive as any law of nature."

"Sounds like income tax," Joe commented sourly. "They started with a simple little tax, I'm told, on just the very rich, and got to the point where there were hundreds and hundreds of books of tax laws. I never could know 'em. Last year I had to pay over two hundred bucks to have my taxes done. And even the guys at the IRS admitted nobody really understood the whole thing. It was just too much of a big mess."

Ruddygore smiled. "Exactly! That is exactly it! I doubt if anybody anywhere understands all that's in those volumes. Fact is, you just live in the world and you aren't even aware that what you live with is one of the Rules. It's just the way things are. And they're constantly being revised and rewritten. Biggest mistake we made was forming a subcommittee to look over the Rules and throw out the bad and resolve some of the basic contradictions that came up. Instead, the fatheads just increased the amount of Rules."

"It's the tax code, all right," Joe said agreeably.

"Only it's worse, since what's in there affects everything and everybody," Ruddygore pointed out. "You have no choice in the matter. And you have no idea—yet—just how petty it can get. And how silly. In fact, that's one thing we will have to attend to right away with the two of you. Right now you're aliens in this land and still pretty much outside the Rules. If we don't attune you to them before you leave Terindell, all those dumb things will fall on you at the same time, and the Creator alone knows what sort of terrible things might happen to you. Poquah, is the lab in good shape?"

"Excellent, sir," the creature replied, and both Joe and Marge almost jumped out of their chairs. Poquah was standing there with a service cart filled with pitchers and tankards—for how long he had been present, they couldn't say. There hadn't been a sound from either him or the service.

Ruddygore chuckled at the two. "I admit Poquah takes some getting used to. He is my closest aide and boss of this place, second only to myself in authority. However, he is an Imir— a race distantly related to those elves you saw, but *very* distantly. The Imir are large, as you can see, and a warrior race if there ever was one."

Poquah served the tankards to the three of them in a good, professional butler manner, but then poured a fourth for himself and took the last chair. He still looked something like a stick-man, bending only at right angles.

The Imir took a swallow from the tankard and put it down on the carpet. "We deny relation to elves," he said proudly. "Except, perhaps, the other way around. We have little in common, elves and Imir."

"His people have a basic gift of faërie,* though," Ruddygore told them, "honed in the Imir's case to a fine edge. You simply will not see or notice them until and unless they want to be seen or noticed. It is a trait many of the magical folk have,

---

* *Faërie* refers to the heritage, magic nature, power, and "realm" of fairies in general; it has a connotation of that which is withdrawn from human ken. *Fairy* refers in more specific manner to individuals, races, traits, and abilities of the fairy folk; its connotation is more that of a normal, day-to-day existence.

but in their case it is a defensive one, triggered by startlement, apprehension, or fear. In the case of the Imir, they can turn it on and off at will—a very handy thing for warriors."

"I can see that," Marge agreed.

"Well, Poquah, what do you think of our two new recruits?" the sorcerer asked.

Poquah looked over at the two of them, those red eyes surveying first Joe, then Marge. "Interesting choices," he said at last. "But as a pilot project, they may do. I am surprised at the presence of the woman, but it adds symmetry to the entire affair."

Ruddygore smiled. "The Imir are not known for tact and diplomacy," he told them. "They tell you exactly what they think."

"Diplomacy and tact are basic dishonesties developed by races who can not fight," the Imir responded casually. "They are unnecessary to the Imir."

Ruddygore sighed and got up. "Very well, then. Let me get a change of clothes, and we'll see to making a proper hero and heroine out of the two of you."

<hr>

CHAPTER 4

HOW TO MAKE
A GOOD APPEARANCE

All persons brought from other universes must be physically acclimated to this one and bound to the Laws and the Rules.
                                        —XX, 210, 116(a)

WHAT RUDDYGORE CALLED HIS LABORATORY WAS A STRANGE cross between a real lab and something out of the Middle Ages. There were compartments, basins, beakers, and flasks very much like those in a school chemistry lab, and there was even a source of natural gas with small Bunsen burner-type nozzles on flexible hoses. There was drainage in the basins, too, although water was strictly a hand-pump affair from several locations. Other parts of the place, though, were what Joe called "strictly voodoo."

There were open areas with all sorts of mystic and cabalistic designs on the floors; long candelabras and incense burners in the shape of odd and demonic idols stood about. Here, too, were braziers and all the other paraphernalia one would expect of an ancient court magician or high priest. There was even an area with an unpleasant-looking altar set into one wall.

Even in the modern part, with its hundreds of little drawers and compartments, things were less than usual. Bat's blood, a jar of eyes of newts, and other things even less pleasant revealed themselves when Joe opened a few compartments out of curiosity. A drawer full of live spiders, quickly slammed shut again, ended his meddling in a hurry.

Ruddygore entered from the rear, near the altar, looking quite different from how he had looked earlier, resplendent now in flowing robes of sparkling gold and wearing a skullcap of the same material.

He smiled and nodded to them, then went over to one of the clear areas near the altar and glanced down in disgust. "Damn. Have to get a mop first and wait for the floor to dry. Damned adepts with their love spells . . ."

Still grumbling, he got a fairly ordinary-looking mop out of the base of an exotic offering stand, pumped out some water from one of the well basins, soaked the mop, and quickly erased the designs on the center of the floor. Replacing it all, he wiped his hands on a towel and came over to them.

"I'll have to wait for the whole thing to dry," he said. "I need to sketch out a few new designs down there." He sighed. "Well, we can use the time a bit to discuss your future."

"That interests me a lot," Joe told him, and Marge nodded.

"Well, let me start with you, Joe. Did you ever imagine yourself off in some other time and some other place as the hero of a big epic? You seem fond of show business, by your remarks. Ever imagine yourself as one of those big, strong heroes?"

Joe thought a moment. "Not really. Not from movies or TV, anyway."

"Not even when you were a kid?"

He thought a moment more. "Yeah, I guess so. I'm more than half native American, you know, mixed with Seminole and whatever part of Puerto Rican is from the old days. I used to like to hear the old folks' stories about how it was before the white man. You know, the great civilizations of the past. A lot of times I saw myself as the great warrior chief, riding down with super power and wisdom, turning back the white man and saving the old ways. Kind of silly for a kid from South Philly, I guess, whose idea of wilderness was Fairmont Park, but it does something to a kid when all the other kids are playing cowboys and you know what you are."

Ruddygore nodded thoughtfully. "I can see that. Can you think back to it clearly? I mean, can you visualize that warrior chief? What he looked like?"

Joe considered. "Yeah. I think I can. Sort of."

"Okay, then. Just hold that vision and don't let go." The sorcerer turned to Marge. "And you? Any super cowgirls? Beautiful princesses? Amazonian warriors?"

She smiled wistfully. "Yeah."

"Which one?"

"All of 'em."

The sorcerer chuckled. "Well, if you had to pick one, some vision of yourself—perhaps as the warrior queen, gutsily defending her splendid golden castle..."

She thought it over and closed her eyes for a moment. "Yeah. I can think of a dozen novels I've practically lived again and again."

"All right. Just keep that vision in mind." He looked over at the floor. "I see it's dry now. Let me make my preparations."

He reached inside the mouth of a hideous bronze idol set in the wall and took out what proved to be a piece of thick, soft chalk. Working rapidly, he positioned first Joe, then Marge, about eight feet apart in the clear area, then started drawing around each of them on the smooth slate floor with the chalk.

The designs were identical. Pentagrams, clearly and solidly drawn, and outside each pentagram a six-pointed star. He got up from the floor and said, "Now, neither of you move. Not an inch outside those pentagrams—not until I tell you. Understand?"

Joe looked nervous and uncomfortable. "The real conjure stuff," he murmured uneasily.

The sorcerer nodded. "The real stuff, Joe. You in particular should understand that you stay where you are at all costs.

Marge, you take it seriously, too." He backed up a distance from both of them, then drew a new, larger pentagram around the two recruits, this time with Ruddygore inside. From a small valise also inside the outer design he removed candles and long candlesticks, which he proceeded to set at each of the five points of the outer pentagram. He lighted each candle in turn with a long stick which was burning at one end, being careful at no time to cross the outer pentagram. Then, stepping back, he proceeded to draw the same design around himself as around the other two, so that he was equidistant from them and facing them. He checked everything visually to make sure it was all to his satisfaction, nodded, and took a deep breath.

"It is a simple spell. Child's play, really. But you get to be an old sorcerer not only from long study but also because you never take even the easy ones for granted. Now, don't be startled by anything that happens from now on. Take it as a show, a magic trick, but for the sake of your souls, do not break your own pentagrams!"

"You gonna conjure a demon?" Joe asked uneasily.

"That's about it," Ruddygore agreed. "A very minor one of little importance, but it owes me. It will appear between us, so I warn you about that right now. It may look fearsome; but as long as you remain totally within your pentagrams, it can not touch you, let alone harm you. It may also sound very decent and civilized, but don't let that fool you, either. At this level, the demons are more raw emotion than intellect and have just about no self-control. If you break your pentagram, it will almost certainly eat you and carry your soul to Hell as its eternal slave. There would be nothing I could do about that—understand?"

They both nodded, and Marge couldn't help thinking over and over, *My god, this isn't a dream or a joke—it's real*! As for Joe, he'd had no doubts from the beginning.

"All right," Ruddygore said, taking a deep breath. "Here we go."

With that he closed his eyes and began chanting, softly, in a language neither of the other two could comprehend. It was an ancient tongue, though, seemingly of some race that far predated humanity, and it was not designed for the human vocal system.

It's no wonder sorcerers also go in for all sorts of potions,

Marge thought, hearing it. *They all have to have chronic sore throats.*

For a while, nothing happened, and the newcomers began to think that nothing would occur. Then, quite slowly, they both realized that the light level was sinking ever so gradually, the torches and lamp flames shrinking in intensity. It was growing, abruptly, quite dark; within four or five minutes, all light sources in the lab were out, except the five candles at the outer pentagram points. Again a minute or two passed with nothing else happening, but the air grew thick with expectancy.

Suddenly, in the space between Ruddygore and themselves, there was a disturbance in the air. It began as a few silver and gold sparkles, but slowly, about three feet from the floor, the sparkles increased in number and intensity and started to swirl, forming after a time a sparkling whirlpool or galaxy shape which quickly widened, took a new shape, and outlined a grotesque figure in its tiny flashing pattern. The sparkles suddenly vanished, and the shape became solid and real before them.

It was a terribly ugly creature, round and squat, in some ways resembling a toad but with a face that was more piglike than anything else, complete with two big, curved, boarlike tusks and lots and lots of teeth. It was hairless, naked, and stood on two birdlike feet. Its eyes were round and bright yellow with black dots in the center, like the eyes of a fish, and, like them, seemed lidless. The skin itself was mottled, gray and greenish, the color of death and mold—and it stank up the place to high heaven.

It looked up at Ruddygore—being only three feet high—and gave a nasty grin. "You don't mind if I check you out?" it rasped in an unpleasant, grating voice. "Even the best slip up now and then."

"Be my guest," the sorcerer responded.

With that the creature waddled around, checking the designs around each of the three humans, then walking the length of the outer pentagram. Finally satisfied, it returned to the middle of the three and again looked at Ruddygore. "They're good enough to restrain me," the demon admitted without sounding in any way surprised. "Wouldn't hold an elemental or anything stronger, though. You're slipping in your old age."

Ruddygore smiled. "It doesn't need to hold anything stronger. You still owe me, Ratzfahr. You know that."

"Yeah, yeah. Damn. Ask a little favor just one time and they never let you forget it," the demon grumped.

"One! You want the list?"

"Aw, okay, okay." Ratzfahr turned his head completely around without moving his body and looked at the other two, then swiveled back to Ruddygore. "They smell funny," the demon noted.

"So do you," the sorcerer retorted, "but I've never let that come between us."

"This is some nutty language you got us talkin', too," the demon went on. "Where'd you get these two, anyway?"

"Earth Prime," Ruddygore told him. "Where else?"

The head swiveled again. "Well, I'll be a cherub! Earth Prime! Been a long time. You figurin' on screwing up the neighborhood?"

"No, but I have need of them," Ruddygore said. "So don't you try any tricks on them, Ratzfahr. They're my guests."

"Guests." The demon chuckled evilly. "I'll bet. Still, what's your pleasure?"

"Acclimatization. The works. Physical. Language. No soul, though. That stays Prime."

"Aw, for cryin' out loud!" the demon protested. "C'mon, you old windbag! That's a hell of a lot! You ask too much."

"No matter what, you must return to Hell," Ruddygore reminded the creature menacingly. "It wouldn't do for everyone down there to know the Profane Name by which you were formed!"

The demon looked genuinely shocked. "You *wouldn't!*"

"You bet I would! And you know it!"

The demon sighed. "All right, all right, you got me where it hurts. You sure about the soul, though? They'll stand out like magnets to them that got the Power."

"I have my reasons," the wizard told him. "Just do as instructed."

"Okay, okay. What language you want?"

"*Makti*, of course. Unless you'd like to give them the Gift of Tongues."

"You gotta be kiddin'," Ratzfahr scoffed. "You know what that would take out of me."

"I do, which is why I ask rather than demand. *Makti* it is, then."

The demon suddenly floated up two feet in the air, turned, and looked at the man and woman critically. "Yeah, I can see they need work," he commented idly.

Both Joe and Marge were tempted to return the insults, but were a little leery about saying much of anything. The demon was certainly not what either of them had expected, but Ruddygore's warning had been seriously taken.

Ratzfahr gave a low whistle. "Wow. They really have high opinions of themselves, don't they? Oh, well. Here goes nothin'! *Raddis on the frabbis! Freebix on the Clive!*" And with those cryptic remarks he started spinning, picking up speed very fast until he was only a whirling blur of motion in the near darkness. Suddenly from him emanated two columns of gold and silver sparkling rays that touched and then seemed to engulf the two humans' pentagrams.

They both felt a sudden falling sensation, as in a fast-descending elevator, and a tingling, like electric shock, only all over their bodies. For a moment, it was all either could do to remain standing in the pentagrams, and each had a fear of falling out and into the clutches of the demon; but while both wavered a bit, they held steady.

There was sound all around, too, now: the cacophony of thousands of discordant voices shouting and competing with what seemed like ten symphony orchestras all playing nonsense and out of tune. It grew and grew inside their heads and all around them until they thought they could stand no more.

And then, quite suddenly, it was over.

Marge shook her head a little as if to clear it, and Joe let out a big "Whew!" Both looked back at Ruddygore, who was again facing the now stationary demon.

Ruddygore said something to them, and it sounded like nonsense. Idiot syllables that hardly seemed like a language at all, but more like the magical chanting he'd done at the beginning. They both just looked at him in confusion, and Marge, at least, worried that the demon had played some sort of nasty trick on them.

Ruddygore, however, seemed satisfied. "How's this?" he called to them. "Do you understand me now? By all means, speak up and tell me."

"Yeah, that's fine," Joe called back.

Marge said, "I thought for a minute something awful had happened."

Ruddygore nodded, mostly to himself. "Good job, Ratty. Now, go! I banish thee back to the realm whence thou didst come! In the name of Hagoth and Morloch, I do send thee to thy world and charge thee remain until called once more! Go!" Ruddygore paused for a moment. "A case of cigars will be sent to you. Enjoy."

"Thanks, T.R.!" the demon responded—and vanished.

"Hold up!" Ruddygore called to the two humans. "Don't go yet. He sometimes likes to pull a fast one!" With that, the sorcerer commenced a long, unintelligible chant.

Suddenly in the air very near them, the demon's voice came. "Aw, *shit!*" it said, and the sense of presence vanished.

All at once, all the lights, flames, and torches in the room flared back into life. There was no sign of the demon. Still, Ruddygore completed the chant, then looked around and seemed to relax visibly. "It's all right now. Let's take a look at you!"

But they were already looking somewhat awestruck, staring at each other.

"Come!" the sorcerer invited them both. "Stop staring and walk with me back here to where the mirror is."

Both hesitantly waited until the sorcerer had walked from his pentagram and crossed the outer one before following, but that didn't keep them from rushing to the mirror once they were assured in their own minds that they were safe.

They stood there, next to each other, gaping at their own reflections as they had gaped at each other.

Joe had been a big man, but now he was even larger. Six foot six, perhaps, in bare feet, and built like a man of iron, muscles rippling with every movement, his skin a smooth, metallic bronze. His face was strongly chiseled, an Indian warrior's face, rugged yet strong and handsome. A young Geronimo, perhaps, or Cochise, with a great mane of shoulder-length, jet-black hair.

Marge, too, had thought taller, but she barely came to his shoulders. Still, she was a vision of her mind—long, pure, strawberry-blond hair, enormous, deep green eyes, with an angelic face and perfectly proportioned supple, athletic, and definitely sensual body.

Joe's voice was now a deep, rich baritone; Marge's, a strong but inviting soprano. It was Joe, after perhaps four or five minutes, who spoke first.

"Hey! We're stark naked!" he exclaimed.

Ruddygore summoned Poquah while he cleaned up his lab, and the Imir took them back to two wardrobes, one with a vast assortment for men, the other for women. The extensive clothing, in a wide range of sizes, told a little more about the land of Husaquahr. Jerkins, tights, and other fashions more at home in a medieval costume epic seemed the rule, although there were hundreds of variations, including elaborate robes, long, satiny dresses, and very ornate male and female clothing. Everything was well made but obviously hand-done in all respects. Poquah told them to select whatever from the wardrobes they would feel most comfortable wearing and assured them that later on they would be allowed to pick more extensively. Right now, this was just to get them started.

Both discovered that undergarments either were not the fashion or hadn't been discovered here. Oh, there were *under-clothes*—more or less full-body types—but they seemed to go with the fancy and uncomfortable-looking royal garb.

Marge finished first, then made her way back to the library, where Poquah had coffee, tea, and pastries waiting. "It is best to eat something, although lightly," he told her. "Your digestive system will need a little help in starting up again without your getting ill."

She accepted his advice, pouring some lightly sugared tea and nibbling on a small croissant. She looked around for a mirror, but there were only books about the place. *Too bad*, she thought. *I still can't believe that that image in the mirror back there is really me*. Still, she had to admit she felt—well, different. Lighter, more agile, more nubile and nimble, and disgustingly healthy.

"Almost feel like a kid again, eh?" came Ruddygore's voice behind her, and she jumped slightly in surprise and turned to him.

"Yes, that's really it," she answered. "I don't think I've *ever* felt this good. And—do you read minds, too?"

"When I have to, but it took no sorcerous turns to guess your thoughts this time," the wizard responded lightly. "I assume Poquah has cautioned you against overindulging for a while?"

She nodded. "That's all right. I don't really feel hungry. Just a bit dry."

"That's natural," he assured her. "Drink anything you want, but stay away from ales and other heavy stuff until you have a few meals in you. I might warn you, too, as a matter of general principle, not to drink any water you haven't boiled, here or anywhere. Fermented stuff, boiled hot drinks, and fresh fruit juices, though, are all right."

"I'll remember," she promised. At that moment Joe entered, and she turned to look at him. She couldn't suppress a chuckle. "Well! Look at *you*!"

"Look at you, too," he retorted, and seemed to mean it.

"What do you mean by *that*?"

Ruddygore decided it was time to step in, although he was vastly amused by the reaction. "Welcome to the Rules," he told them. "Come—sit down and I'll explain what this is all about."

Poquah hastened to give Joe the same cautions he'd given Marge. Joe, though, seemed more disturbed by the exchange than by any cautions.

Marge continued to stare at him. She had hardly gotten used to the rough, burly, dark truck driver, and now here was this young, muscular—savage? No, that wasn't the right word. But Joe had gone along with the body and the image. First he'd chosen a crimson headband to keep his unaccustomed long hair in place, and beyond that a wide leather belt—perhaps four inches or more—with small bronze studs or rivets going evenly around near top and bottom. Aside from the belt, though, he'd chosen a long, thick cotton loincloth, leather sandals—and that was it.

As for Joe, this new, strangely beautiful woman didn't bother him much, either—after all, it had been probably no more than a day and a half since they'd met for the first time—but he could hardly understand why a woman wearing a pretty revealing cotton-lined leather halter and a "skirt" apparently made up of thousands of strands of individually strung red and purple beads that showed practically everything every time she moved had any right to comment on *his* garb.

Ruddygore, still wearing his golden robe, took a couple of

large, fat pastries and sat back down in his chair. Marge sat in a chair to his right, legs slightly crossed, and Joe sat facing them, noting that, from almost any angle, the woman might as well have nothing on at all as that "skirt," whose strands fell away to reveal all, being connected only by a slim and nearly invisible waistband.

"Your reactions to each other's choices are natural, but I can explain it," the sorcerer assured them between bites. "First of all, Marge, you're surprised that Joe chose what he did, so let's take care of that. Joe—why *did* you choose the sword belt, loincloth, and sandals over all the rest?"

Joe looked blankly back at them. "Why, I dunno, really . . . It just seemed . . . *right*, somehow."

Ruddygore nodded. "Volume 46, page 293, section 103(c)— the Books of Rules." He gestured back at the wall of red-bound volumes. "Your mental image, Joe, was, in the parlance of this world, the classical barbarian hero. Now, don't get mad at that word 'barbarian.' It's simply a word applied by a culture to anybody who obviously comes from a different one, one they feel superior to—and which may well be superior to theirs. Get used to it."

"I kinda like it," Joe responded. "Barbarian. Yeah. That's about right. But what was all that volume and page stuff?"

"That particular section, Joe, says, '*Barbarian male heroes in southern temperate climes shall wear their hair long, nor shall they shave their beards, and will dress appropriately in sword belt, loins, and sandals.*' And that's what you did. Of course, since you chose an Oriental barbarian, basically, you won't have a beard or much body hair. But, you see, that's how the Rules work. They don't order you to do something. They just make it so you naturally want to do it."

Joe chuckled. "So *that* explains it. Still, it *feels* right. I don't mind." He had a sudden thought. "But what if I have to go where it's cold?"

"Don't worry about it. Section 103(b) covers it. You don't have to know it. You'll just do it when the time comes. You'll *know*. That's the most positive thing about this land, Joe. You *know*. And if you meet someone similarly dressed, you'll know what he is, too."

"Fair enough. And her?"

Ruddygore turned to Marge. "You realize, of course, that

you're almost more in a state of undress than dress. That's what Joe was talking about."

"Well, yeah, but . . . Oh, those books again."

Ruddygore nodded. "Volume 46 is mostly concerned with appearances. Page 119, section 34(a)—'*Weather and climate permitting, all beautiful young women will be scantily clad.*' It's as simple as that."

She just stared at him.

"Don't blame *me*," the sorcerer responded, reaching for another pastry. "I *told* you they were petty—and in great detail. The current Council is overdoing it quite a bit, I admit, but the basics have been here for thousands of years. They lend stability to the land. In a way, you have to sympathize with the Councils of the past. They were faced with imposing sanity on a world based upon magic. And, truthfully, does your current garb bother you?"

She thought for a moment. "Well . . ."

"Truthfully, now. You didn't even realize it until it was pointed out to you, did you?"

"No, I didn't," she admitted. "It's just that, spelled out like that, there's something that offends me, deep down."

"Both of you may find yourselves compromising some of your principles from your old world, but you have to accept the Rules. It isn't like changing the mind of a legislature or something. In a way, it's close to repealing the law of gravity to change the Rules in any substantive manner. And, by the way, gravity isn't locked in concrete here, either. The universe still operates in pretty standard ways, but don't assume that local conditions do. They most assuredly do not."

She got up and walked over to the wall of red books, pulled one out, and opened it at random. She found it a mess of black, blue, and red squiggles and she couldn't read a word of it. She shook her head and put it back. "I guess we're both back to being illiterate here. That brings up a point, by the way. Just as these books are in some other language, people around here aren't going to speak English, either. Do we have to take language lessons?"

Ruddygore chuckled. "Oh, my, no! That was part of the acclimatization process. You remember just after it was all done I yelled something at you? Something neither of you could understand?"

They both nodded.

"I was yelling in English. Look." He proceeded to give off what sounded like a strange and inhuman series of sounds, then smiled. "*That* was English. Neither of you speaks it any more, nor understands it, either. We are right now conversing in a language called *Makti*. It's the trading language of the river. Although there are dozens of tongues spoken just on and around the river, there is one—a sort of simplified amalgam of them all with its own grammar and syntax—that developed because of the need for it. It's locked in the Rules—Volume 306 is a dictionary, 305 gives the Rules governing it. No matter where you are in Husaquahr, there will be those who understand it and speak it fluently."

"Yeah, but what about words not *in* the language?" Marge asked him. "I mean, I still am a Texan, and that's not a likely word."

"Nor is it one," the sorcerer agreed. "But that word, and similar words, are provided for. They remain in a mental *secondary* vocabulary, still as they were in English, and understandable to a speaker of English. *Makti* is a very flexible tongue, you see, and accommodates local idiom. Otherwise it would be of little use as a trading language. However, with its six tones and shorthand basics, it's not transliteratable into English at all. The language as written is also ideographic, I fear, with a basic alphabet of more than two thousand characters and sixteen accent and tone marks. It takes years to learn if you weren't raised with it, and a full vocabulary, capable of complex writing and reading, say, the Rules, is tens of thousands of symbols. The bottom line is that, yes, you're illiterate—like the vast majority of this world—and probably going to stay that way."

"It sounds pretty complicated to me," she told him. "You mean the other languages are even *more* complicated?"

"Vastly so," the sorcerer assured her. "So much so that *Corabun*, for example, spoken in the area of the Fire Hills and Lake Zahias far to the west of here, has never had a successful written language. Or *Hruja*, spoken in parts of Leander, which is so ridiculous that you *have* to know some ideograms because you have to draw in the air just to talk unambiguously to one another."

"Ideograms," Joe put in. "That's picture writing? Like the Chinese and Japanese back home?"

"Something like that," Ruddygore replied. "But it's not the same language by far."

"It seems this would lock in the hierarchy," Marge noted. "I mean, if you can't read or write, you can't be a trader or businessman, or get a top spot in government. So most of the people can't read those Rules, either, which leaves the magic up to those who can."

"I'll admit to that, in a general way," Ruddygore responded, "but not totally. Remember, here most trades, skills, and positions are passed down from one generation to the next. And whatever literacy is required gets passed along, too. Occasionally somebody with a real knack for it comes along who is, say, a peasant farmer, and then he—or she—rises in society and power if he wants."

"So the farmer's kid *can* be king—if he's somehow able to learn the language on his own, with nobody to teach him, and then get access to all the books he needs. Clever. You hold open the hope to the lowest that their kids *might* rise all the way, while conditions make it just about impossible for them really to do so. It's neat," Marge said sourly.

Ruddygore shrugged. "It works. What can I say? And everybody knows some example somewhere. However, whatever gave you the idea that a king has to be skilled or literate? Most of them are blithering idiots, really. Figureheads for their advisors, councilors, and bureaucracy."

"Pretty cynical, aren't you?" Marge retorted. "But since we can't read or write this stuff, we're stuck on the low rung. Some new world!"

"Oh, my, no!" The sorcerer chuckled. "Barbarians can rarely read—but one or two have seized and held kingdoms. Your wits are your best assets, I assure you. That and training and working at needed skills—and keeping those bodies of yours in peak physical shape. I have a great deal of hope for the two of you and a great set of missions. You are very important to me. You see, right now I have remade you to this world and its laws and rules. Almost all of you. But your souls are still of your native world, and that is important. The forces of Hell must work through agents here, but their magic is far different from any here. They attune themselves to the souls of our world. You are totally vulnerable to the considerable magic of this world and this land—but you will find yourselves invulnerable to the direct sorcery of Hell. It may be of small difference to you, but it may be of great consequence to me."

"I'm not sure I understand anything you just said, but it doesn't sound like either of us is gonna have a long and happy life," Joe grumped. "Seems to me like a pretty high price just to get out of alimony and child support."

Ruddygore smiled. "Long or short? Who knows? You were minutes from death when I pulled you away, Joe."

"So *you* say. I ain't real sure I believe all that stuff."

"Believe it or not as you will, it *is* true. But it is also beside the point now, anyway, and that's the way you should think of it. You are here. You can't get back. Even if I were to let you, you are so changed from who you were that you'd be a strange barbarian in your old world speaking a language nobody could understand. They'd lock you up in a little room and throw the key away. Walk out of here now and you will be in a world you know nothing of and are ill-prepared to live in. Stick it out, Joe. Remember, I said I needed a *hero*, not a martyr. You're no good to me dead, and I'm going to spend a lot of time and effort to keep you alive. Take it like that. I need you, and, at least for now, you need me. Fair?"

Joe considered it. "Yeah, I guess so. For now, anyway. But what comes next?"

"I've been wondering that, too," Marge put in.

"Time is not on my side," the sorcerer told them. "Right now the enemy is slowing to a halt far south of here because it is flood season, and the lower river is one vast flood plain. After that will come the monsoons, which make movements unpredictable. Still, the enemy will be fully on the march again in three or four months, and that means we have six months at best before we either act or fight him at our gates. Not a lot of time, but with a bit of magical help and a lot of experience—and the cooperation of you both—I think we can use that time to good advantage. You'll be seeing little of each other from this point until you are ready. Each of you is now going to school. A most unusual school. One pupil each. If and when you finish, you will be well prepared for the hardships and challenges you might face—and more than able to exist in Husaquahr or anywhere else on our world." He turned to the

Imir, who stood nearby as always. "Poquah, show them to their quarters and notify Huspeth and Gorodo."

"When do you wish them to begin?" the Imir asked him.

"As soon as possible. This evening, if practical or convenient. We have no time to spare."

CHAPTER 5

ANSWERING THE MUNCHKINS' QUESTION

A witch is the term given to any practitioner of potion magic and/ or spells whose practice is based upon a system of religious beliefs.
—IX, 318, 201(a)

LATE THAT AFTERNOON POQUAH CALLED ON MARGE, WHO HAD been relaxing on a feather bed in the small room the Imir had brought her to earlier. She had mostly been just lying there, thinking of how good it was to be alive and anticipating, perhaps, romantic adventures to come. That and examining her new body in minute detail.

I was dead inside, she realized, *and now through an impossible miracle I'm more alive than ever*. Having come so close to death, she wasn't bothered by risk. In a sense, she was already living on borrowed time—and each precious minute was wonderful. The only thing she truly feared and could not entirely shake from her thoughts was that this new life, still so dreamlike and unreal to her practical mind, might end as suddenly as it began. True, total insanity might be like this— and, certainly, she was now living in her fantasies and dreams. *What if I'm somewhere inside a rubber room?* Somehow, deep down, she wondered if she would ever really be rid of that one fear, if she would ever really know. And, even more of a question, did she fear knowing?

"You will come with me now," the Imir told her. "It is time for you to begin your instruction."

She arose and nodded to him. "Where are we going?"

"It was decided that your best potential would be realized by Huspeth in the Glen Dinig," Poquah replied, explaining nothing. "As you know, we were expecting only the man. Huspeth, however, is willing, and is better equipped than we. Can you ride a horse?"

"Yes, I've ridden horses. At least I can manage. Why? Is this Glen Whatsis far?"

"Not far," he said. "But too far to walk. Come with me. We should make haste to get you there before dark." With that he turned and walked out of the room and down the hall. She followed, hurrying to catch up.

They went back down, across the drawbridge, and through the outer ring. Just at the start of the road, two beautiful horses, one coal black and the other snow white, waited, being held by an elf groom.

She approached the horses excitedly. "How perfect they are! But—no saddles, huh?" It was true. The horses were fitted only with bridles and a smooth blanket tied about their midsections.

"Saddles are a luxury. It is best you learn horsemanship without them. Then a saddle will be a convenience, not a necessity."

She looked dubious. "Well, okay, but I hope I can hold on."

With the Imir's aid, she boosted herself up on the white horse, grabbed the reins, and tried to get as comfortable as she could. It felt a little strange being up, and she felt some muscles being stretched in unaccustomed places.

The Imir mounted the black horse effortlessly and looked over at her. "Shall we ride?"

She nodded. "Take it easy, though, at the start, will you? I'm a little wobbly."

"Slow and easy," Poquah assured her. Giving his mount a light nudge with his foot, he started off. Her horse, apparently very well trained, followed the black one at a slow, comfortable pace.

Riding down the slope from the castle was fairly easy, although they were following no trail. Still, Marge's horse swayed and twisted with the land, and it took her several minutes and a few near spills to get anything approaching steadiness without saddle or stirrups.

"Who is this Huspeth?" she called to Poquah when they closed ranks.

"She is a witch who lives in the Glen Dinig," the Imir told her. "She is very old and very wise and very powerful. She is a great one, but she never leaves her forest glades these days."

"Is she a friend of Ruddygore's?"

"Hardly. Huspeth has little use for people in general and for sorcerers in particular. She is greatly feared by many, liked by none."

"Thanks a lot," Marge said sourly. "And I'm being handed over to her? Is it safe?"

"Nothing in life is safe," the Imir responded philosophically. "However, she has her own reasons for wanting this task, which was asked of her but could not be forced upon her. She will do it, not because of the Master, nor for any cause, although our enemy is also her enemy, but because she chooses to do it. We did not expect her to accept, but we chanced to ask."

They went on as the sun sank lower in the fields; with this description of her prospective tutor, Marge's high spirits sank a bit lower, as well.

After more than an hour's ride, out of sight of the castle but just barely, they came over a rise and Poquah stopped. Below, the plain gave way to thick forest, a distinct grove perhaps two miles square between the rolling hills and the River of Dancing Gods.

The Imir pointed. "The Glen Dinig," he told her. "Please dismount." With that he jumped from his horse with a cat's balance and turned to her. She found it difficult to move her numbing legs, which throbbed with pain from the unaccustomed ride, but she managed with his help to get one leg over the other and sort of slide down to the ground. Relief shot through her legs, although she staggered a bit from the painful stiffness.

"Wow! I thought I was a better horsewoman than *this!*"

"Your old body's muscles were so conditioned, probably," he said, "but everything is new to you now. This body is drawn from the energies that are around us and those which made up your old self; it is a new body and it will need conditioning."

She whistled low and nodded, trying to shake the kinks out of her legs. "Yeah. I keep forgetting that." She looked down at the thick forest. "What now?"

"Huspeth never emerges from the Glen Dinig, and I can not enter it. My instructions were to bring you to this point, then direct you to walk down and into the wood. I will return to Terindell."

Again she looked uncertainly down at the forest, which was fast becoming a place of great shadow as the sun sank almost to the horizon. "You're going to leave me to walk into those woods at dusk alone?"

The Imir did not reply. Demonstrating his little trick once more, he was gone, taking the horses. She looked around but could see no sign of him or the mounts, nor hear anything except a slight whistling of a warm wind. She was alone.

She sighed and shook her head. "Well, on your own again, with not even a highway to bail you out." She considered walking back to the castle, but it *was* a fair distance—several miles, anyway—and most of it would be in the dark. She sighed again. "Well, I've trusted old Ruddygore this far. May as well keep doing it now." With this she walked down the hill toward the woods.

It was much cooler in the Glen Dinig, and there was the smell of the damp, with moss and rotting limbs giving it an even eerier look in the gathering gloom. Insects and occasional squirrellike creatures scampered here and there, startling her.

Having no other instructions, she just continued walking, the forest getting thicker and darker as she went. She began to grow nervous, fearing that she might be trapped alone in total dark for the night, and she started having second thoughts about going blindly through the place. She turned to make her way back, but soon realized that back looked the same as forward now. She had no idea how far she had come, nor exactly from which direction. That being the case, and considering the small size of the forest, she finally decided that the best thing to do was to press on in one straight line. Eventually she'd have to reach the edge of the forest or, at worst, the river.

In a few minutes, when things had just turned to a dangerous, nearly pitch-blackness, she came upon a small clearing; in the middle of the clearing was an earthen hut. It was a very primitive affair, looking much like a wood and straw igloo, but there was a fire burning in a pit in front of the little hut—

and some sort of cauldron sat on an improvised stand above the fire, smoke rising from it.

Relieved to see *any* sign of life, she hurried forward.

"Hold, girl!" came a voice, high-pitched and raspy, so grating that it almost sent chills up her spine. She stopped, turned, and looked for the first time on Huspeth.

The woman was not merely old, she was ancient, mostly stretched and wrinkled skin over a bare skeleton. The face was scarcely human, with a long, pointed jaw and a tremendous beaklike nose, and her eyes were like two huge, perfectly round cat's eyes set in a yellow sea that literally glowed. She was medium-sized, but bent over and leaning on a crooked stick. She looked like everybody's bad dream of what a witch might look like, down to the black, full-length robe, scraggly white hair, and small, pointed black cap.

Huspeth looked Marge over critically, head twisting slightly first one way and then the other, as a bird might examine something before pouncing upon it. Finally she said, "So thou art the one they send. Good! Good! Thou fairly *burnest!* What is thy name, girl?"

"M-Marge, m'am. You are—Huspeth?"

The old woman cackled. "Sometimes. Sometimes. But come! Sit by my fire! We shall get to know each other well over what time is given to us. And stop that cowering! Art thou afraid of an old woman like me?"

"I'm told you are a witch of great power," Marge responded carefully. "Power is to be respected, and one mark of this respect is fear."

The old woman roared with laughter. "Fairly said! Oh, truly thou art a goodly one, and clever, too. If thou hast the will, I will take thee farther than thou hast ever *dreamed.*" She hobbled up to the cauldron, sniffed, and looked a little quizzical. "Hmmm...I don't know. Come, girl. Smell and see if thou canst decide if it is ready."

Expecting some foul witch's brew, Marge approached hesitantly, took a deep breath, let it out, then leaned over and sniffed.

"It smells absolutely wonderful!" she exclaimed in surprise. "What is it?"

"A recipe of mine. An old one, but a good one. I will teach

it to thee, and many others. Come! Get a bowl there, and a spoon."

There were two wooden bowls and two small, hand-carved wooden spoons beside the fire, and the old woman used one spoon to fill first one bowl, then the other that Marge held up.

The food had the consistency of porridge, but had various pieces of unknown fruits and vegetables—and perhaps other substances—in it more like a stew. It smelled of all the good tastes Marge could remember rolled up into one, and it tasted even better, at least once it cooled slightly. Suddenly aware of her hunger, she ate unhesitatingly, feeling more relaxed.

Huspeth, too, ate, but said nothing more. Still, she kept looking at Marge with an almost hungry gaze, as if she saw, somehow, something in the younger woman that was of the elder's own distant past, something lost forever but never from the mind.

Only when they both had finished and the bowls and spoons were put to one side did Huspeth decide to speak again.

"I'm sure they told thee a little about me," she began. "Probably not the half of it. They think I do them a favor by taking thee, but I do no one favors, and that is something thou must remember."

"I'll remember," Marge assured her. "Actually, they said very little. But they know you're not their friend."

The witch cackled. "*That* is certainly true! Still, when I first knew of thee, before even they came to me as I already knew they would, I knew that we had a destiny, thou and I. Thou art unique. Virginal and with the soul of another world inside."

"Another world, yes," Marge agreed, "but virginal? Hardly."

"Virginal, yes!" the old woman snapped. "Hast thou still not understood what Bakadur, who calls himself Ruddygore, has done for thee? Thou hast cast off thine old body and with it thy taints and sins. Thou art the one thing that all believe is impossible. Thou art truly a virgin for the second time! Were it not so, we would not be meeting here thus."

Marge just shook her head slowly. "I'm sorry—this is all so new and so sudden. It takes time to accept something like this."

"Time! Aye, time. Tell me, girl, what wilt thou do with thy new life? More properly, what wouldst thou do with it if the choice were entirely thine?"

Marge thought a moment. "I—I guess I really haven't thought that much about it. Right now I'm just going where I'm pointed."

The old woman nodded. "And yet that is the first thing thou must decide, and quickly. Think on it now with me. Dost thou have any skills? How wilt thou earn thy bread and board?"

Marge thought some more. "No skills, I guess. I've been a flop at most things, and my education wasn't good for anything back home and is of even less use here."

"Then thou hast the choices narrowed," Huspeth pointed out. "Even the most base of peasants has great skills in plowing, husbandry, and a thousand sundry other things that assure his bread and board. There are no repair shops here. If thy roof leaks, thou must patch it. If thou art cold, thou alone must know the arts of sewing, weaving, and suchlike, and the uses of tools and devices *here*, not in that odd land whence thou dost come. Thou must see now that, alone in this world, thou hast but one great and fragile asset, and that is thy great beauty."

Marge sighed. "Here, too, I guess, I'm reduced to that. I'm even a total washout in my fantasies."

"Nay. There are two paths. One is easy and comfortable. One such as thou can have many years as a dancer or courtesan, perhaps finally finding a man to serve in marriage."

"I tried that. I wasn't very good there, either."

"There is a second way, though, for thee, but it involves great work, nor is it easy to attain, nor comfortable, nor for the weak in spirit. It will involve pain and great sacrifice, but it has much reward as well, the greatest being freedom, that thou needst do but as thou wilt. But the path is hard."

By the flickering firelight, the young woman turned in a mixture of apprehension and hope to the older. "What path is this?"

"The path of witchcraft, for which Bakadur has uniquely prepared thy body and soul, whether from design or caprice, I know not."

"Witchcraft!" Visions of dark and evil deeds, devil worship, and women who looked like Huspeth filled her mind. "I—I don't know about that."

"Bah! Prejudice! I see the prejudice inside thee! That same foolish, superstitious fear that marks all thy kind! Thinkest thou of witches as servants of Hell? Thinkest thou that all witches look like *this?*"

"Why, I—"

"Some witches," Huspeth continued angrily, getting to her feet, "look like *this*." With that, the entire area around her body began to glow, enveloping her wizened, shrunken form, whirling and dancing as if alive, And out of the brightness stepped a new form, a young woman of stunning beauty and elegance—possibly the most beautiful woman Marge had ever seen. She was beyond mere description, the distillation of all past visions of female grace, beauty, and form.

Stunned by the vision, Marge opened her mouth both in awe and wonder and sat transfixed.

A perfect hand reached out and gestured toward the seated woman. "Arise, child," the vision said in a voice that was the perfection of every woman's voice, sensual, musical, yet compelling. Marge got up without even realizing it, feeling inside that her new body, in which she'd so reveled up to now, was like the old witch Huspeth compared with the one who now stood before her.

"Why dost thou gape?" the vision asked. "Nothing has changed except thy perception of me. I was, am, and remain Huspeth, at least to thee now this night."

Marge managed to find a semblance of her voice. "You—you are the same?"

"The same. It is thy first lesson. Judge not by appearance in any manner. Yet since others *do* judge by thy visage, the one who controls that visage holds power in and of the self. Great beauty and youth yield one set of results, age and infirmity quite another. Such a power, to make others see as thou dost wish, is of the greatest use. Male, female, child, adult—all have their purposes."

"Wh-which are you?"

The vision smiled. "*That* would be telling. But thou must put away thy prejudices here. Hell is as much my enemy as it is Bakadur's. Not that there are not witches bound to Hell. There most certainly are—and they are the most attractive of the lot and the most seductive. But that is not a prerequisite for witchcraft. Witchcraft is a methodology that may be applied to many faiths, but it requires a faith to frame it properly for use."

"I have little faith in much of anything," Marge admitted.

"First, thou must have faith in thyself, and that is the hardest of all. Thou must believe thyself better than the rest, capable of great things, and thou must couple this with the desire and wisdom needed to fulfill thy faith."

"That is the hardest faith of all," she agreed. "How can you know unless you have been tested? How can you have goals when you don't know what is attainable?"

"I will teach thee these things. Think upon it. What wouldst thou do in this world? What is thy desire? Consider well thine answer, for the wrong choices may yet deny thee these things."

She thought about it. Just what *did* she want from this world? "Adventure," she decided and told Huspeth. "Excitement. Challenge. The feeling of doing something *important*."

The beautiful vision smiled. "Ah! Those answers are the ones that bring joy to my heart. Accept my proposition, and I will teach thee faith—and after that power and skill. If thou dost freely join of our order, I will give thee the means to what thou sayest thou cravest. But the way is very hard."

Again Marge thought about it. Freedom. Independence. Adventure. What were the alternatives? Nothing exciting. She suspected, too, that this was what Ruddygore had intended, no matter what the doubts of Huspeth. He didn't seem to do anything randomly—except eat. Still, there were some doubts . . . "You say the way is hard. What do you mean?"

Huspeth considered her reply. "For one thing, the longer thou dost remain virginal, the greater thy powers will grow. They will not vanish when thou dost submit, but they will never increase beyond that point. Dost thou, young and beautiful, consider that too great a price?"

"No," Marge responded quickly. "My life recently has been pretty full of that. Until I can hold my own with the respect of men, I can withhold myself. At least, I *think* I can."

Huspeth nodded. "No man may enter the Glen Dinig, not even Bakadur and his precious Council. Thy testing will come much later and far from here, when thou wilt need thy skills the most. But come! The night is young! Let us begin!"

Huspeth was human once more, but still the figure of angelic beauty. Only those catlike glowing eyes remained, although such perfection was in itself inhuman. She walked over to Marge, unhooked the halter and bead-skirt, and threw them into the fire. "To begin, thou must return to the beginning," the witch said.

She reached down on the ground and picked up a gourd that had been hollowed and hardened into a drinking vessel. "Drink of this completely and do it now," she instructed Marge, who took it, sniffed at it hesitantly, first cautiously tasted, then drank the whole contents. It was a sweet drink that seemed honey-based, but as it went down, she could feel a tingling begin, first deep within, then slowly outward until her entire body seemed covered with tiny little electric pricklings. Her mind, too, was slightly numbed by it. She was wide awake, but content to stand there, not really thinking at all.

"Thou art an empty vessel into which I will pour great truths," Huspeth almost chanted. "Come! Stand before the fire."

In a trance, Marge moved as instructed and waited patiently, aware but unable to do much of anything.

Huspeth positioned herself opposite the fire and raised her hands. The fire seemed to grow brighter and leap up to her, like a thing alive.

"Listen well," the witch began. "In the dawn of creation were Adam and Eve created in the Garden, and of the sons thou knowest, but of the daughters of the first time thou knowest not. While the sons did quarrel and kill, the daughters did reject those ways and sought to recommune with the Creator. One found special favor of the Creator, and it is she who is at the root of our order. Look! Look into the flames and behold Eden as it was!"

Marge looked. In the flames she saw that which had been so needlessly lost, a garden of impossible beauty; a magic garden that was beyond any earthly experience because it was created in true and absolute perfection. To see such total peace and such absolute beauty and perfection fairly tore at her mind, but within her, too, was a great sadness that such a place had been lost forever.

"Feel thy sins, thy doubts, thy fears, leaving thee," Huspeth intoned. "Feel them being drawn out when thou art faced with the vision of the one perfect Garden. Feel them as they fall into the flames and are so consumed. Feel thy past consumed, thy guilt consumed, all consumed and gone in cleansing flames. Thou art the daughter of perfection incarnate. Thou art but one step from the Garden, a daughter of Eve, free of all save the one sin that denies thee entrance."

As Huspeth spoke, Marge felt something drain from her,

pour out from every part of her mind and body. Heavy, dark feelings, things which she had lived with so long that she had never even known they were there. Things from the dark corners where no human looked and where all things of Hell and darkness dwelt. And as each poured out, unseen yet as tangible as tumors excised from the body by a surgeon, she felt an increasing lightness, a total sense of well-being.

"Thou daughter of Eve, dost thou accept they wedding to the First and Perfect One and acknowledge her primacy?"

"I do, I do," Marge responded, meaning it.

"Then, thou daughter of Eve, closest to perfection, linked to thy world and ours, know now the curse of our holy order. Know that, having seen perfection, thou canst never attain it, nor can any whom thou dost know or love. For only in knowing what was forever lost canst thou know how truly cursed is all humankind."

Tears welled up inside Marge and spilled out as she realized the meaning of Huspeth's words. To have known perfection and now to know that one might never attain it . . .

"Gather you, daughters of Eve, about this place and time to see this child," Huspeth commanded. And all around the fire Marge sensed but could not see a host of women, all of great power.

"Do you approve this union?" the witch asked the unseen host.

"*We do, we do,*" came a hundred whispers from the dark beyond the fire.

"Who is our Holy Mother?"

"*Eve, who was first and created in perfection,*" came the response from the unseen host.

"Who is our enemy?"

"*Hell, who carried corruption to our Holy Mother's bosom,*" came the response.

"Who is now the mother of this child?"

"*Eve, who was first created in perfection.*"

"Who shall her mother be among the daughters?"

"*Thou, who bringest her forward.*"

"Child—dost thou accept this covenant and this sisterhood, now and forevermore? Wilt thou be my daughter in covenant?"

"I will," Marge responded.

"*She will. She will!*" the host echoed.

"As a sign of this, child, place thy hand in mine!" With that the witch reached her hand directly into the flame.

Marge was aware that this was a critical choice and that she was free to make it or not to make. It. To put her hand in the fire...

She reached forward, feeling the heat of the flames, and grasped the hand of Huspeth. There was a searing sensation, then a sharp pain, and she knew that a razor-sharp cut had been made in her hand. Blood, not just hers but Huspeth's, dripped from their clasped hands into the flames and hissed.

"Witness the bonding of blood, you daughters," Huspeth intoned. "Witness the act of trust in placing her hand in the flame. She is truly flesh of my flesh, blood of my blood, and is bound over into our holy order and subject to all its strictures and commands."

"*Let it be so*," the chorus intoned.

The hands were unclasped and withdrawn, and Marge somehow had enough control to glance briefly at hers. It was unburned, but there was a crosslike incision on the wrist which was just starting to clot.

Slowly the fire died down to its original strength, and the sense of presences all around diminished and was gone. They were alone once more. Huspeth reached down and picked up a second gourd and walked over to her. "Drink and rest," she instructed gently.

Hardly aware of the pain in her wrist, Marge took the gourd and drank from it unthinkingly, then allowed herself to be led to a soft clump of grass in the small meadow, where she lay down and was soon fast asleep.

Huspeth stood there a moment, then said, "Arise thou by moonlight."

Marge's sleeping form did not stir, but from her body rose a mistlike substance that congealed and solidified into a human form. It was the form of a girl-child, perhaps six or seven, and it bore little resemblance to the sleeping woman as she now was, but a great deal of resemblance, had anyone there been able to know it, to the little child Marge herself had once been.

Huspeth reached out her hand to the child and smiled, and the child-spirit approached and took it, smiling back.

"Didst thou see the pretty Garden, my daughter?" the witch asked.

"Oh, yes, Mommy! It was *so* beautiful!"

"Well, it's not completely gone. Look around thee here, at this glade and this forest. See its beauty and its magic, for it is alive."

The little girl looked around with a little girl's eyes and a little girl's mind—and saw.

The weeks sped by quickly, and Huspeth proved a good teacher indeed. Marge was aware that she was getting a lot of information indirectly, somehow, but she didn't discover how. Still, she found many of her old fears and attitudes changing, and within her grew a new sense of self-confidence.

The forest and glade of the Glen Dinig, which had seemed so lonely and fearsome not long before, became a familiar friend in both day and darkness. It was certainly a magical wood, filled with wonders, yet its most magical quality was its utter peacefulness and tranquility. Not even the insects would bite. The deer and marmots and other natural inhabitants had no fear of her, nor she of them, although they were not tame. There was a balance, a perfect balance, and carnivores were not allowed.

Much of the instruction was rote memory, since she had no means of recording or reading over anything, but Huspeth was a good teacher with a lot of aids for problems. The lessons ranged from the simple—how, in fact, to prepare wondrous meals merely from what was around one, and all vegetarian— to the making of potions from the same plants and the recognition of them. There was magic, too—not only in the potions but in how to sensitize oneself to the energies around one, and to sense the life energy in the trees and grasses, the blaze of a deer in full flight, even the furies of nature.

One day there was a great thunderstorm with enormous bolts of lightning all around. Soaked completely, both of them stood in the middle of the glen, and Marge watched as Huspeth called down the bolts, directed them, and bent the terrible forces to her will. Training mind and will, Marge learned a little of wielding such natural power herself and found, later, that one who could deflect the lightning could deflect other things as well.

There was physical training, too. The use and throw of the dagger, and how to conceal it while wearing only the flimsiest of garments. The sword and saber also had their uses, particularly when one could subtly influence the thrust or direction of an opponent's blade.

Her muscles were hardened and strengthened through long runs and severe exercise including the use of weights. She learned, too, to know her own body, to control its every movement and action. Aided by potions, her physical and mental control slowly jelled into almost absolute mastery. Even Huspeth was impressed. "Daughter," she said, "thou art truly superior to most mortals thou wilt meet."

The training advanced, but it never let up. There were times when there was no sleep at all, and she learned to draw on the life energies around her to sustain her.

Eventually, concealed by spells, they went forth out of the Glen Dinig to observe the ways of fairies and men. It took some getting used to, for at the start Marge was almost overwhelmed by the sense of corruption within all of them, but she learned their ways and their powers, their strengths and weaknesses, as best Huspeth could teach. And she felt more and more remote from them all.

"That is because thou art becoming more than human," the witch told her. "It will mark thee. But thou wilt never forget who thou art or whence thou hast come, O daughter."

Of Huspeth she learned only the very little the witch was willing to impart. She knew, though, that the witch was thousands of years old at the very least, that her power was as great as any on the Council, but that she had become so much more than human that she could no longer abide living in the world among the corruption she felt so dearly. For all that Huspeth had imparted to her, Marge knew that the power and wisdom her teacher contained were as an ocean to her thimbleful.

One day, while out on their look at the world the witch had forsworn but to which Marge knew she would have to return too soon, they saw their first unicorns.

They were fully as beautiful and as grand as legend had made them, far more than horses with curved, pointy horns. Their eyes, too, were very different—almost human. And yet, looking at them, Marge felt a disturbance within the magnificent creatures that shouldn't be there.

The source of that was revealed rather quickly as a deer wandered out from the edge of a wood. The unicorn herd, perhaps ten or eleven, took off after the deer, cut it off from retreat, surrounded it, and began a cruel game of torture for the poor deer.

Tiring, finally, of running the deer almost into exhaustion, sticking it with their horns, and allowing it an escape route only to block it and trip it up, the unicorns moved in—and began eating the deer alive.

"How disgusting!" Marge exclaimed. "Those magnificent animals!"

"The way of the world, as it must be to balance nature. The unicorns are a relative to the horses, but they took a far different path. Their teeth are many and are sharp and pointed, as are the wolf's. They play with the cruelty that children exhibit, for that is what they always are, but then they eat. They did not choose their way, nor did the wolf choose his; they just *are*. But, unlike their brethren, there is great magic within them. Shall we go down and see?"

Marge hesitated. "Considering their eating habits, is it safe?"

"For thee, perfectly. The virgin alone is one with the unicorn. All others they will flee from or, if need be, destroy."

They walked down to the herd, which had finished its grisly feeding and was now relaxing, some standing, some lying down as horses never did. The unicorns eyed the two women warily but did not flee.

"Call one," Huspeth prompted. "Go ahead."

Marge shrugged. "Ah, here, unicorn. Come here, unicorn."

"Not exactly the approved way of summoning, but it works," the witch noted as the nearest unicorn glanced up at the call, looked at both of them, and then trotted right over to Marge.

Hesitantly, Marge put out her hand and petted the unicorn on the neck, as she would a horse. The skin was quite different from what she expected, with the feel and texture of velvet. The unicorn seemed to like her touch, though, and the skin certainly felt nice to her.

"Mount him," Huspeth told her. "Let him take you for a ride."

With her tremendous muscle tone and practiced athletic ability, she had no trouble jumping to the back of the beast, although there was nothing to hold onto but mane.

Still, the beast started off at a trot and quickly accelerated. Marge found that, far from being uncomfortable or badly mounted, she seemed to merge with the unicorn, to become one with the creature, more and more so as it increased speed and sped around the great meadow.

It was a magical and most wonderful transformation, with all of the unicorn's enormous vitality and, yes, sexual energy flowing into and through every fiber of her being. It was a tremendously pleasurable, orgasmic experience that the unicorn gave, and so wonderful that it was Huspeth who had to bring it to an end.

"Thou seest now why the unicorn and the virgin always go hand in hand in legend," she said. "But beware, for just as thou dost take from it, so it takes from thee, and the energy it removes from thee takes many days to replenish, longer if thou hast not the will to stop it in time."

"I'll remember," Marge assured her teacher, still feeling as if she had received a lot more than she had given.

"Now that the two of you are chosen, the unicorn Koriku is wed to thee so long as thou shalt take no man. He will come upon the call of his name by your lips, no matter where thou art, to give pleasure or to rout thine enemies. His strength should be used sparingly, for there is always a cost, but it is there when needed. Beware, too, that Koriku, like thyself, is a mortal creature, and should he die while in thy service, thou, too, wilt die."

Marge shivered slightly at that. "I will remember."

The time flew by. In many ways Marge hoped it would never end. Huspeth was the wisest and most wonderful person she'd ever known, and she loved the witch who was the key to all things wonderful and magical as she had loved no other.

But one day there was a cloud in Huspeth's soul as she emerged from her hut, and a great foreboding filled Marge as she saw it.

"It has come time for the trivial that now becomes the paramount," the witch said enigmatically. "Come, sit beside me, and I will tell thee of this world and its enemies."

"Something's wrong," Marge said nervously.

"The forces of Hell are again on the march. Great battles are taking shape as we speak, and the war advances. The bulk of Marquewood between the River of Sorrows and the Rossignol itself is at stake. If it goes, then the enemy is at our front door, demanding entrance, and there will be few to stop them."

"Who is the enemy, my mother?"

"The same who defiled lost Eden. This time he works, as always, through others, in the guise of armies and wars and philosophies and great promises. Many who march to his tune are willing, many more are unknowing servants, but it makes no difference to him. The Dark Baron himself may be deluded, although he certainly knows for whom he fights, since the gates of Hell must be unlocked to create such a force. All the wizards and sorcerers of Husaquahr traffic to some degree with the demons of Hell, as thou well knowest. But such traffic, which I abhor in all cases, for it involves compromise with the ultimate evil, is the temptation to greater and greater evil. If Hell can wield such powers to the wizard's tune, it can corrupt a wizard's heart as well, and they have got themselves a master wizard totally on their side, self-deluded and thoroughly corrupted by the enemy."

"Who, my mother? Which wizard is it?"

Huspeth shook her head. "I know not at this time. Many of the chief demons of Hell were once the angelic agents charged with the making of our own world. Their power here is as great as in thine own world, and they know all the counters for our magic. The Baron's identity is hidden from all of us, until discovered by other than magical means. But this continual cancer is nothing new to our world. It is an incurable disease that worms its way into every corner and must be continually fought. When it grows too large to control, as it seems it has now, it must be beaten down. The enemy can afford ten thousand defeats, but we can not have one."

"This is not the first time, then?"

"Not even the first time in Husaquahr. But this is a big world, much larger than the one from which thou comest. There are many other continents and many other lands. One, called simply The Land, is so fouled up no one from thy world will believe it's real, even though he be there. Another once put down a dark force under a great wizard, and now that wizard's son, Alateen, refights his father's battles. From Lan Kemar to Lemoria, all the lands that make up our world are continually threatened. Now it is Husaquahr's turn."

"But what can they win, even if they capture the land?"

"Ah, once captured, it will never be freed. But, worse, the Dark Baron's plan is clearly diabolical. He hopes to seize or destroy the lands, castles, and, if possible, persons of a majority of the Council. If he accomplishes this, and he is already a quarter there, he will be able to rewrite, suspend, or even abolish the Books of Rules. Hell will rewrite the Rules and will then have a world of its very own to rule and dominate. *This* will become Hell, and will provide, too, a second front for an assault on the Creator Himself. If Hell wins here, it can devote all its time to thine own world. Armageddon, then, will be fought by Hell from both worlds toward the Creator in the middle. None truly knows the outcome, since Hell rebelled once before and knows what it is up against, should it try again."

"You mean—God could *lose*?"

"It is by no means certain. Sooner or later thou wilt find thyself in the clutches of Hell, and thou wilt know a sample of what waits for all creation if we lose. That is why, now, thou must go."

"No! I mean, not yet. I still have so much to learn!"

"Time later for that, if victory is ours. If not, we all are better dead than what we *will* be. Thou must be a soldier in this battle. There is the adventure and challenge thou didst wish for and the important things to do. No woman of Husaquahr is better equipped than thou to do great things, but all thy studies and training will be for naught if not used. Thou must follow the direction of Ruddygore, who is far more worldly than I, in this matter. He traffics with Hell even as he fights it, and I find him powerful but unworthy of such power—but he *is* powerful, and he is fighting for his very life and so will not waste thee or thy companion."

"Companion . . ." She'd almost completely forgotten about Joe. After all, she'd known him such a short while.

"As for me, I have fought too many of these things. Yet should all fail, and Terindell be besieged, Glen Dinig will fight with Terindell against the common foe. I hope and pray it does not come to that, for it would be Bakadur and I against the Dark Baron and the demons of Hell itself. Thou mayest aid in preventing that from happening, my daughter, if thou keepest thyself as thou art now and if thou dost remember all I have taught. So long as thou dost remain as thou art, thy powers will increase by the day, infinitely so, and new ones will develop as needs arise. Thy true trials and tests lie ahead of thee. Remember well who thou art and what thou hast become."

Marge took Huspeth's hand and kissed it tenderly. "I will, my mother."

Huspeth got up, went into her hut, and emerged with her hands full of various items. "Some parting things, to aid thee in thy future endeavors."

The first was a one-piece garment, both legless and sleeveless, of bright forest green, which had a stretchy clinginess to it yet gave breast support. It was woven out of an unknown soft material that nonetheless was almost silkenly comfortable. Its tightness, though, left nothing to the imagination about the shape beneath, becoming almost a green second skin. It satisfied decency—and the Rules. Also, there was a headband much like a laurel wreath. It held firmly and smelled of forest pine.

"Both wreath and garment are of the forest, of living things magically transformed and transfixed. They will be a reminder of Glen Dinig and the daughters of Eve."

"As if I could ever forget. A part of me will be here forever."

Next came a small green belt that blended with the garment and hung on the hips, but was strong enough for a scabbard shaped like leaves. Into it Huspeth placed a small but ornate dagger.

"The dagger is of faërie metal," she told Marge. "It will penetrate all save iron, which is very scarce here. The blade is fused into the handle of pure dwarf jade. It is the truest and most balanced of all blades, and was once mine when I went forth as thou now goest. In the rear of the scabbard is a small pocket which can be useful."

Next was a little case made out of the purest dwarf jade. Inside was what Huspeth called Marge's "kit"—basic herbs and hard-to-find materials for many potions, plus a small mortar and pestle more or less carved into it. It, too, was designed to be held by a thin belt and was not at all bulky. Finally came a small gourd, useful for all practical purposes and also designed for belt carry, leaving both hands free.

"With those thou canst travel the whole of this world and need no more, with thine own knowledge of the land and its bounty."

"I believe I can now, my mother," Marge responded, meaning it.

"Come. Let us see thee reflected in the pool."

They walked over to the small, mirror-smooth pond at the edge of the glen that had been their water supply. In it Marge saw a far different person—yet a third self. She was dark now; the sun and wind had weathered her and toughened her without in any way lessening her striking beauty. And, as she had discovered shortly after her initiation into the order, her new strawberry-blond hair had changed to a brilliant white, with the exception of a streak of reddish brown running straight down the center from forehead to back—the mark of the order. She had trimmed the hair into something of a pageboy and, with the forest-green garment she wore, it was a perfect complement.

Her legs revealed that she now had the strength of the long-distance runner and more, and her arms, still smooth-looking, took on an almost bizarre quality when tensed, revealing their tremendous muscles. Her brows, of the same reddish brown as the streak, were long, thick, and sloping inward, setting off her large blue eyes; she looked less human than like some great warrior elf. Her appearance was unique and striking, yet her movements still contained the catlike grace and form of the woman she had been.

"All I need is a bow and a quiver of arrows to make it perfect," she mused, more to herself than to Huspeth, but the witch nodded.

"I agree, and thy skill with the bow warrants it." She left and returned with a small quiver made of some plant's green skin, and a bow of true professional beauty.

"Oh, no, I *can't*. You've given me so much already!" Marge protested.

"I insist, daughter of mine. And I expect that which has been given thee to be freely used in the fight against true evil."

"I promise I will not fail you, my mother!"

Huspeth now showed the only real emotion of the day, hugging Marge and holding her close. "I know thou wilt. Now—go. 'Tis time."

Marge went with the utmost reluctance but knowing her duty. She was supremely confident now, both of herself and of her abilities, and ready to prove that she had, at last, found her place. Nothing would ever surprise her again.

But she was not only surprised but almost shocked to find an impassive Poquah waiting atop the hill with the same two horses they'd ridden when coming here.

Poquah did not greet her, but his red eyes looked her over critically for a moment, and then he said, "Ah, yes. A proper heroine indeed. It is well. Come. We must make the castle by dinner."

This time *she* led *him*—at a gallop.

CHAPTER 6

BEING A BARBARIAN TAKES PRACTICE

No physical art may be achieved by magic, nor magical art by physical means.

—VI, 79, 101(b)

GORODO PROVED TO BE ABOUT NINE FEET TALL AND MUST have weighed five hundred pounds, with lots of hair and absolutely no fat. He also happened to be a bright blue color with dark blue hair and had a nose that looked like a blue grapefruit, not to mention a pair of very nasty-looking fangs that stuck out of both sides of his mouth. He grinned when he first caught sight of Joe, and the effect was less a real grin than the kind of playful look a cat would give a mouse just before pouncing.

Joe, who was just beginning to feel really macho in his new muscles, stopped, stared, and gulped.

"So this is the big, bad barbarian they want to train to be a big-shot hero," Gorodo said sarcastically, looking down at his new charge. "Boy! They really demand miracles of a tired, weak old man."

Joe tried to find the tired, weak old man he was talking about.

"What's your name, boy?" the blue giant asked.

He gulped slightly. "Joe."

"Joe? That's a pretty stupid name for a barbarian. Barbarians should have fancy names, or funny-sounding ones, like Conan or Cormac, things like that. Usually with a 'C' sound to start." He sighed. "Well, there's nothin' in the Rules about that, I don't think. Not yet, anyway. Still, a name like Joe doesn't exactly inspire fear and respect. We got to get you a second name, one with real command."

"I already have a second name," Joe told him, confidence coming back slowly with the reasonableness of the giant's tone. "In fact, I have lots of names."

"Indeed. Like what?"

"José San Pedro Antonio Luis Francisco Joaquin Esteban Martinez de Oro, if you must know," Joe responded a bit glumly.

Gorodo whistled. "How in the Nine Hells do you remember all that? Anyway, that sounds just as ridiculous. I mean something strong, like Joe Thunderer or Joe Stormhold or something like that. Well, we'll leave that for now. The Master wants us to get a start today, even though there's little left of it. I'd rather just tell you what we're gonna do and let you get one last night's decent sleep."

"Fine with me," Joe agreed. "I'm not exactly a volunteer. More like a draftee."

Gorodo laughed. "Listen, boy. In the days and weeks to come, I'm gonna put you through a living hell. Bet on it. You're gonna curse me and yell at me and you're gonna hurt something awful. But when I get through with you, ain't nothin' made of solid stuff gonna give you trouble. You're gonna be prepared like nobody's *ever* been prepared. Know why? Not because I was ordered to, and not because I like it, but I would consider your death a personal insult after all I'm gonna do. Understand? You're gonna be the best damned barbarian in this whole crazy world because *my* honor depends on it. Now, go eat decent and get your beauty sleep. Tomorrow's gonna be one busy day."

Joe gladly went and discovered the main dining room almost by accident. The food was good, although the only utensils they seemed to use here were a sharp knife and a wooden spoon.

Few gave him much of a glance at dinner or after, but some elves in plain livery did tell him where he was to stay within the outer castle. The room turned out to be of bare stone, furnished with a straw mattress, a single candle, and not much else.

He lay there for some time, feeling more and more depressed and moody. *Barbarian hero*, he thought sourly. *I'm Joe, from South Philly, that's all, lost somewhere in a land of freaks.* He thought of his ex-wife and his young son, who now had even less chance of ever knowing his real papa. He thought, too, of that girl who was more of a loser than he was. Marge. He'd known her only a short time, and now she was God knew where. He couldn't even really get a clear picture of her in his mind just now, which bothered him, but, though it was crazy, he missed her. She was his one link with what was real and comfortable.

He was lonely as hell, and it took a long time for him to slip into a fitful doze.

The routine didn't vary much. Gorodo got him up at dawn, and he began running—first a mile, increasing as his muscles built up to two, then three. Only then did Gorodo permit a large breakfast, after which Joe was expected to run one more mile just to work it down. Next came weight training, along with general physical exercise to tone up a few muscles.

These extensive workouts hurt a lot, and early one morning he'd protested and refused to do more. That was when Gorodo had exploded, growling and snarling, his veneer of civilization dropping instantly.

Very early in the training, Joe discovered that the blue giant was an expert at beating the living daylights out of one without doing any permanent damage whatsoever. The early choice was pretty simple: it was painful torture to do what Gorodo demanded, but it was even more painful to refuse.

It didn't take long for Joe to get both frustrated with and hateful of the huge blue man, whose only redeeming feature was that he did everything he asked Joe to do. Even that was infuriating, though, since Gorodo showed absolutely no stress, strain, or pain doing what was really awful to Joe.

After a big midday dinner, they would go down to a great stone hall where a number of muscular types, human, non-human, semihuman, and a few inhuman, were practicing with one or another weapon. Here instructors in various types of weaponry worked with him, and at least from them he felt he was getting something useful. Broadsword use. Balance. Timing. Dagger and spear-throwing. Mace and pike. All different, all requiring a special set of skills and a lot of practice. Some were also frustrating in their own right. The broadsword seemed to weigh a ton when he was first introduced to it, and he particularly resented the fact that the instructor was a thin, wiry human a head smaller and a hundred pounds lighter than he— who wielded the sword as if it were made of paper.

But he paid attention, and he *did* seem to have a natural flair for it.

After a heavy supper, he was back to running and weights once more and, by the time Gorodo gave him his freedom for the night, he was so hurting and so tired he could do nothing but head for bed.

Day after day, almost without a break, this schedule was kept, varying only in that, as he seemed really to get the hang of one weapon, a new one was introduced.

After a few weeks of this, the pain lessened but never really went away, though he found himself able to lift increasingly greater weights and run longer distances. The broadsword, which had seemed so leaden at first, now felt as light as a rapier. His body was becoming hard, lean, and even more tremendously muscular from the regular hard workouts, which never let up.

Still, a month or so into the course, the weaponry was relegated to the evenings, and the afternoons were taken up with more practical classes by a variety of humans and creatures. Weeks were spent on horsemanship, and there were even lectures and problems on warfare with the weaponry at hand, and also a good deal of hand-to-hand combat. How to disable. How to kill. Where the nerves were, those critical pressure points. There were classes, too, in primitive first aid—what roots and herbs did what, as well as the basics of tourniquets, setting broken bones, and the like. He was acutely aware, thanks to Gorodo's less than subtle methods of persuasion, of the lack of any decent medical care in Husaquahr, and so he paid particular attention to these practical lessons.

As he progressed in skills, particularly with the sword, he was forced into fighting left-handed with it. It was tough going, and for a while Gorodo gnashed and foamed and growled; but while Joe never quite got as good with the left as with the right, he became at least adequate.

The horsemanship also came very hard; even though he got pretty good at it, he felt he would never be a hundred percent comfortable with any animals. For a man who believed firmly that steaks and milk were created magically at the chain stores, he wasn't as bad as he thought he was.

Time ran on without any real feeling. The weeks stretched to months, and he had no true concept of time or even duration any more. Gorodo was his whole life and his whole world.

The blue giant, for his part, seemed to soften up as things went along, though, not being nearly the hot-tempered beast of those first few weeks. Joe never lost his intense dislike of his tormentor, but he nonetheless developed a grudging respect for what was being done—or at least attempted—by the trainer. He suspected that Gorodo might be a lot smarter and a lot less bestial than the blue man wanted everybody to believe.

Still, Gorodo pushed him and pushed him and pushed some more. Every time Joe felt he had reached his absolute limit in something, the blue man would literally force him to continue. Finally, one day, his resentment boiled over so much in Joe that he took a swing at Gorodo—and connected.

The blue giant was surprised, and then was the great man-beast once again—but this time Joe didn't back down.

It was one hell of a fight—furniture smashed all over the place as two bodies, one large and one larger, tumbled and tossed each other about. It lasted the better part of an hour and a half, a total brawl that brought just about everybody within earshot to gawk at them—elves ran through the crowd taking bets at one point—but ultimately Gorodo, winded, bruised, and bleeding from a number of cuts and abrasions, won out by knocking Joe cold.

Joe awoke in his room with a really nasty headache and a lot of sore spots and abrasions, but all his wounds had been well tended. Gorodo, looking pretty beat up, was there as well, and he didn't even look that mean.

"How're you feeling?" the giant asked, and if Joe didn't know better, he'd have sworn there was real concern in the trainer's voice.

"Lousy," Joe responded.

"Me, too," Gorodo said, sighing and sinking into a chair

he or somebody had brought in. He gave a low whistle. "That was one hell of a fight you put up. I'm proud of you, boy. I think you just graduated."

There was still a little ringing in Joe's head, and he was sure he hadn't heard what he thought he heard. "Graduated? But—you won."

The giant laughed. "Yeah. And I always will, too, sonny boy. At least for quite a while. You're good, though, boy. Real good. Best I ever trained, I'll tell you. Don't get too bigheaded, though, 'cause I said that. As I say, I got one thing you ain't got—and it will be a long time comin'."

"Yeah? What?"

"Experience. I been in a couple of armies. I been a pirate, a raider and sacker, you name it. Fifty years' experience, boy, and I'm still here and still in one piece. It's the one thing I can't give you. But I *will* say that the more experience you get, the better you'll be. There ain't but a few dozen in Husaquahr could a given me the fight you did. What about you? You think you're ready for the real thing?"

Joe nodded, even though it hurt. "I think so."

"Good. I been talkin' things over with everybody else training you here, and we're pretty well agreed. When you're good enough to take me on and hold your own, it's exam time."

"Exam time?"

"Yep. The acid test. Look, you get some rest. You need anything, you call out and somebody will be here on the double to get it for you. Next day or two, when we're both back up to snuff, we'll go into town and raise a little hell. Drink. Wench, maybe. *Then* you'll be ready."

The river town of Terdiera was fairly small—perhaps seven or eight hundred people—but it was civilization itself to Joe after so long in Terindell. The buildings were mostly of straw and mud but were well engineered, and here and there were buildings of stone or brick. The main bazaar was a wooden structure half a block long fronting on a square, with merchants displaying their wares in stalls opening onto the street, and all calling out to every passerby.

"Hoi! Love charms and potions! The strongest of the strong!"

"Hoi! The finest in mystic herbs and spices! More pleasurable than a harem without all the talking!"

"Hoi! The finest in jewels imported from far-off dwarf mines in the mountains of Corimere! Mystic jade said to belong once to the dwarf king Zakar himself!"

It was a bewildering array of products, most of them strange and unusual to Joe's experience. Still, here were leather merchants and stalls with the finest of swords, shields, knives, and daggers. Women were measured and fitted in pretty patterned costumes, and everybody from cobblers to coopers was very busy.

There was money of many sorts, of various sizes, shapes, and designs—possibly from many different lands. Still, all appeared made out of gold or silver, and were worth what the metal was worth rather than what the governments claimed; gems, too, were often taken and given as if they were money.

Gorodo, for all his promises, did not come on this first trip. He begged off, saying he had other work, and something in Joe secretly hoped it was an injury very slow to heal.

Instead, his companion was the grim and humorless Poquah, not much of an improvement over Gorodo in his own way. Poquah, however, was a good lecturer.

"Much of the commerce of Husaquahr is barter, but there is a banking system—and coin, as you can see. Since most of Valisandra's people are farmers and work at a subsistence level, they trade their goods for the products of these merchants. The merchants, of course, totally depend on the farmers for their food and much of their raw materials. It works out rather well."

The bulk of the inhabitants in the town were human, but here and there an occasional other would walk or scamper by, given little notice. The two riders coming into town drew interested glances, but it was Joe, rather than the Imir, who attracted stares. He found he rather liked it, too—that glint of nervousness or hesitant fear in the eyes of many of the men and far different sorts of looks from the women. He knew he not only looked exotic, even by barbarian standards, but could hardly hide the tremendous muscles that made him look like some sort of idealized bronze god. He knew, too, that this was the first reward for all the pain and agony he'd undergone in getting to this point.

The Imir gave him a small sack of gold nuggets, not a lot of currency by Husaquahr standards, but more than enough to buy a few things, should he be inclined, and perhaps a meal and drinks in the town tavern.

He enjoyed the afternoon by taking advantage of that, and he knew he was being scandalously cheated by the merchants he dealt with—but it took some time to get the measure of how much a few grams of gold would actually buy.

At the cobbler's, he traded in his worn sandals for a pair of short, comfortable leather boots with a thin, soft fur lining. The poor cobbler, of course, had nothing in stock for feet like Joe's, but he was both fast and skillful and made a pair to order while Joe went elsewhere.

The leather merchant was handy for buying a thick, comfortable, all-purpose belt with solid brass hooks and rings. To this belt he could attach a scabbard with little trouble, as well as other useful things, and it had a hidden money-purse. The buckle, of intricately worked bronze, was a forest scene, but he bought it because the shape between the trees seemed to form the outline of a diesel truck cab. It was the closest to home he could come.

The hatter was a bit taken aback by what he was looking for; but after some pictures were drawn, she agreed to make it if she could. He was satisfied and, after seeing some intricate and presumably magical designs on some of the more Husaquahr-conventional hats, he also gave her a design he wanted on the front of his own.

By the time he'd finished an adequate but not great dinner and returned, he had what he wanted. It was, possibly, the only such hat in Husaquahr, but to another from his own world it would be instantly recognizable. It was a pretty good imitation of a comfortable cowboy hat of some brown feltlike fur, and right on the front was an outline of a design he knew well, one that here would mean nothing. But he found he could certainly still remember how to write, and on the front, in that mystic symbol, was the alien word "Peterbilt."

He had to admit that the hatter was tremendously skillful, considering she had never seen, let alone made, anything like this in her life.

Feeling more comfortable than he had since reaching this land, the great muscular barbarian, in loincloth, trucker's cowboy hat, and reinforced fur-lined boots—and nothing else—went to the tavern.

People stared when he entered, and continued to stare out of the corners of their eyes as he took a seat at a small table in the back. A barmaid, looking timid, approached and took his order for ale, brought it quickly, and went away. Nobody tried to talk to him, approach him, or in any way make him feel like a human being.

The tavern itself was primitive and basic, with a straw-covered floor and hand-hewn crude furnishings, yet it had much in common with all the bars and taverns he'd ever been in. There was a kindred sort of feeling evoked by the place, with its relaxing men, fresh from travels or the fields, and its rough, worldly-wise women—the kind of place he as a trucker had called home from strange town to strange town throughout a large and distant country he'd once roamed. He could see himself as one of these men, playing a little cards or just swapping tall stories, with very little trouble.

Only, as he was uncomfortably aware, this sort of place was no longer a haven for him, the kind of place where strangers were fast friends. Most strangers, perhaps, but not Joe de Oro. He was far too different-looking and far too potentially dangerous to be invited into any of these groups. That depressed him more, perhaps, than anything up to now and brought back his searing sense of loneliness with crushing force. He wondered what they'd all say here, these strange dark men and women, if they knew that inside that bronze god was a man who desperately wanted to cry but could not.

And so he drank prodigiously, feeling it only a little, and sat in his silent corner and watched the rest of them come and go. After a while he also noticed that, occasionally, burly men and tough barmaids would talk and then leave together, and it wasn't hard to figure out why. Finally, the strong ale lowering his inhibitions a bit, he propositioned the woman who was serving him, more with few words and many gestures than outright, and she thought a moment, looked at his purse, then at him, nodded, and turned. He followed her out, not at all worried about being mugged or rolled.

And he enjoyed it, too, feeling it more strongly and on a more emotional level than he ever had before. The barmaid, too, seemed to have a far more than businesslike good time. It went on and on and on through the evening, as months of frustration and loneliness gushed out of his soul and into the act. When finally done, both he and she fell into an exhausted sleep.

He awoke with the dawn, while she still slept, and he felt a little sense of ego buildup that she slept with a wisp of a smile on her face. He weighed the purse. Not enough for the sword he wanted, but considerable all the same still remained. He knew her intent was to take it all at the end, but he was in better condition than she. He paused a moment, then decided, *What the hell, it's not my money*, and left the purse on the small table near the bed when he departed.

It had been worth every penny, but he knew he could never stand to go this long without sex again.

When he emerged from the little hut down the street from the tavern, he was surprised to find Poquah waiting placidly with the horses. The Imir irritated him with his seeming omniscience and cool manner. They said nothing that was not necessary to each other on the way back.

"Now that you have passed the preliminaries, boy, 'tis time to become a man," Gorodo told Joe. "The final exam. Pass it and you're off to fame, fortune, and glory. Flunk it and I'll kill you myself."

Joe looked at him. "I believe you would at that. If you could. I guess this is some sort of big test of ability and skill. I'm willing to give it a try."

"It's a test of that, all right, but a pretty simple one," Gorodo agreed. "It's real simple but real effective. What we do is this. First, you drink a little potion that kinda knocks you out real gentle. Makes you feel great, though. When you wake up, you'll be stark naked, without stitch, weapon, money, horse, anything at all. We don't tell you where. Just that it's no more than fifty miles from here. Your job is to get back inside the inner wall of Terindell without us catchin' you. No time limit to get back here, really, but one day to the minute after you wake up, Poquah and me and some of the boys will start tracking you down. If we catch you, at any point, you'll wish you never was born."

Joe frowned. "And I'm not gonna have nothing at all? Where the hell do I get what I need?"

"Up to you," the blue giant told him. "Steal it. Make it. Improvise. You been shown the way."

Joe nodded, more to himself than to the trainer. "And what do *I* get if I make it?"

Gorodo grinned. "What kinda question is that?"

"I mean it. You want me to risk my neck on this fool test. What do I win? A gold star for bein' a good boy?"

"It is a fair question," Poquah's voice said, and Joe and Gorodo both whirled reflexively. "It deserves an answer that Gorodo can not give. I, however, can."

"Wish you wouldn't pull that act, ya bastard," Gorodo grumbled.

The Imir ignored the comment. "The first thing you will receive is the satisfaction of knowing you have beaten the best. That is good enough for some. But you will also be awarded an elfsword, a magic blade that is almost alive and is not only one of the best magic swords around but effective even against some magical beasts. Finally, you will have a job with great honor and rich rewards. Those are worthy prizes, are they not?"

Joe thought about it. "Yeah. Not bad, I guess. But you don't sound like you expect me to win 'em."

"We are trained and experienced. We also will know where you started from and exactly what you look like. We will know the lay of the land. Using no sorcery, only our skills and foreknowledge, we will get you. It's that simple."

Once more the Imir's tone rankled him, and he saw the challenge in a different light. If he lost, he was no worse off, really, than if he refused. But if he won . . . Beating Gorodo at his own game and puncturing that enormous self-centered egomaniac of an Imir's pride would be more than worth it. And Gorodo put the icing on the cake.

"Every hunter of you in this test will be one who has passed a similar or identical test," the blue giant told him. "I don't know about that sword crap, but you win the respect of the few who've done it."

"When do we start?" he asked them, getting interested.

The Imir reached down to a small flask on his belt, poured a little golden liquid into a tiny field cup, and handed it to him.

He sniffed it, and it smelled honey-sweet and quite plesant.

"Cheers!" he exclaimed and downed the potion.

CHAPTER 7

GETTING IN AND OUT OF SHAPE

Barbarian luck will not prevail without barbarian intelligence.
—XL, 401, 306(b)

HE AWOKE IN A SMALL CLUMP OF TREES, ITCHING ALL OVER. Jumping up, he looked back and cursed whoever it was, probably Gorodo, who had put him so near that damned anthill.

They were true to their word—he was stark naked and without anything except a lot of ant bites. It was cool and damp, the sun off in the east barely clearing the horizon. *One full day*, he reminded himself. *Then the chase begins*. Still, now was not the time to go running all over the unfamiliar countryside. His training and his common sense told him otherwise. So, moving away from the unfriendly insects, he walked from the trees to the top of a nearby hill, the highest ground within easy reach, already thinking about what he had to do.

First he needed information. The sun told him his directions, so that wasn't a problem. But—in which direction from the castle had they brought him?

The hilltop afforded a nice view for fifteen or twenty miles around. Not a lot of habitation, from the looks of things, but to the left—west—of where he stood, about four miles, was a river. That was all right, but which river? Well, he decided, time to cheat a little. He'd seen more than one map of the region around Terindell, and even maps of the entire Dancing Gods river system. He was certainly no more than fifty miles if their word was good—and it would be an inconclusive test if they had lied—and Terindell was in a little pocket of Valisandra between two other countries.

Truck drivers paid good attention to any maps they saw.

He sat down on the cool grass and thought it out. The odds were that they hadn't put so much time and energy into his training just to kill him off. They'd play it safe, put him where they could control all the factors in the game. That meant keeping him in Valisandra. That being the case, he was either north or west-northwest of the castle. But that river down there was to the west. If it were the west-northwest direction, the Rossignol should be in the east or southeast. That river over there, then, was most likely the River of Dancing Gods—and that meant he had only to follow it down to Terindell.

It was too easy. He could *run* that before twenty-four hours had passed and the chase began. But then, how would they know he'd seen and interpreted the maps? They knew he couldn't read them, but one didn't have to read the words or the legend if one was told that the black block was where one was— Terindell—and what the two rivers were. He decided to make his way first to the river, with the idea that its current flow would either confirm or deny his idea as to where he was.

Running the four miles was easy for him, and he found his natural state no real problem at all. At least, as long as there were only birds and animals around, he couldn't care less. It was kind of fun, as in the old days. He remembered from somewhere that the early Olympics, back in Greece or wherever it was, were run in the buff. All he needed was a torch.

Pacing himself and enjoying it, he took about half an hour to reach the trees lining the riverbank—and he felt only slightly winded. After Gorodo, a free run at his own pace was easy as pie.

The river, indeed, ran to the south—actually, southeast— as it should. He stopped and looked at it for a few minutes, relaxing after his run. It was a muddy river with a fast current, but nothing spectacular at this point—certainly no more than a quarter of a mile across. An easy swim. He considered the idea. Across there was Hypboreya, a different country that wouldn't march to Ruddygore's tune. Not friendly to him, certainly, but not friendly to Gorodo or, particularly, to Poquah, either, the Imir being a somewhat official servant of the sorcerer and the government. If there were any jokers in the pack— and surely there must be—and Joe didn't make it before the chase began, he would swim to the other side. He decided that quickly, as something of an equalizer.

It occurred to him that if he *did* make that swim, he would also no longer be under anybody's thumb. With a few clothes and some honest work in that country he'd be truly free. That might be the ultimate joke on all of them—to have their prize pigeon not make for Terindell at all. He wondered if they had considered that.

He put the idea aside for now, but left it as another option.

A large bird flew down, skimming the surface of the water, and as it did, suddenly the water erupted and a thin, slimy, black, whiplike tentacle shot up and caught the bird, dragging it quickly under. It was all so sudden he was totally shocked and stunned, but it was a reminder of an alien world. This wasn't the Mississippi, nor his old Earth, and things existed, deadly things, that could kill in a flash. If he'd decided to swim the river at that point . . .

He needed a few things as quickly as possible, he knew. He needed clothing of some sort, so he wouldn't have to skulk, and he definitely needed some kind of weapon.

He searched around in the thin forest that hugged the river, looking at deadwood, and finally found a nice, long stick that was more or less straight, looked pretty strong, and, even better, had a rough point at one end and a pretty solid other end. Pointed weapon or club. It would do until something better came along.

He glanced around. Fifty miles. Not much. But, considering that thing in the river, he didn't really want to spend a night out here.

Suddenly, above and behind him came the sound of laughter, as if from some very small children. He whirled, but nobody was there. He stood silently, trying to catch whoever or whatever it was. As he was beginning to feel it had just been his imagination, the laughter came again—and again, above and behind him. He whirled once more, seeing nothing, then stood there gaping for a moment. On impulse, he whirled around again, waiting for the sound—and saw them.

They were about the size of four- or five-month-old babies and looked very chubbily babyish, but their eyes were large and old, and they hovered there, a few feet above his head, on tiny, rapidly beating, white wings.

"Oooo—look! He's naked!" one of them squealed in a playful child's voice.

He relaxed and felt a little rush of anger. "So are you," he retorted.

"Yeah, but it don't bother us none," the small creature said. "It kinda bothers you, though, don't it?"

"Not for the likes of *you*," he shot back, then paused a moment. "Uh, just who and what *are* you, anyway?"

"Gosh, ain't you never heard of cherubs before?" one of them asked, sounding genuinely surprised.

He thought a moment. "Little angels or something, if I remember. You two look like Cupid."

They both giggled. "That's sorta right. I dunno 'bout the angel part, though. Cupids, though, we been called before."

A sudden fright seized him. "You're not gonna shoot me with love arrows, are you?"

They both giggled again. "Love arrows? That's rich. That's a good one! We don't need no arrows to play with you mortals." The speaking cherub paused, thought a moment, then said, a playful smile on his lips, "You're such a big, strong guy. Bet you ain't scared of *nothin'!*"

He frowned. As a matter of fact, he *did* feel a sudden wrongness, a sudden, nameless fear. Trusting his instincts, he looked around, the feeling getting stronger and stronger. He felt suddenly trapped between the river and . . . what? The trees! The trees were something else! Something plotting to snare him! He had to get out fast.

Without a second thought, propelled only by the rising, unreasoning fear, he bolted through the thin line of trees back onto the open plain. Once in the clear, away from those menacing trees, he collapsed on the ground, sweating hard and shaking slightly.

The two cherubs flew out from the trees, laughing uproariously, and approached him. He needed only the smallest glance at them and at their expressions to know he'd been had.

"*You* did that to me!" he accused.

"Awwww . . . Big, bad barbarian scared of a couple of trees," one of the sprites jeered mockingly.

He leaped angrily to his feet, wishing he had some kind of weapon. A stone, *anything*. Common sense told him that these two, flitting around like hummingbirds, would just play with him if he tried to nab them bare-handed.

Suddenly he remembered his big stick, and was almost surprised to see that he was still carrying it. Taking aim, trying to get control of himself and not telegraph his intent, he looked at the two.

"Wow!" one of the cherubs exclaimed. "You're real brave,

mister, if you keep holding onto that *thing* there. It will eat your arm off in a minute!"

Abruptly the unreasoning fear filled him once again, and with a yell he flung away the stick, which was, indeed, still a stick. They had outguessed him.

Frustration overcame anger. Less than an hour into the contest, he was already defeated by two sorcerous sprites. "What are you going to do? Torture me all day?"

"Gosh, no," one of them replied. "It's just kinda, well, you know, *irresistible*."

A sudden suspicion hit him. "Did somebody from Terindell send you?"

They both giggled. "Naw. Nobody sends us no place. But we did kinda get the word that you'd be around."

He sighed. "I should have known. I suppose everybody between here and there will be on the lookout for me. I *knew* it was too easy."

"Probably, if *we* got the word," one of the sprites agreed. They looked identical, and it was impossible to tell one from the other. "So you're in a lotta deep mud, huh?"

He thought about it. "Could be. But if you'll let me go, at least I'll have a crack at it."

"*Let* you go?" One giggled, then flexed a tiny arm. "How are *we* gonna stop you?"

"You know how," he grumbled. "Don't rub it in. I'm a match for any other man, I think, but I can't fight magic."

"Hey! Well, then, maybe we should go along with you for a while," one said. "Maybe help you out on that score."

"Um. Thanks—but no, thanks. Nothing personal, you understand, but you might just get it into your little heads to play some more with me, too."

"Hmph! Just for that we *will* come along. How're you gonna stop us?"

"Yeah," the other one agreed. "We could make you want us, but it's more fun this way."

He sighed. "All right, all right. Maybe you can help at that. That *is* the River of Dancing Gods over there?"

"Oh, yeah. That's what all the mortals call it, anyway," a cherub told him.

"So Terindell is about fifty miles downstream, then, as I figured," he said, thinking out loud. "All right. Let's get going."

He hesitated a moment. "I can't keep calling you 'hey, you' if you're tagging along. You have names?"

"Oh, yeah. I'm Ba'el. He's Lo'al."

Joe gave the trees a nervous glance, then started back for them, not going in but walking along on the plains side. "Okay, Ba'el. You called me a mortal. Does that mean you're immortal?"

"Sorta," Ba'el admitted, sounding uncomfortable. "If you mean growin' old and croaking, nope. But if we're not careful, we can get zapped by somethin' hungry or by sorcery."

"You're both males?"

They giggled. "That don't mean nothin' to us. We got no sex. That's probably why we find it so much fun to watch you folks."

Joe stopped a moment. "If that's true, how do you reproduce?"

"*We* don't," Lo'al told him. "Gee, you're awful ignorant. Everybody knows we come from the egg of the *tardris* flower. Where you from, anyway, barbarian?"

He sighed. "Another world," he replied. "Another time."

Once they decided to tag along, he was almost glad of them, although a bit wary. They seemed intellectually adult but emotionally infantile and easily distracted. He worried mostly about their getting bored enough to start playing tricks with his emotions again. Still, it made sense, particularly when he got out of them that a *tardris* laid just one egg and then sheltered the cherub at night. A new cherub was born only to replace one that did not return in the evening, thus keeping the population stable. The plant itself was almost immortal, it seemed, and it was well known that anyone cutting or harming one would die as it did, so the plants were tolerated where they grew, along lakes and rivers.

The cherubs' tie to their parent flower also heartened him a bit. He wasn't sure of their range, but he was pretty sure they wouldn't go *that* far from their home, particularly when Lo'al let slip that they ate only inside the flower, fed by a fluid it manufactured. They were far too chubby to go long between meals.

The day grew warmer as the sun rose in the sky; within a couple of hours, it was really hot. So far he'd seen or heard no other intelligent beings save his two cherubs, although occasionally in the distance, either from the river or from across the plains, he could hear the sounds of humans calling or yelling or doing something or other.

It occurred to him, though, that going right along the river was exactly what they'd expect him to do. The cherubs were merely a small nuisance, but they'd already shown how impotent he was against such as they. Certainly Terindell's nasty little minds had more challenges ahead, particularly if he kept to the course he was now taking.

Still, if he was to leave the river, he'd need something as a guide. Remembering the map, he recalled that the main road that led from the provincial capital of Machang to Terdiera and Terindell ran down the middle of the little "neck" of Valisandra. The road, he decided, would be much safer until he was closer to the castle.

The cherubs were unhappy at his decision, but didn't put up as much of a fuss as he'd anticipated. He got the distinct feeling that they were already bored with him.

He headed southeast across the plain, glad to be rid of the threat his two companions had posed, and began an easy run. He knew it might be a long distance before he sighted the road, maybe fifteen or twenty miles, but the detour would be worth it. Still, he hoped that he would find some place where he could beg, borrow, or steal at least something to use for a loincloth and some food. It had been a long time since he'd eaten. He also found himself wondering how perfect Eden could have been if Adam had to go to the bathroom the same way as he did. He felt grubby, hungry, and thirsty, and he was ready to do about anything to solve those problems.

About a half hour inland, he came upon a small lake with some bushes but no tree cover. There were a few birds about, but no animals that he could see, save a couple of long-horned cows drinking by the far side.

He looked at the water suspiciously, but there didn't seem to be much of a film and it looked pretty clear. Certainly it looked worth risking a drink and, perhaps, a cleansing swim.

He knelt down by the side of the pond, noting that things were so perfect he was almost looking directly into a mirror. He studied his reflection for a moment, still unable to get used to it, then leaned down to sip. The water tasted fresh and clear, amazingly so for such a small pond in such an isolated plain.

The water rippled where he'd broken it, then slowly settled and re-formed once more into his image. But it was not only his image he saw.

He turned, both startled and embarrassed, to see a beautiful woman standing behind him, fully one of the most beautiful and voluptuous women he'd ever seen. She was also as totally naked as he, which didn't stave off his initial embarrassed feelings one bit.

"Oh, I'm sorry I startled you," she said in a soft, musical voice. "I so seldom get visitors here that I often forget politeness."

He gulped. "Uh, um, I'm sorry myself. I didn't know this was anybody's land."

She laughed. "Oh, it's not my land. It is my pond. I am Irium."

He hesitated a moment, trying to sort it out. For the first time it penetrated that her skin was a pale bluish green, much like the waters of the pond itself. Aside from that and a bit of webbing between her fingers and toes, though, she looked extremely human.

"Uh—your *pond*?" he said questioningly. Something inside him rejected all considerations of her color, webbing, or anything else. She was beautiful . . . gorgeous . . . nothing else in the world mattered but her. Considering his nakedness, his emotions were pretty hard to hide from her.

She smiled at him, and he melted completely. "It's so nice to see someone again. Few ever venture this way these days except cows, and they are poor company."

With that she moved in and closed with him, and all he could think of was her. He didn't even realize that, as she clung to him, she was also edging him close to and then into the cool pond. Waist-deep, then still going in, now neck-deep.

"*Hold*!" The shout was a woman's voice, icy, cutting, and commanding. "Bring him to me or, by Sathanas and Doharic, you shall have no pond at all!"

The threat caused the blue-green beauty to hesitate; then slowly, still without his realizing what was happening, they rose to the surface and moved as if on currents of force back toward the shore.

He was aware only that somebody was butting in, coming between him and consummation with Irium, and this angered him. He let loose his grip from his lady love and turned to see a handsome, striking woman, dressed in long slit skirt and faded brown blouse, standing there, holding a crooked stick of some kind out toward them. "Go away!" he shouted at her. "We don't need you!"

"*We* don't, but *you* do," the stranger responded coldly. Her brow furrowed, and she seemed to be looking beyond just his physical appearance. It was done in a flash, but she nodded to herself. "You have been victimized by some mischievous cherubs who almost killed you." She made a sign in the air, and he felt a sudden deep chill shoot through him. He turned again to his newfound lady love and screamed in horror, pushing away from her and scrambling, splashing all the way, to the nearby land.

The beauty who had so smitten him was a beauty no more, but an ugly, hideous thing, the stuff of long-rotted corpses.

"Flee, wicked sprite of the water, for you shall not have him!" his rescuer called, and the rotting thing gave a gurgling cry and vanished beneath the waters of the pond.

Satisfied, the newcomer approached him as he lay gasping on the beach and looked down on him with a mixture of scorn and contempt. Although a beauty herself, she exuded a strong, confident, powerful aura that was unmistakable. This was a woman used to command.

"Wha—what was it?" he gasped.

"A water sprite. She got trapped in here during a major hurricane and flood, and there's been no getting rid of her. She's really pretty much of an incompetent, anyway—she was rushing to drown you without even the preliminaries. You wouldn't have been such an easy mark if you didn't have that spell cast on you."

He sighed. "Those bastards. Couldn't resist a parting shot."

She shrugged. "It is their nature. They are so childlike they probably don't even remember you now." She looked down and sighed. "Well, you're a real mess. Pick yourself up and come with me. You look as if you could use a meal."

He got up, suddenly conscious of some aches and bruises, and followed her meekly.

Her farm wasn't far away, and it looked very pretty and well tended.

The farmhouse itself was set in an isolated grove of trees,

but all around, the land had been cleared and tilled. Over in the far fields he could see large animals, perhaps oxen, pulling plows—apparently by themselves. Other animals turned irrigation wheels, while over in an uncultivated pasture cows grazed.

Animals, he realized, didn't work without supervision under normal circumstances, but this strange woman had already proved herself a witch or sorceress of some sort. He owed her his life, so he decided not to comment or pry.

The farmhouse was a simple wooden affair with a thatched roof, but it had a good hardwood floor and seemed pretty cozy inside. It was clear, though, that the woman lived alone.

He was acutely aware of his nakedness once more and apologized for it, but she just laughed it away. "Don't worry. I've seen a lot in my life, and it doesn't bother me in the slightest. If it bothers *you*, I suppose I could rig up something, but it would take time. Just sit over there, relax, and I'll see about getting you something to eat."

He sank wearily into the wooden chair offered, finally feeling a little bit more human again. She went into another room and returned with a bunch of home-baked pastries, bread, fresh butter, and a jug of cold milk. "This will at least get you started," she told him, sitting down opposite. He noticed that she never let go of the strange, crooked walking stick she carried, although she didn't seem to need it and hadn't used it at all to support herself. "So," she asked, "how'd you happen to be around the old pond, anyway?"

He sighed. "I'm a little new to everything around here, it seems." Quickly, as he wolfed down the bread and pastries, he told her of having been brought from his own world by Ruddygore, then trained and tested. She nodded, taking it all in.

When he'd finished, she said, "The old boy's off his block, bringing in outsiders. Nothing personal, but from what you've told me just today, you're no match for Husaquahr. Here most humans fall into two classes: the majority—the bulk, really—who do all the work in exchange for protection from all the magical forces around them; and the few who are smart enough or lucky enough to have the power, so they don't fear those forces. The few others like you, adventurers and misfits, mostly, who wander around getting into trouble, were born into this world and know their way around the magic and the politics.

You can't be taught that kind of thing—you have to grow up with all this. And even if it's true that Hell can't handle you—which I most sincerely doubt—it makes no difference. The sorcery of Husaquahr alone is enough to do you in, in ten minutes on your own."

"After this morning, I have to agree with you," he admitted. "Still, what choice do I have? I go along with it or I don't—and if I can't make it on my own in a simple thing like this, how could I make it on my own anyplace around here?" He sighed. "Brawn and common sense, they told me. Well, my brawn hasn't done me much good, and I've shown very little common sense today, for all the good it will do me."

"I think you know you could be of little use to Ruddygore, for all I care of his troubles, but you might be just what I need right now. Come with me—outside for a moment." She got up and went out the door, and he followed, curious.

She gestured with the crooked stick. "You see the farm here. It runs itself, pretty much. Animals are my field of study and my life. Everything I require is produced right here. The locals steer clear of this place, which is why our friend in the pond over there has so few victims. But there are certain husbandry problems I have. Chickens need roosters to lay regular eggs. Cows need a bull to keep the milk flowing. I lost my prize bull the other day to a stupid accident."

He nodded, wondering where she was leading.

"Tell me—have you ever heard of Circe?"

He thought a moment, then slowly shook his head. "I don't think so."

"The legends have Circe as a person, a sorceress. Actually, it is a place. An island, far from Husaquahr. An enchanted island, inhabited entirely by a race of women."

"I seem to remember some old stories of places where only women lived," he told her. "Seems to me they'd die out after a while."

"That would be true," she admitted, "but men are occasionally lured there in collusion with sirens and other allies of the sea. They usually act as expected, waking up on an island of women, and the Circeans let them. In that way the population is renewed."

"Sounds like a fun place to be shipwrecked," he murmured.

"Think you so? I said it was an enchanted isle. After the

people are done with the men, the enchantment is brought into play. A piece of sacred wood, like this, is brought out, and the man is touched *so*." She touched him with the stick. "Then the man is useful in other ways, and Circe is all female once more."

He felt suddenly dizzy and dropped to all fours. "Hey! What—?" he exclaimed, but his talk turned into an outlandish bellow.

She stepped back and looked at him with satisfaction. "I am from that island," she told him. "Exiled for reasons that do not concern anyone but me. Eventually I came here with my enchanted wand and built this place from barren fields. I transform few, for sorcerers such as your Ruddygore could do as they willed with me. But you owe me your life. And you have no future here, as we both agreed. So now you are what you reminded me of the moment I saw you. You are my new bull, bound by my powers to do my bidding and bound, too, to the limits of my land. Your power and your horns will guard the land and herds from unseen interlopers, and you will keep my cows in milk. It's not so much to ask. No petty magic or sprites need you fear ever again, for you are under my protection." With that she turned and went back into her house, leaving him there.

Vision and balance cleared in a bit, and he found what she said was impossibly true. He could turn his massive head enough to see his huge black body, and he could wag his barely seen tail. His vision, he discovered, was poor—after twenty feet or so, things started to blur—and he was totally color-blind, but his powers of hearing and smell were increased tremendously.

He turned and looked back at the house, but knew he could never fit through that door in any case. He needed time to think, he decided, and wandered off toward the fields where the cows were grazing, following—scent? Yes, that seemed to be it.

Almost without thinking, he found himself lowering his massive head and munching the tall grass, which tasted extremely good. But all he could think of was that he'd been suckered again.

He sulked most of the afternoon, munching grass and feeling rotten, and wandered across the farm without really realizing it. He was both shocked and startled late in the day to hear somebody addressing him.

"So you're the new bully boy," a thin, reedy, male voice said casually. "Welcome to the club."

His massive head came up, and he looked around with all the concentration his weak eyes could muster but saw no one.

"Not there, bright eyes," came the voice. "Down here. And watch where you're stepping!"

He looked down and saw in front of him a handsome, strutting rooster.

"So what d'ya want, big boy? A bear?"

"But—you're a rooster!" he exclaimed in a deep series of snorts and grunts.

"And you're a bull. You wanna make something of it?"

"But—you can talk!"

"To you, anyway," the rooster admitted. "And to any of the other former men who are around here. Maybe a couple of dozen. The rest are real animals."

He hadn't considered this. Just the opportunity for two-way communication excited him. "I'm Joe. How long have you been here?"

"Macore's the name," the rooster responded. "Been here forever, it seems. You lose your sense of time, though. Don't much matter, anyway. We're all stuck here."

He didn't like the sound of that. "Nobody ever tries to escape?"

The rooster crowed derisively. "Escape? Man, you're bound to this land by that stick she's got. No need for fences. It's like hitting a stone wall."

"I'll take your word for it." Joe thought a moment. "Say— you say it's the stick that does it?"

"Yep. From her native island. She never is without it."

His mind was suddenly racing with even this tiny glimmer of hope. "But surely she sleeps?"

"Oh, sure. Oh, I see where you're headed. You figure to swipe the stick, maybe hide it or break it up, right?"

"Something like that," he admitted.

"Well, don't think it hasn't been thought of before. You want to risk her catching you and turning you into a snail or worm or something, that's fine with me. Bein' a rooster maybe ain't so much, but it's lot better than the alternatives."

"I wonder. I wonder if everybody's as content as you are to be an animal slave for the rest of his life."

"Hey! Wait a minute! Now, don't get me wrong. If there was a real chance, I'd grab it for sure. But take it all the way. Say we snatch the stick and get away with it. Her hold is gone. We can leave. Hoo-ray! But you'll still be a bull and I'll still be a rooster. The spell's worked *through* the charm, as with all spells. It will hold even if she don't have the stick—and without the stick not even she could undo it. Think about it. You'd be steaks in the Machang markets before long, and I'd be chicken salad. Even if we escaped that, what kind of life would it be? Worse off than here, I'd say. Now do you see why nobody tries?"

Joe nodded, but didn't really accept it all. Something the woman had said kept rattling around in the back of his head, something he couldn't quite pin down.

"You all right?" Macore asked, concerned about the silence. "I know it's tough to accept, but—"

"*Quiet*! I'm trying to think!" he snapped. Something she had said... Yeah! That was it!

"*I transform few, for sorcerers such as your Ruddygore could do as they willed with me ...*"

"How's that?" the rooster asked, sounding concerned.

"Ruddygore! Sure! You've heard of him, haven't you?"

"Oh, sure. Everybody has, I guess. One of the most powerful sorcerers in the world, it's said. Also nuttier than a squirrel's hoard, by all accounts."

"I think you're right on both counts. But what she said, just after she got me, was that Ruddygore was tremendously more powerful than she. She's scared of him. Don't you see? If Ruddygore personally took over, he could break her spell in a minute. He could restore us—and protect us from her!"

Macore thought it over. "I dunno. Maybe you're right. But what good does that do us? These necromancers don't give one small damn about folks like us."

"This one cares about me, for some reason," Joe said, hope returning full within him, and with it a sense of self-confidence. "He suckered me from another world to this one, gave me a new body, then trained me with the best trainers around. If I could get to him and make him know it was me, he'd change me back for sure. And as long as he broke the one spell, he'd do it for everybody. I think I know him well enough to promise that."

The rooster looked and sounded interested. "So Ruddygore's a buddy, huh? How do I know you're not just putting me on?"

Joe sighed. "The best I can do is tell you the whole story," And he proceeded to do so.

The rooster listened attentively, then finally said, "Well, *I* believe you, for what this's worth. But I'm not the one you got to convince. I couldn't possibly lift that stick, even though I could get into the house, and you wouldn't fit through the door. Uh-uh. We need help. I think it's time you met the rest of the boys."

The rest of the boys proved to be a couple of magnificent-looking stallions, two pigs, a gander, four oxen, a ram, and a billy goat. They were harder to convince than Macore had been. Many had been there so long they barely remembered being anything else, and a strong undercurrent of fear of their mistress ran through all of them. In the past, there had been examples made that several remembered clearly. There were a lot of unpleasant things the Circean could turn somebody into, and Joe heard the whole catalog.

"It's not a bad life we have here," argued Posti, one of the horses, "Plenty to eat. Security. An easy job."

Joe just couldn't see it. "Is that all being a man meant to you? I mean, really, is that all *life* means to you? *Agh!* Better she turned you into a carrot! Then you wouldn't even have to think!"

"If you wasn't so damned big and mean-lookin', bull, I'd tear you apart for that," Posti shot back. "What does *anybody* want outta life 'cept food, sex, and security?" There were several murmurs of agreement.

"If that's all being alive means, then you *are* better off here," Joe told them. "If being human means something more— maybe doing some great thing, or maybe being a part of some great enterprise—then you're wrong. Maybe love, kids, learning something new, and teaching it to others count for something, too, though."

"Listen, buddy," Houma the goat broke in, sounding more sheepish than goatish, "what you say may be true for *you*, but not for most of us. I mean, how many people ever can do them great things you talk about? Most of us are just plain, simple folk. Me, I was stuck on a farm workin' my ass off for some duke I never even seen, married off young to a gal who looked worse than Grogha here—" He meant one of the pigs. "—and saddled with a half-dozen kids, all of which looked like her and acted like demons. Hell, wanderin' on this place one day was pretty good luck for me."

Joe looked from one to the other, understanding the problem while not being able to understand fully how people could be like that. He was conscious, though, that he was losing ground in the debate and had little to offer. What kind of men were these, who'd rather stay draft animals? He looked at Grogha the pig. "You, too, hog? You like your life here?"

"It's not bad," Grogha grunted. "Not like what you people seem to think it is."

It was Macore who came to Joe's rescue a little. "I can give you a couple of arguments for going along with the bull here," he said. "The best reason, Grogha, is how you'd like your life if the old bag got a sudden yen for pork chops."

The entire group gave a shocked gasp.

"Yeah," the rooster persisted. "Pork chops. Bacon. Sausage. That's what you'll wind up, you know, when you're too old to produce the little piglets. Same goes for me. I don't like being somebody's chicken dinner. How long do we live in this form? A few years for me at best. Maybe five, six for pigs. Longer for horses and oxen, shorter for sheep and goats, but not very long. How long we been here? Anybody really know?"

"Ten or fifteen years is fine with me," the stubborn Posti responded. "How long was I gonna live back home?"

"Yeah, but you been here the longest, I think," a hesitant-sounding Houma said thoughtfully. "How long has it been, Posti? You ain't as young as you used to be, I know that."

Mentally thanking Macore for the opening, Joe pressed the advantage while it held. "Yeah, Posti. And what happens if you break a leg? All you got to do is make one slip, break down once, and you're nothing but several hundred pounds of dog food."

"Hey! Now wait a minute!" the horse responded defensively, but neither Joe nor Macore was willing to let him off the hook.

"Yeah," the rooster pressed. "What happens to a man with

a broken leg? You get an adept in the healer's art, rest a couple of weeks, and you got it. And how old *might* you grow? To sit around the alehouses and swap the old yarns and be the object of respect—or to that certain fate our new friend here predicts if you remain the same? As for me, I do not look forward to my certain slaughter, but even if, as a man, I were then to die, I would rather die a *man* than live this kind of life."

As with any group of basically pedestrian, unimaginative minds, sentiment shifted with the latest decent argument. Now heads were nodding in favor of Macore's words. Joe decided not to let anybody else swing things the other way.

"A vote!" he called. "Let's have a vote! Those with us will try it. Those not with us can go back to their ways for a while, until fate takes them, or until they are overrun and enslaved by the Dark Baron's forces because they were not there to fight him like men!"

That last, said in the heat of passion, shocked them a little more. He'd forgotten how out of touch they'd be—and he hoped he hadn't gone too far. Macore's rooster head cocked and looked at him a bit dubiously, but there was nothing to be done. "Yes," the rooster agreed. "Let us vote now. In turn, I will call your names and you tell me aye or nay."

"I think—" Posti began, but Macore cut him off by starting the roll call. The early vote was clearly for escape, but beginning with Posti it seemed to go the other way. In the end, it was Joe, Macore, Grogha, Houma, and the other horse, whose name was Dacaro, who voted to escape. The others, the majority of the group, decided against.

"Very well," Macore told the dissenters. "Go back to your stables and fields and vegetate. We will be gone soon."

"Or turned to maggots," one of the oxen snorted. Slowly the nay votes drifted away into the gathering darkness.

Macore sighed. "Okay. Sorry if I have problems, but I have no night vision at all. I make it five of us. We'll need a plan."

Joe looked at the odd barnyard assortment. "I'd say our roles are pretty clear. Macore, you absolutely guarantee we can get off this farm if she doesn't have the stick?"

"If she doesn't have *ownership*, then yes," the rooster assured him. "That means it must be in the possession of one of us or hidden where only we, not she, know about it."

"I have no intention of chancing her getting it back again," Joe said flatly. "Who knows what she might do? So once we have it, I'll take the stick. But I can't get inside her house to get it. Our friends the pig and the goat must be the actual burglars."

"I figured something like that," Grogha grumped. "Hell, she's a light sleeper. She's lasted a long time. Our hooves will clatter on that stone floor of hers."

"Then you must go silently and slowly," Joe told them. "But once one of you has the stick securely in your mouth, both run like hell. I'll be waiting outside and I'll grab it. Then we all start running."

"Damn! Wish I could see in this," Macore swore in frustration. "Well, let's work it out as best we can. First the burglary, then the getaway. We can't afford to get separated once we're clear of here."

"Then let's get to details," Joe responded anxiously.

"When do you want to do this?" Houma asked uneasily.

"Frankly, I'd like to do it right now," Joe told him, "but none of us have had any rest and we'd better be at our best for this. There's no reason for waiting, though. There's just as much chance of getting caught if we rehearse it as if we do it. I'd say tomorrow, at mid-eve, about halfway through her sleep. Macore—you seem to know a lot of her habits. When does she usually go to bed?"

"She's asleep now," the rooster told the bull. "She eats her meal shortly after sunset, makes a final check of the outbuildings, then turns in. There's one help, too—she snores."

"How do you know so much?" the goat asked.

Macore laughed. "I been dreaming of this for a long, long time. But I'm not strong enough to lift that stick, and no good at night. Believe me, though—I've worked it out again and again . . ."

The company gathered in the dark away from the house about an hour after moonrise. Joe didn't like the clear, moonlit night much—it would make them very easy to spot—but Macore liked it just fine. Although his vision was bad, there was light enough for him at least to see what was going on.

They were surprised to find an addition to the night's work—Posti, the leader of the opposition. "I just keep dreamin' and dreamin' about dogs," he grumbled. "Besides, if you pull this off, it might get lonesome around here."

"Glad to have you," Macore said, "but there's little for you to do. Just stand out here with Joe and Dacaro and be ready to run interference if you get the chance."

"When I get the stick, run like hell in any direction except the one *I* take until you're out of sight, then double back to the west gate." Joe looked around, his vision not so hot, either. Finally he saw a small stick—actually the broken handle of a shovel or something similar. "Hey! There's a thought. Find one more like this. Then all three of us tearing off will have something in our mouth. She won't know *which* one to chase."

They scouted around and finally found an old piece of fence. Joe sighed, looked at the company, said, "All right—we all know what we're going to do. If we do it, we're free and clear. If not, well, I'd rather try than sit and say I never did."

They moved slowly, singly or by twos, to the cottage. All was dark inside, and they could hear that Macore had spoken the truth when he said she snored, although it was soft and low and would not mask much in the way of sounds.

Macore perched on Joe's back. "I can't get far alone and I don't want to miss this," he explained. Joe just nodded, then turned to the two smallest members of the team.

Grogha and Houma had been very hesitant about this from the start; but once they had made up their minds, there was no second-guessing.

"I figured we needed a small one or two," Macore explained to Joe. "That's why I got the roll call in that order. The sure ones first, then Grogha and, finally, Houma. I figured, if it looked at first like everybody was going to make the break, Houma'd come in. When it turned out different, he was too stubborn and too proud to back down."

"I never could have gotten this far without you, Macore. I owe you one," Joe told him.

"Maybe," Macore replied, almost to himself. "But maybe I owe you one, Joe."

The pig and the goat had already disappeared inside the house.

The fact was that the witch had little to fear and so had taken few precautions. As long as the spell of her staff was on the farm, anyone could get onto the property, but never off.

Her reputation alone was enough to keep most everybody away, but any who came, perhaps to do her harm, would have raised enough of an alarm among the animals, compelled to defend the place, to result in her awakening in plenty of time to deal with that intruder. She had no reason to fear the animals themselves, she'd thought. A few examples and long domestication had made them fearful and complacent, she was sure. Nor was she concerned with the possibility of a rebel in the newcomer. He was far too large to fit through her door.

But the newcomer was not a rebel, but a rebel leader. Now came the revolution—if that pig and that goat could pull it off.

Inside the cottage, Grogha and Houma were moving slowly in the near total darkness, almost too scared to breathe. They were both well aware of how impossible it all seemed—and that they would be the ones to bear the consequences of failure.

The snores were somewhat reassuring, but then Grogha brushed against a chair, which scraped slightly, and both he and Houma froze as the snoring abruptly stopped. Their hearts felt as if they were about to leap from their chests while there was total silence; but finally they heard her turn slightly and begin to snore once more.

Cautiously, Houma the goat approached the bed. He had the best night eyesight of the bunch, and the strongest jaws. Grogha was backup and support only, one who considered his presence in the room mostly for the purpose of moral support.

They feared that the magic stick might be in a holder, or sequestered away in some secret place, but it was not. It was right there, on the floor beside the bed as Macore had assured them, ready to be grabbed in an instant should the woman wake. Had it been smoother and straighter, she might have slept with it.

Houma opened his mouth wide and gingerly wrapped it around the stick, then clamped down tight. Slowly, cautiously, he turned his head to bring the stock horizontal—and there was a crash. The woman hadn't been all *that* trusting—she'd tied a thread to it that brought down the pots and pans!

She was up and turning in a flash as Grogha screamed, "Too late now! *Run like hell!*"

Houma hadn't waited for the advice, but had kicked off on his hind legs and made for the door, stick in mouth. The thread hadn't broken, though, and trailing him came a large iron frying pan, making all sorts of clatter. Unable to get to the goat, the woman grabbed the frying pan and pulled, hard, at almost the same instant Grogha decided that it was act or die. Leaping forward, the hog ran right for her legs and into them, toppling her backward.

Houma jerked around on the line, falling as the woman on the other end of the string fell backward and pulled; but in a flash the pan came free of her hand as she screamed and hit the floor.

"Hurry!" Grogha yelled. "Get out of here! I'm right behind you!" And, with that, pan still clattering behind, both went out the doorway. Feeling lucky even to be alive, Houma dropped the stick at Joe's feet and took off, followed as fast as he could by the porcine Grogha.

The witch had recovered quickly and was now also coming out the door, yelling and cursing at the top of her lungs. Joe seized the stick, and she again made to grab the frying pan, jumping on it and holding tight, but this time the force at the other end was no scrawny goat but a huge bull. The string snapped, and she fell backward once more, still grasping the frying pan.

Macore yelled, "Move it!" from atop Joe's back, and Joe and the two horses took off as agreed.

Now the moonlit night helped rather than hindered, and Joe was able, even with his poor vision, to follow the route Macore had mapped out for him, getting him in a roundabout way to the west gate. He clutched the magic stick in his mouth for all it was worth and feared only that he was going to trip and break a leg or at least lose the stick. In the dim light of the moon, it was unlikely that he or his passenger could find it again.

Ultimately they reached the gate, where the others could already be heard waiting nervously. At the sight of Joe, they gave an irresistible cheer.

The gate was just that—a wooden gate, barred with a simple wood latch that was incorporated into the long fence line. Joe decided not to wait for the niceties—he lowered his head and charged, hardly feeling it as his massive head hit the gate, shattered the wood, and broke him into the open.

The others followed, and they were off on the barren dirt road. Once away a bit, Joe slowed, allowing the others to catch up. The two horses made it almost on his heels, but it took a little longer for the smaller goat and particularly for Grogha the pig to reach the gathering.

Macore crowed in spite of himself. "Whoopee! We did it! We're *out*!"

Suddenly Joe, who'd been running mostly on emotion, realized it, too. "We're free! We're really free . . ."

"Not for long if the old bag catches up to us," a breathless Houma reminded them. "Let's put a little distance between us and the farm—and ditch that stick where she'll never find it."

They made their way down the road, Joe and the horses valiantly trying to be slow enough to accommodate the goat and the pig. Finally the road turned sharply southward, and they realized that they were coming upon the junction of the main road to Terdiera.

Joe stopped. "Any of you with better eyes see a place where we can rest for a while?"

"There's a grove of trees over there that will give us some protection," Houma said. "To your right—near the little pond."

Joe looked up. "Little pond? How little? Does it look deep?"

"Hard to say," the goat replied. "Why?"

"Well, it wouldn't be a bad place to toss this stick, now, would it?"

"Say! You're right at that!"

Macore was more cautious. "I wonder if we might not try to break it, at least in two, first. That won't help us, but it might make it hard for her to go back into business if she ever *does* find the pieces."

They nodded and made for the pond.

Joe, Posti, and Dacaro took turns trying to break the thing, but finally it was a combination of Houma's goat jaws and Joe's weight that did it. Joe didn't know what he'd expected— some weird magical lights, something—but it seemed just like any other old stick. Somehow, the lack of a reaction at its breaking was disappointing.

Still, having broken it, they tossed one piece in the pond, not knowing if the water was inches or yards deep. The other piece Joe chewed on for a while, then finally dropped in an area in the woods where there was much deadwood on the ground. "No use in making it easy to put the thing back together again, if she can," he noted.

With that they decided on a schedule of guards and tried to get some rest. It was hard, coming after the excitement, and they soon started talking.

"Posti, you were the one who kept the others from coming," Joe noted. "Now you're here. Don't you feel any regrets?"

"Naw. Not really. I just never really figured you could do it. Fact is, I'm still kinda happy bein' a horse. It just makes it easier to be free of that old witch. Besides, if you think on it, the others are free, too, if they wanna be. So I'll string along and see how this goes."

Joe looked over at Dacaro. The sleek black stallion had said barely a word, from the initial debate through now, although he'd done his part and had, at least, said enough to vote for the plan. "What's with him?" Joe asked Posti.

"He don't talk much, but he's a good man," Posti responded. "I dunno much about him, but I got the impression he's not too unhappy bein' a horse, either. You wonder what *he's* runnin' from—or to. Me, you know about."

Joe nodded, After a while, conversation petered out, and they did get a little fitful sleep.

The next day was cloudy and humid, with occasional light rain in the air, which suited them all just fine. The poor weather would reduce commerce on the main road and perhaps give them a little edge in avoiding trouble.

They decided to parallel the road rather than follow it, as much as the land and fencing would allow, avoiding any complications. By midday, Terdiera was in sight, looking a little less than festive in the gloomy weather. They gave the town a rather wide berth to the north, then returned to the road connecting the village with the castle. By midafternoon, the familiar walls of Terindell were in sight.

Joe stood there looking at the great castle and shook his head in wonder. "I can hardly believe it. We made it!"

"Yeah, with no real fuss, too," Posti responded, a little awed by the luck.

"So far, so good," Grogha agreed, "but now what? Are they just gonna let us barnyard animals wander in? And if we *do* get in—how the hell are we gonna tell 'em who we really are and what we need?"

"We spell it out for 'em," Dacaro said, startling them all. Every head turned to the taciturn stallion.

"He talks!" Houma said with some surprise.

"Shut up and listen!" Joe snapped, then looked back at Dacaro. "How do we do this? Anybody here know how to read and write this stuff?"

"I do," Dacaro told them. "As to the how, we just scratch it with hooves or spell it out with a stick in the dirt. I don't know how much will be necessary, though. I think in *that* castle they will be able to *see* an enchantment."

"Can you show us the marks to make—just in case?" Grogha asked cautiously.

"Just one will probably do in a pinch," Dacaro responded. "Look." With his right front hoof he scratched a simple pattern. "Like this."

They all stared at it. "What does it mean?" Macore asked.

"Basically, the few lines inside indicate an enchantment or spell," the stallion told them. "The shape of the border, with its six sides, says that the sign refers to us. No animal would or could make that sign. Can you all remember it?"

It *was* simple, and all agreed that they could. With that Joe said, "Well, let's get on down there."

They went down from the hill to the road itself, now something of a sea of mud. The great outer castle wall loomed ahead, and the drawbridge inside was down, as usual. It wasn't a real problem, considering the magical reputation.

Dacaro continued to puzzle Joe. "Where'd you learn to read?" he asked.

"Long ago, and in this very place. I am no friend of the one you call Ruddygore, nor is he a friend of mine."

"But you came with us."

Dacaro's proud head nodded. "Yes. I came. But not for the reasons you think. It was not any problems back there, but what you said at the last that made up my mind. About the Dark Baron."

"Yeah, I *did* say something. At the time I thought I shouldn't have."

"It was well that you did." Dacaro looked around as they passed through the outer castle gate. "Ah, what memories I have. Not good memories."

None of the usual elf gardeners or other staff seemed about, although it wasn't that surprising, considering the weather. There was inside activity, though—fires glowed through windows, and the master kitchen's chimney flowed with white smoke and good odors.

They stopped in the middle of the courtyard, feeling a bit nervous and dwarfed by it all.

"Well? So where's the welcoming committee?" Grogha wanted to know.

Across the courtyard a door suddenly opened, and a tall, lean figure emerged. Joe recognized Poquah the Imir instantly, but, for once, the Imir did not recognize him. In fact, at first Poquah seemed not to notice them standing there as he walked across the courtyard. Suddenly he stopped, turned, and began to frown as he looked at them. Finally he came over to them, without any apparent apprehension.

"Draw the sign! Somebody draw the sign!" Grogha prompted.

"I thought as much," the Imir said. "Enchantments. A Circean spell, if I'm not mistaken. Why do you come here?"

"How the hell can we tell him?" Macore grumped.

"Well, you could just tell me," the Imir responded. "Do you think so simple a spell would be a barrier to *me?*"

"We've come asking for the aid of Terindell," Dacaro said smoothly. "Obviously, those who would receive aid will serve in payment."

The Imir's arrowlike brows rose. "Indeed? And why should we have need of such as you? Go on your way. Fate and your own unwariness have cast your lot. You must accept that. Such spells as we would give you here would be worse than any you might suffer as you are."

"I *told* you it was all for nothin'," Posti grumped.

"Listen, you hawk-faced overgrown elf!" Joe snapped. "I'm Joe de Oro, damn it, and I don't think Ruddygore wants me to stay like this!"

The Imir seemed thunderstruck for a moment. Then, suddenly, his granitelike face began to quiver, as unaccustomed muscles were brought into play. And, slowly, Poquah did the one thing none who had ever known him would believe possible.

Poquah laughed.

Suddenly aware of how his demeanor had broken down, he got himself under quick control and stared at the bull. "*Really?*" he managed.

"Yeah. Really, damn it."

"I must admit we never expected *this*," the Imir said. "We had the whole river region staked out as well as the Valisandra Road. Gorodo must be having fits out there right now." He stood back and shook his head wonderingly. "Actually, you are much improved this way in all except disposition. I assume you decided to cut cross-country and ran into that old witch with her shaping-stick. Yes. It makes sense. Stupid, but it makes sense in your context."

"Well, save your opinions and get Ruddygore!" Joe snapped. "I want release. My friends here, too. I couldn't have busted out without 'em and I owe them."

"That will be up to the Master," Poquah responded. "Remain here and I will see if he's in and prepared to receive you."

"You can also tell him that I won. Fair's fair. I passed your little test."

That, too, seemed to rock the Imir. "You *won*?"

Joe was starting to enjoy this. "Sure. I was to get back here, inside the castle, with no time limit, before anybody from the castle caught me. Well—here I am!"

"A highly unprecedented method," Poquah said, "but you may have a point."

"Just go see about Ruddygore."

"As you wish. I am not quite certain how he is going to take this." He turned to go, then paused and turned back to them. "The Master may not be in, or he may be otherwise occupied. Just stand around and munch grass, or whatever it is you do. He will attend to you in his own good time."

"Thanks a lot," Joe muttered, absent-mindedly munching grass.

CHAPTER 8

BUILDING A COMPANY IDENTITY

Companies must be composed of no less than seven individuals, at least one of whom should not be fully trusted.
—XXXIV, 363, 244(a)

THE DARK HOST WAS IMPRESSIVE IN ITS ORDERED MARCH AND fairly dripped of evil. Ruddygore, in astral form, looked down upon the enemy forces from his high vantage point and was amazed at their number and organization. How many? Ten thousand, surely, if there was one. The multitude of races, both from Husaquahr and from realms far beyond, was also startling. When the Dark Baron conquered, he gained forces and additional loot with which to hire the best from afar.

They were a sinister bunch, but even evil had its beauty, which was one reason it was so attractive. Huge, beaked *tarfur* in their great flowing robes of black and gold perched atop swift, multiwinged suggoths. Behind were the bat-winged *gofahr* and at least two small legions of hoglike *uorku* and the horned riders of far Halizar. There were elves and men as well down there, the elves biologically identical with the gardeners of Terindell, yet were somehow rough, hard, and ugly, with eyes either burning or empty. The humans ran the gamut from tall, fierce-looking barbarian mercenaries to professional soldiers, opportunists, and obvious conscripts.

The Dark Baron had doubled his forces since the start of the flood season, and more were coming day after day, Ruddygore knew. Everybody feared a winner, and the Baron certainly looked like one. Queasy leaders in a dozen places were making very certain that they would be positively remembered if the Baron's forces conquered all of Husaquahr—and beyond. He knew that many of those far-off leaders, with their own evil forces and marching armies to face, understood that the Baron was merely an agent for the same dark powers that moved all of the others on this huge world of sorcery. Across the mighty oceans, on far-away continents and in countries unknown in

Husaquahr, other dark and powerful leaders were also pressing, as they always were; in many cases, the leaders of those forces were the only ones who fooled themselves that they were not tools of a greater master of evil, one forbidden for the past two thousand years to vie directly for control of the worlds, who instead had to use the egomania and greed and lust for power of more worldly agents to do his evil work.

And he and they did it very well indeed.

In the great tent city that was in the process of being struck, the generals plotted their strategies and awaited orders from their supreme commander, whose identity even they did not know, as to where to march next.

Yet already here in Zhimbombe, the legitimate authorities had been reduced to living in caves in the eastern mountains, those who had not broken and caved in to the dark power.

But even those still defiant were refugees. They had been beaten, and the enemy spent the flood season in and around the Zhafqua and in the ruins of the formerly beautiful capital of Morikay.

With the flood plain now drying, the enemy forces were preparing to march, certainly to the River of Sorrows and the border of Marquewood. Would they now flank to the east, or perhaps attempt a second line by crossing the River of Dancing Gods?

They had a hundred miles to the River of Sorrows, which would buy Ruddygore some time. Some, but not much. A bit more time to construct some sort of temporary bridge across the receding but still swollen Sorrows, or work out some way to cross the Dancing Gods in force. *That* would be some trick—between the Sorrows and the Dabasar, the Dancing Gods was already two miles or more wide and over forty feet deep in mid-channel.

East? West? North? East was slow, mountainous, and would leave their supply lines long and ugly, while they would be fighting in the best areas for Marquewood to defend. North lay the Valley of Decision, named for an earlier great war's climactic battle, when the invader of that time was forced to channel his forces through a narrow and uneven valley with gorges at two points. Sorcery or not, anybody at the bottom was going to have a pretty nasty time, and those hills and ledges were hollowed-out castles and fortifications, running for miles and built right into the hillsides. But west he had to cross the River of Dancing Gods. Easy going all the way to Stormhold that way, but—how to cross? And how to supply his armies if they crossed? The wealth and booty of Leander was far to the west, and High Pothique was poor and treacherous.

Still, the sorcerer who called himself Ruddygore reflected, the Baron would *have* to cross the Dancing Gods and count on supplies by river from the City-States.

The time to hit was during that crossing, when the Baron would be weakest and most vulnerable. Either that or abandon all until Stormhold and equal turf were reached. Valisandra and Marquewood, he decided, needed a navy and an air force.

He was about to withdraw from the scene when he felt a presence, a crimson force, in the headquarters tent. Drawn to this strong feeling of power, he peered down and saw the Dark Baron himself.

The crimson aura was incredibly strong and visible only to those well versed in the Arts, yet it was not a distinctive, personal aura as much as part of the mask; had it not blotted out the Baron's true aura, Ruddygore could have instantly identified the evil leader.

His temporal disguise was also impressive, cloaked as he was in shining black armor from head to foot, his head masked by a demon's-head helmet whose eyes burned with an inhuman yellow light.

The defenses, both magical and temporal, were perfect, as always. Although the figure towered at far greater than seven feet, it was impossible to guess the true height or build of the sorcerer inside, or even the gender. More than once, Ruddygore had suspected that the disguise hid far more than mere aura and features, but there was no way to know for sure.

Ruddygore stared down at the massive, giant figure and thought, angrily, *I know you. I have eaten and drunk with you, perhaps exchanged jokes and tricks of the craft. You have been my guest, my friend, my rival in the world we both pledged to serve, not destroy. Which one are you? Who are you, who has sold his body and soul to Hell? In whose name do you ratio- nalize the violation of your most sacred trusts? Damn you! I will know you one day! I will know you and be present to witness and participate in your total destruction—I swear it!*

The force of his hatred and his will seemed to penetrate to

the huge dark figure standing below. The demon's mask looked upward, as if searching him out. A right hand came up, and a gloved index finger traced a searing orange pattern in the air, a pattern which, when completed, suddenly sped up toward Ruddygore, growing and blazing intensely as it approached.

Unwilling to face the Baron with a strictly astral form, and not wanting to give that evil one the satisfaction of knowing that there was somebody really watching, Rudddygore rapidly withdrew, making sufficient countersigns to divert the blazing pattern. Nothing clear, nothing obvious. A quick retreat. Let the Baron wonder if it was real or only nerves, the sorcerer decided.

He was quickly back at Terindell. After a brief glance around to make certain he was not followed by anything, he floated over the castle walls. The center quad looked like a barnyard, he noted curiously. He would have to see what was going on. Still, one horse there—an aura of pale greenish blue in a pattern that was vaguely familiar to him. A horse with an aura?

He decided not to investigate until back in human form once more. Some animals could see astral bodies, and he didn't trust that horse with the aura at all.

His own body lay on his bed in his inner chamber, protected by the strongest of spells, apparently asleep. Quickly he approached and merged with it. The body yawned and stretched; the eyes opened. He was starving, he realized. Astral projections always did that to him. He looked around, found a couple of pounds of chocolate-topped butter cookies, and tore into them. They would be just about right as a snack while he undid enough of the door spell to get out.

It was a little more than half an hour before Ruddygore emerged from his building inside the compound and approached the animals there. The ever-attentive Poquah followed slightly behind, and had obviously briefed the sorcerer of Terindell. For his part, Ruddygore seemed somewhat amused.

He looked them over critically. "Hmm . . . Not a bad spell for the old bat. Still, she probably had to use some of that stinkwood. She's going to be very unhappy and vulnerable without it." He turned to Joe. "So—you claim you have won?"

Joe looked up at him and tried to see him clearly with his

poor vision. "Sure I did. Nothing about shape or form was in the rules one way or the other."

The sorcerer nodded. "That's true. But nothing said we had to change you back, either. Still, you're right. I didn't go through all this to have you go out making cows happy, and your very survival and return here show that you have the three qualities I counted on you to have. The first is luck—blind, dumb luck that gets you out of jams. Don't sneer at it. It's essential, to be anybody around here. The second is self-confidence, which you have aplenty, it seems, or you wouldn't have returned here no matter what. Finally, you use your head—when it would have been easy to accept your new lot in life meekly, you wasted no time in planning and organizing the opposition and carrying your escape off. I approve. I think, too, you've learned a valuable lesson here—that you can trust nothing and no one, and that almost everyone is out to get you in one way or another." He sighed and looked thoughtful. "I'm tempted to leave you a reminder of all that. The tail, perhaps, or the horns. But—no. This is too serious a business."

Ruddygore's hand came up, and he made a series of apparently random signs in the air. Joe suddenly felt himself restored. He was there in the pasture, on his hands and knees, a clump of grass still in his mouth. He spat it out, sputtered, and got to his feet, looking down at himself and feeling all over just to make sure. "Hey! I'm really back!" he couldn't help exclaiming.

Ruddygore nodded and smiled. "We'll get you some food and clothes and a good night's sleep. After that, we'll talk."

Joe made no move to go, but instead just stood there, looking at the sorcerer and the remaining animals. "Uh—what about them? They helped me. I couldn't have done it without 'em." He cleared his throat a little embarrassedly. "I, uh, kind of promised..."

The sorcerer nodded. "You promised what you couldn't deliver and suckered them into helping you, and now you want me to bail you out. That's about it, isn't it?"

"That's about it," Joe agreed a little sheepishly.

"I knew it," Houma sighed. "He's going to leave us stuck."

"Not necessarily, my horny friend. Who might you be?" Ruddygore asked.

"Houma. Formerly a farmer on the lands of Cohorn."

"Uh-huh. And how did a farmer from Cohorn happen to wander onto that farm and get turned into a goat? That's a hundred miles or more from Cohorn."

"Um. Well, sir, we broke a plow, and Cohorn village had no spares, since it was very old, and they sent me to get a new bracing custom-made for it."

"Hmmm... A good liar, too. Come, now—what was it, really? Women? Drink? Dishonesty? Or just plain oath-breaking?"

The goat sighed. "Not as bad as all that. We was out workin' in the fields, and a friend of mine, Druka, got caught up in a runaway plow team. Got pretty tore up. Well, this highborn son of a bitch rides over, jumps off his fancy horse, and starts screaming that we've screwed up the production schedule and loused up a good master plow. Loused up a good master plow! With Druka there all cut and bleeding to death! So I slugged the bastard. Felt good. He looked real surprised and went down like a sack of meal. Then I dragged Druka out. Finally I saw he was dead. Chain had broken and snapped back, probably broke his neck. Well, sir, I knew what would happen if that fellow came to, him more concerned about plows than men and all. I figured I either had to kill him or cut and run. He wasn't worth killin' like that, and I'd hardly get a fair fight, so I cut and ran. Bummed around for a while, took odd jobs, and finally applied for work at the old bat's place."

Ruddygore nodded. "I see. And now you want—what? To be restored and returned to Cohorn?"

"Oh, no, sir! There's no time limit on hittin' a highborn. Uh-uh. I'll be happy to join up, work for you or whatever, but if you're gonna send me back or turn me in, you might as well leave me a goat."

The sorcerer laughed. "Well said, sir!" He turned to Joe. "He meets with your approval?"

Joe nodded. "He has real guts, I'll say that. I don't know what you two have been saying, but this fellow sneaked in, got that wand, and didn't panic. I think I'd trust him at my back."

"Then that is where he should be," Ruddygore replied. Again he made a series of signs in the air; suddenly a spindly, knock-kneed fellow with a light beard appeared, on hands and knees. He looked uncertain, almost wondrous, as he made his way unaccustomedly to his two feet. *He looks like a young Uncle Sam*, Joe thought.

Next the sorcerer looked at Macore the rooster. "And you, sir?"

"A tradesman. I sharpened and serviced household gadgets door-to-door and farm-to-farm. I picked the wrong customer, that's all."

Ruddygore turned again to Joe questioningly.

"Macore was the first to agree to the plan and talked the others into it," Joe explained. "He also had almost all the information we needed."

"Hmmm . . . Macore, huh? Seems to me I heard of a Macore a few years back from someplace in Leander. Funny. He was in the same business you were. Only he had a reputation for leaving with more things from the various farms than he should have. You wouldn't be any relation to him, would you?"

"No comment until I've seen a lawyer," the rooster responded.

Ruddygore laughed and turned back to Joe. "What the fellow was, actually, was a common thief. Not even a fancy one. Pretty good, though. He would have valuable skills for us— but I wouldn't trust him too far. He is too clever to have to steal for a living—he did it because he liked the work."

"I'll take the chance," Joe answered. "Besides, I owe him that much."

Again the sign, and now Macore was revealed—a small, slightly built man with a large hawk nose and tiny, deep-set black eyes. For once Joe wondered about the choice of animal the Circean had made. Macore looked more like a weasel than a rooster.

Next was Grogha. That pig looked up expectantly at the sorcerer and eventually told his story about the shrewish wife and mean kids. Like Houma, he was willing to do anything in the service of Terindell, but, rather than go home, he'd remain a pig.

Ruddygore had no problem with him, and the Circean pattern was once again revealed to be fairly consistent. He was a middle-aged, fat man, short and stocky, with a round face and an enormous wide mouth.

Next came Posti. Joe told Ruddygore about the hesitant

horse, but emphasized that Posti, once committed, had acquitted himself well indeed.

"So you would like to be restored and join our Company?" the sorcerer asked. "I detect some hesitancy in you."

"I—I'm not really sure *what* I want," Posti admitted. "I know I was a pain back on the farm, and I know, too, that I came along mostly because I was damned bored. I wanted to see more of the world, get in a little more real living. But I ain't too keen on bein' *me* again, either. I wasn't no beauty. I had a club foot and a cleft chin and I mostly did the haulin' and dirty work, anyway. So y'see, sir, why I was torn. On the one hand I wanted to feel like I saw *something* of this life, more'n most folks, but, hell, sir, I mean, I'm a really *pretty* horse. Strong, too."

Ruddygore thought a moment. "Do you understand what we are doing here? We are fighting a war."

"Aye, sir. I'm willin' to do my duty."

"Suppose . . . Just suppose . . . Suppose we keep you a horse? A horse for one of these men? We'd have a horse with your courage and the intelligence of a man, and you would participate and do your part. You would also get the travel and adventure you seem to crave. How about that?"

"I was kind of thinkin' along them lines myself," Posti admitted. "But I sorta thought it would sound crazy."

The sorcerer grew thoughtful once again. "Still, we must have a way for you to speak, and you just don't have the equipment for it—nor can I really give it to you without changing your nature. However, I think perhaps I have a spell for it." Again the mystic patterns in the air. "There. Now you will be able to communicate with anyone who sits upon your back— and only that person under that circumstance. You will, of course, retain your present ability to talk to others similarly bewitched and to some of the fairies. What about it?"

"I think that will do fine, sir," Posti answered.

Ruddygore turned at last to Dacaro. The sleek black stallion with the odd aura had remained silent and apparently disinterested in the proceedings until now. The head came up, looked down at Ruddygore, and Dacaro said, "Hello again, Ruddygore."

Ruddygore frowned. "Well, I'll be damned! No *wonder* that aura was familiar. Dacaro, isn't it?"

"You know it is."

"I had clean forgotten that you were exiled to the Circean's care! But I have not forgotten why," Ruddygore added darkly.

"I did not think you had," the horse responded.

Ruddygore turned to the others, who, except for Posti, could follow only the sorcerer's part of the conversation. All knew, though, that something was wrong. "This man did me a great disservice once," the sorcerer told them. "He alone was there by force, not by accident."

"He was helpful to us, though," Joe said.

"Yeah, and he could read, too," Grogha added.

"Still, this presents a problem," Ruddygore told them. "Dacaro was an adept here at Terindell several years ago. I'm afraid he had the talent but not the self-discipline for the arts. On his own, he opened the gates of Hell and almost destroyed this place—and me. I was faced with a deep breach of trust and faith and also with the fact that he knew far too much of the darker side of necromancy to be allowed simply to go. He was too ambitious and too easily seduced. He would right now be with the Dark Baron, had I let him leave."

"That's not true!" Dacaro shot back. "In fact, that is the only reason I joined in on this breakout, and certainly the only reason I returned *here*, to you of all people. You forget I have looked into the face of the ultimate evil that sponsors the Dark Baron. Were you right about me, I could have easily cut and run to him after the escape."

Ruddygore thought about it. "What you say has merit, I admit. But I look inside you, Dacaro, and see your tragedy. It is a tragedy I do not think you yourself understand—or, at least, will admit to yourself. What you say is true—but there is inside you something that draws you wrong. You have the makings of a Dark Baron yourself, Dacaro. *He* really doesn't think he's evil, or controlled from Hell. He has fallen completely into self-delusion, which the seduction of ultimate power brings. It's inside you, too."

"I disagree."

"Obviously. And yet my original judgment stands. In your present condition, your powers are somewhat limited, although still there—as is your considerable knowledge. But I simply can't take the chance of restoring you. Not now, particularly. After this is over, perhaps. But not now."

"I thought as much."

"Still, I'm not about to throw you into the arms of the Dark Baron, either," the sorcerer continued. "What say you to the same deal I gave Posti there? Joe can use your magical knowledge and your language abilities. The whole Company can. Will you join the Company of your own free will?"

"As a horse?"

"As a horse. For now, anyway."

Dacaro thought it over for a moment. "All right. For now, anyway. But I do not wish to die a horse."

"You have my word. Prove yourself once more, and perhaps something can be worked out. Deal?"

The black stallion sighed. "Deal."

Ruddygore again made some signs, this time showing obvious concentration.

"What are you doing?" Dacaro asked nervously. "I need no spells from you to communicate!"

Ruddygore kept on, and Dacaro saw ribbons of gold and blue and yellow flow from the finger of the sorcerer and weave the signs in the air—the only one there, other than the sorcerer himself and Poquah, who could see such things.

"You are bound by a stronger spell than the old one, which was so easily broken," Ruddygore told him. "I wish you to face your choices squarely. None but one of the Council could undo my spell."

Dacaro thought about it. "I see. You expect me to run to the Baron in the end."

"Self-discipline is the key to your growth or corruption," Ruddygore said. "Let's see who is right." He sighed and turned to the others. "Now we are almost complete. Joe, Dacaro will be your mount, and you will be able to communicate with him. Listen to him. He has enough of the art to keep you out of some trouble or advise you on the rest."

"Glad to have him," Joe responded.

"Posti, I'm going to give you the last member of the Company as your rider."

"Last member?" both Joe and Posti said.

Ruddygore nodded. "Have you forgotten, Joe, that you didn't arrive here alone?"

The big man snapped his fingers. "Damn! I really *had* just about forgotten! How *is* she?"

"Changed. In some ways greatly changed. In others still the same. We will all dine together tomorrow evening. At that time we will do the last things that must be done, and then I have a job for you. All of you, in fact."

"So soon?"

"Time does not wait. Already the Dark Baron's forces strike camp. In ten days, perhaps a little more, they will be at the River of Sorrows to the south with nothing to stop them. In four weeks or so, we will know where he is going and, therefore, the best point to make our stand. There will be a great battle. I have no time to waste, nor do any of you."

"Four weeks..." Houma repeated. "You mean we're that close to a fight?"

"Closer. You see, I have a far different but no less vital task for you. There is a possibility, at least, that the outcome of that battle and perhaps the war turns on your mission. Now go with Poquah. Relax. Those of you who are again humans, enjoy it. Tomorrow those of you who need it will be outfitted and equipped, select horses, and the like. At dinner tomorrow you will know your task. The morning after that, you will be riding far from here. Some of you may not return again."

CHAPTER 9

ALL THE INGREDIENTS FOR A QUEST

Magic swords for quests must be named.
—XVII, 167, 2(c)

RUDDYGORE LOOKED MARGE OVER KEENLY AS SHE ENTERED the room and he liked what he saw. "You have progressed beyond my wildest hopes," he told her.

"I had a good teacher," Marge replied. "No fan of yours, though."

The sorcerer chuckled. "I daresay not. Think of us as members of the same family who went in different directions. Both were of equal potential and inclined, say, to, painting pictures—but one saw the old school as outdated and uninteresting and became an abstractionist and cubist; the other painter saw all that newfangled abstract stuff as nonsense and painted realistic portraits. Neither of them could discuss the other without each one's philosophies of art getting in the way. But even though they disagreed on the nature of art, they saw in each other a sincere belief in art itself. That's roughly the analogy between Huspeth and me."

"But she said she would be with you if the Baron reached Terindell, I remember."

He gave a soft smile and nodded. "Indeed. We disagree on just about everything concerning our own, ah, art, and we can't say three civil words to each other without getting into a fighting and clawing match. Just like our realist and our cubist. But both of those painters would be on the same barricade fighting together the forces of those who would wish to burn all pretty pictures. You see?"

She smiled and relaxed. "Now that you put it that way . . ."

"I had hoped she would see you as I did—the potential there. Tell me—can you perceive and read auras?"

"I can *see* them—sort of. You're a fuzzy purple and yellow pattern. But I can't really tell much from them."

"That comes with experience. You're already much further along than I would have expected. Enough to be considered an adept, at least, at the lower levels. If you wish, as time goes on, I can add to your knowledge and instruction."

"I'd like that," she told him. "I find the whole thing fascinating. But sooner or later I'm going to have to learn to read to go anywhere."

"There are ways around just about everything here," he assured her. "If you have the will, the way will open. But nothing's for free. Not even the training you've had so far. And Huspeth's developmental pattern for you contains a number of potential future problems, too."

Her eyebrows rose, and she waited for him to continue.

"First of all, have you looked at yourself—really looked at yourself—in the past few days?"

"In the pond. Why?"

He pulled himself out of his chair and beckoned her to follow him back into the lab. Again he pulled out the full-length mirror. "Look there and tell me what you see," he said softly.

"A well-stacked Peter Pan," she responded dryly; except

for her obviously feminine, well-proportioned figure, she *did* have very much the Peter Pan look, even to the hair, particularly in the clothing Huspeth had given her.

"Nothing else?"

She looked hard. "The ears look a little funny," she decided.

He nodded. "Slightly pointed and angled back against the head. That and the streak in your hair. They are marks of the fairy folk. In order to get as much into you as the time allowed, Huspeth took some shortcuts, I'm afraid. To sensitize you to magic, she infused into you a measure of fairy blood, and it tells. The more you use this new magic art, the more dominant that fairy strain, that changeling strain, will become—and it will show."

"You're telling me, then, that the more magic I use, the less human I'll become. Is that it?"

He nodded.

"But she never told—"

"I know. You think of Huspeth as a kind and powerful teacher. But the philosophical differences with her run a lot deeper than you suspect. She idolizes the fairy folk. Always has. With that bent, she has come, wrongly, to believe that humans are the source of the world's corruption—the gate through which Hell must work. In a sense, she thought she was giving you a gift that would guard you from corruption later. There's no undoing it, either. There isn't time, for one thing, and also, those qualities will be more than useful. But the more of fairy you become, the more those restrictions applying to fairies will also apply, and things you wouldn't think twice about could be dangerous."

Marge looked worried. "Like what?"

"Well, for one thing, even now I would stay away from iron of any kind. There's no natural iron in Husaquahr, by the way, but some of the mercenaries from other lands have iron weapons. The dwarves, whose power derives from their ability alone in faërie to handle iron, always have access to it. Magic swords, too, often have an iron alloy in them. Right now iron will burn and make you a little sick. If you progress, it could kill you with a touch."

She whistled low. "Any other nasty little things like that?"

"The nineteen volumes of Rules covering basic faërie powers and limitations are a bit much to go into now. Let's say that the general restrictions will be self-evident; the specifics can be boiled down to an old Rule that applies to folks like Huspeth and me, too—the more on the magic side you are, the more vulnerable you are to magic as well. Just keep it in mind—if you're tempted, or need to use any powers you might have."

"Not much chance of that," she assured him. "Most of my powers are chemical, not signs and spells. We didn't have much time to get into that."

"More will come to you, with the temptation to use it, as time goes on," he cautioned. "Just remember what I say."

They walked back out into his library. "Say—what would happen if I *did* change all the way over to fairy?" she asked. "Would I wind up looking like Poquah or something?"

He chuckled. "Oh, no. Actually, it's pretty hard to say. But the nonhuman blood would force out the human all the way, eventually. No matter what you became, you'd lose your mortality to age and time."

"That sounds like a good deal."

"Perhaps. Perhaps not. The difference between the fairies and us is that our mystical part, our souls, is hidden from each other—and often from ourselves. With the fairies, what you appear is what you are. Thus, humans may die—and yet not die. There are other planes and other paths. If a fairy dies, though, it is gone."

She considered that, but decided that the concept was too abstract for her right now. This was a new world and a new life—and she wanted to get started in it.

"Let us go to the banquet hall," Ruddygore said. "It's time you met the rest of the Company—at least that part of it that is human. Afterward, I'll tell you what this was all about."

Joe was stunned at the change in Marge's appearance, and she at his, but both still felt inside themselves a certain comfort and kinship with each other that they did not share with the people of Husaquahr. They hardly knew each other, it was true, but both knew where New York and Paris were, and the best Polish jokes—and why one shouldn't tell them. They were from the same world; the others knew it not.

They had a fine meal with the convivial Ruddygore as host. He talked between mouthfuls of this and that and practically everything—except what he had in mind for them. Joe, at least, couldn't shake the uneasy feeling that the condemned were eating a last hearty meal.

Finally all was cleared away, and only Ruddygore appeared to be still capable of eating anything. He passed around cigars, which were mostly declined, then settled back in his big chair and looked them over.

"Well, we've all had a nice evening," he began, "and now it's time for business. I trust that there was something here for everyone. I made it heavily vegetarian, I'm afraid, to accommodate the lady here."

"No problem," Macore responded. "I'm gonna have trouble eating chicken ever again, and I'd guess the rest of 'em have the same kind of problems."

The sorcerer nodded. "That's what I figured. You'll work into it, though. Ah, as you know, the two animal members of our company did not join us, but Poquah is briefing them as we sit—and they have been well tended." He looked at each face in turn. "Are you ready to go to work now?"

"Not particularly," the portly Grogha replied honestly. "But that don't mean we won't."

"Fair enough. First, let me tell you what is going on. The Dark Baron has raised an army of at least ten thousand from a dozen or more races and, now that the floods have subsided, they are preparing to move northward."

Macore whistled. "Ten thousand!"

"And growing more by the day. Valisandra, Marquewood, and Leander are preparing a master conference to decide strategy. We still don't know which way they are going to move, or how, but there's a battle, possibly decisive, in the works about a month or two from now."

"You mean we're enlisted?" Houma said.

"Drafted, you mean," Grogha put in grumpily.

"Well, we can certainly use all hands at the right time," Ruddygore admitted. "If we fail to hold them this time, the next battle will be right outside those walls there. But I don't propose that you all trot off and join the army. Not right now, anyway. There is a side errand that must be run, and it is of vital importance. If anything, it must be completed *before* the decisive battle, so time is also of the essence." He looked at them, "Anybody ever been to High Pothique?"

"I have," Macore told him. "Cruddy place. Not a real country at all. Just a lot of small holdings. Why?"

"In Starmount, just beyond the Vale of Kashogi, a thing of great value has just been discovered, something believed lost to Husaquahr for all time—and better left lost. But now that it's been found, it must be returned to its rightful owner. If the Baron gets his slimy hands on it, he may win a major objective of his war without firing an arrow or raising a sword. It is nothing less than the Lakash Lamp."

"Long ago, in the ancient fires that birthed the world, a greater demon cheated on the laws agreed upon to govern the world," Ruddygore told them. "It was not so much a cheat, really, as a shortcut, a solution to a problem that the demon found no other way to solve. In order to establish certain of the laws of magic, it was necessary to have a safety valve, a wild card, an exception to those very laws. And so, out of those early fires was fashioned the Lamp of Lakash, named for its demon creator.

"To make certain that such a dangerous thing as the Lamp would never fall into the hands of one fully prepared to use it, the Lamp was not left in the world but transferred, taken to the other Earth whence Joe and Marge have come. There, up until roughly two thousand years ago, it remained—occasionally falling into the hands of a person who used it and causing a great many stories and legends about evil genies and magic lamps. But then new rules were placed upon both Heaven and Hell, and all matter which had been displaced from one world to the other was instantly returned to its world of origin, the Lamp included. Thus, the Lamp came to Husaquahr.

"It went through many owners here, but all were eventually trapped and defeated by its curses and limitations. Still, attention was drawn to it, and it came into the hands of my predecessor, Jorgasnovara of Astaroth. When it came time for him to pass on to the next level, he left the Lamp in my care, here in Terindell, where I'd already set up shop. And here it remained for a very long time—until, eventually, an error was made. An inevitable error, considering the time involved, I suppose, but an error all the same.

"There was an adept at that time named Sugasto—a very talented adept, who was on his way to becoming a great sorcerer someday. Sugasto was so good that I was blinded somewhat to his great character faults and, as a result, I stupidly told him one day of the Lamp's existence. He was seduced by its potential, particularly since it could be wielded only by mortals using magical arts—and were he to attain full wizard status, he could not directly use it. He begged me to show it to him, but I refused again and again, regretting I'd ever brought it up. Jorgasnovara, after all, only told *me* about it some weeks after he died. But somehow, Sugasto found out where the Lamp was. It took him several months, but it had become an obsession with him.

"I said he was good at the Art—and he was. *Very* good. To get at it, he undid spells that would have defeated some very good sorcerers and he stole the Lamp while I was away on the other Earth plane. Knowing that I would sense the undoing of those spells and hurry back, he ran from here, ran south and west. We pursued, of course, and nearly caught him near Stormhold—but he fooled us by going up into High Pothique, and there vanished forever from our knowledge. All we knew was that the Lamp was no longer in mortal hands and we could not sense or trace where it was. That was more than two centuries ago.

"But now, just recently, we have found the ending of that story. Piecing together legends and old documents and working with the Xota People, who've consented to talk to anybody human only in the last few years and then just slightly, an explorer and trader named Vaghast discovered that my wayward apprentice had fallen straight into the hands of the Xota, who were upon him before he could use the Lamp. I suspect that he was so reluctant to *use* the thing—waste it, to his mind—that he died of his own greed and lust for power. At any rate, the Xota sensed the tremendous power of the thing, even if they didn't know what it was, and they put it in their god-cave, a sacrificial place, and their own shamans placed protections upon it. Supposedly the cave is guarded by a horrible monster of unknown shape, size, and nature, held there by spells and bound to destroy all who would enter the cave.

"We know the general location of the cave and we know now for certain that the Lamp is still there. Unfortunately, the Dark Baron knows this as well. I am quite certain that the Baron is one of the Council, and it was to the Council that all this was reported not two days ago. It's a sure thing that even now some of his forces ride to the cave. We must beat them to it."

Macore whistled again. "That's pretty wild—and pretty hairy. First of all, last I heard, the Xota were still as nasty as ever, even if they did talk to this guy, and that high mountain country is theirs for sure. Even if they were friendly as pet dogs now, they'd still be savages when it comes to anybody disturbing their god-cave."

Ruddygore nodded. "That's true. They'll be fairly noncommittal now, but once the *first* group to get there betrays its goal, they'll be ferocious."

"I'm more concerned with that horrible monster part," Houma put in. "So we fight or sneak our way through this horde—and once we go in, this thing just gobbles us up."

"That's a possibility," Ruddygore agreed. "But I didn't form this Company for an easy job."

"All the while the Baron sends a small army," Macore added. "Less and less do I like this."

"*That* is not a concern—at least the army part," the sorcerer assured him. "First of all, it's no mean trick to cross the Dancing Gods below the River Tasqom, particularly with a large force. Second, such a force would be set upon by Marquewood and would have a hard fight through Stormhold, only to have to climb and pass through the Vale. Not likely. No. He will send a small company, somewhat under cover. They won't be pleasant folk, but they, too, will know they have to get there by stealth, not a fight."

"Okay, so that puts 'em in the same shape as us," Joe said. "It still don't sound like a picnic."

"Neither was the Circean, and you managed," Ruddygore noted. "You, Joe, and you, Marge, are particularly well prepared. Dacaro has a great deal of knowledge to aid you, should it be necessary, and Marge has the means to use that knowledge."

"Okay, so we won't be completely disarmed," Joe responded. "Still, the odds look pretty bleak."

"As bleak as escaping from Circe's grasp and regaining humanity?" the wizard teased. "Joe—all of you—trust me a bit. We are not alone in this fight, you know. The Baron has the forces of Hell, but the other side is pretty effective, too. They told me that you were the one, Joe. They sent me over to get you. I did—and at the time, I didn't even know why. Frankly, I *still* don't—but I know you're their choice. Your very survival the past few days proves it. You know you were very, very lucky, Joe. Lucky the Circean came along just when she did to save you from the water sprite. Lucky to have succeeded in your crazy scheme to steal the rod and escape. Well, Joe, there's no such thing as luck. Not really. Good luck and bad luck are the terms we lesser ones give to angelic and demonic forces. For some reason, Joe, you have friends in high places. They'll help you out."

Joe chuckled dryly. "Friends in high places. Guardian angels. Man! I sure ain't no saint!"

"There's no way to understand them—they are beyond us and very alien from anything we know or understand. But they're real. It's how they've operated the past two millennia. Why they choose one over the other, why they let good men be tortured and killed and evil ones march, I can't begin to understand. But I go with the flow, Joe, because it's also in *my* best interest. And you're it."

Joe sat back, trying to accept what he'd been told and having trouble with it. "Well, I'll be damned—uh, I guess if you're right, maybe I won't be, huh?"

Ruddygore laughed. "Maybe you will, maybe you won't. Dante put most of the popes in Hell, remember. So don't let it go to your head. And don't count on it. They can drop you, or make you a sacrifice, as easily as they can take you all the way. But they have forearmed you a bit."

"Huh?"

"You have a Company of brave men. You picked up this young woman on the road, and she has proved a talented adept. You have—by chance?—Dacaro's knowledge and understanding of the magical arts. And these three men know the territory, more or less. One has been near there; the other two still are more accustomed to *this* world and are valuable as, say, native guides. And I'll add one additional factor before we leave here tonight. For now—any more questions?"

"I think I have a bundle," Marge said. "For one thing, why is this Lamp so vital?"

"Surely you recall the legends of magic lamps," the sorcerer replied. "What were those magic lamps like in the old stories?"

"Grant wishes," Grogha said brightly.

Ruddygore nodded. "Yes. Grant wishes. With this Lamp you can more or less suspend both Laws and Rules, magical or physical. Within limits, of course, or the Lamp could destroy the structure of the universe. Still, whatever mortal holds the Lamp of Lakash has the wishing power. And contrary to all those stories you may have heard, one wish and one wish only is what you get."

Marge frowned. "Only one? Isn't it always three?"

The sorcerer smiled. "*That* is the curse of the Lamp. Almost everyone believes it that way, and there are few to tell you different. And so, consumed by power, you make a second wish, secure in the old tales that you will get it."

"And what happens?" Houma asked, breathless and fascinated.

"Interestingly, you get it. But you get something else as well. Come! Come! What is the other thing that comes with the Lamp?"

Marge thought a moment. "A genie?"

"Exactly!" Ruddygore cried. "A genie! But what is the nature of this genie? What sort of being is he, and whence does he come? The answer is rather simple—*the genie is the last person to use the Lamp more than once!*"

"But they always called the genie the slave of the lamp in my old stories," Grogha noted. "What does he do, anyway?"

"He is, in every respect, the slave of the Lamp, bound to serve whatever mortal next possesses it. And I *do* mean slave. You must do *whatever* the possessor commands. And you're stuck that way until somebody else makes the same stupid mistake you did and replaces you. Now you see the greatest curse of the Lamp. If you don't get rid of it—literally give it to somebody else—you'll eventually be trapped. And if you do, then *they* will have a wish—so you had better trust them absolutely, since you no longer may use the Lamp. Of course, no matter what, the Lamp's possessors eventually run out of a chain of people they can trust. And that's why it's best in the hands of somebody like me. I can not use it and, therefore, can not be cursed by it. And I will seal it away so that no one will get to it unless there is dire need—and under my control."

"Hey, now! Wait a minute!" Joe jumped in. "If *you* can't use it, then neither can this Baron, right?"

Ruddygore nodded. "That's correct."

"So what harm is it just to let him have it?"

The sorcerer sighed. "Joe, surely your own experiences show that mortals can be placed under a *ton* of spells and told to do just about anything at all. Remember your cherubs? The Baron wouldn't need to use it himself—but he has an endless supply of people he owns and controls body and soul to make wish after wish *for* him."

"Yeah, I guess he could just wish he'd win the war and that'd be that," Houma speculated.

"No," the wizard assured him. "I said the Lamp was quite limited—and it is. First, the wish must be personalized, and confined to a specific localized magical event. So all right, he could wish for a fog before the battle, or that our horses take sick. Even for an earthquake, if he were losing. But a battle has too many people, human and nonhuman, with too many variables for the Lamp to handle it properly. He couldn't even wish for the enemy army to turn to stone, since that wish would affect only the mortals in the army and would be limited to his specific area of battle. It would allow him to escape a desperate situation, but not to win or lose. It could, however, tip the balance in his favor."

"If it works only on mortals, does that mean we can't wish this monster somewhere else?"

The sorcerer shrugged. "Probably you could. I doubt if you could wish it dead, though. And you can never be sure if you've properly phrased your wish. That's another little curse. For example, saying 'I wish we didn't have that monster to worry about any more' gives the Lamp a lot of leeway. It could allow you to die—and then you wouldn't worry. If *I* wanted a sure thing, I would wish that the monster was friendly toward me and my companions and would not bother us in any way. *That* would be pretty sure."

"*I* see," Marge nodded. "Make the wish about *us* and our relationship to the threat."

"Man! You could still wish yourself filthy rich! Or maybe immortal!"

"'Filthy rich' is an interesting term," Ruddygore noted. "Knowing the Lamp, I imagine it would probably put your gold at the bottom of a great cesspool. Yes, you could wish for wealth—but even there you must be careful. Being rich or noble does you no good if your riches and title are in some far-off land. As for immortality—I suspect that that wish would be a real curse, particularly if you could never remove it. And once you make that wish, beware of any loopholes you leave, such as about whether or not you'd age. The rules are basic. Keep it simple, very specific, and very personal. And be careful about random wishes. The possessor of the Lamp has only to preface a statement with 'I wish' and it is one. So, saying 'I wish I had a drink' or something like 'I wish I were dead' can at best be wasteful and surprising—at worst, fatal. Even something as simple as 'I wish I knew' would do it."

"You seem pretty confident of us," Macore noted. "What makes you think *we* won't be corrupted by that power?"

"Oh, some of you probably will," he responded cheerfully. "However, I have laid a *geas* on you that will require you to get the Lamp back to me."

Marge thought a moment. "Can't we just wish us all back here as soon as we have the Lamp?"

Ruddygore sighed. "I wish it were that simple. Unfortunately, the Lamp's transportability is somewhat limited. A rule of thumb would be that, if you can't see it, you probably can't reach it. Actually, the possessor alone could wish himself anywhere at all and probably get there—but only the possessor. For a group, its power is limited—more or less to line of sight. Say, fifty miles."

Joe sighed. "Oh, great. One of us can escape, but we'd leave the others stuck. So we have to make a run for it, anyway."

"That's about it," the sorcerer agreed. "In and out. Unless, of course, there is only one of you left."

That thought sobered them. "I wish you were coming with us," Grogha said. "Then it would be easy."

"Not so easy, with me or not, for there are some things beyond my powers," he replied. "In any event, I am needed to aid and coordinate the battle that must come, no matter who wins the Lamp—if anyone does. But regardless of what else may happen, I must be assured that the Lamp either is in friendly hands or is impossible to get by either side. If the Baron gets it, we may fail. I think we have forces that are a match for him. It is much better to defend than attack. But if I must spend all my time negating the Lamp, the Baron will be free to aid the battle. The Lamp's power is considerable, no matter what I've said. I *think* I can cancel or negate anything it does, if I work fast and furiously—but I can not handle the Baron *and* the Lamp. Better *we* have the Lamp and the Baron have the problem. See?"

"Negate . . ." Marge repeated, thinking. "You mean we might get the Lamp and then find the Baron lousing us up?"

"You could. And a negated wish still counts. Remember that." He sighed and got up. "Well, I have done what I could. Dacaro can help with advice, although he can't use the Lamp himself." Again he paused. "You understand now why I had to be so harsh with Dacaro? He was—is—very, very much like Sugasto. I simply could not take the chance with him after he, too, violated a sacred trust. Come."

They walked out into the darkness and to Ruddygore's library. He went over to a wall, pressed a hidden stud, and the bookcase moved back and then to one side, revealing a small chamber. He entered, then returned with a long, heavy object wrapped in silk cloth. He went to the table as they all watched and carefully unwrapped it.

They crowded around and gasped when they saw what the silk masked. It was a sword—a great, magnificent sword. Its fancy hilt looked like polished gold, and its blade was sharp and shone with an unbelievable brightness. The blade, however, was totally encased in a solid block of what looked like transparent amber.

"Long ago I did a service for one incredibly high," Ruddygore told them. "This was a reward, of sorts. A true magic sword, forged by the ancient dwarf kings thousands of years ago. It's one of a number of such swords, all made during that time and all given only through supernatural will. It's rare, though, in that it remains as it was when forged. It has never been used. I had no need of it, and nobody before was worthy enough of it. Now, I think, Joe, it is time to put it to use."

Joe looked down at the sword. "It's beautiful," he breathed. "But why is it magic?"

"First, the blade is an alloy of steel better than any ever seen. Most blades here are bronze, as you know. Steel contains iron, which means the blade is fatal to most fairy folk except dwarves. Just a wound, the merest prick, would do it." He turned to Marge. "Don't *you* touch it, either! Even if it's necessary!"

"I'll remember," she assured him, looking at the beautiful sword nervously.

"Additionally, such swords as these are harder than diamonds. They will cut through rock, metal—you name it— amazingly easily. And they have something of a life of their own. No one, save the owner, so long as he lives, will be able to wield the blade—and the sword itself will pick its next owner, so it can not be stolen. It may have other powers that will manifest themselves—it's hard to say."

Joe looked at it hungrily. "It's great. Just what I needed. I didn't have enough to buy a sword at the market." He frowned. "But it's stuck in this plastic or whatever."

"The amber prevents anyone from using it but the right one," the sorcerer told him. "There! Take the hilt. Raise it high. Let's see if it will accept you."

Joe reached out and took the sword in his hand. It felt extremely heavy, but he managed to lift it, even raise it over his head.

There was a strange humming sound, and a moment passed before they all realized it was coming from the sword itself. The humming grew louder and louder as he held it—and finally the vibration from the sword cracked, then shattered the amber casing, which fell to the floor as so much dust.

"Hey! It's suddenly real light! Almost like a fencing foil!" Joe exclaimed.

"To you," Ruddygore told him. "Only to you, Joe. Nobody else will even be able to pick it up. It accepts you. It is yours— one with you. Use it well. Its relative strength is unknown— but it is very possible that it could even kill the Dark Baron himself if you gave it a chance."

That thought pleased Joe. "Wouldn't that be somethin'!" He lowered the sword, which seemed to have taken on a glow, and placed it in the scabbard on his newly purchased sword belt. The glow subsided and was gone when he let go of the hilt.

"You must name it, Joe," the sorcerer told him. "It is a virgin sword. You will name it for all times."

"Uh—name it?"

The sorcerer nodded. "Just take it out once again, hold it in front of you, and give it a name with real meaning. You should be honored—few have the opportunity, and this may be the last unnamed magic sword anywhere."

Joe did as instructed. The sword glowed and hummed softly in front of him. He thought for a moment, then seemed to brighten. "Okay. Uh, let me know if I'm doing this wrong. I name this sword, my sword—Irving."

"WHAT!" It was Marge who screamed. "Irving? That's ridiculous! Joe—haven't you ever read *anything?* Magic swords are named things like Stormbringer or Excalibur. Fancy, exotic names."

Joe looked puzzled. "But I *like* the name Irving. That's the name I gave my son. I never could have him, but at least I got somethin' here named in his honor so I don't forget him."

Marge looked frantically at Ruddygore, who shrugged. "The sword has accepted the name," the wizard noted. "Irving it is. Somehow it is fitting that a barbarian named Joe has a sword named Irving. I don't know *why*, but it is."

Marge shook her head, started mumbling to herself, and went over and sat down in a chair, still shaking her head and saying all sorts of unintelligible things.

"I kinda like the name," Grogha said, trying to be cheerful. "I mean, it's *different*."

"It sure is," Ruddygore muttered, but Joe beamed at the comment and sheathed the sword once more.

"Now, then," the sorcerer continued, "let me show you a couple of tricks. Joe, remove the sword again and place it back on the table there. Go ahead—do it."

Joe looked uncertain, but did as instructed.

"Now move back—over by that chair. Ten feet or so, I'd say."

Again the trucker turned barbarian complied.

"Grogha, pick up the sword and bring it to Joe."

The portly man went over, took hold, and tried. He tried very hard, until sweat rolled off his brow. Finally he gave up and turned to Ruddygore. "Man! That *is* a heavy blade!"

"Anybody else?" the sorcerer invited.

Each in turn, except for the unconsolable Marge, also gave it a try—and failed. "That thing's nailed there," Macore grumbled.

"All right—now, everybody over by Marge, out of the way of Joe," the sorcerer instructed. "Ah. That's fine. Remember, Joe, try this only when nobody you like is in the way. Call the sword. Put out your hand."

Joe put his hand forward.

"No. Not like that. As if you were going to catch the hilt."

Joe looked puzzled, but did as instructed.

"All right. Now call it. By name."

"Uh—heeere, Irving!"

"It's a sword, Joe! Not a dog!"

Joe cleared his throat. "Irving! To me!" he shouted. In an instant the sword flew threw the air and right into his raised hand. The movement was so sudden and startling that he almost fell over from the shock and surprise—but he didn't drop the sword. Recovering, he looked down at it. "I'll be damned!" He turned to Ruddygore. "How far is that effective?"

"If it can hear you, it will come—no matter what's in the way. Farther than that, if you have a clear line of sight from it to you."

"Wow! That's really neat!"

Marge looked up at him sourly. "Really neat. I don't *believe* you."

He looked back at her, frowning again. "But it is."

She sighed. "If you say so. Jesus! Irving!"

"And now, my friends, you should all get some sleep," Ruddygore told them. "Tomorrow you begin—and very early. Macore, you remain. Since you've been in Pothique, I'll give you the terrain and trail maps. Before you leave tomorrow, Poquah will brief you on the basic route, although he's already briefed Dacaro and Posti. The rest of you will have more conventional horses, but Dacaro will have power over them. Oh, by the way. Rather than my original idea, I think I'll let Marge have Dacaro, and you, Joe, will ride Posti. It makes more sense to have the magic application and the magic knowledge together."

"Whatever you say," Joe told him. "Hell, I'm ready to go now. If I'm stuck here with all this, I guess I'd better get into the spirit."

Marge sighed. "Think of it, Joe," she prompted. "Don't you remember Ruddygore once saying that the fantasies of our world are the truths of this one? This could be the start of an epic! *The Chronicles of Marge and Joe!* Think about *that*!"

He thought about it. "Not bad. *The Chronicles of Joe and Marge.* It has a ring to it, I guess. I doubt if I'd ever read it, though."

"You make light of that possibility, yet you may regret labeling your adventures an epic in times to come," Ruddygore warned them.

"Huh? Why?"

"Oh, we'll cross that bridge when we come to it. For now, don't dream too much of immortality in legend. First you have to earn it. And I might as well tell you, the odds of any of you surviving this mission are beyond those any bookmaker would give or take."

CHAPTER 10

OF TROLLBRIDGES AND FAIRYBOATS

Unlike all other forms of energy, magical energy may be created and destroyed by applications of positive and/or negative spells.
    —II, 139, 68.2(a)

JOE, MOUNTED ON POSTI, LOOKED AROUND AT THE REST OF the Company and found the group somewhat imposing. Marge seemed almost dwarfed on the sleek black Dacaro, but the other three looked well matched to their more normal steeds. Ruddygore had said that seven was the proper number for a Company, according to the Rules, but this Company included five humans and two transformed ones upon whom he and Marge rode. He had to trust it to Ruddygore that the number worked out.

Macore rode up beside him and pulled out the map of the region. "We'll have to cross the Rossignol east of Terdiera," he pointed out. "That's the only bridge for a hundred miles, and it wouldn't do to backtrack any more than we have to."

Joe shrugged. "So? What's the problem?"

"Trolls," the little thief replied, a sense of distaste in his tone. "Damn them. Only really decent bridge builders in Husaquahr."

Joe gave another shrug, and they started off, enjoying the early morning air. As they rode through a not-yet-open Terdiera, Joe looked around for familiar places and faces and saw more of the former than the latter. Early risers stopped to gape at the five riding through the town center, and particularly at their leader, who thought he looked pretty good in his loincloth and trucker's hat.

On the other side of town they departed from the main road, down a narrow side street that quickly became a dirt track when it left the town behind, going down to the river. It was a fairly well traveled path, to judge from the deep ruts and gouges in the road, but there was nobody on it this early in the day.

The bridge was nothing fancy, but still was impressive engineering for the technology of Husaquahr. A wooden structure supported by thick pylons made from the trunks of hardwood trees, it stretched the thousand yards or more from shore to shore and even curved up in the center to allow barges to pass under. The channel was not wide but was fairly deep. The bridge, also, wasn't very wide—they would have to pass single file to feel safe, since there were no guardrails or other safety devices or guides.

"Whew! I'd hate to have to drive a wagon and team across that thing," Grogha noted. "I'm not too sure I feel thrilled riding it now."

"The bridge is perfectly safe if you don't panic but just go straight," Macore assured them. "However, this is no free ride. See!" He pointed and they all looked.

The sign contained a series of pictographs and accompanying very formal-looking text, the former for the mostly illiterate locals, the latter for the unwary traveler who, being most likely a trade or political figure, would be able to read and needed a more detailed explanation. The sign's pictures fascinated them:

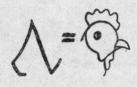

Joe frowned. "Now what the *hell* does *that* mean?"

"Dacaro is reading the sign to me now," Marge told him, but it was Macore who spoke up first.

"That's standard picture writing," he explained. "It says, 'STOP! PAY TROLL! Pedestrians one chicken each, horse and rider one pig, wagons and drivers one pig per axle or one cow for the whole load.' What did you expect? It *is* a trollbridge, after all."

Joe looked quizzically at Marge, who nodded. "That's what the writing says, according to Dacaro, except that the text adds, 'Or equivalent.'"

"Pretty steep," Grogha noted.

Joe looked at Macore. "So what do we do? We don't exactly have a barnyard handy."

"I'm not sure I like that live pig business," Grogha added nervously.

"Oh, you're not a pig any more," Houma scolded. "You'd probably be worth a whole wagon as you are."

Macore looked back at Marge. "You're the keeper of the treasury. You have those silver coins Ruddygore gave us?"

She nodded, reached down on her saddle pack, and removed a heavy sack. "How much will we need?"

"Well, if a pig's the fare, we need five pigs. That'd be about eleven of those coins at today's prices, I think—but I'm a little out of touch. May as well go down and find out." He turned to Joe. "Now don't panic or start swingin' that sword when the troll comes up," he warned. "They're liars and crooks and really nasty, but even if we took the one or two on this side, they'd have us on the bridge. Better to pay."

Joe just shook his head sadly. "Yeah, I know. I'm used to these things."

They went down to the bridge itself. There was no structure or sign of life or authority anywhere around, which puzzled Joe. "What's the matter? They not up yet?"

At that moment there was a great roaring sound from beneath the bridge, and the water erupted. A gigantic blue creature climbed out, covered in woolly hair, with two enormous eyes and a teeth-filled mouth that went the two-foot width of the eerie, vicious face.

The creature looked at the Company hungrily for a moment,

then said, in a voice much like an angry bear's, "You wanna cross?"

"Why else would we be here at this ungodly hour?" Macore shot back, sounding totally unintimidated. "Five horses and riders. How much in coin?"

The creature looked over the people waiting and licked its lips with a huge purple tongue. "I'll take two of the horses and you can all go," it suggested.

"Uh-uh. No horses. We have a long way to go. Coin. How much?"

"Twenty-five for the lot."

Macore sounded shocked and hurt. "Twenty-five! That's robbery! We'll go back up to the village and buy five pigs when the markets open and save a bundle."

"Yeah, but that's three hours from now." The creature smirked. "You want special service, you pay the extra freight."

Macore sighed. "C'mon. We can kill three hours." He made as if to turn.

"Wait!" the creature called to him. "All right. Special. Twenty."

"Ten."

"You rob me! I tell you, little one—how about I just eat *you* and the others go free? What about it, the rest of you? You should be happy to be rid of such a robber and thief as this."

"Sorry," Joe told the troll. "But I think ten *is* too low for such a fine bridge. How about twelve?"

The troll roared and splashed the water in very real-looking mock anger. Finally he said, "Eighteen! Low as I go!"

"Split the difference," Macore suggested. "Fifteen. It's a good profit. Either that or we wait for the markets to open—which won't be very much longer if we keep this up, anyway."

The troll growled and gnashed his teeth and somehow managed to foam at the mouth. They all thought he was going to attack them in rage, and Joe's hand went to his sword hilt, but finally the great troll calmed down. "Pay me!" he snarled.

Macore reached back, got the fifteen coins from Marge, and flung them at the troll, who frantically grabbed for them with massive clawed hands. He missed a bunch, and they went into the water.

"All right, gang," Macore said. "Now—listen closely and I'll tell you the rules. We go single file and keep a fair distance apart. Take it *real* show. We've met his price, so he and his kin can't molest us in any way—that's the Rule—but they may try some funny stuff to panic us or our horses. If any of us fall in, we're fair game and they can eat us. Understand? So keep real control of your horses, and ignore *anything* that happens on either side of the bridge. You all understand?"

They nodded but looked slightly uneasy. "I'll lead," the little thief told them and guided his mount onto the bridge past the fuming troll.

Joe went next, then Marge, then Houma, with Grogha nervously bringing up the rear.

All went well until Macore reached the point at which the bridge arched sharply upward over the main channel. At just that point the water erupted on both sides of them, with giant trolls growling and screaming menacingly. There seemed to be a dozen or more, all as repulsively ugly and nasty-looking as the gate troll.

Posti gave a start but held, and Macore had firm control of his mount, while Dacaro ignored the commotion, but Houma's mount reared in shock and he almost toppled in. Grogha, having the same problems, was just a little more in control than his friend in front.

Macore turned angrily and screamed above the noise, "Get those mounts under control, you two! As soon as you get 'em calmed, everybody dismount. Let's *lead* the horses from this point!"

Both Joe and Marge found it difficult to ignore the roaring and screaming trolls, but Houma got his horse calmed a bit and slid off, followed by the rest.

Macore turned to the nearest foaming troll. "Ah! Your mother was a fairy princess!" he yelled derisively.

The troll roared and foamed all the more and slapped the water.

"Your father was a fairy princess, too, pumpkin-nose!" Macore taunted.

While this made the troll all the more furious, it had a different effect on the other huge creatures, who stopped their panic acts and started laughing uproariously at the obvious discomfort of the target of Macore's insults. This, of course, infuriated the target all the more, and it took a swing at the nearest fellow troll. In a few moments, they were all oblivious to the travelers and swinging away at one another.

Looking smug, Macore led his mount up the center span and down, followed at prudent intervals by the other four. They crossed the rest of the bridge without further incident, the sounds of the fight still clear behind them.

"Trolls are good engineers and savvy bargainers, but outside of that, they ain't so bright," the little man said, chuckling. The Company mounted once more and followed the dirt track on the other shore for a quarter of a mile or so until it hit a main road. At the junction was a large sign. "Welcome to Marquewood. Obey local ordinances," Marge repeated Dacaro's reading of it.

"Well, onward and upward," Joe called. "I'm beginning to feel as if I'm back on the road again!"

About a mile farther down, the road split into three directions, and there was a roadhouse and inn. Joe looked at the place hungrily, but Macore cut his impulse short. "I think we better make time today. We got seventy miles to the Dancing Gods, and that's a good two, three days. Best we stop when we *have* to or we'll *never* get there."

Reluctantly, Joe nodded, and they rode past to the junction itself, well marked but totally unintelligible to them.

Marge rode up to the signpost, letting Dacaro do what he wanted, and the black stallion looked at the signs. "The extreme right road is the one," his voice came into her mind.

Although they'd talked a bit before, it was still startling to her to hear the horse speak to her. Dacaro was no conversationalist, and she hadn't had time to get used to the fact that her mount was more than a beautiful, sleek, intelligent animal.

Marge pointed to the road. "Dacaro says this way. Any objections?"

Macore looked at his map. "Nope. That should be right."

They traveled most of the day, and it was past dark when they reached a small inn on the road. Macore cautioned them to say as little as possible about their origin, mission, or destination, "because you never know who's gonna sell you out, particularly in places like this."

Joe nodded. "We better have some kind of cover story, though," he suggested. "Just to keep it straight."

"Hmm . . . All right. You two—" Macore indicated Houma and Grogha. "—are merchants. Get it?"

"What kind?" the practical Grogha asked.

"Anybody asks you, you tell 'em it's none of their business," Macore replied. "But you're picking up some raw materials for clients in Valisandra. We're your associates, see? You say that and everybody will figure we're your guards, anyway. Don't pick fights or start conversations. Let me do the talking. The less we say the better. Got it?"

They all nodded.

"And, lady, you get Dacaro to give you a neat little spell for that money, huh? We need it bad, and they'll lift it at the first opportunity."

Marge nodded and then paused, as if listening to something none of the others could hear. Finally she said, "We'll take out what we need ahead of time and leave the rest in the saddlebag. He's got a pretty fair spell for it, and it will be right there in the stable, where he can protect it and raise the alarm if the spell fails."

"Good enough," Macore said. "Take out—oh, a dozen, I suppose. I don't think we'll need more; if we do, we can always come out and get it. Right?"

Marge paused again. "He says twenty and forget coming back. It's a pretty strong spell to undo just to make change."

"I'll go along with that," the little man told her, and soon they were at the inn and settled down.

The roadhouse was almost deserted, and the family that ran the place seemed willing to ask no questions of paying guests. The night passed uneventfully, which was fine with them all. It had been at best a tiring day.

The next morning Macore was enthusiastic. "We have a little more than thirty miles today, according to the innkeeper, to reach the River of Dancing Gods," he told them. "Looks like we might be in High Pothique by this evening."

"I understand that this High Pothique isn't really a country at all," Marge said between bites of breakfast. "Will we have any trouble on the roads there?"

"Oh, I wouldn't worry about the roads," the little man assured her. "They're pretty well traveled. But there isn't much of a central government in High Pothique—too many magical domains and freeholds under minor sorcerers and the like. Right along the river are a few villages that will be okay. It's when we cross the low mountains into Stormhold that things might start getting a little dicey. It's kind of a magical free-for-all, if you know what I mean."

"I'm not sure I do," she replied, but pressed no further. She began to wonder, though, as had Joe, who had appointed the little thief as leader of this expedition. Still, they were helpless without him—his knowledge of the country had already proved itself out with the trolls. Marge just hoped he was as widely traveled as he pretended to be.

On the trail later that day, she decided to press him a bit on her doubts. "Have you ever actually been to this Stormhold?" she asked him.

"On the edges," he replied. "At the limits of navigation on the Sik, a tributary of the River of the Sad Virgin, which forms the southern border of High Pothique, there's a town called Kidim. It's something of a trade center for the interior—at the river limit and also at the foot of the Vale of Kashogi, which is the only real way into the interior, considering that the mountains are two miles high on both sides. I once got to Kidim." He looked suddenly thoughtful, then shook his head. "Naw. They'd have forgotten about that by now." That last was said mostly to himself, but in the same loud tone which he used normally. "At least, I hope so," he added, sounding a little nervous.

Joe, who was following the conversation, gave a chuckle. "Returning to the scene of the crime, huh?"

"Aw, it was nothing, really. They're a bunch of hicks up there. Close-knit little community, never go anywhere or do anything—solid burgher types. Nice-looking gals, though. Still and all, they make all this money brokering among the races and rulers of High Pothique and the rest of the world and they don't do anything with it. Who can figure them? So I figured I'd liberate some of that dough." He sighed. "Well, I found out that the one thing they *do* spend money on is burglar prevention. Those spells were so good I doubt if *they* can get their hands on it."

They rode on to the south, approaching the great river that was the life of Husaquahr. As Macore had hoped, they reached it in late afternoon.

"How do we cross this one?" Houma wanted to know. "More trolls?"

Marcore laughed. "You couldn't build a bridge over the Dancing Gods. Too wide and too deep, that's for sure. The only way you can cross is by boat. See? There's the river. I don't see the fairyboat, though."

"Another ferry," Joe muttered. "I'm still not too thrilled about the last one I took."

They made their way down to a landing, actually nothing more than a cleared area of hard dirt, and looked out. Anchored to a piece of solid rock a few feet from the river's edge was a thick cable that went out into, then dipped under, the river.

Joe got off, went over, and looked at the cable. "Damn! Looks like *steel!*"

Macore came over and examined it. "Well, I'm not really sure what steel is, but I can tell you what *that* is. It's fairy-spun rope, from the forest elves of Marquewood. It's incredibly strong and waterproof to boot. You can tell it's fairy—see how it's actually fused with the rock, not tied to it?"

Joe nodded, then turned and gazed out at the river. It had been extremely wide around Terindell, but now it was positively huge. Two other rivers, the Rossignol and the River of Sighs, had merged with it at this point, along with a hundred minor creeks and streams, and the extra volume had added a mile to the width of the Dancing Gods. Across on the opposite shore, little beyond a green smear could be made out, although behind that smear rose a series of imposing and barren, domelike mountains.

"Where's the ferry?" Joe asked nervously. "And why the cable?"

"Oh, it's probably on the other side or on its way back," Macore told him. "Don't worry about it. They'll be making trips, even at night. As for the cable—it holds the boat, of course. If it didn't, we'd wind up forty miles downstream with this current."

They settled back and relaxed a bit, aware that this was the last really calm moment they could expect for some time. Once across the Dancing Gods, with the great river to their backs, they would be in hostile territory.

"We'll put up at a coastal inn tonight, I think," Macore said. "It will probably be dark or a little after when we get across, anyway."

"Sounds good to me," Joe responded. "Say—about this boat. Who runs it? Some more nasty critters?"

Macore laughed. "Fairies run it. Why else would they call 'em fairyboats?"

"Um, yeah, uh-huh," was all Joe could manage.

Grogha stared out at the broad expanse of the river, then frowned and shaded his eyes for a moment against the glare off the water. "Yep! Here she comes!"

They all got to their feet and looked out. Still far off, they could now make out a dark shape against the waters, approaching with agonizing slowness. Try as he might, Joe couldn't get a good idea of what the boat looked like.

It wasn't until it was very close that he realized why. It was a large flat made of wooden planks, with big log bulkheads on both sides. The cable went through a long tube on the right side of the boat, keeping it in position but doing little else. The motive power, however, was rather startling.

The motive power for the huge skid was eight small forms on each side of the boat, all wearing harnesses that were attached by cables to the boat and all of whom were flying their hearts out. This was no mean feat for the sixteen of them—they were quite small, perhaps two or three feet tall. Obviously, Joe reflected, they had a lot more strength relative to their size than people.

The boat was not empty; a very heavy-looking wagon loaded with something and pulled by four draft horses was on board, as well as a few individual horse-and-rider combinations.

The tiny fliers pulled the glorified raft right up onto the hard landing; then the forward pair dipped down to the ground and tied off their pulling cables to studs set in the ground.

The wagon lost no time coming off and headed away. Two of the riders did likewise, but the third approached the Company, waiting its turn to board.

"Good afternoon," he said in a sonorous voice. "Might I inquire how far it is to the nearest inn up the road?"

Macore studied the rider. He was tall and gaunt, possibly of mixed human and elvish ancestry, with a gray goatee and wide-set, reddish eyes. He wore a totally black riding outfit, with cape and broad-brimmed black hat.

"About nine miles north," the little thief told him. "What is the situation on the other side?"

The stranger paused to think. "The situation, sir, is unpleasant. All sorts of strangers flooding into Pothique's river towns, looking very secretive. I fear the war is approaching."

Macore nodded seriously. "I suspected as much. But what of inns along the river? We'll need to stay over tonight."

"Try the village of Jaghri a mile south of the landing," the stranger suggested. "There should be reasonable rooms there— but watch your valuables and keep on guard." He looked at the trail. "Well, I must be going. I don't like to be on strange roads after dark."

"I don't blame you. Have a good journey, sir, and a successful one!"

"And you the same," the stranger responded and rode off down the road.

Joe approached Macore with a quizzical look. "What was *that* all about?"

"Either he's a spy for the Barony—which I doubt, since he's so incredibly obvious—or he's running scared. More likely scared. I think we take his advice and be on extra guard tonight—and every day and night after."

"Hey! You two! They're waving us on!" Grogha called, and they turned and got on their mounts.

Dwarfed by the riders and the wagon, one of the fairies they hadn't noticed until now stood on the deck, acting as loadmaster. He was a curious sight as they passed him and stopped where directed. He looked something like a tiny man—about two feet high and very well proportioned, much like a Greek statue—with a crop of purple hair between two overlarge pointed ears; from his back sprouted a set of transparent wings that were configured much like a butterfly's and were as large as the rest of him. Around his waist he wore a pair of leaves as a loincloth, and around his head was a garland of what looked like seaweed.

He both walked and flew—*flittered* was the word that came to Marge's mind—from spot to spot, showing each of them where to leave their horses, apparently trying to balance the load. Still, the raft could take far more than five horses and riders, and it wasn't much of a problem.

Once positioned, the fairy got a series of stakes that seemed to fit into holes in the deck and lock there and placed them so that all five horses could be tethered.

Then the fairy rose straight into the air and gave a high-pitched whistle; the crew on each side of the boat rose with the paddles, kicked off to the boatswain's chant, and got in unison. The boat began to move.

Once it was under way, the loadmaster fairy settled down, so that he hovered about five feet off the deck, making him roughly equal in height to the humans, now dismounted and stretching once again. The tiny creature approached Joe, and there was no mistaking his intent, so the big man gestured back to Marge.

More of the precious silver pieces were eked out, more than for the trollbridge, but it wasn't the same, somehow. Hearing and seeing the effort put into moving them and the craft across the broad expanse of water, they all felt that this money was well earned.

The crossing took about an hour and forty minutes, and the sun was almost behind the rounded granite domes to the west when they pulled up on the opposite shore and disembarked. There were no signs of either direction or welcome, but they had sighted the lights of a small town just a bit downriver as they crossed, pretty much as the stranger had told them, and they headed there at a moderate pace.

Still, as the fairyboat pulled out once more for its last run of the day, they all felt a certain additional loneliness. The great river now lay as not only a physical but a mental barrier to the land they'd known, and they were heading into unknown realms with that water barrier at their backs. For the first time, all of them felt truly on their own.

The village of Jaghri was a ramshackle collection of wooden shacks and a warehouselike inn around a boat landing. The design was slapdash and primitive when compared with what they'd been used to, and the whole thing looked weathered. Clearly it had seen better days.

The stableman was a little hunchback with the face of a prune and the disposition of sour milk. His round eyes were offset, so he looked as if his face were at an angle when it was not, and he drooled and spat with no regard for people or property.

Dacaro and Posti, however, assured the others that they'd be fine, even if they had to take care of themselves, and Dacaro suggested this time that the saddlebags be taken inside with the group and kept under close guard. He reminded Marge of the spell that would safeguard them.

The inn itself was a stinking waterfront dive. Where the past night's roadhouse had been clean, modern, well kept, and not very crowded, this place was in every way an opposite. It was crowded and it stank.

Those inside were also a rough-looking lot, and a minority was human. Even those who were human, though, didn't look very friendly—or too human themselves. All eyes were on the five as they entered, and there was a slight drop in the noise level, but it quickly rose back to normal.

Macore looked around, spotted a bartender, and went over to him. "You got any rooms to rent tonight?"

The barman, who apparently had never bathed, gave a grin that revealed yellowish, rotten teeth and said, "Yeah, we got a couple upstairs and more in back. What d'ya need?"

Macore thought for a moment. He was about to suggest the same as the night before—a quad for the men and a single for the lady—but he decided that nobody had better sleep alone around here. "Two rooms," he told the barman. "One for three, one for two."

"Eight grains in advance," the bartender grunted. "Pit toilet's in the back."

Macore nodded and counted out the money, which vanished even faster than the fairy had made the boat fare vanish. "Show me the rooms."

The bartender gave an evil grin. "Rooms? You want rooms? Sorry. Just rented the last two."

The little man stared at the bartender for a moment. "I play no games and give few warnings," he said matter-of-factly. "Either you stop this game now and give us our rooms, or you are dead. I will count to five. If your life is worth eight grains, let me count down."

The bartender laughed. "Who's gonna do it? You, little squirt?"

The thief was swift, drawing his shortsword and leaping at one and the same time, pushing the bartender right in the face and landing on top of the bigger man, sword at his throat. "*Five*," Macore said icily and made a small cut on the man's throat. Blood trickled.

There was dead silence in the room, and the other four, who had remained to one side, placed their hands on their weapons.

"Upstairs, first two on the left," the barman rasped. "Let me be now!"

"Not until you give us our change," the little man responded, as cold as before. "Ten grains I have coming. *Now!*" The sword hand moved slightly once more.

"You bastard!" the barman snarled. "I only charged you eight!"

"That's true. And I charged you ten. Shall I count to five again? Don't worry. If we have a decent sleep and are unmolested, I might give you a big tip tomorrow. Perhaps ten grains' worth. Understand?"

"You win." The bartender sighed. "Let me up."

Macore backed off with an athlete's grace, sword still at the ready.

"I'm gonna have to reach under the counter here to get your money," the bartender told him. "Just take it easy, friend." He reached into a small compartment, brought out some coin, and took out a ten piece, putting it on the counter. "There. See?"

Macore nodded, picked up the piece with his free hand, and relaxed a moment.

"I'm beginning to feel useless around here," Joe muttered.

Macore grinned, sheathed his sword, and turned back to them.

"*Macore!*" Houma yelled as the barman reached back under his counter and took out a menacing-looking dagger. The little man dropped and rolled, pulling out his shortsword as he did so, and Joe brought his great sword from its sheath and leaped over the thief to the barman with a yell.

Taken off-guard, the barman, who'd been ready to throw the dagger or plunge it into Macore's back, instead tried to shield himself with it against Joe's attack. Not really wanting to kill the man despite his manner, Joe ignored the dagger and brought the flat of the sword down on the barman's head.

Sparks flew from the point of contact; as a startled Joe yelled, there was a sudden flash of smoke, heat, and light— and the barman was gone.

The would-be barbarian stood there, getting his breath, looking stunned at the spot where the barman had stood. "What the hell . . . ?"

Macore got to his feet and put his sword away once more. "He wasn't human, Joe. He *looked* it—sort of—but he wasn't. You touched him with iron."

Joe whistled. "Well, I'll be damned . . . I never really killed anybody before."

"Well, if it's any comfort, you probably still haven't," the thief responded sourly. "He was sure a nobody if there ever was one." He looked around. The crowd had stopped to watch the show, but was now slowly returning to drinking and gaming once more. Nobody seemed the least upset at the fight, and particularly at the fate of the bartender.

Macore let out a breath. "I must be getting old. Houma— Joe. I owe you both one, that's for sure."

"That's why we're a Company," the lanky Houma responded modestly. "You'd do the same for us."

Macore gave a slight shrug, but did not otherwise reply. Instead he said, "Well, let's take our rooms—at least see if there really *are* two vacancies upstairs."

There were. They weren't much—the linen was stained and the whole place could have stood a fumigation, but it would have to do for the night. "Joe, you and Marge take the first room. The rest of us will take the second," Macore said. "That way the numbers and experience are on one side, the power on the other. Good enough?"

They all nodded. Joe went over to the door and saw that it could be barred by a large board. There was a small window with just a piece of burlap for a curtain, but there was no bacony, and it was a good thirty feet to the ground. The room would do.

Marge looked at the door and the window thoughtfully. Finally she said, "You know, the same security spell Dacaro taught me for the money would also work on the rooms, I think. But you'd be stuck here until we came and got you."

"That might not be a bad idea, anyway," Macore replied and looked at the other two. "Any objections?"

"Nope," Grogha said. "Might help me actually get some sleep."

"I'll second that," Houma added.

"It's settled, then—if you're up to it," Macore told her. "But first let's put the spell on the bag and go down and get something to eat. If anything this place serves can be eaten without eating us, that is."

"Let's just hope the cook isn't related to the bartender," Joe responded nervously.

CHAPTER 11

A COMPANY PICNIC

Energy for minor magicks is transformed from the practitioner's own energies.

—I, 346, 89(b)

MARGE PREPARED ONCE MORE TO PERFORM THE SPELL ON THE saddlebag, after first removing a few coins for use and giving them to the other four. She was acutely aware of her powers and her lacks in the process. To work magic required three things—an inborn sixth sense that was the ability to see the forces, the training to recognize and control what you could see, and the ability to understand and, if necessary, solve complex mathematical equations. For, of course, that was what all spells were—equations involving the magical energies and forces. The more complex the spell, the more complex the math involved.

She certainly had the ability to see the forces, at least after Huspeth had finished with her. In fact, the witch had probably not given her the talent at all. She had the strong feeling that she had always been able to see and sense those forces—but failed to recognize them for what they were. Huspeth, too, had shown her how to recognize those forces and spells; the meanings of colors and auras—not just for people but for everything. To work the forces was also simple for Marge, although she was aware that none of the others in the Company save Dacaro—and possibly Macore—could see what she could see. But the equations were beyond her, at least for now. She had been good in literature, the arts, and social sciences like history. Math had never been her big subject, not since she'd barely limped through high school algebra. Thus, she was dependent on Dacaro. Prevented by his equine form from shaping the forces, he yet knew from his training the necessary math and could pass it along. Neither was powerful individually; as a team, they were a complete minor sorcerer.

Most of the chants used in spells were mere devices, either to aid in concentration, as memory tricks to bring forth the equations, or simply to confuse onlookers. The actual practice was quite simple—you just concentrated on the person, place, or thing you were working the spell upon, then moved your finger or hand and let the energy flow from you into the object itself.

This spell consisted of yellow lines, glowing yellow strings that looked like paint on air. She looked at the saddlebag, repeated the little mnemonic Dacaro had given her as a memory aid, then pointed at the bag with her finger and drew the yellow lines, as if with crayon or marker. When she had finished, the saddlebag looked normal to the rest of them, but to her it was covered with a complex child's scribble of yellow lines. At least, it looked like a child's scribble—in actuality, it was an equation expressed that way. Anyone meddling with the saddlebag would find the results extremely unpleasant; anyone wanting it now would have to undo that yellow stringy mess exactly the opposite from the way she'd done it, with no slips.

Such a task would be child's play for a sorcerer like Ruddygore or a powerful sorceress witch like Huspeth, but the spell was more than adequate for average men and fairies. In a sense, it was like a good burglar alarm system—it wouldn't keep out the competent pro, but it certainly discouraged the amateurs, who were ninety-nine percent of any threat.

She rejoined the others, and they went downstairs. The same motley crew was still there—and there was a plump, middle-aged woman now behind the bar—but the only notice taken of them was that folks tended to move away from them as they took a table. They had gained a measure of respect, if nothing else.

They were briskly attended to, though, by a small, sad-faced waiter who gave them no trouble and no extra words. They had some problems finding a proper vegetarian dish for Marge—the others' repugnance to eating animal flesh had lasted only until the first roadhouse—and when the food came, it was greasy, overcooked, and tasted like an unwashed stove, but it *was* filling and there wasn't any more to be said. They talked little while eating, except about the quality of the food.

Afterward Marge excused herself to go out to the stable and see Dacaro. "I want to be sure of the spells," she told them, and they agreed.

"Want me to come along?" Joe asked her. "You never know whom you're going to meet."

"If I can't manage that much, I have no business being here," she responded and left.

It was quite dark out and humid now. The smell of the river was rich in the air, but she had no trouble walking the block to the stables and finding the stableman. He was a little amazed that all she wanted was to sit on the horse, but he simply muttered about having seen everything in this business and left her.

Once she was upon the black stallion, rapport was instantaneous.

"Anything wrong?"

"No," she assured him, "but it's not the world's nicest inn." Quickly she told him about the evening's exploits and the kind of spell she wanted.

Dacaro thought a moment. "I think it is time you received some instruction. Perhaps it will be a good way to while away the miles from here on out. You seem determined to practice the art."

"Of necessity," she responded, "although I admit it fascinates me. I know I'll never be great at it, but it is something unusual that I can do."

"Ruddygore explained to you the price of such dabblings? The fact that you are a witch's changeling?"

"Something like that. I'm not sure I understand it and I'm certainly not going to let it bother me."

"The principle is simple. Only the masters of the art may create magical energies. All else must come from the practitioner. The more difficult spells can literally take a lot out of you, energy that must be replenished slowly. In your case, the replenishment is not of flesh and blood but of the nature of faërie. The more energy you expend—send from yourself— the more faërie will replace it. If you lost blood, your body would eventually replace it with new blood. But if you lose the plasma of magic, it must be replaced from magical sources. Your sources are attuned to faërie. If you continue, your entire body will eventually be so replaced. You will *be* of faërie."

"Is that necessarily—bad?"

He considered this. "It depends on how you look at it. The more you are of faërie, the more magic of the minor sort will be instinctive, requiring no training. But you will be subject to the magic of mortals and the rules of faërie. Never having been of faërie, I can not say if this is good, bad, or indifferent. But it is certainly *different*."

"We'll cross that bridge when we come to it," she told him. "For now, the protection spell for the rooms."

"Simple. You have a good memory. Remember this spell and do it so." He sketched out in her mind a pattern and a rhythmic chant to aid the pattern's symmetry. "Try it. Just a bit. Just in the air here."

She concentrated and tried it, going just a little ways. The color of the bands was orange, and they were a little thicker and harder to manage, but not by much. "How's that?"

"It will do. Go now. Get some rest. We have a busy day tomorrow."

She left him and returned to the inn, where the rest of the Company was still at the table drinking ale. Joe and the portly Grogha seemed in the best of spirits.

After a while, they went upstairs. She first checked the saddlebag and found it undisturbed. That didn't mean that no one had tried, but certainly the spell had worked. After bidding the other three good night, she stood back and worked the protection spell, first on the window and then, from outside, on the door. It looked really pretty, she decided.

She and Joe went one door down to their room. From inside this time, she traced the spell once more on door and window. Joe watched her, fascinated, seeing only a chanting woman waving her right hand about, but he knew that something was indeed taking place.

She felt a little tired when she finished and sat down on the bed of straw.

"I just happened to think of something," Joe said.

"Huh?"

"We had a lot to drink. What if I have to go to the can?"

She smiled and pointed under the window. "See that pot there? That's a chamber pot, as in the old days."

He went over, looked at it, and frowned. "Umph. Some privacy! But I suppose if you gotta go you gotta go."

She nodded and lay back on the bed. "I really am starting to feel worn out. I think maybe I'll just go right to sleep."

He came over and knelt down beside her. "Sure ain't Texas, is it? Or South Philly, either."

She smiled. "No, it sure isn't. And I'm glad it isn't. I wouldn't go back for anything now, I think. We have something everybody dreams about at one time or another but almost nobody ever gets, Joe. A new life. A second chance. It's funny. Here we are, in a dirty roadhouse in an ugly foreign country, about to put ourselves into real danger—and I've never been happier in my whole life. Never. You understand that?"

He nodded. "In a way. But only in a way. Me, I'm still on the road for somebody else, stopping at flea traps and risking my neck for not much. And I got nobody, really, to be doin' it for—just like back home. This stuff ain't so glamorous, either, when you bean somebody with a sword and electrocute him or something like that. I got a feeling that the only thing that's really changed about me is that now I'm gonna get paid for killin' folks instead of haulin' their stuff."

She thought about it a moment. "Maybe you're right, Joe. But it's the only life we've got now. Let's play it out. It could be fun, too."

He sighed. "I dunno. Maybe—maybe you and me will be a team, huh? We're different, you and me, from any of them. We're from someplace else. Someplace different, if you know what I mean."

She leaned over and patted his arm. "I think so. We'll see."

She snuffed out the lantern. It was an eerie scene for her after that, with the orange bands of the window and door and the yellow on the saddlebag aglow, yet reflecting not at all the rest of the room. To Joe, of course, it was pitch-darkness.

"Marge?"

"Yes, Joe?"

"I'm just lonesome, is all. I have been for a long, long time. Long before comin' here, I mean."

"I know."

"Marge?"

"Yes, Joe?"

"I'm horny, too."

"I figured as much. Not now, Joe. Not for a while. Not between you and me, that is. Let's just be—friends for a while, huh? Companions from another world."

He sighed once again. "What's the matter? Afraid it will louse us up?"

"No, it's not that. Look, Joe, I can't be as strong as you. And this is even more of a man's world than ours is. My only chance to be independent—to be free—here is through the magic. The place Ruddygore sent me, well, it was sort of like a convent. I joined their order."

"You mean you're a nun?" He sounded genuinely shocked.

"Think of it that way, if you can. It's not to say that—someday—I might not bend. When I think the time is right. When I'm ready. But as for now, the longer I stay celibate, the stronger my magic power gets. Once I break it, I can never get any stronger. I just told you what the magic means to me, Joe. So I have to pay the price."

He was silent for a minute, then finally said, "You ain't the only one payin' a price." But then he rolled over and was soon snoring. She had no trouble joining him in that endeavor.

It was Joe who was up first, shortly after dawn, and he tired rather quickly of just lying there and waiting for her so he could leave. He gently shook her awake.

"Hope you don't mind—but I'm trapped," he said apologetically.

"No, I don't mind at all," she told him. "In fact, the lack of clocks and wake-up calls is a real pain around here. How come you got up? Trouble sleeping?"

"Nope. When you're on the road and time is money, you get so you can mentally set yourself to wake up at a particular time. It's no big trick—just a practical necessity."

She got up, yawned, and stretched. "I always heard about people who could do that, but I never could." She rubbed her eyes and blinked a few times. "Right now I wish we had some running water. I'd like to wash my face off and get the sleep out."

He laughed. "And you were the one who really loved this place."

"I didn't say it couldn't stand a few improvements." She

laughed back. She got up, yawned once more, then turned to the saddlebag. "Easy stuff first."

Having made the pattern in the first place, she knew exactly where to start and how to retrace the pattern backward. It was so quick and effortless that even Joe was surprised. "You're learning that stuff pretty good," he told her.

She nodded, then sighed and looked up at the window. "Seems almost a waste to undo the window, but somebody may have to jump out of this firetrap someday." The orange bands were still a bit bulkier to manage but no real trouble. The door was a bit slower, because of the greater complexity and sheer size of the pattern, but it took only a couple of minutes. Finally she said, "Okay, Joe. Lift the latch and let's go spring the rest."

He did so, and the door opened without trouble. She grabbed the saddlebag and they went to the next door, where another two or three minutes was spent undoing the spell. Joe then pounded on the door, and was greeted by a sleepy "Who's that?"

"It's us!" he called. "You can open your door now! Time to hit the road!"

There was the sound of grumbling on the other side, then the sound of the board being removed, and the door opened. All three were sleepy and grumbling, but were ready to go by the time Marge had removed the window spell from their room. She looked around at them. "I suppose it's too much to ask for there to be a bath in this place, but let's at least wash up and get breakfast."

Grogha yawned and scratched. "You ain't got no spell for fleas, have you?"

"Maybe we can find something," she replied. "A bath would be best—but I'm not too sure I want to expose myself around here."

"Bath?" the portly man repeated, as if it were a totally alien word.

"Yeah, you might try one sometime," Macore prodded playfully. "You should do everything at least once in your life."

Marge washed herself off at the outside pump, as did Joe and the others. Then they went back inside the inn, almost deserted at this early hour. Strong coffee was available, though, and some fruit and pastries, which suited them all just fine.

When they had eaten, the stout woman who'd taken over the bar the night before came over to them.

"You owe eight for the rooms and two for the breakfast. Jajur is on the house. Skimmin' like that's not proper. At least not so up front."

"Jajur?" Joe asked.

"The bartender. Though I should charge you for me havin' to work extra hours last night."

Marge thought a moment. "How about twelve and call it even?"

"Fair enough."

The money was counted out and paid, and they headed for the stables. The five-grain charge there seemed a bit stiff, but they paid it without complaint. Macore looked over at the moneybag. "How much more we got in there, anyway?"

Marge shrugged. "About a hundred grains in various denominations, plus some gems."

"Let's see some of the gems."

She reached in, took out a few, and gave them to him. He looked them over with an appraiser's eye, then whistled. "Not bad. These three ought to be enough." He kept them and handed her back the rest. Then he sought out the stablehand to ask about outfitting, and they went further into town, leading the horses, until they came to a weathered store. It wasn't open yet, but the owner was inside setting up, and it didn't take much to get him to start business a bit early.

By the time the little thief was done, they had a mule, pack, and harness, bedrolls, canteens, and a small camping outfit. There was a lot of haggling, but, as Macore had predicted, the three stones proved sufficient.

Joe and Marge were impressed. "All that for three of *those*?" Joe asked incredulously.

Macore nodded. "And he got the best of the bargain. One thing, our Master Ruddygore is not stingy, I'll say that for him."

Marge looked at the overloaded mule. "Is all this really necessary?"

Macore took out the map. "I think so. I doubt if we'll make it more than halfway today to Kidim, and that means a camp-out in the wastes. Tomorrow we'll be climbing and maybe we'll make it, maybe not. Besides, *after* Kidim we'll be fresh out of stores, anyway, so we had to buy some of this sooner or later. Why not now? It will only be a lot more expensive as we go further inland."

The next step was letting the horses and the mule drink and filling the canteens. By that time, the first of the open-air markets was open, and they were able to buy a fair amount of fruit and some dried meat, as well as coffee and tea. Checking the map once more and getting information from the fruitseller, Macore was able to lead them on the proper path, first back to the ferry junction road, then a bit north, where the shore road forked, one way following the river, the other turning first west, then south, into the mountains.

That road was clear, but it was obvious that it was not widely used, particularly from the approach to the Bald Mountains themselves. The mountains weren't high, but they were barren granite domes of some ancient volcanic origin, and a natural climatological barrier.

The trail led up to them, then began a series of switchbacks, taking the Company up a thousand feet or so in slow stages. The summit was only thirteen or fourteen hundred feet high, but that was a lot when one was starting from the bottom.

Once the travelers were through the pass, the trail descended much as it had brought them up, but the landscape had changed dramatically. Almost up to the foot of the Bald Mountains, the river-fed earth had been green and lush. Now it was mostly desert, a desolate yellow, purple, and orange landscape of dry beauty, marked with mesas and buttes wind-carved into fantastic shapes.

"Looks like the Badlands," Joe commented.

At the bottom of the descending trail, they hit another junction, unmarked as had been all the others in High Pothique.

"Inland route," Macore told them. "Used mostly by caravan traders who don't want to be that obvious. We go straight, though. Through *that*." He pointed at the desolation. "See those mountains in the distance, almost blending with the sky? Well, they're the really big mother mountains, and that's where we're heading."

"Lead on," Houma called to him. "You got the map."

The hot sun bore down on all of them as they went, and Joe cracked that he should have brought his suntan lotion from the truck, but he knew, somehow, that he would not burn. By the evening, though, he was already several shades darker than when he began, and all their faces and hands showed weathering.

Dacaro was as good as his word to Marge. "If you are determined to master the art, then I will help you," he told her.

The theory of it was not all that esoteric—since they were talking applied rather than theoretical magic—but to move from doing presupplied spells to creating one's own to suit whatever purpose one wished was something else again, something not mastered in a day.

It was with some inward fascination that she couldn't help but think of it as being much the same as learning computer programming—something she'd once taken a course in at one of those fly-by-night business schools back when she was still looking for a job. Up to now she had been using pre-prepared "software"—the spells furnished by Huspeth or Dacaro. Now she was being taught, in slow steps, how to build them herself. Of course, she'd graduated from the course, but not with any decent handle on programming. Her math was just a bit too slow—and so it was here, with no pocket calculators to help her out.

Still, Dacaro was patient and reassuring and seemed delighted to be able to do something finally with the knowledge he'd gained over his years as an adept.

At one point she asked him point-blank what he'd done to incur Ruddygore's wrath.

"I went on a trip with him—to your world," he told her. "A most smelly and confusing place, I must say, but one with a lot of things I thought would improve our situation here."

She was surprised at this. "Does he go to our world often?"

"Fairly often. Two or three times a year, perhaps, for a week or so each time. He sees shows at theaters, mostly, and buys horrendous souvenirs of places—tacky stuff even by your world's standards. He did not show you his collection?"

"No."

"He will. You will be appalled. I argued with him that bringing back some of the technology of your world would ease a lot of misery here. He adamantly refused, even though he admitted it. He talked about intangibles, values this world had that had been bred out of yours by your technology. I did not agree with him then and I do not now. So I disobeyed him.

I brought back something which I thought could be useful here in our eternal fight against the enemy. I brought it back mostly to study and have copied. But he discovered it, sensing the iron in its construction, and so we had our bitter falling out that left me in this state."

She grew curious. "What was it you brought back?"

"A—revolver, I think you call it. Or is the word 'gun'? And five hundred rounds of ammunition."

She whistled. "Why a gun?"

"I argued with him. I asked him to imagine our brave forces lined up against those of the Baron, armed with these or more efficient versions of these, instead of swords and spears and arrows."

"Sounds reasonable to me," she agreed. "What did he object to?"

"He told me that I was looking at the problem the wrong way. I was to imagine the Baron with such weapons. But *we* would have then first—and we could always improve upon them. It would end war as we know it!"

"Yes, it would, Dacaro," she said sadly. First one side would have pistols. Then some would be inevitably captured by the other side, and *they* would copy the design and make their own—only better. Maybe scale them up. What was a revolver but a miniature cannon? And then the other side would . . . Was there uranium here?

She knew too much about that sort of pattern to be on any side but Ruddygore's, and she could understand why Dacaro so frightened him—and why poor Dacaro would never understand the reason. She gently changed the subject back to magical spells and did not refer to his problems again.

Although the sun was still up, they made camp at a small water hole right in the middle of nowhere. The horses and the mule had no hesitancy drinking from the stuff, even though it looked a little stale, so they didn't, either. It tasted odd, but they suffered no ill effects.

The watering hole hardly qualified as an oasis—the pool was barely ten feet around and looked to be a place where the bedrock had weathered away at a soft spot, allowing an underground river a small outlet. There were some bushes, but no trees, and it looked as if it were used, but seldom.

"As far as I know, this is the only water between here and

Kidim," Macore told them. "Of course, all I know is the map. I never actually crossed this way before." He frowned and looked southward. "Still, I'd say we should make the town before dark tomorrow." He sighed. "Man, I'm hot and tired!"

"We all are," Houma replied. "It is desolate country indeed. Still, it is open country, too. Less likely to bump into funny things."

"Don't get too confident!" Macore shot back. "The last time I was real self-confident, I tried to sell sharpeners to a nice lady who ran a farm all by herself—remember?"

There seemed no way to reply to that. Joe looked around. "We should build a small fire. I doubt if it will attract much attention, but it might make anything that lives out there think twice about us, not to mention keeping us from stumbling in the dark and drowning in the pool. It's gonna be mighty dark here soon."

"Good idea," Grogha said. "I think we can use some of this dead stuff in the thicket and maybe spare a couple of frame boards from the pack mule."

"Or you could use the wood in the gray pack in the middle there, as I intended when I bought it," Macore said laconically. They all glared at him, but they had their fire going before darkness fell, as it did with amazing suddenness.

Grogha proved a pretty good field cook, considering the limited makings he had to work with. After cleaning up and putting everything away, Marge looked at the packs, and the mule. "Do you think I should put a spell on them—just in case?" she asked.

"Better to be safe than sorry," Joe responded. "Go ahead. Be kinda hard to protect *us*, though, so we'll have to stand turns at watch."

"Yeah, but how will we know when to change watch?" Houma asked worriedly. "No town clocks in sight."

"Candles," Macore said. "Actually, I can't take credit for this. The merchant suggested them." He got them out of the pack and lighted one in the fire. "They take two hours to burn down. Simple, huh?"

"Good enough for me," Joe told him. "Who's first?"

"Me," Marge said. "I'd like a little time more or less to myself."

They started to protest, since none of them had even thought of her for the duty, but she silenced them, and they knew better than to press it.

Another hour or so was spent sitting around, talking about nothing in particular and watching the spectacular stars that appeared in the desert sky, then most were ready for bed. Marge helped them get their bedrolls settled, and Joe suggested a semicircular arrangement around the fire. Within two hours, all were asleep except her.

She first made the spell on the mule pack—removed, of course, from the mule—and on the all-important saddlebag, finding it easier and easier. Like writing her name with a pencil, she thought, pleased. Dacaro had told her that the more she practiced any magic, the easier it would all become.

It was deathly quiet, without any sort of breeze, and the air had not cooled off much at all. Idly, she started practicing some of the simple exercises Dacaro had taught her. So simple . . . She could draw faces with the spell light, twirl it around like a lasso, and hurl the energies where she willed, at least within her line of sight.

She pointed her finger at the ground from a standing position and traced a pattern. Once the pattern, in light blue, was established, her index finger became a stylus, allowing her to carve shallow designs in the rock itself.

The world is pure mathematics. Know the proportions and the relationships of any given thing and you have the potential of doing anything with it. That was the key, Dacaro had said. *And when you can look at a tree, a rock, a bush, or a person and see the pattern in their auras, then you will take the final step to sorcery.*

She concentrated on a nearby bush. *Pattern . . . pattern . . . find the pattern . . .*

And, to her surprise, she saw it. Thin, impossibly complex spiderwebs of white plasma. She turned to the fire, which was getting dangerously low. There was still a lot of combustible material there, but it had not caught for some reason. She concentrated on the fire and the unburned wood and saw, after a while, the magenta pattern of the fire and the white of the wood. *Tie one to the other*, she thought, *and maybe . . .*

She found an end on the magenta strand and another on the white and willed them to move, move toward each other, touching, combining . . .

The fire suddenly roared up, looking like a Roman candle, and she laughed aloud in delight. Suddenly conscious that she might wake someone, she stopped and willed the fire back to normal levels. It went obediently, as she knew it would. She had the pattern. Still, she could make it dance, rise up and down, gyrate—until the wood was completely burned, anyway.

She turned to the water and saw its golden weave. In a sense, it was simpler than the fire pattern, which was in turn simpler than that for the wood or the bush. So simple to ripple it, or cause a small eddy...

Suddenly she tensed, sensing something else where she looked. There was certainly something other than water there, something alive. It was not close, but it was down there, somewhere. She could feel it, knew it with absolute certainty.

She stood at the edge of the pool and made a decision. It was a huge job to work the room preservation spell over the mouth of the underground water hole, and took her quite some time, but she made it doubly strong and extra tight, blue bands forming a virtual net over the opening.

Whatever was down there might be able to break it, but at least the thing would have a hard time, if indeed it was a threat at all. But she somehow knew it was a threat, something ancient and repulsive that fed on those who used the water hole. Not us, she decided determinedly. Not without a fight.

She went back over to a rock near her bedroll and sat, feeling suddenly tired and a bit drained. Parts of her face hurt—too much sun, she decided, now taking its toll. She looked over and saw that the candle had burned out. How long she had been watching she didn't know, but she was certainly ready for sleep now. As gently as possible, she shook Joe awake.

He yawned and groaned. "Anything?"

She shook her head. "But there's something living at the bottom of that pond. Something nasty," she told him. "I put a protection spell over the whole thing. Whether it will try and come out I don't know. If it does, I don't know either whether or not the spell will hold it, but keep an eye on it."

"I will," he assured her. "You get some sleep."

She needed no urging.

*   *   *

It was still dark on Houma's watch when there was a sudden roar from the pond that awakened them all and startled the horses as well. A roar and a lot of splashing. They were quickly on their feet, adrenaline racing, and Joe pulled a burning ember from the fire to use as a torch, grabbing his sword in the other hand.

They approached the fuming water cautiously, not knowing that to expect. What they saw in the water was a sort of face—a huge, incredibly old, demonic face, full of hatred. It exuded a sense of terror none of them had ever known before, but the hatred was only partly directed at them. It was straining, struggling against the surface of the pond, and Marge understood that, at least for the moment, the spell was holding.

She felt a nuzzle at her back and almost jumped a foot, but then realized it was Dacaro. She understood what he meant immediately and quickly jumped upon his back.

"Dacaro! What is it?"

"I have no idea," he replied, "but it's sure a good idea you put that spell there. It's not going to hold, though. You can see it unraveling around the edges. This thing isn't very bright, but it has a hell of a lot of sheer power. Ask Joe if he can stick his sword into the water and hit the face. Let's see if iron does anything."

"Joe! Can you stab it without losing your sword or falling in?" she called.

"We'll see!" he shouted back, revolted by that hideous face, yet unable to tear his eyes from it. The sword hummed and glowed in his hand. He poised, waiting for the face, which filled most of the pool, to get a part of itself in a no-miss spot against the edge, then plunged the blade into the water and quickly withdrew it.

The face roared its pain and hatred, but only redoubled its efforts to break its bonds.

"Well, scratch that," Dacaro told her. "I really doubted it was that easy, anyway. This is going to test us both, woman." He thought furiously for a moment. "Okay, we'll try something, but it's damned complicated. I'll feed it to you slowly, and you do it as I tell you. Got it?"

"I'm ready." She looked at the men near the pool. "Hey! Everyone get back! We're going to try some sorcery on it!

Keep your weapons ready, though! Be prepared to strike, but not until I tell you!"

Slowly, cautiously, the four men backed off, giving both Marge and Dacaro a clear field.

"Here goes," Dacaro said and began feeding the spell to her. It was enormously complex, far beyond her ability to understand or comprehend, at least at her level. She had begun mastering arithmetic, she realized, upon seeing this thing; now Dacaro was feeding her incomprehensible calculus. She had no choice but to follow through.

The energy field that formed like a wall in front of them was of all the primary colors and perhaps a hundred shades. She had never seen anything like it, nor did she have any chance to appreciate it, but she could feel its awesome power.

"Joe!" she called, relaying Dacaro's orders. "We're going to let that thing come out! When it does, it will run headlong into the damnedest spell you ever saw, like a net that will close on it. When you hear me yell again, get in on the side and hack that whole damned head off *behind* the face! Understand?"

"Got ya!" Joe called back, too charged up to feel afraid right now.

Quickly, Marge, using a Dacaro shortcut, removed the blue bands from the pool. "What if *this* doesn't work?" she asked worriedly.

"Then we run like hell," the equine adept replied.

Freed of the protection spell, the face roared up and out of the water and onto the rock.

"I'll be damned! It's some kind of worm!" Grogha shouted. "Yuk! Look at that slime!"

The demon worm was six feet out of the pool when it hit the new and more powerful shield. It reacted to the great net of force much as it had done to the blue—pushing into it with a terrible rage.

"Good . . . good . . ." Dacaro said, mostly to himself. "It really can't see the spells, as I figured. It's just so big and strong it's used to pushing its way through anything."

Marge watched as the thing plunged directly into the net of force, which gave a bit in the middle, enveloping the evil face.

"It's giving way!" she called nervously.

"No!" Dacaro shot back. "It's designed to do that. Tell Joe to be ready."

She did, and Joe brought his sword up. Grogha and Houma also brought their bronze swords up, ready to tear into the demon worm from the other side.

The face was now completely enclosed in a bulge in the magical netting, and Dacaro gave the word. "Now!" Marge shouted.

Coming in behind both net and face, all three started swinging and hacking at the wormlike flesh in back. The face howled in rage, but seemed unable to understand what was happening to it, or where. Pieces of giant worm flew as they hacked away and finally severed it. The severing was so sudden that both Joe and Grogha almost fell into the mess and barely backed away.

The remainder of the body flailed around for a moment, then slid with astonishing speed back into the pool. The head, apparently suspended in air to the human onlookers, continued to snarl and snap for a while.

"We've won," Dacaro told her. "Now do this." He fed her a small set of instructions, and she translated them into a huge mental shove at the face in the net. It flew back, rolled, flopped a bit, then rolled again into the pool, where it sank rapidly.

Again following Dacaro's instructions, Marge pushed back the net, at one point having to shout Houma out of the way, then laid it, like a tabletop, across the width of the pool. Only after attaching it to the pattern of the bedrock did she relax and realize that she was sweating like mad. She felt suddenly very, very tired indeed. Before she knew it, she fell off the horse.

CHAPTER 12

ALL THE CIVILIZED COMFORTS

Virgins are uniquely useful for certain magicks, yet they have draw-backs beyond the obvious.

—CX, Introduction

WHEN MARGE AWOKE, SHE FOUND HERSELF ON A MAKESHIFT litter being pulled by Dacaro. They were on the move again, that was for sure. A worried Joe rode an equally worried Posti behind the litter. When her eyes opened, he gave a shout that brought the party to a halt.

Joe jumped down and went to her. "How do you feel?"

"Lousy, but I'll live," she replied. She looked around. "What hit me? Where are we?"

"You just keeled over," he said. "Luckily for you, one of the bedrolls was underneath. I don't think anything's broken."

"I feel good enough to ride," she told him, not sure if that was really the truth. "Untie me from this thing."

With Macore's help, Joe did as instructed and lifted her to her feet.

"Woosh! A little dizzy, and I have a couple of bruises in places I never had 'em before, but I think I'm okay." She looked around again. The tall mountains loomed ahead, not more than ten miles away. "So where's the pool?"

"Way, way back there," Joe told her. "We talked it over and figured it was better to move with you this way than to risk another night with our slimy friend back there."

She nodded. "I agree with that. But—didn't you kill it?"

He shook his head negatively. "I doubt it, and so does Dacaro. What brains the thing had weren't in its head at all. It will probably nurse its wounds down there, regenerate a new face, and be ready for the next suckers."

She thought of that hideous face and shivered. "You know, up to now, I've believed in good and bad and in between, but that thing was true *evil*. Could you feel it?"

They all nodded. "Something from the dawn of the world,"

Macore said. "Some terrible force in that form. Maybe it once thought, but now it's nothing but pure hatred and rage."

"And appetite," Grogha added.

"That, too," Macore agreed. "You want to try riding now?"

She nodded. "I'll manage. But help me up on Dacaro. He may have some spell that can relieve me."

They helped her up, then disassembled the litter and packed it on the long-suffering mule.

"Glad to find you back among the living," Dacaro told her.

"So am I," she responded honestly. "I don't know what came over me."

"That spell. It was far too complex and draining for a novice—but it was necessary. It took all your reserve. Hurt much?"

"A lot of bruises. I feel as if I had been run over by a truck."

"Didn't you say you had a witch's kit? Isn't there something you could brew up for yourself?"

She felt foolish. "Sure there is. Damn. I almost completely forgot. Uh—if we have any water."

"The water from the pool was all right—in the morning," he told her. "The canteen's full."

"How long was I out?"

He thought a moment. "Hard to say. Several hours. It's past midday. But better whip up your witchery before we push on again."

She called out to the others, and they obliged, watching as she mixed certain herbs together from her kit, then brewed them into a tea and drank it all, even eating the mixture.

"Taste good?" Grogha wanted to know.

"Terrible," she told him. "But I can already feel it starting to work." She folded up her kit and put it on her belt. "Let's get moving."

Back on the trail, Dacaro explained to her his correct guess about the nature of the evil worm. "It was all rage and hate," he said. "When I saw how it simply tried to bully its way through your spell, I knew it was pure emotion. Its sensory apparatus was all in its head, while its brain was protected back in the tail someplace. But it seemed to have no way of telling anything without the information that head provided—and it just pushed on straight ahead. I gambled it wouldn't even know where it was being chopped—and I won. Once the head was severed, it was blind, deaf, and dumb."

"I think I've had enough of monsters for a while," she remarked. She suddenly had a thought. "Uh—Dacaro. That big spell took a *lot* out of me, right?"

"Yes. All you had, really."

"And—it's being replaced slowly out of faërie?"

"Um, yes. I was wondering when you'd think of that."

"Have I—changed?"

"A little," he answered honestly. "But it will be gradual in any event."

"Will it be—enough? To push me over the edge, that is?"

"I can't say. The external changes first, though, that much I know. But you won't be beyond mortality until your wings grow out, so you can at least tell from that."

She thought about it. "Wings. You mean like those the little fairies had on the boat?"

"Perhaps. There are lots of wings. I don't expect you to shrink much, since that would have been among the first things to notice. So the wings would have to be different—they have to support a different mass. Why? Having second thoughts? Nervous?"

"Nervous? Yeah. Because I don't know what to expect, what price I'm paying. Sort of like selling your soul to the devil. At the time you don't even realize it's gone, but when the time comes, you sure miss it."

"Perhaps, when this is over, you can talk with some of the fairies," he suggested. "But, regardless, you either stop or go on."

"It's not that much of a choice, really. Like last night. It was me or nobody."

"I think I might have done it—differently—through Macore. He has the sense of the art, but absolutely no knowledge or training. It might have killed him, but I could have done it."

She sighed. "Some choice. But that's not the only factor. Magic's my edge. It's what I *do* here. If I give it up, I might as well open a stall and sell potions."

"Suit yourself. I wouldn't get so worked up about this changeling business, anyway. We'll probably all die in this mission."

She chuckled. "Optimistic, aren't you?"

"We'll see."

The pass through the mountains showed clearly now. The slope was steep, but gentle enough for horses and perhaps a wagon team if need be. The pass itself was quite wide, although it looked to be a very slow and relaxed climb of a couple of thousand feet, at least. They started up and were soon surrounded by high mountain walls.

Within the first couple of hours the temperature had dropped considerably, and they all were feeling chilled. Although there was no snow evident in the pass, it was all around not too far above them.

"We're going to have to buy some warmer clothes for this place, if we don't freeze to death right here," Joe muttered. "Near naked's all right for the hot stuff, but it's nothin' to be in a snowstorm."

The others, who were dressed better than he but not for this, could only nod in agreement. Making matters worse, the sun was already low enough to be masked by the surrounding mountains. Marge shivered and called to Macore, "How much longer to this town of yours? Will we make it before nightfall?"

"Hard to say," the little thief called back. "Remember, I never came in this way before. But I do know that it's in a glacial valley just below this pass on the other side. It will be touch and go between us and night, but we'll have to do what we can."

It was early evening, and there were flecks of snow in the air when they finally made the summit of the pass and could look out to the other side. There was little sun left, but it was still light enough for them to see, and the village just below was as Macore had promised.

Kidim was set inside a U-shaped glacial valley carved out long ago. The valley was almost a bowl set in the mountain, not terribly deep but about a mile and a half wide. Its water was glacial melt, which formed a formidable lake in about half the depression; but while it was fed by mountain snows, it overflowed away from the village part of the bowl, over in an imposing, tall waterfall that dropped into another bowllike lake several hundred feet below. That lower lake was in turn the source of the River Sik—incredibly, navigable from that point all the way down to the River of the Sad Virgin and eventually to the great Dancing Gods itself. The lower pool was fed not only from the waterfall but also from countless rivulets and small streams, some gushing right out of the mountain.

Kidim, however, was above all that, in the best defensive position. It reminded Marge of nothing so much as a Swiss village, the kind they used for the Olympics or bobsled runs. It was a town of perhaps seven or eight thousand living in elaborately painted and decorated clapboard and gingerbread-style houses, and it was alight with life.

Joe looked around. "Not bad. They could hold that pass back there with a relatively small force; nobody would be safe charging up here from down there. It's almost a perfect natural fortress."

Macore nodded. "And those walls are heavily fortified. They can close it off in a moment and withstand a tremendously long siege. It is said, too, that caves in the mountain itself, known only to the townspeople, are stocked with food and weapons—and even offer escape routes. Their treasures are stored somewhere back there, which makes them so hard to get at."

Cold and miserable, they anxiously headed for the town gates, the pillars of which were carved out of the natural granite. The gates were open. Although there were guards atop the walls looking down on them, there was no challenge or attempt to stop them.

The town was busy at dusk. Sidewalk cafes were filled, and from the various brightly lighted buildings that so resembled chalets could be heard the sounds of entertainment, eating, dining, and general merrymaking.

"Now *this* is more like it!" Marge exclaimed. "I'd begun to give up on High Pothique!"

"It varies widely," Macore responded. "This little City-State is extremely rich and fat. But it gets that way because of its position here. Anyone who wants the valued raw materials of High Pothique's interior deals through here. Anybody wanting to sell anything to the remote tribes and nomads of the interior has to go through here. This is a classic case of geographic greed in action!"

First they found the stables and, for a very high charge, got the horses and mule taken care of and the supplies stored in a bonded and guarded storage area. It was clear from the almost ten grains they were charged, though, that Kidim knew it had travelers where it wanted them.

At Macore's urging, they decided they would splurge for this one night, staying in the highest-class inn—actually called a hotel—in the town. Each would have a separate bed this night—a soft, down-filled, luxurious one with silken sheets and fine wool blankets. Again they took two rooms, using the same arrangement as before.

They skipped the hotel dining room, though—it looked a bit too posh for such burned and unwashed travelers as they—and opted instead for a small, friendly restaurant down the street. The food was wonderful, the wine choice, and when Macore got the bill and told them what it was, they could only wonder what the hotel dining room would have cost.

Afterward, since they wanted to walk off their stuffed feelings, Macore counted out some money to each of them so they could wander about and perhaps pick up some warmer clothing.

They walked around together for a while, but Marge got interested in a clothing store with exotic fashions, Macore wanted to check out some old haunts, and that left three. Grogha and Houma were soon at home in a bar with the promise of live female fairies performing erotic, unnatural acts on stage, and that left Joe.

He wandered down the street, stopped in a clothing store for men, and finally found a wool jacket and high-top, fur-lined boots that would be good in mountain country. Feeling warmer and much, much poorer, he just ambled around for a bit. He was feeling lonely again, and there wasn't much he could do about it.

A young woman—she couldn't have been more than sixteen or a few months older—approached him coyly. She looked too clean and well dressed to be a prostitute, but here one never knew.

"Sir?" she whispered conspiratorially.

Well, maybe they *were* clean and well dressed here. "Yes?"

"Sir—you look like a gentleman. Would you care to seduce and abandon me tonight?"

He chuckled over the phrasing. "Sed—how much?"

She looked shocked. "I'm not a common whore!" she snapped. "I would not dream of charging!"

He was immediately suspicious in the extreme. It sounded like one of those too-good-to-be-true offers—which they always were. *Sure, honey. Go with you, then get waylaid by thugs, robbed, and maybe murdered.*

"Uh-uh, honey. Not tonight," he told her regretfully and walked on.

He hadn't gone another block when a totally different woman, perhaps even younger than the first, beckoned and made the same offer. Again he refused, although she almost pleaded with him.

Finally he said, "All right—what's this all about? Why does every young girl in this town want to be—seduced and abandoned—tonight?"

She looked a little apprehensive, then pulled him gently into an alleyway right off the street. "You have been propositioned before tonight?"

He nodded.

She sighed. "We're all trying it on every stranger we meet. It is impossible to get anyone local to do it. They would insist on marriage or we'd be dishonored because it would be found out. But a stranger could do it—and no one would know. Lots of girls have done it. What's wrong with *me*?" She pouted almost like a small child.

He stepped back a moment, still confused. "Let me get this straight. Are you telling me you're a virgin?"

"Of course!" she came back proudly. "Otherwise, what would be the point of this?"

He coughed and swallowed back a snappy reply to that one. Only a virgin would make that kind of a comment.

"What is it—some kind of bet? Or maybe some magic spell?"

"Oh, of course not! It's the dragon!"

That stopped him. "Dragon? What dragon?"

"You *are* new here. Just a little over four weeks ago a dragon was spotted flying to and from a new eyrie in the high mountains just behind us. It's been seen almost every night since, flying to and fro, probably establishing its nest. Once it does, it will— hunt." She looked up at him desperately, and there were actually tears in her eyes. "Don't you see? Dragons are attracted to virgins!"

He leaned back against the building wall, feeling the need for support, an expression of utter disbelief on his face. "Let me get this straight," he said again. "There's a dragon in the area?"

She nodded. "First one in more than a century in these parts."

"And dragons eat virgins?"

"*Everybody* knows that."

Well, everybody didn't, but ... "Are you trying to tell me that every virginal girl past puberty is sneaking out at night in this town and begging to be—" He groped for a word she'd understand instead of the ten that came immediately to mind. "—*violated* by every strange man she meets?"

"Well, of course! Why else would we be doing this?"

He broke into a big grin. "And about how many of you virgins are there?"

"A couple hundred a month ago," she told him. "Maybe half that now. It's kind of—hard—to bring yourself to do it. But the Books of Rules state that the dragon could start hunting any time after establishing its eyrie, and that takes thirty days. So you see why ..."

He shook his head in wonder. *A trucker's paradise*, he thought. *As if you died and went to heaven* ... Not, he told himself, that he didn't feel sorry for the poor girls. He understood their fears—he thought. But—a town full of willing virgins whose honor would force them never to tell? It was the most absurd thing he'd ever heard. Funny, too. He no longer felt very tired at all ...

It was quite late when Marge got back to the hotel room, and she was surprised to find none of the men there as yet. She sighed and shook her head. She felt really done in and about as grimy as she ever had.

She spread out the garments she'd bought with almost all her money. They were practical ones, good for mountain work, but the fur was soft and fitted snugly about her. She couldn't be certain what the fur was—the term used by the saleswoman had been unfamiliar to her—but she decided it was probably better not to know. Still, with these clothes, she'd be extremely warm; and with the small, pointed-toe boots and tight-fitting gloves, she'd look almost like an elf.

Like an elf? She wondered about that. Casually she undressed and went to the full-length mirror in the luxury room and looked at herself once more. *Had* she changed?

The image looking back at her from the mirror was not really a familiar one, of course, but it *had* changed since she'd last examined it. Her ears, for example, which Ruddygore had noted were turning back and changing, had changed more. They were fully pointed now and sharply back on her head. Elflike ears that looked fine, even exotic, with her streaked hair—but were definitely not human in the slightest. Her eyes, too, seemed huge, sad, and teardrop-shaped, with unnaturally long lashes. They were beautiful, erotic eyes—but they were not human eyes.

She thought of the fairies on the boat two days earlier. They had all been male—sort of, anyway—but they had this sort of ear and something subtly similar about their faces. Not the eyes, though, or the general facial shape she was developing. It was not *their* kind that she was becoming.

She went back to the clothes on the bed and just lay there for a few moments, fingering them. Suddenly she stopped and looked at her hands, then sat up and looked closer. There was no doubt about it. Some sort of—webbing—was growing from the points between each of the fingers. It was only a tiny extra mass of very thin skin now, perhaps an eighth of an inch from the base of the hand, but there it was. Her fingernails, too, seemed extra hard, somewhat silvery in appearance, and were taking on a different nature, perhaps more—animallike? She couldn't decide.

Before she could think on it further, though, there was an officious knock at the door. Acutely aware, suddenly, of her nakedness, she called out, "Who's there?"

"Concierge, madam," came an equally officious reply. "You had asked at the desk if a bath could be arranged?"

She frowned. "Yes—but they told me it was too late in the day."

"A clerk checked with me, and I discovered that there was more than sufficient hot water. It won't keep, so we thought you might wish to use it tonight."

She smiled. A bath! A real bath! "Hold on, let me get something on," she called back and quickly got back into her dirty jerkin. Picking up the new clothes and a large towel, she walked to the door and opened it. Only then did she think how trusting she had been—how she had only his word that he was the concierge.

But he *was* the concierge. She had seen him at his desk in the lobby. "Follow me, please, madam," the little man said, and she followed him down the hall, down to the lobby level, and then below. The bathhouse was small—not even the well-to-do took many baths in Husaquahr, it seemed—but surprisingly modern. The sunken tub was steaming with clear, hot water brought in from coal-fired tanks that also provided some heat for the main floor, and there was a large bar of soap, a full supply of bath linen, and even a white towel-robe, imprinted with the symbol of the hotel.

"I will see that no one disturbs you, madam," the concierge assured her. "When finished, please stop by my desk in the lobby and let me know, so that we may drain the tub."

"I'll do that," she promised him, eager for the water. "And thanks!"

He left and shut the door behind him. She quickly laid out all her stuff, got undressed, and slipped into the tub. The water was quite hot, but that didn't matter at all. It wasn't *too* hot, and the warmth penetrated her body, eased her bruises and muscle tension, and just felt absolutely wonderful.

It was in the wee hours of the morning, after the last bar had closed, that Joe returned to the hotel. He felt tremendous, despite the long day, but he was really tired now. All he wanted was sleep.

He knocked on the door of the room, softly, just to warn Marge of his impending entrance, but then didn't hesitate to open the door and walk in.

He stood there for a moment, puzzled. She wasn't there. The oil lamps were still on, and there were signs that she'd been lying on top of the bed at one time—but that was all. Idly wondering if the Rules also specified boy virgins, he looked around for a clue. He dismissed his thought about the boy virgins in a minute. That wouldn't make sense. She had that celibacy thing. He stopped and thought a moment. Everything was closed now, he knew, so there was no place she could have gone to, except maybe to the wall to look at the night view—but that was unlikely. She'd had a hard day, and even her potions weren't a hundred percent effective. She'd been tired and achy when they'd first hit town, and she'd said after dinner that she was going to get some mountain clothes and then try for a bath and go to bed.

He snapped his fingers. A bath! Sure! He looked around, saw that the big towel was missing, and nodded to himself. Then he stopped for a moment, puzzled. A bath at three in the morning? This wasn't like back home, where one just went into the bathroom . . .

He turned and walked back down to the lobby. He didn't immediately check with the desk, but saw a pictograph indicating baths on a floor below. The desk clerk and the concierge watched him but did not say or do anything as he went down the stairs.

He checked both the small bathrooms. Nothing in the first, but the second showed signs that somebody had used it recently. He went over and tested the water temperature of the bath. Cool, like the other—but the other had been clear. This was soapy and still messed up. He glanced anxiously around, then found in a small pile her old clothes and the new ones she must have bought. Only the towel had been used.

Knowing now that something was terribly wrong, he bounded back up the stairs to the lobby and approached the night clerk first. The clerk smiled and looked up at the big man, nodding. "Yes?"

"The woman who checked in with me—do you know where she is?"

The clerk shrugged. "Sorry. I haven't been on very long. Try the concierge."

Joe went over to the little man at the concierge's desk, who also looked up expectantly. Joe noticed he seemed abnormally nervous and couldn't quite sit still.

"The young woman who checked in with me," Joe repeated. "Have you seen her tonight?"

The concierge frowned and pretended to look thoughtful. "Young woman? Sir, we have many. I can't be expected to remember *everyone*."

"Streaked hair, big eyes, pointy ears," Joe responded, getting a little steamed up.

The man seemed to think hard again, and was about to speak when Joe added, "She took a bath tonight—downstairs."

Sensing that he couldn't conceal obvious facts without

sounding worse, the concierge brightened. "Ah, yes! But I *do* remember her! She went down to the baths *hours* ago. Why, is something wrong!"

"She's missing, that's what. You been here all night?"

"Except for a couple of calls, yes."

"Do you remember her coming back up from the baths?"

The concierge thought a moment more. Sweat was breaking out on his brow. "Uh—yes, I believe I do."

Joe reached out, temper flaring, and literally picked the little man out of his chair with one hand. "*Liar!* You forgot to remove her clothes! They're still down there! *What have you done with her?*" With one mighty move, he pulled the man across his desk so that they were face to face, all the while keeping him suspended off the floor by the grip on his clothing.

The concierge, deathly afraid and sweating like mad, yelled, "Codoary! Help me!"

With an angry shove, Joe threw the concierge halfway across the lobby, where he struck a stuffed chair and toppled over. In the same moment the big man whirled, his face a fury, to see, not just the desk clerk, but two other men, all with swords, coming at him.

In an instant his great sword leaped to his right hand and hummed brightly. "I hope none of you got any fairy blood," he growled at them, "'cause I got to leave one of you alive to torture!"

The three advanced in a semicircle, threateningly but not very professionally. It was obvious that none of these men were hired thugs or assassins. They looked like shopkeepers, hotel clerks, accountants, that sort of thing—and they looked mighty uncomfortable facing a barbarian warrior.

He didn't wait for them to make up their minds. With a mighty yell, he leaped at them, and his sword hand moved with swift and terrible precision. He didn't even have time to think about it—it was as if the sword itself were alive and doing all the right things.

In an instant's time, or so it seemed, the humming sword slashed off the nearest assailant's sword hand at the wrist, then came back up under the next and knocked the sword away and into the air. With his left hand he punched the disarmed middle man in the stomach, and he fell back and collapsed on the floor.

This left only the desk clerk, who was aghast and scared to death. The shock of what had happened to the first two totally unnerved him. With a squeal, he dropped his sword, raised his hands, and cried, "Please! Don't hurt me!"

Joe approached him, then pushed him rudely against a pillar and brought the sword up to the frightened man's throat. The clerk made a noise and looked so close to pure terror that, for a moment, the big barbarian was afraid the fellow was having a heart attack. Still, he was the most conscious of the four, so it was best to start with him.

"You see my friend here? His name's Irving." Joe pushed the point to the throat so the clerk could really feel it.

Even so, the clerk managed to gasp back, "*Irving*?" in a disbelieving tone.

The big man nodded. "Think it's a funny name, huh? He don't like it when he thinks people are makin' fun of his name." Joe paused a moment, genuinely angry but thinking. "All right—you know what my friend Irving's good at? *Cuttin'!* How about it? Shall I let him cut off a hand, maybe, like your friend's there? Then another hand? Then maybe the legs—and what's between 'em?"

The clerk whimpered.

"All right, you tell me what they've done with the girl, and *now!* I'm not a patient man!"

"Please! You got to understand!" The clerk was almost gibbering. "The dragon. It had to be appeased. Our daughters—"

"Dragon!" Joe stormed. "What the hell does this have to do with the dragon?"

"W-we saw that she was a virgin. Duoqua, who's the town elder, can see the magic. She was the first virgin stranger we'd seen! Honest! You gotta understand! My own sister's pregnant by some outland stranger because she was so scared! We *had* to!"

"What did you do with her—scumball?" Joe roared. "Where is she?"

"C-castle rock! They took her to castle rock! The altar there!"

"Where is it? How do I get to it?"

"I—I *can't!*"

"Either you can or you're dead," Joe snapped coldly, and

he meant it. "I have no time for you to think about it. Your friends are coming around!"

"I'll take you! Let me loose!"

Joe let the clerk lead the way—down again toward the baths. "If there's any trickery, just a little, *anything*, not only will you regret it but, I swear by all that's holy, so will your whole stinking town. Forget that she's an agent of the sorcerer Ruddygore! Forget that she's sister to the great sorceress Huspeth! She's my rider, damn it!"

At hearing the first two names, the clerk swallowed hard and muttered, "Oh, my god!" They were apparently sufficient to strike in the man the realization that, while armies could never conquer Kidim, enemies like those could cause terrible desolation and hardly feel it. The clerk gave Joe no more trouble.

Through a service door they went, then down again, into a maze of well-lighted tunnels with steps and railings, past rooms with symbols for various Kidim banks and merchants on them, others with pictographs for various kinds of foodstuffs, and even a whole chamber full of wine. Joe knew that this was the labyrinth in the mountain of which Macore had spoken. For a moment he regretted not rousing the other three, but there wasn't time, really. Right now Marge could be staked out, with a horrible monster circling to strike . . .

"I'm surprised you don't have guards all over the place," Joe remarked as they went.

"Don't need 'em," the clerk told him. "There are spells and magic guardian beasts all over those rooms—and as for the labyrinth, once in—how would anybody find his way out? It's booby-trapped, too."

"It better hadn't spring any traps on me," Joe warned.

"It won't!" the clerk cried nervously. "Ruddygore . . . Huspeth . . . God! Did we pick the wrong one! But you gotta understand . . ."

"Cut the moral justifications! Just get me there as quick as you can!" Joe snapped. He was becoming increasingly irritated by both the time it was taking to get where they were going— if the clerk was playing fair with him—and the growing knowledge that *labyrinth* was the right word and that he had very little idea of where they were and less of how to get out of there.

Suddenly they emerged outside. The cold wind hit them in the face, and they were on a stone walkway along a mountain ledge. Joe and not been conscious of much upward movement in their walk, yet they were either above the town or on a different side of the mountain at about its level.

Someone had lighted torches all along the way, their flames whipped by the wind, but they showed the path. It wound sharply up, around a curve, then out to a lookout station that seemed suspended in space.

"Anybody guarding this path?" he asked nervously.

"With a dragon around? Are you kidding?"

That sounded reasonable enough. "All right—stop. She's out there—on that ledge?"

The clerk nodded. Suddenly he gave a sharp cry. "The dragon!"

Joe didn't wait for anything more. He slugged the clerk hard, knocking him cold and thus preventing him from easy escape or raising an alarm, then started running up the stone walk at full speed.

Something suddenly flew over and quite near him, raising a wind so large it almost bowled him over. He stopped and turned, sword at the ready, and saw the dragon. He could not get a clear look at it in the dark beyond the torches, but it was a *big* sucker, he kept thinking. He stopped to get his bearings on it, knowing timing would be crucial, and saw that the creature seemed fascinated by the lookout and was, in fact, slowly and warily circling it.

Joe took off again, knowing that this probably meant that the dragon had not yet taken its sacrifice, but that it could and would at any moment. The trail took a sudden slight and unexpected dip, and he stumbled and cursed, then got up and took up the chase once more. The trail wound around now, putting him for just a moment out of sight of the lookout itself. But the dragon's huge, dark shape was too great to be hidden, and it descended, just in front of him, where the overlook would be. *I'm too late!* he thought frantically.

At that moment the mountains echoed with the most terrified, horrible scream of fear he had ever heard. Crying out in frustration, Joe rounded the bend to the overlook, determined that he and Irving were going to avenge Marge, at least, or die in the attempt.

CHAPTER 13

A BATTLE IN THE VALE

Dragon motives are inscrutable.
—C, 228, 167(a)

JOE WAS PURE EMOTION AS HE ROUNDED THE BEND AND SAW clearly the scene on the lookout. He was so charged up that what he saw only penetrated his consciousness when he was halfway to the makeshift altar to which Marge had been tied. Only then did he realize that, although tied down stark naked on the altar stone, she was unharmed.

Just beyond, on a huge stone ledge overlooking the lookout, the dragon perched, gazing down upon the scene below with unconcealed terror in its great crimson eyes.

"You all right?" Joe called anxiously to Marge.

She managed to turn her head slightly. "Yeah, I think so. If my heart's started again."

"When I heard you scream..."

"But I *didn't* scream," she told him. "*He* did." She gestured with her head toward the dragon.

Joe kept one eye on the great beast while he edged closer to Marge. Once there, he started to cut the ropes with his sword, but she cautioned, "Watch it! If that sword touches me, it could kill me!"

Joe risked looking down at her, then carefully cut the arm and leg ropes binding her to the structure. She sat up, massaging her wrists and ankles, all of which bore discolorations and minor rope burns. Finally, though, she felt well enough to stand and joined Joe, who was staring at the dragon.

It was a magnificent-looking beast. The old legends had never done the dragon proper justice. It was sea green except on its underside, where it was a dull rust-red, with massive scales protecting its vulnerable points. Its great, leathery wings were a curious mixture of silver and black in a pattern. The piercing crimson eyes seemed aglow with a light of their own, neither reptilian nor mammalian, but filled, somehow, with a great alien power. There did, indeed, seem to be little puffs of smoke coming from the large, flared nostrils at the end of its perfect reptilian snout, and Joe suddenly grew nervous that it might breathe fire on the overlook and cook them both.

At that moment the dragon opened its great mouth . . .

And whimpered.

Joe frowned. "The damned thing acts as if it's scared to death."

"Maybe it thinks you're Saint George," she suggested.

He shook his head. "No. It screamed and backed off while I was still out of sight. I don't get it. I thought they were supposed to *love* virgins."

"Well, I, for one, am sure glad things aren't that cut-and-dried around here," she responded. "I thought I was a goner for sure."

"Snarfle," added the dragon, which sounded as if it had to blow its nose.

"For my part, I'm all for getting the hell out of here before somebody rushes up and reads it the Books of Rules on dragon preferences," Joe muttered. "Besides, you must be half frozen."

"I'm still too scared to be cold. Later I'll get frostbite."

Joe started edging Marge and himself back from the altar, at all times facing the dragon, Irving still in hand and at the ready. The dragon's eyes followed them, but it still looked as nervous as they were. They were almost to the path when a gruff voice yelled, "How *dare* you! How *dare* you! Six weeks' work, down the drain!"

Joe risked a turn and saw, coming toward them from farther up the trail, a medium-sized figure that looked at first to be a walking bush. It was running, though, on what seemed to be enormous, bare human feet. Out of the mass, two thick arms, raised high in fists, gestured angrily at them.

Joe pushed Marge behind him and made ready to meet this new threat. The creature or whatever approached fairly closely, oblivious of the sword, and they could see that it was a manlike figure completely covered with thick, matted black hair. Other than the arms and legs, the only things visible were two huge, yellow, oval-shaped eyes peering from beneath the brush.

It went past them and out to the altar. Joe let it go, still aware of his precarious position on the trail but too curious to run.

The hairball, as Joe thought of it, reached the altar, turned, saw the cowering dragon, and stopped. "Oh, poor Vercertorix! What have those nasty people *done* to you?" he called out, in a tone one would use to a small child.

The dragon snarfled some more, then sniffed and seemed about to break into tears.

"I think I've had about enough of this," Joe muttered to Marge. "Hey! You!" he called out. "On the overlook there! What in hell is going on here?"

The hairball turned. "Ruining a month and a half of hard work!" the creature snapped angrily. "Not to mention scaring the poor thing half to death."

"*We* didn't do anything!" Joe told him. "The villagers kidnapped this woman and stuck her out here as a sacrifice to that 'poor thing' there!"

"Bah! Ignorant, superstitious fools! I'd have Vercertorix here destroy that pesthole if his nerves were up to it!"

"They think he made a nest up here—that he was going to attack the town, anyway," Joe called out. "That's why the sacrifice of this innocent stranger."

Naked and cold though she was, Marge was madder than anything. "Don't you snap at *us!* Who the hell are you, anyway?" she demanded.

At the sound of her voice, the dragon whimpered and tried to press himself back into the rock, causing no small landslide.

"Nest, indeed!" the hairball scoffed. "Why any self-respecting dragon would want to nest in this hole, I can't tell you. But will you *please* stop scaring him, woman? You're only making him worse!"

"How am *I* scaring him?"

The dragon had another minor fit. "Don't *do* that!" the hairball screamed angrily.

"Do *what?*"

"Talk. Remind him of your presence. He's got enough problems without being tortured. Have you no humanity?"

"But he's *not* human," Joe noted. "He's a dragon."

"Semantics! Bah! That's why I went up high into these mountains seventy years ago and why I haven't had any truck with human civilization since. Stupidity, greed, war, superstition, bureaucracy, and semantics. Stupid ills for stupid people!"

Joe thought it over for a minute. "This dragon's been visiting you each night, then. Why?"

The hairball sighed. "Isn't it obvious? We may as well shout it now. The damage is done. Everybody will know, and his shame will be such that we'll probably have one less dragon. They breed only once every thousand years, you know!" He sighed, calming down slightly. "I've been treating him for his neurosis, of course. He has a complex. Isn't that obvious?"

All Joe could see was the fairy stories of his childhood collapsing like houses of cards. "You don't mean . . ."

"Certainly! He has a morbid fear of fair maidens! And *now* look at what you've done!"

"*We* didn't do *anything*," Joe retorted. "Besides, if he's scared of pretty women, why'd he come this close to begin with?"

The hairball took a tone of utter impatience with such stupidity. "If you had a brain, barbarian, you'd figure it out. Dragons are as curious as cats. Sensing something alive staked out here and seeing the torches, he *had* to investigate and find out what it was. That's his nature. And as you see, he wasn't ready yet."

"Thank heaven!" Marge breathed.

Aware of how cold it was, Joe took off his jacket and put it around the freezing Marge. She was thankful, despite the fact that it fitted like an army tent.

"And who are you?" Joe asked the hairball.

The strange man cackled. "They call me the Old Man of the Mountains, I'm told. I'm a scientist, of course. I specialize in dragons and other endangered species."

"Well, see to your patient, Doc. I think we'll go back down now."

"Wait!"

"What now?"

"I see that the lady is a halfling," the Old Man of the Mountains noted, sounding friendlier. "And I recognize that sword. It was given a thousand years ago to a man I once knew. How did you come by it?"

"I got it from the sorcerer Ruddygore," Joe told the hairy one. "If that's any business of yours."

"Ruddygore? The name is unfamiliar. Huge, fat man with a beard? Always eating?"

"That's him."

The mass of hair seemed to bend in a nod. "I thought so. So he's still alive, huh? Come on up the trail a bit. I have a cave nearby with a warm fire and some strong drink where I was waiting for Vercertorix here. I would like to talk to you."

"No, thanks," Joe told him. "We have to get back to town."

The Old Man of the Mountains chuckled. "And how are you going to do that? Could you find your way back through that rabbit warren of theirs? Come to think of it, how'd you find your way here?"

"There's a clerk from the hotel down there. I knocked him cold. He'll get us back."

"Oh, yes? Well, go on down for a moment, if you will— but you will find, I think, that you did not hit him hard enough. He is gone."

Joe didn't have to go down. He figured that the hairball was telling the truth.

"Come up to my cave," the Old Man invited again. "I'll get you back."

"Won't we—scare that friend of yours?"

The two big, yellow eyes glanced over at Vercertorix. "You just stay there and get calmed down," he soothed the dragon. "When you're confident, go to your nearest den and sleep it off. It will all be better in the morning. Then see me tomorrow night as usual. We'll get this straight. And I'm sure these nice people will not spread your problem around."

The dragon whined a bit, and there was a huge tear in its left eye. Having no choice, but not relaxing his guard or his sword grip, Joe followed Marge and the Old Man of the Mountains up the trail.

"Dragons are unusually intelligent," the hairy one, who introduced himself as Algongua, or just plain Doc for short, told them. "Almost as smart as the average person. And they're a lot more powerful and mobile. Of course, they get a bad reputation, but any carnivore that has to eat a minimum of five hundred pounds of meat a day just to keep up strength is not

going to be exactly beloved. They aren't hostile to people—
not really. They kill people only when those people are a threat
to them. Actually, they prefer cattle most of all, or aurochs."

"But that thing in the Rules about virgins..." Marge in-
terjected.

"Ah, that thing's caused more problems than it's solved.
Basically, it was intended to *protect* humans. If a dragon must
eat a human for food, he'll choose a virgin every time. That's
the Rule. And why? To give the rest of us a chance. Somehow
it's gotten all twisted by superstitious folk into a demand for
sacrifice. Stupid. Dragons want as little to do with human folk
as possible."

They reached his cave, which was well concealed, and then
they still had to squeeze through a narrow, twisting corridor
in the rock to get to the main cavern.

It was surprisingly luxurious inside. There was a roaring
fire in a large, conventional fireplace and a thick rug on the
floor. There was also a wall of books, including some—perhaps ten or fifteen—of the Books of Rules.

It was, in fact, rather warm and cheerful. Joe wondered idly
where the chimney came out.

The drink was strong, but it tasted good to both Joe and
Marge after the chill on the ledge, and the fire was particularly
welcome.

Finally feeling relaxed, Algongua took a stiff drink and sat
in front of them. "Now, then—what's this all about? You're
not here for your health. Not from Malthasor."

"Who?" Joe responded.

"Ah—Ruddygore, I think you said he was calling himself
now."

Marge grew interested. "I've heard another name for him,
too, but it wasn't that one. How many names does he have?"

"Probably hundreds," the hairy man responded, cackling a
bit. "None of them his real one, of course. Sorcerers never tell
their real names to anybody—it can cost them. But he's basically a good man and a strong wizard as well."

"You knew him well?" she pressed.

"Long ago, as I said, we both had the same—er—employer, let's say. That was long ago and far from here. So—
if I may be so bold—where are you headed in his service?"

Joe thought about his answer. He didn't want to alienate

the strange man, but he had only Algongua's word that they were on the same side—and, come to think of it, the Old Man had never as much as said *that*, either. Only that he knew Ruddygore. "We go up the Vale of Kashogi," Joe said at last. "There is something in Starmount that was stolen from Ruddygore and which he wants us to retrieve."

The hairy man whistled. "Starmount! I'm sure the Xota will not be pleased. I wouldn't like to take an army into there!"

"The Dark Baron might—he wants what we want," Marge put in, sensing Joe's caution and understanding it. "We are a small Company—we hope to sneak in."

Algongua laughed. "Sneak in! Well, perhaps it can be done. But this Baron, you say, may march on it? That should be most interesting."

It was obvious he had no idea who the Dark Baron was, and Marge decided to tell him, giving as much detail as she herself knew.

The strange man sighed. "Always another archvillain! The Dark This and the Black That and the Prince of Something Else. They're all the same. Ridiculous. No sooner do you beat one than another comes along. I long ago gave that up as nonproductive. I am beyond these petty temporal battles and wars." He sighed. "But that doesn't help you, does it? Here—let me think a moment. Starmount . . . hmmm . . . Yes, I think I can remember a few things."

"Can you tell us what the Xota people are?" Marge asked him. "That alone would be a great help."

"They're a degenerate race of fairies. Ugly brutes, with bat's wings. More animal than anything else. Expect no mercy or quarter from them! They'll eat people, other fairies, even themselves. They sacrifice to primitive, bloody gods. Still, my dear, I'd kill myself if I were you, rather than let them capture me. *You* they won't kill. You're a halfling, and they'll just complete the process and keep you as a slave—and they do terrible things to women slaves."

"I'll keep that in mind," she assured him. "Still—since we're on the subject, you said they'd 'complete the process.' I'm a little curious and nervous as to what I'm turning into even now. Can you tell?"

He looked at her with his big eyes and cackled again. "Too

soon to tell, really. Depends on what your fairy parent was. I gather you don't know."

She decided not to go into her true origins—or Joe's. "No, I have no idea. It began when I served an apprenticeship with the witch queen Huspeth."

"Huspeth!" He made a sound that was definitely derisive and sounded something like *bleah*. "Who knows, indeed? But, I assure you, she didn't start the process. Halflings are born, not created—and remain human, and occasionally ignorant of their nature, unless heavily exposed to faërie or given to dabbling in sorcery. Since I see you're well along and *he* certainly is human enough, I assume you're an adept of some sort."

"A rank beginner. Otherwise I wouldn't have been surprised in the hotel tub, knocked out, and carried out to that overlook."

"Still—enough. From your looks, I'd say you were probably in the nymph family, which is common for changelings, but there are a hundred types and tribes of nymphs, all different. Well, you'll find out soon enough." He thought a moment. "Starmount. Hmm..." He got up, went over to the bookshelves, opened an old book and took out a small piece of yellowed paper, then returned to them. "This is, if memory serves, a map of the Vale and the Starmount Gateway." He unfolded it. "Yep. As I thought. There's an old high trail. Real narrow—single file for horses a lot of the way, and a long way down if you slip—but at the three-thousand-foot level most of the way. See?"

He laid it out for them and they looked at it. They couldn't read the script, but the trail and many natural features were well marked.

"Once you're in Starmount you're on your own, but this should get you there—if you're plucky enough to use it. Also, I can't vouch that the trail's maintained at all. This map's two hundred years old. But you have a fighting chance if it is."

Joe felt a sense of excitement rising within him. What was it Ruddygore had said? *Luck rode with the barbarian hero.* And here was just what they needed—handed to them.

"I don't want to be ungrateful, but we'd better be getting back," he told the strange hairy man. "We've had a long travel day and a longer night—and no sleep as yet."

"Of course, of course. I was just enjoying conversation

again. But—how well will those meddling fools receive you down there?"

Joe thought about it. "I don't know. They can't be too friendly—after all, I *did* beat up two of 'em and take one's hand off right in the hotel lobby. But they kidnapped Marge. I figure they better *hadn't* do anything."

"Come, then. I have a small complex of caves here that tie into theirs. I'll get you back."

He was as good as his word, although the route was even more tortuous and confusing than Joe's had been on the way out. Still, once more they stepped into the bath level of the hotel. When they turned around to thank Algongua, he was already gone.

"Wait a minute," Marge told Joe. "Let's see if they left me my clothes." They checked the bath room, but it had been drained and cleaned. There wasn't a sign of anything that was hers. It wasn't just the clothes—her kit had been there as well.

"So they even steal my stuff!" she stormed, sounding really angry. She took off Joe's coat, which had almost reached the ground on her, and gave it back to him. "Well, I hope they're easily shocked!" And with that, stark naked, she marched up the stairs into the lobby, Joe following, curious to see what she was going to do. He was by no means certain of their reception and put his hand on his sword.

There was a new clerk and a new concierge on duty when they came up, and the mess from the fight had been cleaned up completely, but there was no question from the shock both men on duty showed at the sight of them that they knew full well whom they were facing.

She marched up to the concierge. "You! You'll get me my clothes and have them cleaned, neat, and ready when I call for them in the morning!" she commanded, then whirled on the clerk. "And you—we will be staying one more night. All five of us. On this hotel. That's just for starters. If you don't agree, I will cast a spell on this place that will make it fit only for worms like those miserable creatures who run it!" And with that, she stormed up the stairs.

Joe looked around, noted that neither man had so much as breathed during that, grinned, and said, "If anything is out of place while we're here, this hotel and all who work for it will be destroyed. Even so, I assure you its reputation for what was done tonight will be spread the length and breadth of Husa-quahr." He sniffed. "First-class, indeed!" Then he followed Marge upstairs.

There were snores coming from the room of the other three, so they didn't disturb them, but Marge insisted on putting a full protection spell on the room she and Joe were in. She collapsed on her bed and sighed. "Oh, god! I feel as if that dragon *did* eat me! Don't wake me, no matter *what* you do."

"Don't worry—I won't," he assured her and blew out the light.

The events of the previous evening were the talk of the town by morning. After the fight in the hotel lobby, there had been no real way to keep anything secret. Most of Kidim sympa-thized completely with the men who'd done the deed, but were now acutely embarrassed by it, particularly since it hadn't worked. A merchant and trade city like Kidim fed on reputa-tion, and its reputation was for honorable transactions and a totally safe and secure haven in the midst of a barbaric country.

Thus, while Macore, Houma, and Grogha had no idea what had gone on when they awakened, dressed, and went down to a late breakfast, they were more than pleasantly surprised to discover they could not pay for anything at all—whatever they wanted was theirs, with hopes that the "incident" would not be held against the whole town. They were so pleased by the reception that they took full advantage of it for several hours before they could find somebody to tell them what it was all about.

Joe and Marge did not appear until midday. Marge was delighted to find outside the door both sets of clothes—the old ones laundered and neatly folded—and all her belongings from the bath. She donned the brown skin outfit and packed away the skimpy green one for better weather.

Grogha had come up every hour or so to check on them, and so they were just about ready to go out when the portly man, seeing the clothing taken in, had pounded on the door. He quickly told them of their treatment by the town, which pleased Marge no end.

"Just remember, they're only being this way because they aren't sure they could kill all of us," Joe warned. "But I think they know it won't bottle up forever, regardless."

They had a large brunch on the hotel and noted that they were being stared at again and again by various townsfolk. This would be one those people would tell their grandchildren.

They decided to spend one more night, simply to get their systems back in order, and they supplemented their supplies and weapons—on the house, of course. Marge even had another bath the next night—although with full protection spells around this time. Joe, too, took advantage of the bath and got his meager regular clothing cleaned as well. The other three couldn't see the sense of it.

Still and all, the town was mighty happy to see them go the next morning.

"Maybe we should have told them that the dragon was no threat to them before we left," Marge suggested.

"No!" all four men responded in unison, then looked sheepish. "Ah, that is," Macore added, "they don't deserve it. Let 'em worry. I doubt if they'll try this kind of trick again."

"Besides, finding out it was no threat might lose us our status—which is pretty nice—while increasing their sense of guilt," Joe continued smoothly. "They deserve to sweat." He was, however, amused by the frantic reactions of the other three. So he hadn't been the only one to have a full night, it seemed.

They reached the point where Algongua's map said that the higher trail branched off, but it took them a half hour to find what they hoped was it. It was overgrown, worn, and weathered and only hinted that it was a trail—but it went west at roughly the three-thousand-foot level, and that was what the map claimed.

There were several rocky stretches where any semblance of a trail just gave out, and they spent some time hunting to pick it up again, but it did not prove in the early going too difficult to follow. As it thinned and hugged the granite sides of the mountains, it became more definite. But a trail that was no more than three or four feet wide on the side of a sheer cliff and that had a drop on the other side of more than fifteen hundred feet at the minimum was by no means comforting, and parts of it had been weathered uncertainly, while small streams and waterfalls crossed it and wore deep grooves in the face.

There were actually some clouds below them, but after a while they disappeared, and the main road up the Vale of

Kashogi to Starmount and beyond could be clearly seen. It looked pretty deserted, but Macore thought at one time he saw the dust of some riders far ahead. It might have been a wisp of cloud or some optical illusion, he admitted both to them and to himself. But the enemy forces had been conspicuous by their absence so far, and there had been no real sign in Kidim, although even Ruddygore had thought they would be thickly represented there.

"Perhaps they were," Dacaro suggested to Marge. "Those are merchants and bankers, and most are educated men. Who stirred up the dragon fears? Who could read the Rules—and only those parts on dragons guaranteed to scare the hell out of people? And who suggested they do what they did to you? I suspect more than meets the eye there. Evil is often best when it is the most subtle, reasonable, and invisible."

"But they failed—if in fact it was them at all," she noted. "That means we have to expect another try."

"Yes. More of a brute-force one, I would suspect. They won't have any easier time with the Xota than we, if that's any comfort. And they may not know about this trail—although they'll draw some conclusions when we fail to show up down there. We will have to take things as they come. The enemy may even be at the cave already."

She didn't like to think of that. Not after all this. She did, however, tell Dacaro about the Old Man of the Mountains and his comments on her.

"I don't know who—or what—he is," the equine adept told her, "but he is certainly correct in that halflings and changelings are not made. Not by Huspeth, anyway. It is something that, considering your unique origins, I did not take into account before. But, yes, Ruddygore himself must have cast you like this—and let Huspeth take the heat for it."

"But why?"

"Only a guess. He saw that you had an aptitude for the art, but also understood that you had not the time, nor the ability, perhaps, to learn the complexities of the spells. And certainly your lack of reading ability as an adult is also limiting. So he took the path of best advantage—for him. As one of the fairy folk, you would have natural, instinctive uses of magic and total sensitivity to it."

"Algongua said I would be a—nymph, I think he called it.

I know what the old legends are on nymphs, but not what that means here. Can you tell me?"

"Well—yes and no. Basically, a nymph is a race of faërie, all members of whom are female. They are closest to human in size and general form and are quite often extremely oversexed in all senses of the word. A nymph has the ability to mate with *any* male of *any* species, whether fairy, human, or animal—you name it. Her progeny, then, are always halflings themselves, generally human in form, but if they become involved with fairies or in the art, as you are, then they will change into their fairy form. The results can be quite bizarre. Satyrs. Centaurs. The small winged ones. Strange amphibians. Depends on who—and what—the father was. Whole new races of faërie have been created in that way. Of course, if the child is female, it has a fifty-fifty chance of being another nymph, so the race doesn't die out. As to kind, there are wood nymphs who live in and are linked to trees, field nymphs, water nymphs, all sorts. You name it. But I still sense the potential for wings in you, so you may be an aerial of some sort. We will see, won't we? It should be interesting to discover what happens if the transformation is completed."

"Huh? What do you mean?"

"As primarily human, your powers gain with celibacy. As those of a full nymph, your powers will gain with the opposite type of conduct."

"What! You mean . . ."

"Precisely. Since the magic of faërie is innate—the potential is there and develops automatically under certain circumstances rather than having to be learned—the more times you do it with anybody, the stronger you will become."

She was silent for a while. Finally she said, "You're amused by that, aren't you?"

"I'm sorry, but I must admit I am. Don't be too angry. Would you rather have *your* problem or mine?"

There really wasn't much of a comeback to that.

They camped out early in the evening, at the first area they came upon, with enough room, not wanting to chance being on this trail after dark with no place to turn into. It was damned cold, but a small waterfall provided water, and there were some scrub bushes for the horses. It was still a cramped evening and a nervous one that high up and in the cold.

The next day dawned cloudy, but they were anxious to get

going. During the morning they made good time. Early in the afternoon the clouds descended to the trail level, and travel became something of a nightmare. With so little tolerance, they soon were chilled, wet, and unable to see the tail of the horse ahead of them. It was sheer luck that they came upon another wide place—narrower and even less comfortable than the previous night's, but enough—and found themselves having to stay the afternoon and through the night. Quarters were really close then, and they had to be careful simply not to step in and slip on the horse droppings, but they had to stick it out and remain through the second night.

The third day showed not much improvement, and they feared that they would be stuck yet another full day in that cramped space. But after a couple of hours, the sun broke through and burned off the fog. Not all the way—still, the cloud level was a hundred feet or more below the low points of the trail. While there was no guarantee of safety, they were all willing to chance it. Dacaro, with his bulk, was particularly uncomfortable and offered a fog dispeller spell if need be rather than remain there any longer. He didn't normally want to risk any spells until he had to—the enemy below might be sensitized to such things.

On the fourth day, about midmorning, the trail started down in a series of hairy switchbacks that left no margin for error. They almost lost Grogha when his horse came close to losing its footing, but he was able to keep control in the nick of time.

Macore and Joe consulted Algongua's map and decided that they were coming down to join the main trail—which was rising to meet them. The Starmount Gateway, then, would be only a few miles ahead of them—and where, again, they would be on their own. Still, it was supposedly only eight or nine miles from the Gateway—actually a natural pass that opened onto the great Starmount Plateau—to the cave they sought. That brought another sobering realization—the Xota could be anywhere, starting now. As fliers, they could leap down from hiding places above, or swoop in in aerial attacks. The Company was suddenly acutely aware of how exposed it was on the high trail.

The junction was certainly not far, perhaps just around the next bend, from the looks of it, when Macore put up his hand, halting them, and turned and put a finger to his lips.

Joe, just behind him, frowned and whispered, "What's the matter?"

"They're ahead of us. Probably laying for us," the little thief whispered back. "I can almost smell 'em. But I heard a horse snort and shuffle."

As quietly as possible, Joe relayed the message back.

"Horses!" Marge exclaimed to Dacaro. "Then this won't be the Xota."

"No. These are the ones we have feared. Obviously they got here ahead of us and set ambushes at this end of both trails."

Macore slipped off his horse, aware that he had very little room on the trail. He drew his sword and made his way forward, in front of his horse. Slowly, with a thief's skill and practice, he crept ahead and soon more or less *oozed* around the bend in the trail.

They all drew their own weapons, but aside from Joe's getting in front to hold Macore's horse, there was little he could do. They waited anxiously, fearful that the little man had been taken.

Finally, though, Macore slipped back around as quietly as he'd gone. "There are six of them," he whispered softly to Joe. "They picked a nice position, too. We would have been exposed at least three hundred yards on the trail. They may have been there for some time. They're all dismounted and seem to be mostly sitting around looking bored. That will change the moment we appear, though."

Joe thought about it. "No way to sneak up on them?"

"Not unless you can fly," the thief told him. "Three hundred yards to a broad, flat rocky area with some trees and bushes where we join the main road. It ain't much when you just gotta walk it, but it's ten miles when you're fighting. And this drop is all the way to the junction, almost. There's a mighty big hole until the trails join."

Joe nodded and looked down. He could see the other trail, only forty yards or so away on the other side, but in between was about a four-hundred-foot-deep gap. He thought furiously. "All downhill?"

"You said it. *Real* grade, too."

"I wonder—considering none of us can fly, and we'd be suckers for crossbows..."

"So? So?"

"How about a charge? You sure they don't know we're here?"

"Pretty sure. Did you say a charge?"

"Uh-huh. As soon as we round the bend, go for a gallop. Full charge, yelling and screaming, weapons brandished and ready."

"Are you crazy? The horses will probably lose their footing and fall into the ravine!"

"Yeah—but if they don't, it will sure surprise the hell out of those men, won't it? They'll have to pick up and aim their weapons; maybe some of 'em will have to mount up. Three hundred straight downhill yards . . . I figure maybe twenty, thirty seconds at full gallop at the worst. Maybe even ten."

Macore shook his head wonderingly. "It's impossible."

Joe grinned. "That's what *they* think, sure. You go tell the others." He looked back and sighed. "I wish Posti was in front, but you'll have to do as the leader," he said to Macore's brown horse.

Macore went back, talked to the others, then made his way forward again. "They all think you're nuts, too."

"Anybody got another idea? We can't back up—not enough room. We can't fly over that ravine. We don't have any way of climbing down, even if we were willing to desert Posti and Dacaro. And the longer we stay here, the more likely it is that one of us or one of the horses is going to give us away."

Macore nodded glumly. "I know, I know. But if we must commit suicide, why do you have to be so logical about it?" He looked at his horse. "Who leads?"

"You take Posti—and brief him. He'll come through. I'll take yours."

"*That* I won't argue about," Macore responded honestly and made his way back once more.

"When I raise my sword, be ready to follow," Joe called after him. "When I drop it, we start."

They all drew their weapons and waited tensely, eyes on Joe. Both Marge and Houma had small crossbows with a supply of bolts conveniently in front of them; the other three held swords at the ready. It wasn't much of an attack force, but it would have to do.

Macore glanced nervously around. "I hope he's as good a rider as he thinks he is," he muttered aloud.

"I hope we're all better fighters than I think we are," Grogha responded worriedly.

Joe raised his great sword, positioned himself, and was ready to begin when he heard Marge say, "Wait!" in a loud whisper. As tense as he was, it was almost enough to start him off, anyway, but instead they all turned and looked questioningly back at her.

"I can call a friend," she told them. "One who will cause one hell of a ruckus. That will give us the diversion we need to go in."

"A friend?" Macore repeated, frowning. "*Here?*"

"A unicorn," she told them. "My—protector." *I hope*, she added silently to herself. "I don't know why I didn't think of him earlier."

Joe was skeptical. "How the hell can a unicorn get here in time?"

"I don't know, but it all just came back to me. What have we got to lose?"

He thought it over and knew the answer was "Not much." He nodded and said, "Okay, give out the call. The rest of the plan stays the same, though. If this unicorn comes thundering by, it's the ball game, so as soon as we're sure they've seen or heard it, in we go. Got it?"

They nodded, but none, not even Marge, really believed in any sort of unicorn savior.

"Stay away from the unicorn no matter what," Marge warned. "He's friendly only to me." With that she sat back, tried to concentrate, and said, more mentally than physically, "Koriku—come! I am in great danger and need your help!"

For a moment nothing happened, and Joe relaxed, turned, and raised his great sword once more. Then abruptly there was a roll like thunder and the sound of hooves, and they saw the great magical white beast coming toward them, riding the air above the ravine, level with their road. Marge smiled, then gestured for the creature to move to the opposite, main road and continue, The signal was taken and heeded.

Around the bend, there were sudden shouts as the men in the ambush both heard and saw the creature charging in upon them. At that moment Joe dropped his sword and kicked his horse in the ribs. The time for thinking was done, The others quickly followed, yelling, as was Joe, to add to the confusion.

Posti kept Macore almost in the rear end of Joe's mount, showing the guts he had displayed so long ago at the Circean's farm. Next came Marge and then Houma, who released their initial crossbow bolts as soon as they could see the men in the wooded clump. Grogha brought up the rear, his horse pretty much taking him along, and tried mightily not to fall off.

The sight of the great unicorn bearing down on them was a complete shock to the defenders, who had been very lax up to now. They looked up and saw the charging white, single-horned apparition and were frozen for a moment; then they moved as one to counter it, toward the main road and away from the high path.

At that moment, the riders came around the bend with their yells, and the defenders were caught, divided in their attention and ducking the first bolts sent their way, even though those were far short of any mark.

Two, though, were clearly pros, archers who jumped up, bows ready, and let loose two wild shots in the direction of the exposed party. While neither hit the mark, the archers were shooting and reloading with a fluidity that seemed almost inhuman.

Koriku sensed the immediate threat in the archers and lunged for them with a snort that became something of a roar, landing on both and knocking them down. Suddenly he was the enraged carnivorous beast Marge had seen in the fields, spearing men with his great horn and rending flesh with row upon row of sharp, pointed teeth set in powerful equine jaws.

By this time Joe had reached the guardpost itself. In maneuvering around the unicorn, he exposed himself to the no longer dazzled defenders. He felt an arrow pierce his side and he whirled and bore down on a crossbowman who was now trying to reload, running over the hapless man and trampling him. Joe's horse went down, rolling on top of a swordsman who screamed in agony, but Joe managed to jump off and come up on his feet, the arrow in his side now causing some bleeding he was too charged up to notice.

Between Joe and the unicorn, the defenders were turned inward, allowing the rest of the party to make it in relative safety. Posti hit the ledge with his hind legs, kicked off, and

landed full on top of another archer, who also went down—
as did Macore, who flew from Posti's saddle and spilled onto
the rocky ground, losing his sword for a moment.

Marge and Houma had managed to reload, and each took
out a swordsman, one of whom was running for his horse,
which was tied up in the rear. Another soldier leaped from a
rocky bluff and carried Grogha over onto the ground. The portly
man struggled with his larger assailant for a while, but blood
was trickling from his month and he was in great pain. When
it was clear that Grogha was out of the fight, the soldier abandoned him to writhe and moan there and turned to Macore,
just now getting groggily to his feet. The soldier, a huge,
bearded man in black uniform and chain mail, towered over
the little thief, and the first blow of the soldier knocked Macore's sword away; a second, with the flat striking Macore's
head, sent the little man reeling backward, coming to rest in
a bush where he groaned once, then fell back, still.

Now the soldier smelled victory and turned on Marge. Koriku, finished with his archers, saw the move, turned, and in
a great leap was upon the bearded man, first pushing him down,
then knocking the sword from the man's hand with his great
horn. As the huge equine head came down and the gaping,
blood-soaked jaws filled the soldier's vision, all confidence
vanished and he screamed in terror.

Joe, for his part, took on another swordsman. It was quite
a duel, since the soldier was extremely good and obviously
well trained, but Irving's magic always seemed to provide the
proper counterblow and move into every opening. Finally gain-
ing the upper hand, Joe flung the sword from the other's grasp
and then plunged his own into the soldier's abdomen. The man
gave a terrible cry, bent over backward, then collapsed in a
heap.

Marge saw another uniformed shape come from behind a
rock, sword in hand, toward Joe's back. She let loose a bolt
that penetrated the attacker's chain mail, and the man gave a
horrible cry that brought Joe quickly around. Irving wasted no
time in finishing the man off.

Houma looked around, saw the bleeding and broken Grogha,
and cried out the man's name, riding swiftly to him. Joe spotted
Macore's limp form in the bush and ran to him. Marge leaped

off Dacaro and ran first to Macore, examining him for vital signs.

"Is he dead?" Joe asked worriedly.

She shook her head. "Not yet. But he's in a bad way, I can tell. Help me get him down here on the grass and keep him still. I'll see about Grogha."

Houma was leaning over the portly man, and there were tears in his eyes. "Grogha, you filthy pig, don't you dare die on me!" he shouted. Marge had some trouble getting him away, but then she bent down and examined the fallen man's wounds. Her moderate powers of witchcraft came to the fore, for they included diagnostic and healing arts. She tried to soothe Grogha, who was conscious but in terrible pain, while she probed his body.

Finally she sighed, got up, and went back to Joe, who asked her, "How is he?"

"Beyond my powers," she responded sadly. "So is Macore, although he's not nearly so bad off. Macore's got at least a nasty concussion and a broken rib or two; Grogha's got bad internal bleeding. I'm afraid a rib may have punctured a lung."

Joe thought frantically. "Wait a minute! Magic's gotten us out of a number of scrapes. Don't they use it instead of doctors here?"

She looked up at him, suddenly a little cheerier. "I'll ask Dacaro," she said and jumped up on the horse. "Can you do anything?"

"Perhaps," the adept replied. "Perhaps not. It will depend on the nature of the injuries. But there is no good way for me to treat them as it stands. It's not like spoon-feeding you a spell. I will have to project myself inside each and effect whatever repairs, major and minor, are needed as I go." He paused a moment, thinking hard. "There *might* be one way, though. Do you trust me enough to let me take over your mind?"

The question startled her. "Can you do that? If so, why should I object if you can help them?"

"Because if you consent and assist, I *can*. But consider— I do not have to reverse it once it is done. You will have to trust that I will do so."

She understood what he was saying now, but she looked at the unconscious Macore and the limp form of Grogha, which, even now, had only the most tenuous of threads to life, and made her decision. "What do I do?"

"I'm certain Huspeth taught you the trance state. Clear your mind. Make it as blank as possible. You will feel me enter— but do not resist, for that will simply seal me off. Let it happen. Understand?"

"I can do it. Let's hurry, though. I'm afraid we're already too late."

"That is up to the gods," the adept responded fatalistically. "Let us do what we can."

One of the archers was badly wounded but still alive. Joe checked all the soldiers' bodies out, finding little or nothing on them, and then went to the archer on whom his horse had fallen. The horse itself was in bad shape, he could see, and would probably have to be destroyed. Posti, at least, had come through with nothing more than a bruise.

Like the others, the injured soldier was dressed in a silver-trimmed black uniform of some kind, chain mail, and a partial helmet, and was ruddy-faced and bearded. The man writhed and groaned in agony, but stopped when Joe approached and just stared with eyes blazing hatred at the man who'd done him in.

"How many did the Baron send to the cave with you?" Joe asked coldly.

"Barbarian!" the soldier gasped defiantly. "I die, but I tell you nothing!"

"You die slowly, friend," Joe noted and looked up, then back at him. "Already the buzzards and other scavengers are gathering. You could last a long time here—picked alive by beak and claw. It's a pretty unpleasant way to go."

"Do what you will," the man responded.

"I'll pull you out from that horse and give you swift release," Joe offered. "Swift release and burial from those that eat the dead. I'm not asking for a betrayal. Only the answer to a couple of questions."

The man seemed to think it over, and Joe knew he'd hit a nerve. "What does it matter, anyway?" the soldier asked mostly himself. "What questions?"

"How many in the Baron's party?"

"Thirty-six of his best fighters."

Joe felt uncomfortable. If that was the truth, there were still thirty like this man ahead.

"How far ahead are they?"

"More than half a day," the soldier told him. "They left at dawn."

That, too, was disturbing—but if it was only a few miles to the cave, why hadn't they returned by now? Joe wasn't sure whether he should feel better or worse that they hadn't returned. The fact that they hadn't meant they'd walked into some big trouble—and they were thirty seasoned army men. As of now, he had Marge, himself, and Houma in any shape to go on.

"One more question. They went up the main road here?"

The dying soldier nodded. "Yes. There really is no other way."

That was enough. He looked down at the man and drew his sword. "Too bad you're with the bad guys," he said softly, "but you're a good soldier, a gallant fighter, and you die with honor."

The man looked genuinely pleased and touched by that. "Hold, barbarian, one moment. That sword is a magic one that will slay me. Which great name does it bear?"

"Irving," Joe replied.

The man looked aghast. "Irving?" he repeated unbelievingly.

Irving came down and severed his head from his body at that moment. Then Joe tried to get the body out from under the horse, and almost made it, when he suddenly felt dizzy and collapsed over the horse's torso.

CHAPTER 14

THE GENIE WITH THE LIGHT BROWN HARE

All magic lamps, charms, etc., shall be guarded well.
                                              —LXXX, 494, 361(b)

HE WAS ROLLING DOWN INTERSTATE 80, A BUXOM BLONDE AT HIS side, a beer in his hand, and Merle Haggard on the tape deck as the miles flashed by. It was a wonderful, satisfying life, and it was good to be alive . . .

"He's coming 'round!" a voice called out from somewhere, somewhere far from I-80 and the blonde and the beer.

"Clean towel!" another voice ordered, wrenching him farther and farther away. Something was wrong, really wrong, and even Merle Haggard was singing English madrigals in a foreign tongue . . .

He opened his eyes and looked around. It took a minute or so for him to remember where he was, and who these people were, and the details of the day. He could see that it was dark now, and there was a small fire in the wooded glade. He saw Marge come to him with a towel soaked in hot water, bend down, and wipe his face.

"Wh—what happened!" he managed, his voice sounding like a croak.

"You had an arrow in you. Went almost through you, too. You're very lucky, Joe. Dacaro says a one-inch difference and you'd be dead now. As it is, the wound's already healing, although you might feel it for a few days yet."

"Macore? Grogha?"

"Much worse off, I'm afraid. Macore will recover, but he'll need a couple of days before he's up to riding. Grogha, however—he was real bad, Joe. His back is broken. I've given him a potion that's knocked him out, but even the magic's no good unless you know exactly what to do. Dacaro's a good sorcerer, but he's no healer. He was able to repair your hole pretty well and fix up Macore's leg and ribs, but Grogha lost a lot of blood, mostly internal, and he's too cracked up for anybody but a specialist. The nearest specialist would be in Kidim. I doubt if he could stand the ride."

Joe whistled, coming out of it now. "I don't know. Until today it still was something like fun and games. That bartender, it didn't seem real somehow, and none of the rest made much difference. No matter what *we* did, no matter what scrape we got into, we always got out of it. Now this." He suddenly grew tense. "The rest of the Baron's men—any sign?"

She shook her head from side to side. "We've been watching. Nothing. Not a sign."

He sighed. "Well, keep a watch. But, somehow, I don't think we have to worry about them. Just a feeling. Still—we'll know soon enough." He pulled off the moist towel and brought himself to a sitting position. It hurt like hell in his side when he did, but it was bearable. "I'll be okay. Just whip me up something to dull the pain a bit, give me the night, and I'll be ready to ride tomorrow."

"Tomorrow! How can we possibly go tomorrow?"

"We have to," he told her. "For one thing, either those nasties *are* going to come back, in which case we're dead if we stay, or they aren't—in which case the reason why they aren't is going to come sometime to see who else might be in the neighborhood. We're too close to stay put. Besides—we got a wishing lamp to get, huh? Maybe one of those wishes can be used on Grogha."

She thought about it. "Yeah! You're right! It may be the only way. But if thirty hardened soldiers couldn't do it . . ."

"We have no choice. And we have to know what's going on in advance." He looked up. "That's almost a full moon up there. Where's Houma?"

"By Grogha."

"Get him."

She did as instructed, and soon the lanky farmer and former goat was by Joe's side. It was clear he'd been crying some, and Joe didn't hold it against him at all.

"Houma, I'm sorry I got you both into this mess," he said sincerely.

"Oh, hell, you didn't exactly torture us," the other replied.

"We did our share today, didn't we?" There was a certain pride in his sad tone.

"You sure did. But you know we're going to lose Grogha unless we get the Lamp."

Houma brightened. "Sure! The Lamp! I damn near forgot! Then there's a chance!"

"A slim one," Joe said. "Look, not too far ahead, the road reaches Starmount Plateau. It's a clear, moon-bright night, so it should give a good view of where we're going. If these Xota are fliers, and if the Baron's men were trapped by them in daylight, chances are they're day folk themselves and will be licking their own wounds tonight."

"I getcha," Houma said. "You want me to go up and find out what we're up against."

Joe nodded. "This wound's pretty painful, but I think I can live with it. I'd rather get a night's sleep, but if things look good, I'm all for trying it tonight."

"Are you out of your mind?" Marge practically screamed at him. "You're too banged up!"

But Houma was game. "I'll take Posti. That way, if anything happens to me, he might be able to get back with the word."

"Good. But don't take any chances—and get back as soon as you know anything."

With that, Houma was off. Marge sat down beside Joe and shook her head in wonder. "I don't know what I'm going to do with you. You're crazy."

He chuckled. "Well, you were the one who wanted adventure, right? I'm going to keep going with my impulses. They've been pretty good so far."

Marge looked over at the two motionless forms across the fire. "Yeah. Real good."

"We're all still alive. That's more than anybody would have figured at this point. This close to our goal, I don't want to lose now." He sighed. "It's not a simple world any more, though."

She looked at him strangely. "Yeah. You and those close to you can die here."

"No, not even that. That soldier I talked to. He wasn't some nasty, evil, menacing Baron or supernatural wart on the world. He wasn't evil at all, I don't think. Just an honorable man doing the job he was best at. That makes it a lot tougher, really.

It's easy to fight and hate your enemies when you think of them as some kind of supernatural monsters. I dunno. I just figured the kind of folks that would ride with the Baron would be more like, well, Nazis or something, at least. Now I find out they're the same kind of folks we are."

Marge sighed and leaned back for a moment. "Yeah, I think I know what you mean. This *should* be a kind of romantic world—you know, knights, dragons, that sort of thing. But it's a real place, not some fairy tale. It's a place where most of the people are owned by feudal lords, where the garbage is still tossed out the back window, and the same kind of people still die for the wrong causes. Even the supernatural side isn't all that glamorous, with these silly Rules and hung-up dragons seeing psychiatrists. I wonder if maybe it's the price we pay when and if our fantasies ever do become real?"

"These aren't *my* fantasies," he grumbled.

She smiled. "Are you sorry you came?"

He thought about it. "I'm not sure. Even now I'm not sure. Ask me when this heals and this stuff is over and done with." He paused a moment. "Where's your friend the unicorn, by the way?"

"Gone. I don't know where. I'm not even sure just *what* he is. Until recently, I thought of unicorns as just, well, pretty animals. Now I'm not sure what they are. I'm not even sure if whatever they are is good, frankly, or whether that's a proper question. You see, there's a price I must pay for that. It was much too busy here for me to pay it now, but Koriku will remember the bill and collect. Oh, don't look so upset. It's not that bad—but I'm not sure what it is, either. Don't worry about it for now." She sighed. "I want to look at Macore and Grogha. Then we all better get some rest—you in particular."

She left him there to ponder all that had been said, and he managed to drift off to sleep without the aid of Marge's potions.

He was awakened gently about four hours later, in the dead of night, by Houma. He was so glad to see the lanky man that he didn't even grumble at being awakened.

"I got almost to the cave itself," Houma told Joe. "Had to make the last part on foot, though, to keep close to the rocks. Posti would have stuck out."

"Any sign of the Baron's forces?"

Houma nodded grimly. "They're all over the place. It was pretty ugly, Joe. Their bodies, and the bodies of their horses, were spread out all over the flat about four miles up. Most of 'em were badly torn up, and a lot of the bodies of both the men and the horses looked—*gnawed*, if you can believe it." He shuddered. "It was the worst thing I've ever seen."

Joe sighed. "Did you count the bodies?"

The farmer nodded. "I think it's all thirty. Couldn't be positive, since I didn't really want to go out there too far, and there were some—things—working on a couple of the corpses."

"Xota?"

"Naw. Don't think so. Looked like animals. I didn't see any signs of them Xota people."

Joe struggled to his feet. "That settles it, then." He got up, staggered a bit, then winced and stretched. "I'll do." He looked at the two sleeping forms. "Marge—you stay with them. Houma and I are going to take a little trip."

She looked stubbornly at them. "Oh, no! Even if you manage somehow to get by and in that cave, which I doubt, don't forget there's some kind of monster in there. You need me, Joe. Dacaro gave me a number of spells that may or may not do any good, but I know enough to know that you shouldn't go in there without me."

"But somebody's got to stay here with them," Joe pointed out.

She nodded. "Houma will stay. He's done enough tonight."

Houma's expression was a cross between protest and relief. Still, he said, "I can give a good fight."

"No, she's right," Joe told him. "This is as far as the Company can go for now, and you might have to protect them and this camp. Marge and I will go. If we're not back by tomorrow evening, though, don't come after us. Do what you can for those two and get back. Ruddygore must know what happened to both expeditions."

Houma sighed. "I guess you're right. If you ain't back by this time tomorrow, poor Grogha will be dead, anyway, and I guess me on Posti and Macore on Dacaro—tied down if need be—could make it on the low road." He paused, then suddenly leaned over, kissed Marge, and gripped Joe's hand hard. "You two be careful. I already lost Grogha, I figure. I don't want to lose you, too."

"Neither do I, my friend," Joe answered sincerely, then looked around. "Where's Irving?"

The road went up through the pass, then down onto what appeared to be a wide plain. They knew that this was Starmount, the great plateau at twenty-eight hundred feet that stretched for almost seventeen miles westward into the interior of High Pothique. It was aptly named, with a full view of the sky and a great moon now far lower than it had been earlier in the night, but still bright enough to see by. The cave was supposed to be against the mountains to the right of the road, and they turned their horses northwest to hug the rocky side of Starmount.

In a short while they came upon the scene of an earlier battle. It was much as Houma had said, but they did not try to get close to see the grisly details. There were dark, four-footed animal shapes out there, and some snarling could be heard. Best to leave them alone, they decided.

And then, at last, they came upon the point where the mountain wall became smooth and sheer. They dismounted and looked across the way—a clear stretch of perhaps a quarter mile, with no cover whatsoever, to a dark spot at the base of the mountain wall.

"Right where it should be," he muttered, and she nodded. "That moon's getting awful low. Shall we ride or leave the horses here?"

"I think leave them," she told him. "I feel more confident on that open flat on foot—and without cover, there's no point to taking the horses, anyway."

"Speed," he pointed out.

"Yeah—and noise. They'll attract whoever killed those soldiers. And we'll have to tether them right outside the cave. We couldn't advertise better."

"You convinced me," He sighed, thinking of his aching side.

She thought of it, too, and handed him a gourd off her belt. "Here. Drink this. It will deaden the pain a little and give you some extra energy."

He took it gratefully, sipped it, almost spat it out, and said, "Yuck! This is as foul as sewage water!"

"Most of 'em taste awful, but they work. Drink it down."

He held his nose and finally managed it, making a terrible face afterward. But he had to admit that within two or three minutes he felt far better, with less pain and less tiredness. They gave a light tether to the horses, hoping it would keep them there but allowing them to pull free and run if spooked. There was nothing else they could do.

"Let's go—slowly and carefully—while we still have some moon," he said, and they were off.

There was an eerie stillness about the whole place, one that was more than a little unnerving, and they moved toward the cave, weapons drawn, looking in all directions, expecting something or someone to rise against them at any moment. But nothing did, and after a suspense-filled fifteen minutes, they were at the mouth of the cave itself.

Now that they were there, facing it, they could see that there was light inside. Torches flickered, not right near the entrance, but farther in, giving enough light for them to see but not to betray the cave to any distant onlooker.

"Looks as if we were expected," Marge whispered.

"Or our monster is scared of the dark," Joe replied. "Well, it's now or never."

She nodded. "I just wish somebody knew what this monster was."

They entered, Joe first, and kept cautiously to the walls of the cave. It was a narrow and winding entrance, but shortly it opened up, until they were on the edge of a huge chamber, perhaps half a mile across and almost that wide. It was here the torches were set against a far wall. There was a huge altar, and before it were stacked an enormous number of bodies of black, winged creatures. They stared at the scene, and Marge absently counted.

"There are more than fifty bodies there," she whispered to Joe. "No wonder the Xota are off licking their wounds somewhere. Those soldiers made them pay for the attack."

He nodded, looking at the altar itself. "That carved altar there. See the larger shape carved around it? Remind you of anything?"

She stared, then frowned. "A rabbit?"

"Yeah. A rabbit god. I'll be damned. Never heard of *that* one before."

At that moment they heard a fierce, screaming noise, like

a beast in a terrible rage. There was no way to tell where it came from—the echoes in the cavern masked any source. Both of them tensed at the sound. "The monster," Marge breathed.

Joe looked around what he could see of the cave. "Say! Look—out there in the middle! Those are two of the soldiers' bodies! Some *did* get this far!"

Marge stared at the two forms. "They look squashed flat."

"Yeah . . . squashed." He looked around once more. "Where would you say they'd keep the Lamp?"

She shrugged. "The altar's the only place I can see that looks used."

He nodded. "And that's where the two soldiers lie—between here and the altar. But what kind of monster could do that? It looks as if they were swatted with a giant flyswatter."

Marge thought a minute. "Listen! You hear heavy breathing?"

"My heart's too loud," he responded. But now that she mentioned it, he *did* hear it. It sounded as if the whole cavern were breathing. "Still can't put a handle on where it is. But anything that big—we ought to be able to *see* it."

She sighed. "Maybe it's invisible. Well, I guess it's time to use one of those spells. I want to see what we're up against before going out there."

"What are you gonna do?"

"Dacaro figured we might be able to confuse a monster. If this spell works as advertised, you and I are going to walk across that cave in a couple of minutes—while we're both here."

"Huh?"

"Just shut up and watch." She turned to the cave, put her hands to her temples, and concentrated on the spell Dacaro had made her memorize. It had been easy to get a number of such spells while he'd been inside her head, and she had taken full advantage of the opportunity. The only trouble was, of course, that neither she nor Dacaro knew what spells would come in handy in an unknown situation—they had to guess.

The air shimmered in front of her, and slowly the images of two people faded in before them. As the images grew clearer, Joe could see that they were taking on the shapes of him and Marge.

In another minute the visions had solidified to the point

where he could almost swear he was looking at himself and Marge. The illusion was, in fact, uncannily real. She sighed, looked up at them, and said, "Walk to the altar."

The two simulacra turned stiffly and started walking out onto the cavern floor toward the two squashed soldiers. Marge kept looking directly at them, which Joe understood was necessary to preserve the illusion, but he was under no such compulsion. He started looking around for the monster once more, hoping that it could be fooled by this trick.

Suddenly there was a roaring sound, the same as they'd heard before, followed by a sharp and sustained odd sound that reminded Joe of nothing more than a giant's fart. And down on the two replicas fell the great monster of the cave from its hiding place above.

"My god! It's a giant bunny rabbit!" Joe said, amazed.

"It's the biggest damn Texas hare I've ever seen," she admitted. The thing was *enormous*—twenty feet high, not counting the ears, and terribly muscular, the Mr. Hyde of hares. Its face, too, was not the passive hare's face, but an ugly, contorted version; its large, yellow eyes were burning with fierce hatred, and its two great buckteeth were flanked by saber-toothed fangs.

Its giant legs struck the two replicas full, then did a dance on top of them. Had they been real, it would have flattened them for sure.

Marge wasted no more time keeping up the illusion, but couldn't help staring at the rabbit, then up. "There are no ledges up there for something that size," she noted. "Where did it come from?"

The great hare god roared its conquest, then quieted and glanced around. They ducked back for a moment into the cave mouth and were certain they hadn't been seen. Joe peered out again, just as the hare roared and screeched once more, looked at the altar, roared at it, then did something that neither Joe nor Marge expected.

Its great mouth opened, and it inhaled—and kept inhaling. As it did, its great brown body seemed to fill up and stretch like a balloon, until it was as big around as it was tall. And with that, the enormous hare floated up the sixty feet or more to the roof of the cave, becoming almost invisible in the darkness, its brown hair blending with the weathered limestone.

"So *that's* it," Joe breathed. "This is crazy. How can it float up there like a helium balloon on just plain old air?"

"Because it's not a normal monster," she responded. "It's some sort of magical creature, a demon, perhaps, in the form of a hare. I was taught that true demons have no form. Their form is made for them by the ones who bring them into the world, and can be almost anything. Somebody, long ago, decided that the Xota people needed a god. Who knows? Perhaps one of their most powerful magicians once tried to control a demon, or accidentally let one in, and it took on the form of the common hares that might be all over these parts. If it were trapped here, this might be the result."

"That's all well and good, but how do we get this gasball demon out of the way? Got any spells for that?"

She thought a moment, then looked up at the cave ceiling. "I can see where it is now that I know what I'm looking for. Hmmm . . . Well, disguising ourselves as Xota is out. I don't know how to do that one." She unhooked her crossbow from her belt and loaded a bolt. "But I think I can shoot it."

He whistled. "Man! If you miss—or if you only wound the thing—it will go nuts."

She nodded. "Don't I know it. But that's a chance we have to take. I'm pretty sure it's too big to get at us in here."

"Yeah—but it's loud enough maybe to bring the neighbors at our backs," he responded nervously. "Still, I don't have any better idea." He stopped a moment, thinking furiously. "Or do I?"

She turned to him. "Got something?"

"I doubt if an ordinary bolt would do it," he told her. "But if we could shoot Irving . . ."

She looked at him thoughtfully. "Yes. I think I *could* jury-rig it so that we could shoot the sword. But it would be terribly unbalanced, and so heavy it might not make the distance."

"I can always call it back to me," he assured her, then caught her frown. "What's wrong?"

"Joe—I can't touch that sword. You know that."

"That's all right. I've had training with the crossbow. Have I ever! Hand it to me—hey! Uncock it first! Yeah. There. Now—stand back."

He drew the sword and tried loading it in the simple crossbow. He failed several times, and Marge felt frustrated that she dared not reach out and show him how to adjust it; but finally, with her coaching, he managed to load it and cock it. Still, it looked ridiculous and unwieldy. "I don't think it's going to work," Marge said worriedly. "The bow just wasn't designed for this."

"All it has to do is give Irv a boost," Joe assured her confidently. "This sword has a mind of its own. It won't fail." *I hope*, he added mentally. "Irving, speed true to your target and puncture it."

The sword seemed to glow slightly and hummed in response. Joe took a deep breath. "Well, here goes."

He stepped out into the cavern, looked up, spotted the quivering ball above, and took aim. "Hey! Gasball! Come and get it!" he yelled.

The hare god roared and started its drop. At that moment Joe lifted the bow and shot the sword right at the descending mass. The sword flew from the crossbow and, as Joe had said, seemed to take on a life of its own, flying straight and true. It was helped by the fact that the hare god was descending toward it, and the sword struck and penetrated the flesh of the horrible creature.

There was a loud bang, like a cannon shot, that almost broke their eardrums, and they yelled in pain. Joe was sure he was deaf. All around the cavern, however, bits and chunks of flesh fell in a grisly rain.

Ears still numb and ringing, Joe stepped into the cavern again, shouted, "Irving! To me!" and held out his hand.

From somewhere far across the cavern, the great sword hummed and flew like iron to magnet right into his hand.

Their sense of hearing returned slowly. "It burst like a balloon!" Marge laughed.

He nodded and grinned. "Yeah. That's all it really was. A big bag of air. Come on. That noise is bound to bring somebody curious. Let's get to the altar." They made it on the run.

The bodies of the gargoylelike Xota were grisly even without their gaping wounds and injuries, and they smelled as all decomposing flesh did, but Marge and Joe went around the large bier of dead to the stone hare itself, carved into the solid rock. Behind the bier were a lot of things, many of which looked quite valuable, but it was on the stone hare's "lap" that they saw what had to be what they sought.

"It looks just like Aladdin's Lamp in the old fairy tales," Marge noted. She bent over and picked it up. "I wonder if it currently has a genie? And, if so, how you get him—or her?"

"Rub it—right?" Joe suggested, remembering the stories.

"Yeah. Here. Let's see." She rubbed the Lamp—and, almost immediately, from the spout flowed an ethereal shape that took form as a young man dressed in odd, baggy clothes. He looked around and smiled.

"Well, I'll be damned! Somebody finally got it!" he exclaimed.

"You're the slave of the Lamp?" Marge asked. "This is the Lamp of Lakash?"

"Yes and yes," the man responded.

"And who are you?"

"I am Sugasto," he told her. "If that means anything to you after so long a time."

"Sugasto! Ruddygore's adept!" Marge cried. "So you *didn't* die!"

He sighed. "Hardly. I made a very stupid wish on it for power and wealth—and wound up having to travel to High Pothique to claim both. I got cornered by the Xota. They killed my horse, my companions, and their horses as well—it was pretty absolute—and they had me totally trapped. There was only one thing I could do, and that was to use the Lamp again. I wished that I would be safe from harm from the Xota—and got my wish, as you see. As the slave of the Lamp, I can not be harmed, because I'm basically a spirit, not solid at all. I just look that way. The second wish made me the genie, freeing a most unpleasant old woman who was immediately torn apart by the Xota. Of course, since they saw the old bag emerge from the Lamp and me flow into it, they knew it was magic— and so they brought it to their all-too-real god. I've been stuck in this damned hole ever since."

Marge thought a moment. "You've got to do whatever the possessor says, right?"

He nodded. "That's about it. Not much I *can* do, though, being a spirit."

"And I'm the possessor?"

"As of now. I can not tell a lie or fail to answer a question— to you."

She hooked the Lamp on her belt. "Well, come on, then. We have to get out of here—and fast."

"I go where the Lamp goes," Sugasto noted. "I have no choice."

They made their way across the cavern floor once more and around the narrow, winding entrance until they reached the cave mouth.

"Uh-oh. It's gotten to be daylight," Joe muttered. "That's bad. Even if the Xota didn't hear all that commotion, they're probably back now."

Marge turned to Sugasto. "How about it? Can you reconnoiter for us?"

"I can."

"Okay, do it. That's not a wish, now. Just an order."

"That's the way you play the game," he agreed and sped from the cave mouth out into the early morning. It didn't take him long to return.

"Well?" Marge demanded.

"You've got troubles," He sighed. "Half the Xota nation's out there right now. There are forty or fifty directly above the cave, ready to pounce on whoever comes out, and maybe six or seven hundred staked out along the two miles from here to the road."

She thought a moment. "We couldn't wish both of us back to our camp, could we?"

"You could," the genie replied, "if your camp's not more than forty or fifty miles from here. I can check. It would have to be within my range from the Lamp."

"It's at the trail junction outside the Gate," she told him. "Go."

In a flash he was off once more, and back within twenty or thirty seconds. "Yes, you can transport out. But as much as I would like you to overwish and free me, I don't want to suffer the fate of my predecessor—particularly not now that I'm out. You've got a small army of black and silver uniforms not ten miles farther on. Maybe a hundred pretty tough-looking soldiers. If you transport out, you'll be a sandwich between the Xota and the soldiers—who, I assume, are not your friends, considering the dead bodies around here."

"You're right about that," Joe agreed. "We'll fill you in on the political news later, though. Hmmm . . . What about sorcery? Anything we can do to trick those people conventionally? You were supposed to be an adept of some kind."

"I was pretty good," Sugasto huffed with pride. "But I'm way out of practice, and in this form I can't do anything, anyway."

"I can carry out your spells," Marge told him.

He looked surprised. "Can you, indeed?" He thought a moment. "Still and all, this isn't exactly a situation I can spell us out of. If I could, I wouldn't *be* here in the first place."

He had a point there. "That means the Lamp or nothing," Marge said, thinking furiously. "But I'll have to get the wish exactly right."

"And fast," Joe noted. "They won't wait all day without coming in to see if we got smashed by their god." He had to chuckle. "Wonder what they're gonna do for a religion when they find we popped him?"

"Quiet! I'm trying to think!" she snapped. She looked back up at the genie. "I don't suppose they left us our horses."

"Breakfast, I think," Sugasto replied ruefully. "Sorry."

She sighed. "Well, so much for that. Hmmm . . . Wait a minute. How compound can this wish be?"

"Not too much," Sugasto told her. "One magical event, that's it. You can't wish yourself invincible, immortal, and rich all at the same time."

"All right. But could I wish for a *single* solution to the problem of *both* armed forces?"

Sugasto thought that one over. "Maybe. Depends on how you put it."

"I think I've got it. If not—Joe, it will be your turn."

"Go ahead," he invited. "I'm a little uncomfortable around that thing."

She held the Lamp tightly in both hands. "I wish that our entire Company would be rescued from all our enemies this day by a powerful force friendly to us."

"Done!" Sugasto shouted.

Outside, there was a sudden, tremendous roaring sound.

CHAPTER 15

FROM THE JAWS OF VICTORY

Companies must break up before an objective can be truly secured.
—XXXIV, 319, 251(b)

JOE HAD NO PARTICULAR TRUST IN WISHING LAMPS, BUT HE had to see what was going on out there regardless. Sword held at the ready, he approached the cave mouth from where he could see the plains of Starmount clearly. Marge came close behind him.

Just then a huge, dark shadow flew over the cave, and they heard another mighty roar and felt the heat of great flames not far away. Joe jumped back a bit. "Jeez! Did we get the Marines with napalm?" he wondered.

"No! We got Vercertorix!" Marge replied, pointing. Joe crept again to the cave mouth as a number of flaming bodies fell from atop the cave to the area just in front of them. Off in the distance, they saw the great form of the enormous dragon, wings spread, looking both noble and magnificent as it made pass after pass at the cave walls, occasionally bumping rock and starting landslides, but more often barbecueing the Xota with tremendous blasts of flame from its great mouth.

Some of the Xota, who were flying creatures themselves, took to the air and managed to get into a reasonable attack formation after the dragon had passed. Bows and spears at the ready, the Xota, perhaps fifty or sixty of them, waited almost suspended in midair for the great beast to turn once more and come swooping back in. The flying force could hardly hide themselves from the dragon, but they stood their ground and waited until they could almost feel the dragon's breath before letting loose their weapons.

"The little bastards have guts, I'll give 'em that," Joe muttered, fascinated. "It's like pygmies against an armored tank."

For a moment it almost seemed as if Vercertorix were going to fly directly into the formation, but at the last minute he pulled up and beat several times with his massive wings. The Xota tried to get off their arrows and throw their spears, but the downdraft the dragon caused was so tremendous that their formation was suddenly broken, sending them tumbling. Vercertorix, who'd expected that and planned it, did a magnificent loop-the-loop in the air and came back again on the same tack, now letting loose his flaming breath at the broken Xota formation. It was no contest, and more small bodies fell burning from the sky.

"How can something that huge fly that gracefully?" Marge asked, awestruck.

Joe was more pragmatic. "I couldn't care less—just so long as the Xota don't have a fair maiden to drag in front of him."

The dragon made one more sweep of the terrain, scattering the last of the Xota and making sure that no major force remained, then came in for a pinpoint landing near the cave.

"Hey! My friends! Aré you still alive in there?" they heard a familiar voice call to them. "If so, come out by all means!"

Even Sugasto was impressed. "There's somebody *riding* that thing!"

"Algongua!" Marge cried. "It's the Doc, Joe!" She was ready to run to him, but Joe put out a hand and restrained her.

"Hey, Doc!" he called. "Won't Marge cause—problems?"

"I think not!" the hairy man called back. "Come and see!"

That was all they needed, and out they came. The dragon glanced over at them as they emerged, and looked a little dubiously at the woman but did not flee or yell.

"It worked! It worked!" Algongua exulted.

They came up beside the dragon and regarded the hairy man on its back. "*What* worked, Doc?" Joe asked.

"Therapy! We owe it all to you two, really. After six weeks of my treating him, it took only one look at the lovely lady here to cause a complete relapse. I was angry at the time, remember, but the more I thought about it, the more I was sure I'd been on the wrong track. You see, his fear stemmed from an encounter a few months ago with a powerful sorceress— young and beautiful-looking, too. She caused him some great pain, and that set up his problem. It really wasn't a fear of fair maidens at all—that was just a symptom. It was a loss of self-confidence! So, I reasoned, if I went with him and we eased into a battle, with me shouting encouragement and sharing the risk, it might restore him. And see? It worked!"

"Snarfle," the dragon agreed, nodding.

Marge frowned. "But now I *am* confused. Did my wish cause this to happen—or would it have happened, anyway, in which case I wasted it?"

"The Lamp is like that," Sugasto told her. "It's always a little perverse if it gets the chance. My guess is that reality was subtly altered with minimum—perhaps no—damage by your wish, which made this rescue possible, even inevitable. But we'll never really know."

Joe was more concerned with the reality of the dragon and the hairy scientist. "I thought you were the hermit, beyond battles and such."

Doc shrugged. "Maybe that's been my problem. I can divorce *myself* from the miserable world, but I can't divorce my patients and studies from it. Oh, well, it was fun, anyway."

"Marumph!" Vercertorix agreed.

Marge snapped her fingers. "I'd almost forgotten! This is only half the battle. A company of the Dark Baron's soldiers is almost to our camp now. Poor Houma's there with two very injured men!" She looked up at Algongua. "Can you stop them, too?"

The scientist thought a moment. "How about it, Vercertorix? Want to try some soldiers? The ones we saw on the way in?"

"Grausch!" the dragon responded, nodding slightly.

"All right. Why don't you three hop on—I think you can hang on here—and we'll drop you at your camp. Then we'll take care of those soldiers."

Marge turned to Sugasto. "Why not get back in the Lamp until we reach the camp?"

"Whatever you say," he responded, sounding a little regretful—and flowed back into the Lamp on her belt.

Algongua was fascinated. "A real genie! How *about* that! So that's what the old boy sent you for!"

"We'll talk later," Joe told him. "Give you the whole story. Let's get those soldiers first."

They linked up, Marge grabbing Algongua and Joe grabbing

Marge. It was pretty nerve-racking when the dragon began to move and spread its massive wings, and even worse when the great head suddenly came up and they lifted, but in a matter of no more than two minutes they were level and headed at great speed toward Starmount Gateway.

In another minute, no more, the dragon reached the Gateway, circled once, and landed just down the trail from the junction camp. Joe and Marge wasted no time jumping off and getting away from the great beast, and Doc waited only long enough to assure Vercertorix clearance before taking off once again. Joe and Marge had to brace themselves to keep from being blown over by the backwash, but the dragon was soon up and out of sight.

They were less than half a mile from the camp and reached it quickly. Houma was both astonished and overjoyed to see them, and they were pleasantly surprised to find Macore sitting on a rock, smiling and waving to them.

"It will take more than a cracked skull to get me," the little thief told them. "Now if it had been any place other than my *head*..."

Marge was bubbling over to tell Houma and Macore about their adventures and reassure them about the dragon, and she was halfway through before she suddenly stopped and said, alarmed, "How's Grogha?"

Both the others' faces fell. "He's gone, lady," Houma said sadly.

"It was all for the best. He was in such great pain..."

She got up and walked over to the other side of the camp, where Grogha's body had been carefully wrapped in his bedroll, and looked down at it. Tears welled up in her big eyes, not only for Grogha but also for her failure to remember him right from the start. Most of all, she was frustrated by the fact that she had the Lamp, but too late, too late...

"Damn!" she swore aloud. "I wish we'd been in time to save him!"

Suddenly she heard Sugasto cry exuberantly, "I'm free!" Then things happened too fast and too confusedly to be sorted out properly.

There was a blurring, a dizziness that overtook not only Marge but each of them, and then they were all there again, in the same places—but Grogha was no longer dead and wrapped, but lying there pretty much as they had left him, moaning and groaning in pain.

The Lamp fell from Marge's belt as if the loop had broken. She bent down, still confused, to pick it up and found that her hand went right through it. "What's happening?" she cried, in something of a panic.

A very solid Sugasto stood near her. "You made a second wish and it was granted," he told her. "Now you've paid the price for it. *You* are the slave of the Lamp."

Joe was over checking the supplies and, except for the slight dizziness, which he put down to lack of sleep, didn't seem aware that anything was wrong. Houma and Macore, however, *had* seen it and, while confused, went over to her and to the stranger now suddenly in their midst.

Sugasto pointed to the Lamp. "If you want to save your friend, pick up that Lamp, one of you, and wish him whole and healthy once more. I'd do it quickly—he won't last long, And since I can't use it or touch it ever again, it's only fitting that the lady's sacrifice not be in vain."

There was a greedy gleam in Macore's eyes as he realized what the Lamp was, but it was Houma who picked it up first, held it, turned to Grogha, and said, rubbing the Lamp, "I wish Grogha was whole and well, healed of all ailments and afflictions."

The bloody, broken body of Grogha shimmered, then solidified, and all traces of the illness, loss of blood, wounds, and lacerations were gone. He opened his eyes, looked confused, saw them all, shook his head, and said, "I—I had the most *horrible* dream . . ."

Houma was so pleased and excited that he dropped the Lamp and rushed to embrace Grogha, tears of joy in his eyes.

Seeing his opening, Macore grabbed up the Lamp, smiled, then turned to Marge. "Inside the Lamp until I call you out!" he commanded.

Suddenly she felt a tremendous force drawing her, like a vacuum cleaner, into the Lamp's mouth. It was a strange, eerie sensation, and the limbo in which she found herself was neither dark nor light, but an odd, formless land that went on and on. She could hear no sounds at all. No—wait. There *was* something. A voice. Macore's. He was talking to somebody—but she could not hear any response, none at all. She was attuned to his voice and his voice only. But something *was* happening to her . . .

Forms, concepts, and a great deal of information poured into her mind from out of nowhere, almost as if they had been there all along, but unknown and untapped until now. She knew everything there was to know about the Lamp of Lakash, its powers and limitations, and her own nature, bonds, and powers. She also suddenly knew the plane of existence she was now on and understood that it was not empty at all . . .

Macore stared suspiciously at Sugasto. "You were the genie?"

"But no more," The Adept replied. "Nevermore. After a thousand years!" He sighed. "It's good to be alive once more, particularly with the new knowledge I've gained from the Lamp."

Macore looked crafty and thoughtful. "She was telling us before that wish that you were the guy who stole it in the first place. That true?"

Sugasto shrugged and bowed.

"You're some kind of adept, right?"

"Something like that," Sugasto agreed.

"Well, we're workin' for the guy you took it from. If you don't fancy meetin' up with him again, you better use what powers you got to get that guy Joe and these two off your back."

The Adept thought about it. "And off yours?"

Macore grinned. At that moment Joe finished checking the supplies and walked back to them, looking confused. He didn't think Sugasto's appearance was unusual, since he didn't think of him as flesh and blood, but he glanced around. "Where's Marge?"

Sugasto smiled and made a few signs in the air in Joe's direction. Joe suddenly froze, then looked even more confused. "I forgot my train of thought! Damn!"

"You asked about Marge," Sugasto reminded him.

The big man frowned. "Marge? Who's that?"

"Nobody important," the adept responded smoothly, then turned and made the identical gestures in the direction of Houma and Grogha, who hardly noticed. "Why don't you see about Grogha?"

Joe nodded. "Yeah. Good idea." He walked over and bent down beside Grogha.

Macore looked impressed. "That's some trick."

"A simple one. It won't last long, you know. When the dragon returns, Vercertorix and Algongua will know, and it would take a lot more work to make them forget. The dragon is only here because of her—and so their return will precipitate a return of memory."

"But that could be any minute!" Macore protested. "Some trick!"

"There are other tricks," Sugasto bragged.

"Yes, there are," Macore agreed, touching the Lamp. He suddenly became stiff and glassy-eyed. "I wish Sugasto and Dacaro would exchange bodies, curses, and *geases*, and that Sugasto would then be subject to and obedient to Dacaro in all matters."

Nothing seemed to happen at all, but Sugasto's look of astonishment suddenly changed into a broad grin. He flexed his arms for a moment, then reached out and took the Lamp from the still-stiffened Macore. "Thank you, Macore," he said, his voice and inflection subtly altered. "I knew I could count on your greed to get this Lamp sooner or later."

He turned to the three men now excitedly talking to one another, oblivious of the little drama that had just taken place, bowed his head, and concentrated for a moment. Grogha, who was just getting to his feet, slumped down again, and Joe and Houma fell into a heap on top of him, unconscious. The adept then turned back to Macore, pointed to the ground, and snapped his fingers, and Macore, too, collapsed.

Feeling satisfied, he walked over to the two remaining horses, the gray spotted Posti and the black stallion that was Dacaro, but who now looked at him with frightened and puzzled eyes. He carefully saddled Dacaro, then placed the Lamp in the saddlebag, got up on the horse, and turned to Posti, who stared back at him.

"Don't look so shocked, Posti, old friend. You can explain it all to them when they come to, which won't be very long from now. But tell them not to look for me. Warn them. I wish none of them harm, for they are good people, but I will do whatever I have to to protect myself—and I am now *very* powerful."

"Who are you?" the gray horse challenged. "And who's now inside Dacaro?"

The man sighed. "You never *were* too bright, were you? While in the mind of Marge to heal Macore, I was able to cast spells—and I cast one on Macore, certain that the opportunistic little thief wouldn't rest until he'd gotten his hands on the Lamp. I triggered it, and dictated his wish, from my own mind. I'm your old friend Dacaro, Posti, and I have no intention of letting that bastard Ruddygore keep me a horse." With that he reined around, then urged the horse forward, riding off on the upper trail.

Posti was still confused, and tried to sort it out in his mind. For a moment he considered chase, but realized that, alone, the way he was, he had little chance of it. He remembered that upper trail, though. There was no way off until almost to Kidim. Dacaro might think he was smart, but he was trapped.

Joe, Grogha, and Houma came out of it rather quickly, as did Macore. Of them all, only Macore realized what had been done, and he was none too anxious to tell anybody about it.

Doc Algongua had brought them around when he returned and found them out. He was no slouch on practical magic, either, it seemed. Sorting it out, even with Posti's help, wasn't quite so easy.

"So Dacaro planned all along to steal the Lamp," Joe said, shaking his head. "Ruddygore never *did* trust him. But Marge did—more and more. We needed his knowledge. And all he did was lead us on until he had what he wanted. But—where will he go now?"

Algongua thought a moment. "Not back to Ruddygore, that's for sure. You remember he added that bit about transferring *geases*?"

They all nodded.

"That means he's freed from any obligation to get that Lamp back to Ruddygore. Sugasto—the real one—now has the *geas*, much to his discomfort, probably, but he's totally subject to Dacaro's orders. I would say that Dacaro has no intention of using his wish any time soon, and he's got enough power and self-control not to waste it. That means he's got some greater game in mind."

Joe thought a minute. "Marge said the whole thing between

him and Ruddygore was over his trying to smuggle a gun into
this world." Briefly he explained what a gun was, and Algongua
seemed to get the general idea. "That means either he's going
to use his wish to open up the route between my old world and
this one to him, or he's going to the Dark Baron."

"Probably both," Doc replied. "He can't ally himself with
Ruddygore or with anybody who's a friend of Ruddygore's.
Any member of the Council he might turn to would demand
the Lamp and would then have him. That leaves the Baron.
He's got a lot to offer. His own considerable powers, the Lamp,
and the way to the other world, a world he knows and has been
to."

"Poor Marge," Joe sighed. "Trapped in that Lamp as a genie.
Slave to his wishes." As Sugasto had predicted, memory had
returned with the dragon's arrival.

"Well, she can't help us—or herself," Doc noted. "Looks
as if I'm going to be involved more than I figured. Vercertorix
and I will go the length of the upper trail and see if we can
pick them up. His powers will be few against a true dragon."

They all brightened. "Yeah! He wouldn't have figured on
the dragon! He thinks he's left us here with one horse!"

"Well, he's got several surprises," Algongua told them.
"First of all, you ought to be able to pick up a soldier's horse
or two or three not too far down from here. We finished them,
but a number of horses escaped unharmed." He sighed. "I'm
afraid I may have made another mistake about Vercertorix.
Now that he's had two battles, he wants more. It's like eating
peanuts—he just doesn't want to stop. I'm afraid he wants to
get into the war itself now."

They searched what they believed to be every inch of the
upper trail, and the lower one, too, but found no trace of the
elusive Dacaro. He was incredibly powerful in the magical
arts, that was clear—so much so that Ruddygore had not trusted
him with the human form to operate his skills. Now he was
joined with an adept of additional great powers subject to his
command—Sugasto, in the body of the horse, whose skills
and knowledge could be called upon when needed, as Marge
had used Dacaro.

About the only solace Joe took from any of it was that
Sugasto had thought he'd been freed and now he was captive

and slave once more. He certainly deserved it, as much as
Dacaro did, but there was little real comfort in that knowledge.
Marge was still captive, and Dacaro had all the high cards in
his favor.

After getting Vercertorix to scare a few of the runaway
horses toward them, Joe bade Algongua fly to Terindell with
the news, taking Macore with him. What was left of the Company would return by trail and, hopefully, pick up Dacaro's
tracks somewhere.

For Dacaro's part, the spells of concealment and invisibility
had been simplicity itself. He was confident that, while they
might follow him, even chase him, he was more than a match
for the lot of them. His only fear was that Ruddygore would
get personally involved.

The first night, he rubbed the Lamp and brought forth Marge,
mostly to have conversation with somebody other than the
seething Sugasto. He saw, somewhat to his surprise, that she
had changed more physically. She was somehow less human-
looking, more exotic than ever; her complexion was becoming
a light brown, and the webbing between her fingers and toes
was nearly complete. Her nails, too, were becoming harder,
thicker, more animallike, and sharp. All of which meant nothing as long as she was in spirit form, unable physically to
manipulate any material thing in the real world, but it fascinated
him nonetheless that the process continued even in this state.

She was, of course, by no means very happy with him, and
he finally got tired of her cracks and ordered her to speak only
when spoken to. Ever obedient as required, she shut up, but
couldn't disguise her contempt for him regardless.

"Sugasto tells me that those of the Lamp don't live inside
it, but rather on a different plane," he said. "Is that true?"

"It is," she told him. "The land of the djinn. It is fascinating."

"Tell me about it. Describe it."

"What you ask is not possible. There aren't any words for
it. The frame of reference is different. It's like trying to describe
our three-dimensional universe to a one-dimensional being. It
took me a while just to be able to perceive it myself. Even
now, I'm not sure what it is or what I'm perceiving, and I
certainly have no way of describing it. There is no way to relate
it to anything we know or experience."

"So even the command of the master of the Lamp has limits," he muttered. "You can't tell about what you have no frame of reference to relate to. Still, there is intelligence there—and knowledge?"

She nodded. "Vast knowledge. Since the realm has no physical existence at all, as we know it, it is a realm of pure magic. But the Lords of the Djinn impart little they don't wish to impart."

"The Lords of the Djinn..." he repeated thoughtfully. "I wonder. I have heard of their realm and of them, but I had no idea that the Lamp was a gateway to it. In the end, the entire Council studied there before becoming the most powerful. Yet I find Sugasto's added knowledge from that realm to be mostly petty or useless. Is it so with you?"

"It's not much," she admitted. "They are mostly concerned with my triple nature—from another universe and a changeling. Still, I find my mind much clearer on magical principles and procedures, and my understanding of spells and incantations is far greater, even for the short time I've been there. It's like learning a foreign language, I think. The best way to learn one is total immersion—going into an environment in which only that language you wish to learn is spoken. Substitute magic for language and you get the idea. When magic is everything, learning is easier—and you learn or you go nuts."

He nodded. "Do they have a sense of what is going on here?" he asked her. "The battle between the Dark Baron and the rest?"

"They know of the battles between the greater forces, Heaven and Hell, and that's all that concerns them. They take no sides because they feel no threat from either side. Nor will they deliberately help, hurt, or in any way interfere with events here. That's in the laws of magic they obey."

He shook his head in satisfaction. "That's good enough for me. I would like to go there sometime and see and learn for myself. But, as of now, I know of only one way to do that— and I am not willing to make *that* kind of sacrifice. There is another way later. Perhaps the Baron will complete my training to the point where I can go on my own."

He ordered her back into the Lamp and got some sleep.

Even a man with Dacaro's considerable powers was still a physical and mortal being. As such, he required the same three days back that he'd needed getting to the Gateway, and he also required food, shelter, and rest. He risked Kidim because he had to, but used a spell to alter his features subtly so that they might not betray him to later inquisitors.

Kidim, however, was more crowded than usual, he found. More of the black-liveried soldiers were about, mostly relaxing as they waited for the rest of their parties to return from Starmount, still ignorant that those parties would never return.

After a day or so in the town, he had a good idea of who was who among the Baron's forces, and had overheard a hundred conversations. He was satisfied and confident enough to approach an officer of the rear guard.

"I'm an adept, formerly with Ruddygore," he told the man, a Captain Thymir. "We have had a falling-out. In the meantime, I have acquired something that your master wishes very much."

The captain was distrustful. "How do we know you're not a spy or double agent?"

Dacaro chuckled and, in the privacy of his room, showed the captain the Lamp and brought forth its increasingly exotic and beautiful genie. The captain was convinced and very impressed, but discovered quickly that Dacaro was no pushover. If the Lamp were to be taken from the adept, it would have to be by one far more powerful in sorcery than Dacaro himself.

"All right," the captain said, after being forced within a hairbreadth of spitting himself on his own sword, "what is it you wish?"

"Safe and rapid passage from here to your lines," Dacaro told him. "After that, as soon as practical, an audience with the Baron himself."

The captain thought a moment. "All right. I think it can be arranged. We'll take one of the boats downriver tomorrow. All I can promise, though, is to get you to somebody higher up. I've never even seen the Baron myself, so I haven't the slightest idea of how to go any further."

Dacaro nodded. "That is satisfactory. But I remind you of my own powers. Any attempt on me will bring a most unpleasant slow death. Do you understand me?"

The captain looked at his sword, on which he was so recently almost impaled against his will, and shivered. "Don't worry. As much as we want that Lamp—who wouldn't?—I'm not about to go after it. But I'd suggest you keep it hidden. I'll tell no one else until I report to my superiors, understand?"

"Agreed," Dacaro said. "Oh—my horse must go along. Can you manage that?"

"If you speak the truth about our men, I can," the captain responded. "The way you tell it, we won't have nearly so many goin' back."

A day before Joe and the remaining Company reached Kidim by the lower road, Vercertorix returned—but the rider was not Algongua.

"Poquah!" Joe shouted. "Are we glad to see *you!*"

The impassive Imir looked his usual grim self. "Had we time, it should have been and would have been the Master himself. But there is a great battle shaping up, perhaps only days away, possibly only hours. If he were here tracking down the traitor, he would get satisfaction, and probably the Lamp, but it might cost the war."

"You'll do," Joe told him. "Where do we start?"

"First I'm sending Vercertorix back to Dr. Algongua, who is still at Terindell," the Imir said. "Although I have never heard of a dragon of Husaquahr taking part in the wars of men and fairy folk before, this one seems most eager, and we are happy to get him. Then we four will go into Kidim. It is certain that our man stopped there, although probably in good disguise. I think I can penetrate it, even if he has already flown."

Their return to the town was hardly welcome news to the townspeople, but was final confirmation to the soldiers, too, that what Dacaro had told their captain had been correct. They were too far from their forces to cause trouble in Kidim now, though, and so they made preparations to leave and return. They, too, had gotten word of an impending battle.

Joe, Grogha, and Houma let the Imir do all the detective work. It was magic they needed to penetrate, and magic was Poquah's game. It didn't take him long, either. They were never certain of his methods, but he was most thorough and positive.

"Dacaro is here, and he and the horse are on one of the transports in the lake below," Poquah told them.

Joe jumped up and grabbed his sword hilt. "Well, let's get down and find him then!"

Poquah sighed. "Your heart and spirit are commendable, but your common sense is addled. There are still seventy of the enemy against us four. Dacaro, being of mortal stock, also has the edge in any magical confrontation with me, our relative powers being equal. And he has the Lamp, against which even the Master might have problems if the wish were suitably nasty and well phrased, as it would be. I know this Dacaro. He is a terribly dangerous man, all the more so for being sincere. He believes the modernization of Husaquahr is a cause, a way to lift the people into a better life. As a result, he sees himself as the good side in this contest and is willing to go to any lengths to achieve his goal. In this he is much like the Baron, who is also self-deluded yet quite sincere."

"I like things simple. You're complicatin' everything up too much," Houma grumbled. "The bastard's an evil traitor. If I get the chance, I'm gonna cut his throat."

"Me, too," Grogha added.

The Imir shrugged. "Have it your own way. I agree he must die. But don't confuse what I say with what must be done. He *is* evil, and he flees to an evil master, but no evil leader ever thinks he is evil. The subtleness of Hell in this world or any other is that it is always built on good intentions. That is why it is so pervasive."

Joe understood him, but the other two remained unconvinced. "Still," the big man asked, "if we can't go after him now, what can we do?"

"We must take him when he is least prepared," the Imir responded. "Therefore, we must first find out on what boat he sails, and follow that boat and its occupants. If we have no opportunity before to get at him, we must continue to follow him—all the way to the Dark Baron himself, if need be." He looked at Houma and Grogha. "But not all of us. The two of you—with Posti—should join our forces. This is not a job for all of us—our chance of discovery and betrayal is too great."

Both men protested vigorously, but Poquah was adamant, and they accepted his decision with a lot of grumbling. The Company had been dissolved. Now Joe and Poquah must go with the enemy to catch a powerful fish.

CHAPTER 16

THE DARK BARON

Those aligned with evil may cheat, but must always leave an opening, however tenuous, for the virtuous.

—II, 112

POQUAH'S MAGIC MADE THE SOLUTION TO THEIR PROBLEM OBvious. Knowing that a force of this size probably would have been put together only for this mission, and thus not everybody would know everybody, the Imir cast a spell on both him and Joe so that they appeared to be common soldiers to everyone who looked at them. And, with that, they simply joined formation and marched onto one of the boats when the main force was withdrawn.

It was not the boat with Dacaro aboard, but Poquah was relieved at that. "These disguises are more than sufficient for man or fairy," he told Joe, "but a good adept would see through them in an instant. Best we do not get too close to him until we are ready to strike."

"It's lucky that most folks aren't magical, or I'd feel downright uncomfortable," Joe noted.

"You would feel more than that, my otherworldly friend," the Imir responded. "This place would be an insane asylum. It almost is now."

They sailed down the Sik and joined the River of the Sad Virgin, still pretty much in neutral territory. But the four boats pulled in before they reached the Dancing Gods, and crews busily changed the appearance of two, adding camouflaging, redistributing and adding masts, and repainting. It was clear that the boats were designed and the crews were trained for this sort of thing. By the end of the day, they looked like two merchant freighters, exactly what they should be in this kind of commerce, and flew the Kidim flag and sail markings.

Neutral merchants.

The soldiers, too, changed their uniforms for civilian clothes, those of merchants, sailors, and the like, causing Poquah to have to alter his spells as well. Particularly interesting was the fact that the soldiers' beards were shaved and their hair trimmed short. Now they hardly matched any description of the soldiers seen at Kidim.

Poquah had used his powers of persuasion to find out as much information as was known. Of the four boats, they were on the third in the convoy, while he was quite certain from the crew's comments that Dacaro was on the boat directly in front of them. Joe, in fact, was certain that he spotted the black stallion with the others in the rear tethering area. But their boat was not one of the ones changed.

Four boats had left, but now crews and passengers consolidated into the two that looked like Kidim's. With over a hundred and fifty of the company missing, it was no real crowd—and it made their progress down the river less conspicuous. The other two, including the one they'd been on, were scuttled.

Now they found themselves on the suspect boat and had to be careful. It took Poquah no time at all to establish that there was, indeed, a very special passenger none had seen, staying in the captain's cabin. It was all very mysterious, but the troops were good soldiers who asked few questions and started lots of wild rumors.

"Maybe we'll get lucky," Joe said hopefully to the Imir. "I mean, maybe we'll get overhauled and taken."

"I doubt it. First of all, our side has a weak navy with little experience. I suspect these two crews are more than a match for any on the other side. But in any event, I hope not. That would simply force him in to the open, and he still has his wish. That's his insurance policy in case the Baron proves less than accommodating."

"But Ruddygore said either he *or* the Baron could probably negate the Lamp," Joe pointed out. "Some insurance."

"That's true if it is used against them," the Imir agreed. "But it need not be so. It can be used to elevate Dacaro's status."

"I just wish there was some way to get to him."

"He never leaves the cabin. His meals are brought in. Yesterday I volunteered for galley duty, with the thought of poisoning the food he eats."

"And?"

"I succeeded. But there is no report of any problems, so he

apparently has a routine cleansing spell in use, as I feared. So far he has made no mistakes. The spells on the cabin are so strong he would have a lot of warning, even if a member of the Council went to work on them, and I am far lower than that. We will have to wait. Sometime, somewhere, he *must* make a mistake."

Joe understood that this was more a hope than a certainty. Where was his great luck now, all of a sudden? So far it had saved his neck, but had mostly aided the wrong side.

It was another three days of hazardous travel downriver once they reached the Dancing Gods. Below the Sad Virgin, the river meandered all over the place and had countless bars, eddies, and islands. It took a tremendous amount of skill, experience, and flawless navigation to get through the extremely long stretch, and Joe's admiration for the crew transcended his loyalties.

Now they passed the Dabasar, and the River of Dancing Gods was more than three miles wide and tremendously deep but, if anything, even more treacherous, since they were now within the flood plain, and the annual great flooding always changed the river's course and nature.

Poquah was a little concerned in the later stretches. They were deep within the enemy's area of control, and he was afraid that, on horse detail, he had been penetrated by the equine Sugasto. He did not tell Joe, who was worried enough, and hoped that, if true, the ancient adept either would think nothing of someone with a disguise spell or would keep quiet. Sugasto had no love for Dacaro, certainly, and although he was bound to do his bidding, there was no need to volunteer information.

Before nightfall they made their landing. Joe and Poquah were both relieved—at least now their quarry would have to reveal himself.

Their patience did not go unrewarded. Late in the evening, the captain came on deck, followed by a mysterious-looking stranger in dark clothing. He didn't look quite like Sugasto, whose body Dacaro wore, but Poquah was no more easily fooled than Dacaro would have been in spotting him. He did not allow that spotting to occur, though, and Dacaro certainly had no reason to be suspicious of enemies from Ruddygore at this stage. The adept would be much more concerned with treachery by the Dark Baron and his men.

Joe and Poquah ducked out of sight as the two men walked back, selected their horses, then led them off the gangplank to shore.

"If they're going far, we'll have to steal some horses," Joe noted. "And it's gonna be hard not to get pressed into duty around here."

"Has my magic failed you yet?" the Imir asked him, and together they slipped off the boat.

The two men made no move to mount their horses, but continued to follow a road from the river landing for a few hundred yards, leading their mounts. Soon they were in the midst of a huge tent city, flags of many nations and peoples flying before them, and a lot of hectic activity that actually helped conceal the pursuers' true nature.

The captain and the dark stranger reached one particular tent, not very distinguishable from the others but flying no flag, and tethered their horses in front. The captain walked over to the guard at the entrance and whispered a few words. The guard nodded, and the two men entered the tent.

"The captain has already sent runners on ahead," Poquah told Joe. "It is certain that they wait here for the Baron himself, when he can spare the time from battle preparation. I think we must move before the Baron gets here—or we will be totally outgunned."

They turned off the main path to the tent and walked casually around in back, making their way closer and closer by a circuitous route. So far, nobody had paid them the slightest attention, and they were able to reach the rear of the tent they sought without problems. They bent down to see if they could perhaps get a piece of tent up and crawl under, but as they did so, something fell on both their heads and they went out like a light.

They came to in the tent. Both Joe and Poquah had been stripped naked, and hung from a support beam by thick ropes tied to their wrists.

In the center of the tent was a plain oak table and a few chairs. The captain from the boat stood near the doorway opposite them, putting down a large bundle of stuff on the tent floor—Joe saw that it was their clothing and swords, Irving included.

The other man, whom they now recognized as Sugasto—at least in body—looked at them and smiled. The precious Lamp of Lakash hung on his belt.

"I see you're awake," Dacaro said cheerfully. "You went to so much trouble that I thought you should not be denied meeting the Dark Baron. And you, Imir—you'll find your magic nullified quite handily. I've learned a few new tricks since we studied together at Terindell."

The Imir's face contorted with rage and contempt, the first display of pure emotion Joe had ever seen on the creature, and he spat in Dacaro's direction. "You bastard! The Master was too kindhearted, but most certainly correct about you. You are unworthy to lick his shoes!"

Dacaro shrugged. "New ways are coming, Poquah. The best of the old with the new technology from the other world. Neither you nor Ruddygore can cling to your power much longer and you know it. The new ways we will introduce will break your feudal hold on the oppressed people of this land."

"And replace them with a newer and even more bitter oppression," Poquah shot back.

"We'll see. Or, at least, *I'll* see. I doubt if you two will have to worry about things one way or the other. Oh, by the way—I spotted you the first night you came aboard our boat. Or, rather, Sugasto did. He doesn't like me very much, for some reason, but he fears the wrath of Ruddygore far more. That's why he's where he is and I am where I am. I am neither fearful or in awe of Ruddygore. He represents a dying and bankrupt way of life."

At that moment there was a commotion outside, and into the tent burst an awesome figure. He was enormous, towering over the others—but still below the suspended captives. He wore a full set of shiny black armor covering every part of his body, including gloves and a fighting helmet, visor down, whose aspect was cast in the shape of a terrible demon. He had the kind of commanding presence that seemed inborn, that of regal bearing and total self-confidence. Even masked and featureless, the Dark Baron captured everyone's immediate attention. Dacaro seemed slightly awestruck by the presence, which was a far cry from the fat and slovenly Ruddygore.

The Baron wasted no time getting to the point. "You have the Lamp of Lakash," he said to Dacaro in a deep, commanding voice that Joe couldn't help comparing to one electronically disguised—although that was obviously impossible. "I am here to receive it."

Dacaro was certainly awestruck and totally aware that he was facing someone as far beyond him as Ruddygore was beyond Joe, but not so awestruck as to buckle under. The stakes were too high here. Instead, he unclasped the Lamp and held it in his right hand. "I have the Lamp, my lord, here. It is my intent to present it to you—but I must have certain assurances of my own before I do."

The Baron seemed slightly amused. "You propose to *bargain* with me? I do not drive bargains to receive what is mine by right. And, since you are here in my camp and in my presence, you are in a poor position to bargain."

"I am Dacaro, formerly adept to Ruddygore," he began, but the Baron cut him off.

"I know exactly who you are and what you are. I have no time to dawdle or dicker. The battle begins with the dawn and I must be there. You will hand me the Lamp *now*."

Dacaro gave a slight smile. "I wish you would accept my terms and conditions for handing it over," he said mildly.

The Baron started a bit. "So you have not yet used the Lamp. Very well—what terms do you suggest?"

"I wish to have my training completed so that I may be elevated to full rank and initiated as a true sorcerer. Then I would aid you as, say, sorcerer to one of the armies, in the balance of the war. After we are victorious, I would like to be installed at Terindell."

The Dark Baron chuckled. "Only that, huh? You wish to be elevated to the Council and replace Ruddygore. Well, my treacherous friend, we see no reason for trusting traitors. The man who would so willingly betray Ruddygore for such power has no honor, and without honor he would as lief betray any lord and all oaths of fealty and allegiance. *I will take that Lamp now!*"

The veneer of self-confidence Dacaro had worn now crumbled in total confusion. "But—but I *wished!* You can't go against the *wish!*" He took a step backward and looked about nervously. "Slave of the Lamp! Attend me!"

Smoke poured out of the Lamp and congealed into the figure of Marge. Joe was struck by how much she'd changed, but he was too concerned with the drama being played out in front of him to think much about that right now.

Dacaro looked at Marge. "Why didn't it give me my wish?" he demanded.

Marge seemed to take some satisfaction in her answer. "Because this is not the Dark Baron," she told him, "but another in his armor. And the other within is not of this earth, nor of any earthly kingdom, and, as such, is not bound by the Lamp at all."

The Baron's hands went to the demonic helmet, unfastened it, and lifted it off, showing the head beneath. It was the same as the mask—a terrible, demonic face, only not fashioned by craft of metal but in a blue-black, leathery skin. "I am Hiccarph, Prince Regent of Hell," the creature told him. "The Baron sends his regrets, but he has a war to fight." And then the demon prince laughed.

Dacaro screamed. "No! No! I wish you back to Hell! Begone!"

"Free!" Marge, breathed and stepped back from the two now facing each other.

Dacaro gave a laugh. "You haven't won me, Prince of Hell! I go to the land of the djinn!" And, with that, he faded into smoke and poured back into the Lamp, which had dropped on the floor of the tent with his second wish.

The demon just stood there a minute, thinking. He moved, then, to get the Lamp and picked it up.

Joe realized that, because he was hanging so high, the demon's head was now between his hand and Irving. Held painfully by the wrist, he nonetheless managed to open his hand. The magic sword was on the floor, with Poquah's weapon and their clothing. The idea had come into his head from the start, and now was the first and perhaps only time it might work. With a little silent prayer he yelled, "Irving! To me!"

The sword flew from the bundle of clothes right at the demonic head, striking it and knocking the creature back, then continued on to Joe's hand. With a flip of the wrist that was tremendously painful, he brought the blade around and it sliced neatly through the rope. One arm free, he brought the blade up and cut through the other rope, falling to the floor.

The demon had been knocked over, losing the Lamp, but now the terrible creature rose to its feet. Its face was the face of nightmare, its power something that could be felt by all in the room.

Marge dived, scooped up the Lamp, and pitched it to Joe.

The demon got to his feet, smiled, and said, "Now feel the powers of Hell, mortal!" He threw out his hand and Joe instinctively drew back—but nothing happened.

The demon looked puzzled. "What in . . . ?"

Joe gave him no more time. "I wish all in this room and its contents were now with Ruddygore!" he yelled, holding the Lamp.

In a moment, they all winked out of the tent.

To say that Ruddygore was shocked and surprised was an understatement. One moment he had been alone in his tent thirty miles across the Valley of Decision from the enemy army, meditating for added powers, when suddenly in popped Joe, Marge, Poquah, a strange soldier looking scared to death, and a full suit of the Dark Baron's armor.

Joe whooped and hollered, waved his sword in the air, then tossed the Lamp to the astonished Ruddygore. "It worked! We did it!"

It was Marge's and Poquah's turn to be astonished. "But— how?" they both asked at the same time.

The black-clad captain, still in a state of shock, looked around fearfully and squeaked, "I surrender! Won't somebody accept my surrender?"

Ruddygore was the first to regain some sense of self-control. He walked over to the fearsome armor, kicked it, and frowned. It was empty. He turned to the captain. "Just put your sword over there and sit down like a good fellow," he told the frightened soldier. "We'll get around to you when everything's sorted out." The captain complied.

"Now, then," the sorcerer continued, "just what *is* going on here?"

As quickly as possible, the three sketched the events in the tent. Ruddygore listened attentively. Finally he nodded his head affirmatively and sighed. "Well, I think I can at least explain it. The Baron, knowing that he was vulnerable to a well-stated wish even if he could block moves against himself with the Lamp, drew upon his ultimate power and raised Hiccarph. Now, Hiccarph's powers are quite limited on this plane—he has, in fact, no more real existence than the genies of the Lamp—but he could move that suit of armor and, most important, he was totally invulnerable to any magic of Husaquahr. Using the armor, he could pick up the Lamp and take it to his ally. When you summoned Irving, Joe, the sword struck the upper part of the armor. In the summons it was an irresistible force—so the armor went sprawling. That was quick thinking, by the way."

"I'd hoped it would run the Dark Baron through, damn it," Joe muttered.

"Be content. This was a major victory from the very brink of total defeat. It's a good thing I wasn't in Terindell, though—or you and the Lamp would have gotten there, but not the rest. I shudder to think what might have happened to you."

Marge frowned. "But the Lamp was completely powerless against this demon! And he seemed amazed to be powerless against *us!*"

Ruddygore nodded. "The forces of Hell would not be directly subject to any of the Laws or Rules, because they have no physical existence on this plane. They must work through humans—in this case the will of the Baron that placed Hiccarph in that armor. But as to why Hiccarph had no power over you, Joe—it was because you are not a native of this world. Your soul is still your soul, and it is of a different place. Hiccarph was summoned by a native of this world and, as such, he was attuned totally to the things of this world. Since he had no physical being beyond the armor, he could only reach out for your soul—but he was wrongly attuned. That's the best way I can put it. On your native world he would have plucked your soul from your body and carried it with him back to Hell itself. But *here*—let's just say he was on the wrong frequency. That's what I counted on. It is the extra edge you and Marge have over anyone else." He paused a moment. "I fear it will also mean both of you are now marked. Hiccarph and his bosses will never rest until they know why they failed against you. They will be after you."

Joe grinned. "Let 'em come! We faced down the Prince Regent of Hell a few minutes ago." He leaned over, grabbed a startled Marge, and kissed her on the lips. "We're ready for *anything* now." He paused and looked at her and smiled. "Welcome back to the land of the living."

She smiled and patted his hand. "What of Dacaro?" she asked. "He's now in the land of the djinn."

"And there he'll stay," Ruddygore assured her. "Nor will he get what he seeks there. They will string him along, but give him nothing of substance. And one day I will pay him a visit there, and he will learn that the Lords of the Djinn may be disinterested in our affairs but *do* value old friendships."

A military officer entered, bowed slightly, and said, "Sir— it will be dawn in less than half an hour. Lord Kasura awaits your pleasure."

Ruddygore turned and looked suddenly very tired. "Tell him I will be there straightaway." He turned back to Joe, Marge, and Poquah. "The three of you have done what you can, and it is more than any man had a right to expect. Get something to eat at the mess tent—anyone will be able to tell you where it is—and then get some rest. The outcome of this day will no longer depend on your labors, but our cause has certainly been fortified by your deeds."

Poquah, who was pulling on his clothes, said, "Master, I will be with you. My place is not to rest during a battle."

"As you wish, old friend. But ours is a different sort of battle from what those brave ones will face."

"I can still fight," Joe told him, and Marge nodded as well.

"No. It is time for the professionals now. A battle requires planning and discipline, and you were not a part of the training. Remain here, or go up the heights nearby at the command post and watch it unfold as best you can. But fight not today— unless we are lost and overrun." And, with that, he turned and left, Poquah following, trying to get his pants fastened.

The captain stirred in the corner. "Won't somebody take my surrender?" he pleaded.

Joe looked at him. "Go. On your word of honor, go to the river and join your own forces, but do not fight us until you are with your own."

The captain shook his head from side to side. "Oh, no. I'm going to surrender. *I looked into that thing's eyes.*"

Joe sighed. "Then turn yourself in to the captain of the guard. I'm sure they'll have a place to accommodate you." Then they, too, walked out, leaving the prisoner alone.

They found the officers' mess tent with no trouble. They filled plates from a cauldron of scrambled eggs, and Joe, at least, took slices from the roast of pork on a spit as well. Both sipped abnormally strong black coffee.

After a while they felt somewhat themselves again and began to relax a bit, although the tension throughout the camp was too thick to ignore. Still, in the moments before things broke loose, Joe took advantage of the little time remaining. "Well— you sure have changed, that I'll say."

She looked a little embarrassed. "The djinn accelerated the process. It was only a few days, but time there didn't pass like time here."

He nodded, although he didn't quite understand. Certainly her short pageboy hair was now down to her shoulders, and was a true silver color except for the ever-present streak in the middle, now a burnt orange. Her elfin ears stuck out cutely, and it seemed that her whole face and figure radiated an unnatural sexuality. Her figure had become so exaggerated that the clothes she wore bulged and pulled, and he knew they wouldn't last long. "You're going to have a hard time with that nun's vow," he noted playfully.

She sighed. "I know. But maybe that's for the best. Huspeth will never understand, though."

His brows went up. "Then she didn't do this?"

"No. Ruddygore lies when it's convenient. It's his sort of practical joke on Huspeth, I think. I can see why people get irritated with him."

"So you're still glad you hitched a ride?"

She smiled. "Very glad, Joe. Very glad. And you?"

"I'm beginning to get the hang of this place. I think maybe I'll stay a while. Have you thought of what you're going to do—after today? Assuming we win, of course, and we aren't on the run."

She shrugged. "I don't know. I'd like to go to the realm of faërie for a bit, to complete this and to learn more about what I am and what it all means. That will determine the future, more or less, I guess. But I haven't had my fill of this land. I'd like to see all of it someday. What about you?"

He shook his head. "I don't know. I think I can hold my own here now. I guess maybe I'd like to travel, too. Just sort of let things take me along, like that river out there. Go with the current and the flow and see where I wind up."

"Still—we made a hell of a good team, didn't we, Joe?"

He grinned. "We sure did, Marge."

Trumpets sounded across a broad area outside and seemed to echo and go on forever. Officers still in the mess grabbed their weapons and ran out, while the cooks started frantically cleaning up the place. Drums began to beat, and there was the sound of massive numbers of horses and men moving into positions.

Joe sighed. "I think I'd like to see this battle."

She nodded. "Me, too."

With that, they got up and walked out into the breaking dawn.

CHAPTER 17

THE BATTLE OF SORROWS GORGE

Although magic may play a significant part in any battle, victory must be secured by soldiers supported by sound strategy.
                                             —XIX, 301, 2

"NOW IS THE TIME FOR SWORDS AND SORCERY!"

With that ritualistic exhortation required by the Rules, the commanders of both forces urged their men into battle.

From the heights overlooking the great battlefield, the leaders of the northern countries watched and plotted. Behind them, apart from the rushing messengers and great birds and winged fairy folk bringing reports and taking out orders to the field, Ruddygore stood alone, dressed now in his robes of gold and looking quite imposing. He sat in a large wooden chair that seemed almost like a throne, and his arms rested on the arms of the chair, while his eyes were closed.

Poquah saw Joe and Marge and came over to them. "The Master is right, as usual," he sighed. "I am far too weakened to do more than assist." His slitted eyes seemed to burn, though, and they knew he wanted to be out there with the moving armies.

The sight was imposing. Huge masses of men and equipment

marched in formations, while the nonhumans and people of faërie formed their own ranks, covering the human foot soldiers. Ahead, almost a thousand massed cavalry stood, barely holding back their mounts.

"Looks like a Roman epic from the late show," Marge noted. "Only this is for real."

"I don't understand why they waited for dawn," Joe said to Poquah. "This looks all too set for a guy with a reputation like his."

"Crossing the River of Sorrows is no mean feat," the Imir told him. "Our own forces harassed but could not prevent it. We didn't have the time to get sufficient armies south. By the time our troops were gathered, most of his were across, and so it was better to take up defensive positions and wait. The Baron has a real problem, you see—he's in Sorrows Gorge, his entire force with its back to the River of Sorrows and the Dancing Gods. If he loses, he could lose a lot of his main force. But if he wins, he can break through the mountains there and have a clear plain for hundreds of miles and an unimpeded run to Terindell."

Joe shook his head wonderingly. "I'd have used all that to cross the Dancing Gods. From the map, it's much easier going on the other side."

"True—but he would telegraph his move weeks in advance and he would be in essentially the same position at the Sad Virgin. That is why the Valley of Decision has always been the place would-be conquerors have come, and why none have yet breached it."

Marge gazed out nervously at the assembling forces. "How good a chance does he have to win?"

"About even, with the Master here," Poquah told her. "But if he punches through here, there is nothing much to stop him."

The defenders had dug trenches and built effective-looking earthworks, and Joe didn't envy anybody having to come against them. There were also large catapults and other less familiar machinery of war, but no permanent fortifications in the area.

The sky was suddenly alight with hundreds of fireballs, rushing in toward them, landing, and bursting, spilling their fiery death in a random manner. Poquah watched them come in. "It has begun," he said softly.

The defenders took cover and generally weathered the storm of fireballs, the catapult equivalent of heavy artillery. It was merely a softening-up measure, for all its spectacle. While the fireballs did little damage, they made certain that the main field was clear for the attacker.

Now, across the field, perhaps ten miles from the command post, a huge thing like a black snake moved across the length of the battlefield. It took a little thinking to realize that what they were seeing was a line of men almost a mile long and perhaps ten or fifteen deep. It was not merely impressive—it was downright awesome.

From defensive earthworks, a similar line began to march out from the defenders' side. It was not quite so deep or so wide, but *they* didn't have to march over a mile or more of open ground. These were the elfin *hacrist*, master bowmen, and they took their positions and stood their ground, waiting for the approaching line to get within range. Behind them formed cavalry, so many horsemen it was impossible to count them from the command post. They formed into company-sized detachments and waited, about a hundred yards behind the *hacrist*.

When the two forces were within range of each other, the bowmen let loose with a tremendous hail of arrows that nearly blackened the sky. They concentrated on the center of the attacking line, which suddenly seemed to turn into a solid wall as the soldiers held their shields horizontal, forming something of a roof. The closer they were and the better the discipline, the more absolute that roof would be.

Soon there were holes in that roof, as such a concentration of arrows and bolts as none there had ever seen struck with great force. Without exception, the men who fell were left, with those behind falling in and taking their place in the relentless advance.

From behind the bowmen, the catapults of the defenders went off in perfect series. Some were firebombs, but most contained as much as a quarter of a ton of junk, rock, and scrap metal that would tear into or crush flesh.

The catapults took their toll on the advancing marchers, whose roof was certainly caving in at a number of key spots— spots on which the bowmen now concentrated.

Joe frowned. "They're not going to get here *that* way," he noted.

Poquah nodded. "Yes. They have something up their sleeves, that is certain."

In his great chair, Ruddygore, too, was thinking the same thing. A frontal attack was useless unless supported by a flank; if this kept up very long, the edges of the force would be the only attackers and could be disposed of long before they could close the vise. He rose up into the air, his astral shape taking in the entire battle scene, but he could see nothing—and he determined that the great mass of the Baron's troops was, in fact, committed. They looked to be about the numbers and types of beings he'd seen in his earlier reconnaissance. Something was definitely wrong here . . . But what?

On a hunch, he swung over his own forces, jubilant in their easy victory, and beyond, in back of them, to the ox bows near the River of Dancing Gods. He saw almost immediately that his hunch was correct. Four thousand infantry together with flying *cosirs*—perhaps several hundred, in nine flying companies, all wearing the colors of Marquewood—approached. They were now less than two miles from the rear camp of the defenders. They flew traditional Marquewood colors, but the *cosirs* gave them away.

Abruptly, Ruddygore's physical body stood up from his chair and he screamed, "We are attacked from the rear by men in our colors!"

Two of the generals turned and frowned. "How?" one asked.

"They must have been carried in small groups up the river and stayed dispersed until last night," the sorcerer told them. "They wear the colors of Marquewood, but who of Marquewood would be supported by nine companies of *cosirs*?"

As suddenly as that, the Baron's true strategy was revealed, along with the fact that there were far more of the enemy than believed. The fight was no longer one-sided, but at least even. Even if the new enemy were exposed, a large percentage of the defenders would have to shift to open field fighting in their rear, weakening the frontal assault. Now, instead of the defenders having the Baron with his back to Sorrows Gorge, they were caught in a vise themselves with no place to run to.

Either the Baron or some other sorcerer with the rear force must have sensed Ruddygore's astral presence; from behind, even as orders were being issued for a defense of the rear positions, committing the reserves to that fight, the *cosirs* came silently out of the sky directly at the command post and reserves.

The creatures were as large as men, with folds of skin between arms and legs, yet they were also feathered and taloned and had tails that were vertical, acting almost like aircraft rudders. Their orange and blue coloring made them things of lethal beauty, and their faces, a curious blend of bird and elf, were triumphant as they swooped down in well-disciplined columns. The early ones carried cauldrons of some thin, foul-smelling liquid which they poured on the ground, the tents, and whatever forces they could reach. The latter ones carried only torches, and it was clear why, without thinking much about it.

The reserve bowmen took a good toll of *cosirs* as they swooped in; perhaps one in three was struck, and more than half of the whose were knocked right out of the air, but that was not enough.

Joe drew his great sword and swung around, ready to help the reserves. Then, at that moment, he saw that Ruddygore had chosen to ignore all this and was sitting calmly back down in his chair, eyes closed once again.

The archers started aiming specifically at the *cosirs* with torches, preferring to smell like oil rather than boil in it, but many of the torchbearers made it through and dropped their loads. Suddenly the entire command post and reserve center were on fire, and men and fairy folk screamed and scattered, writhing in pain.

Joe ran past the flaming holocaust to the rear, where he could see that the approaching enemy force was moving with astonishing speed for infantry toward their positions. Officers tried to regroup their troops and set up some sort of defensive line in all the confusion.

Marge looked at Ruddygore, then at Poquah, with alarm. "How can he just sit there like that? They'll get him for sure!"

"No, he is well protected," the Imir assured her, "although I can not for the life of me understand what he is doing right now."

At that moment Ruddygore came out of it once again, rose, and looked around in anger. "No!" he shouted to the generals. "Continue concentrating on the frontal assault! Frontal attack! Forget the rear guard! Press them back against the river!"

One general, a very noble-looking man with experience in his eyes, frowned. "But we must defend the rear!"

"No! *I* will defend the rear! Trust in me as you have trusted no one since weaned from your mother's milk, but do as I say, Prince! Do what I say or we are lost!"

With most of the fires out or burning tents beyond redemption, Joe saw officers rounding up men and pulling them back toward the original attack. He frowned, but followed, determined to see this out no matter what. Still, he spotted Marge and Poquah and ran to them, confused. "If they're all fighting forward, who's gonna take out the thousands that are about a quarter mile back?"

Marge looked at him, then past him, and broke into a big grin. "That's who!"

Joe turned and saw, coming in low over the flats, the dragon Vercertorix.

The dragon had practiced on smaller numbers back in High Pothique, but now it faced a formidable array and it did not seem too worried by the greater number, even announcing its presence with a monstrous roar. It was obvious from the start that Algongua or someone else was telling the dragon what to do—or, at least, making suggestions—because Vercertorix approached the columns with careful precision, carving zigzag paths of flaming breath through the ranks, forcing the breakup of the columns and general disorganization.

After doing as much initial damage as possible, the dragon then concentrated on keeping the main force back. The object wasn't so much to fry all four thousand—that would have been next to impossible—but to keep them scattered and falling back toward the relative protection of the silt mounds around the ox-bow lake. Heartened by the sight of the great dragon routing their enemies, what was left of the reserves and support troops on the command post hill began cheering, which let those below, who were fighting the main battle, know that something good was happening at their backs and taking the pressure off.

Cavalry moved forward into the wrecked ranks of the Baron's main force with a vengeance, breaking the attack column into smaller units which infantry moved to mop up. The Baron's officers and field commanders, realizing that their rear attack had at least stalled, if not failed, tried valiantly to regroup and fall back to defensive positions against the river gorge.

Ruddygore stood on the hill overlooking the battle, suddenly grim-faced even despite near certain victory. Marge looked and saw what few others could see—a tremendous field of magical force embodying every color imaginable and in such a tight pattern that its complexity was beyond her abilities to follow. The source of the magic flow was clearly from the Gorge area, and she understood that the Dark Baron was making himself felt.

Now the field of force congealed and took on a new and more animated pattern, becoming a gigantic, three-headed monster, all jaws, teeth, and claws. Although outlined in the near unreality of the magical lines of force, it was truly the most horrible and loathsome creature she had ever seen, and she gave a gasp at both its terrible visage and its enormous size—it seemed to encompass the entire battlefield.

Joe turned to her. "What's the matter?"

She pointed. "Can't you see it? It's—horrible!"

He looked, and saw only victory in the making.

"The Baron's trying to reach Vercertorix!" Poquah told them. "It must be black for him indeed to take such a chance. Now we'll see the Master in action!"

Joe just turned and looked at them, then at the battlefield, and shrugged.

To those who could see magic, many things were happening. Ruddygore, who'd stood there watching the approaching monstrous shape, suddenly flared and changed into a shining giant being of near blinding white light. As huge as the monstrous creation now approaching, this was far different in color, texture, and form, almost as unbearable in its beauty as the Baron's monster was in its hideousness. It floated eerily out to meet the monster, and the two met over the battlefield. So great was the force of their meeting that clouds came in from all directions, rumbling and shooting thunder, congealing around the spot where the two great creatures of powerful sorcery grappled. Even Joe could see this phenomenon, and stared at it, fascinated.

The clouds, turning all sorts of colors and rumbling threateningly, began to swirl about them, kicking up a wind and bringing the smell of ozone and a deadly sort of chill. They swirled around the battlefield at an unnatural speed, as if being pulled into some sort of drain, but in the center of the drain—the hole—where the great beasts fought, the invisible battle was clear and eerily sunlit.

The patterns in the mixing of the two beasts were almost beyond endurance. Merely watching them started to give Marge a terrible headache and a sense of disorientation. This was power—pure, unadulterated power, both of magic and of will, between two whose powers were greater than the sum of all magical powers she had witnessed in the past.

The soldiers on the battlefield seemed aware of what was going on above and around them. The forces of Marquewood and Valisandra did not break, but took advantage of the swirling winds and terrible lightning and thunder. They were going to press the enemy to the Gorge, and the hell with the weather.

The sight to the attackers, however, was simply one last terror that had been visited on their proud forces this day, and they retreated steadily before the advancing Marquewood-Valisandran infantry.

Commanders still at the command post pulled back all surviving rear-guard troops, those not actually engaged in the press, and sent them immediately rearward. While this was little more than a thousand soldiers of mixed specialties, Vercertorix was having the time of his incredibly long life evening the odds. In fact, the dragon seemed to be making a game out of how he could split up, chase, and panic groups of soliders. One entire company of the Baron's rear troops fled before the fiery breath of the dragon straight into the ox-bow lake itself. Unfortunately for them, most were wearing full battle armor, and the lake was about ten feet deep.

The intense power generated by the fight of the two sorcerers over the battlefield finally became too great for those onlookers who could see it to bear. Marge felt dizzy, then swooned and collapsed, and even Poquah had to turn away, looking sick and weak. Joe demanded to know what was going on.

"The Master and the Baron are directly engaged—out there," the Imir managed. "It is the greatest confluence of magical forces I have ever seen, and is too much for those of us of faërie to bear, though we live in magic constantly."

Joe thought about it. "If they're evenly matched, though, it's a draw. And that means the Baron can't get to us. Ruddygore only has to hold, not win—our boys on the ground are doing that."

From the vortex in the center of the battlefield, suddenly a voice rang out; a cold, mechanical voice that all could hear, not only those of the art but everyone on the battlefield.

"Hiccarph! Rally your forces to me or we are lost! Forces of Hell, attend me now, for I have served you well!"

And behind the great beast on the field, the Princes of Hell appeared to those who could see them; great, giant, ghostly outlines of creatures too horrible to look upon, mounted on vicious black creatures forged from the fires of Hell itself.

And from the opposite forces, another great voice spoke. "You have failed, Baron, because of your *own* overconfidence, your *own* tactical errors. We will allow a withdrawal, but we will help you not, for it is beyond redemption. Another day, another time, another battle . . ."

The Baron's voice, so cold and mechanical, broke, and he cried out in anguish, "Noooooo . . . !"

The storm that swirled around the warring sorcerers broke suddenly, the rain coming in so great a torrent that it was almost a physical force. The battlefield turned quickly to slippery mud, spilling horses and men and knocking the flying fairy folk out of the air. Lightning struck constantly, creating with the tremendous rain a huge wall that flowed out of the storm and into a great barrier between the forces.

The Baron's terrible three-headed monster broke from its fight and faded into the wall of water and lightning, quickly becoming one with it and then vanishing entirely.

To Joe, who watched the storm become the wall, it was merely very impressive and a little frustrating. "Damn! They're going to get away behind it!"

"Yes, a withdrawal will be possible," Poquah responded, "but not without great cost, more to them than to us. We have won. The Baron failed to anticipate the dragon, and now he pays for it. But such a cost to us as well! Such a cost . . ."

Joe turned and gently picked up Marge, taking her back to one of the few tents still standing. Poquah ran to the spot where Ruddygore had stood before the great battle and found his Master there, sprawled out on the grass. When the Imir turned him over, it could be seen that the sorcerer was still alive, but looked as if someone had tied him down and beaten him severely.

"Master!" Poquah cried. "Master! Do not desert us now in your triumph!"

The body of the fat man seemed to shudder slightly, and his breathing became more regular. With an effort, Ruddygore opened his eyes, groaned, and looked up at the anguished Poquah. "Don't worry, old friend," he gasped, his voice cracking and weak. "You shoulda seen the other guy . . ."

The Battle of Sorrows Gorge was over, and the defenders had held, but the mopping-up operation took several days. The sight of the battlefield the day after was sobering to the most romantic in the group. Bodies littered the field, wearing all sorts of colors, many human but many not. Joe was both shocked and sobered at the sight; it made him feel a bit sick.

The Dark Baron had sent eleven thousand across Sorrows Gorge and another forty-six hundred in the rearward force. Of that number, he managed eventually to extricate slightly more than half. Fewer than eight hundred, almost all from the rear force, had been taken prisoner. The rest lay dead upon the field.

Roughly ten thousand total had defended. Of that number, only a bit over fifty-one hundred remained, many of those wounded or maimed. It had been a costly battle indeed.

Ruddygore was taken to Terindell by boat, along with Joe, Marge, Poquah, and a number of others associated with that castle. Of Grogha and Houma, who had been in the fighting force, there was, as yet, no word, although things were still extremely disorganized. Macore, however, who was still recovering from his wounds suffered in High Pothique—or so he claimed, anyway—had remained behind at Terindell and greeted them upon their return, wanting to know all the details.

It was clear Ruddygore was in very bad shape, and they all relaxed and waited at Terindell until there was some word on him, some sort of reassurance about his condition. Unlike physical wounds, the wounds on Ruddygore's body had been physical stigmata of the inner spiritual wounds he had suffered in the fight with the Dark Baron.

During the next three weeks they saw the sorcerer not at all, although there was a steady stream of visitors and dignitaries to the great castle and lots of gifts and well-wishes.

Joe and Marge again talked of what they might do now, but all was put off until Ruddygore was well. It would be unthinkable to leave him without knowing, without a parting word.

Near the end of the third week, two weary knights appeared on horseback, one on a gray spotted horse, and there was great rejoicing all around. Both Grogha and Houma looked very much as if they'd been in a terrible experience, and both had suffered many wounds, yet they were cheerful enough to start telling and embellishing their battlefield exploits until only a few days later they told how they'd won the war.

Algongua, too, arrived, although not on Vercertorix, to say his farewells. He was going back to High Pothique, more convinced than ever that people weren't worth it. Still, he was more worried about Vercertorix. "I'm afraid he'll never be happy with an occasional cow again," he sighed. "Oh, where have I failed!"

Four weeks after the Battle of Sorrows Gorge, word came that the Baron's forces were regrouping and re-forming and that a new alignment of commanders had been established to the south. Lacking forces sufficient to counterattack and retake the southern areas, the north knew that it had indeed won a great battle victory—but no war.

And, too, on the same day as that word came, Poquah went first to Joe, then Marge, and asked them to come to Ruddygore's library that evening. The sorcerer wanted to see them.

They went anxiously, not knowing what to expect, but the sorcerer received them, looking fairly fit if still a bit gray and weak. He'd certainly lost a good deal of weight and was, possibly, down to a mere three hundred pounds. But the bruises and lacerations had faded, and he moved with far less stiffness and discomfort.

They dined with him that evening and felt secure and relaxed, now that the sorcerer not only was going to make it but was his old self again.

"I've been back to your world, you know," he told them.

"Oh?" Joe responded. "Why?"

The sorcerer laughed. "I like it—for a visit. Besides, there was a Gilbert and Sullivan theater festival in San Francisco." His eyes twinkled slightly. "I could hardly pass that up. It was good therapy, too." He relaxed in his plush chair and lighted a cigar, then grew a bit more serious. "Have you two thought of what you'd like to do now? Seriously?"

"Nothing definite," Joe told him, "but I do have sort of the wanderlust."

"I'd like to find my exact tribe and go to them for a bit," Marge said. "I'd like to know more about myself and what I'm becoming."

"I can tell you the who, what, and where of that," Ruddygore assured her. "I'm afraid I played something of a cruel trick on you, but I couldn't resist doing it to Huspeth."

"I don't mind. Not any more," she told him. "I'd like to go to Huspeth one last time, though, and explain the situation. I'd feel better about it."

He nodded. "You can do that any time. Poquah will arrange for a proper horse and give you the route. It's not far." He sighed. "But I think now, considering how much your service has meant to me, that I'll play completely fair with the two of you. I'd like to give you a series of options and let you pick."

"Go ahead," Joe urged, interested. "But I don't see that we did all that much for the big picture."

"What you did was incalculable! With that Lamp, the Baron would not have had to engage me. He could have knocked Vercertorix into the ground, even masked that entire rear-attack force until it was upon us! Getting that Lamp was the difference between victory and defeat. You can be very proud. It is because of you that so many of our brave people did not die a vain death. Control of the Dancing Gods is still not the Baron's, and the bulk of Husaquahr is still free. It was the job you were summoned here to do—and you did it well."

They both smiled. "I'd like to believe that, anyway," Marge told him.

"Well, it's the truth. And because of it, I'll lay out *all* your options. First, you can remain in the service of Terindell as honored folk. We have won a battle but not a war, and there will be much more to do in the future. The Baron will not be so overconfident again. Of course, I'd give you both whatever time you wanted or needed, and transport you anywhere you wanted to go, before sending you on any more missions. That is option number one."

He paused, puffed a few times on the cigar, then continued. "Now, option number two is that you both go your own way. Find your own lives here. I won't hold you. But I *do* think the two of you make a good team, a near unbeatable combination of beauty and magic on the one hand and quick-thinking brawn on the other. That business in the Baron's tent, Joe, was sheer brilliance." Again he paused, looking thoughtful. "There is a third alternative, of course."

"Huh? What?" Joe wanted to know.

"You could go back. I could send you back. Your souls

still belong elsewhere, and so you could return—as you are, in fact. New lives. Marge, you could have every male eating out of your hand back there. A little cosmetic alteration on the ears, perhaps, and you'd be the most exotic and erotic woman since Helen of Troy—and she was vastly overrated. And, Joe, with that body and quick mind of yours—and some quantity of gold I could give you—you could be or do almost anything you want."

They were thunderstruck by this last option, since both of them had abandoned any hope of ever returning. Joe had often thought of it, of course, but he'd never expected to have the choice offered to him.

Marge smiled at Ruddygore. "No, I don't think I want to return. Maybe someday for a visit, but never for good. I've been in this world perhaps only a year, but I've lived more than I have in all my previous life. It's not the wondrous, romantic world of my fantasies, true, but it *is* a wonderful place nonetheless." Both she and Ruddygore looked at Joe.

"You know, ever since I met you, I've been aching to go back. It's all I dreamed about. But—I don't know. Call it inscrutable Indian perversity, or maybe just an old trucker's whim, but there really *is* nothin' there for me. The funny thing is, I might have still taken you up on it until we got back here. Just seein' folks like Macore, Houma, and Grogha—you know, I got more friends in this world than I have in the other? And I'm still my own boss here, still on the move, only here one place ain't so much like another."

Ruddygore sighed and nodded. "All right, then, that's settled. As for the other, perhaps I wasn't playing *quite* fair with you."

Both of their heads snapped up and looked at him suspiciously.

He sighed. "Remember back at the start of this thing? Remember, Marge, when you labeled it the start of an epic?"

She chuckled. "Yes, I remember. I didn't know how true that was when I joked about it."

"You still don't," he told her. "The Books of Rules, Volume 16, page 103, section 12(d)."

"Yeah? So what's that crazy set say about us?" Joe wanted to know.

"*All epics must be at least trilogies*," Ruddygore replied, and laughed and laughed and laughed . . .

ABOUT THE AUTHOR

JACK L. CHALKER was born in Norfolk, Virginia, on December 17, 1944, but was raised and has spent most of his life in Baltimore, Maryland. He learned to read almost from the moment of entering school, and by working odd jobs amassed a large book collection by the time he was in junior high school, a collection now too large for containment in his quarters. Science fiction, history, and geography all fascinated him early on, interests that continue.

Chalker joined the Washington Science Fiction Association in 1958 and began publishing an amateur SF journal, *Mirage*, in 1960. After high school he decided to be a trial lawyer, but money problems and the lack of a firm caused him to switch to teaching. He holds bachelor degrees in history and English, and an M.L.A. from the Johns Hopkins University. He taught history and geography in the Baltimore public schools between 1966 and 1978, and now makes his living as a freelance writer. Additionally, out of the amateur journals he founded a publishing house, The Mirage Press, Ltd., devoted to nonfiction and bibliographic works on science fiction and fantasy. This company has produced more than twenty books in the last nine years. His hobbies include esoteric audio, travel, working on science-fiction convention committees, and guest lecturing on SF to institutions such as the Smithsonian. He is an active conservationist and National Parks supporter, and he has an intensive love of ferryboats, with the avowed goal of riding every ferry in the world. In fact, in 1978 he was married to Eva Whitley on an ancient ferryboat in mid-river. They live in the Catoctin Mountain region of western Maryland with their son David.